CENSORED

A Novel

James A. Fleming

Libreria Fleming
Publishing

Also by James A. Fleming

Broken Border

The House on Glenheather

"To see the right and not do it is cowardice."

Confucius

Ca. 551-479 BC

"Employ your time in improving yourself by others writings, so that you shall gain easily what others have labored hard for."

Socrates

Copyright © 2023 **Libreria Fleming Publishing**

All rights reserved. No part of this publication may be reproduced, distributed, or transmitted in any form or by any means, including photocopying, recording, or other electronic or mechanical methods, without the prior written permission of the publisher, except in the case of brief quotations embodied in critical reviews and certain other non-commercial uses permitted by copyright law. For permission requests, write to the publisher, addressed "Attention: Book Rights and Permission," at the address below.

Published in the United States of America

ISBN 978-1-959173-92-2 (SC)
ISBN 978-1-960159-60-1 (HC)
ISBN 978-1-960159-38-0 (Ebook)

Libreria Fleming Publishing
924 Burnt Hickory Cir. NW
Marietta, Georgia 30064
www.stellarliterary.com.

Ordering Information and Rights Permission:

Quantity sales. Special discounts might be available on quantity purchases by corporations, associations, and others. For details, contact the publisher at the address above.

For Book Rights Adaptation and other Rights Permission. Call us at toll-free 1-888-945-8513 or send us an email at admin@stellarliterary.com.

This is a book of fiction. The characters are imaginary. Names of any actual persons are entirely coincidental and not intended to be a reflection of any person, living or dead. Reference to actual places is used fictitiously as a literary device and may not be accurate. Opinions, viewpoints, and perspectives are solely those of the author.

JAF

TABLE OF CONTENTS

CHAPTER 1 1
CHAPTER 2 8
CHAPTER 3 17
CHAPTER 4 22
CHAPTER 5 44
CHAPTER 6 54
CHAPTER 7 76
CHAPTER 8 80
CHAPTER 9 100
CHAPTER 10 103
CHAPTER 11 108
CHAPTER 12 118
CHAPTER 13 122
CHAPTER 14 141
CHAPTER 15 149
CHAPTER 16 157
CHAPTER 17 187
CHAPTER 18 196
CHAPTER 19 199
CHAPTER 20 208
CHAPTER 21 218
CHAPTER 22 238

CHAPTER 23	274
CHAPTER 24	276
CHAPTER 25	307
CHAPTER 26	320
CHAPTER 27	324
CHAPTER 28	326
CHAPTER 29	328
CHAPTER 30	330
CHAPTER 31	334
ACKNOWLEDGEMENT	336

CHAPTER 1

"Are you in any pain?" the cardiothoracic surgeon asks, her voice muffled by a protective face shield.

"No. I'm fine," replies the woman on the operating table. Her face exhibits no signs of discomfort or apprehension. The surgeon, Dr. Myong Soon, stands beside the patient, gloved hands folded as if in prayer. She silently watches the beating heart for another two minutes. Satisfied, she looks across the open chest and says, "Will you close, Dr. Nam?"

The surgical team is completing the complex "beating heart" operation. OPCAB is medical shorthand for Off Pump Coronary Artery By-Pass. It is a surgical procedure Myong Soon perfected at a German-owned hospital in the booming New Delhi exurb of Gurgaon. The surgery causes little pain and doesn't require blood thinners or general anesthesia. Patient recovery time is shorter than with traditional by-pass surgery, and the costs are minimal. The actual operation on the heart takes less than eight minutes. Preparation time for the procedure, the opening and closing of a patient's chest, and everything else, takes hours.

Surgery is not a difficult skill for Soon to master. She learned early on the difference between a good surgeon and a superior one is judgment; learning to anticipate problems and knowing how to prevent problems is the key. She encounters no problems this day, and the last of three heart procedures is completed in less than seven minutes, a personal best for her. It is a source of professional satisfaction, and mental fatigue.

Backing away from the operating table, she pushes through an adjoining swinging door into the pre-op room. She snaps off her gloves, kicks off her OR shoes and removes her face shield. She exits into the surgical corridor. The doctors' surgical lounge is a hundred steps from the operating room.

The Hanyong University Medical Center complex in Seoul, South Korea, is huge. There are hundreds of surgeons in the booming metropolis of 20 million people. In addition to the excellent medical facilities, Seoul is the largest producer in the world of flat-screen televisions and cellphones. Capitalism is working. The economy is booming.

Dr. Soon was kidnapped by the North Koreans in 1970 when she was two years old. The government provided her with parents. She was one of hundreds of South Koreans kidnapped by North Korea in the 1970's and 1980's. From the very beginning of her education, at every grade level, she performed extremely well. She entered university at 17 and medical school three years later. Shortly after becoming a doctor she moved to rural North Korea to serve the poor, and minister to a small orphanage supported by a French non-government organization (NGO). She was fulfilled in her only ambition: serving those in misery and poverty.

Soon's brother-in-law, Han Chong-Kyun, was decidedly different. He saw the evil in Kim Jon Il, a pathologically monster indifferent to the suffering of his own people. Chong-Kyun had high level access to secret information about the government's nuclear weapons plans, which he passed to the Americans. However, in a matter of months, he was discovered by the People's National Security Bureau (NSB), arrested and imprisoned in Camp 20. Reportedly, he died of mysterious circumstances. He left behind a memory stick – flash drive - with secret information of incredible value to the U.S. government. This information Dr. Soon passed to Charles Sewell, a half Korean, or so she believed. Truth be told, Sewell was the Central Intelligence Agency's cover name for Jon London. Anyway, she and "Sewell" escaped from North Korean to South Korea via China. As a reward for her assistance to the U.S. Government, her South Korean citizenship was restored and she was offered a faculty appointment at the Hanyong Medical Center in Seoul. She never learned what ultimately became of Charles Sewell.

In the women's changing room of the doctors' surgical lounge, Myong Soon takes off the green disposable scrubs and deposits them in a medical waste receptacle. The décor in the lounge is utilitarian at best; two large flat screen televisions adorn the walls opposite each other, one continuously scrolls through a 24-hour operating room schedule and status. It displays projected beginning and completion times of operations (or cancellation or postponement), followed by a brief descriptor of the procedure, and posts the surgical team. Soon notes she is listed for a heart valve replacement procedure the following morning at 6.

The other flat screen is a traditional television, carrying 24-hour local and world news, interspersed with various hospital announcements and notices, and a live feed from the OR for unusual or interesting surgical procedure, such as a double transplant.

Everything in the lounge is a light shade of green. Even the fresh towel Soon takes from the metal towel rack is green. She wraps it around her waist momentarily, and seconds later takes it off and hangs it on a green ceramic peg outside the shower stall. A hot shower revives her. After stepping from the shower and drying off, she goes to her personal locker and retrieves a white bra, size 34B, and size 4 bikini white panties, and puts them on. She takes a boar-hair brush from the top shelf of the locker and walks to a nearby mirror. For a time longer than usual she brushes her shoulder-length ink black hair. Then she returns the brush to the metal shelf. From one of two plastic hangers in the locker she removes a knee-length brown wool skirt, and a white silk blouse. After dressing she sits on a padded bench facing the lockers, hands at her side and mind in neutral. For several minutes she sits quietly, eyes closed, breathing deeply and resting her tired feet. Then, as if awaken from a nap, she takes her fashionable leather boots from the floor of the locker, slips them on, and zips them up. She puts on a dark brown leather jacket, closes the metal door, and spins the combination lock.

As she walks from the doctors' surgical lounge to the elevators she considers restaurants for dinner after patient rounds. Seventy hours weeks – sometimes more – leave her little time to think of anything but medicine. But sometimes she steals a moment to think of her narrow, solitary life. Although it has been more than two years, she misses in her life one person.

Eight hours later – when Soon fails to return to the Medical Center for the scheduled heart procedure – the Chief of the Cardiac Surgery Service goes to see the Hospital Administrator. He stubbornly insists something is seriously wrong. "Dr. Soon would have to be dead to not come in," he stresses, dramatically.

"Let's not panic," the Administrator calmly suggests. "I'm sure there is some reasonable explanation why she is late. What have you done to try and contact her?"

Five minutes after the Cardiac Surgery Chief leaves his office, the Administrator picks up the phone and dials the private number for the Chief Superintendent General (CSG) of the Seoul Metropolitan Police Agency (SMPA). The phone is answered after a few rings. The Administrator expresses his concern that something is amiss with one of his doctors and asks for assistance. Further, he says, the surgeon does not answer her page or repeated cellphone calls. When a staff member was sent to her residence to check on her, he adds, there was no response. He's worried.

The Chief Superintendent General, previously a heart patient at the Medical Center, has a vested interest in staying on good terms with the Hospital Administrator. He quickly sets in motion a police investigation.

Halfway around the globe from Seoul – beside the high and slippery banks of the San Juan River - is the remote village of El Castillo, Nicaragua. It is a backwater stop on the road into Hell

El Castillo is far removed from a different kind of hell - the political turmoil and riots in Managua. The Sandinista National Liberation Front does not shy away from mob violence to further the cause of social unrest. And the rebuilding of communism in Central America. The swift waters of the river keep cash-strapped El Castillo solvent, but the mosquito-infested frontier town remains frustrated by poverty. Summers are hot and humid. Life is hard and cheap. There are numerous infectious and parasitic diseases lurking along the river: Central American liver flukes, lung flukes, blood flukes and intestinal flukes compete with tapeworms and hookworms for an animal or human host. Hepatitis B, rabies, and malaria occasionally afflict the villagers. Birds and bats carry fungal spores that humans can inhale. Desperately poor people compete with rats and large snakes for food. The U.S. Army Veterinary Corps estimates that for every rat seen, there are nine unseen. The nearby jungle is a quietly deadly place.

At the western end of the main street is Hotel Elizabeth. It charges US$25 per night with air conditioning, but very little hot water. A destination hotel – and the best and largest one for many miles along the river - it can accommodate 30 guests at one time. As wilderness hotels go, Elizabeth is a five-star; by urban standards it is not quite a one-star. Its main clientele are ecotourists and adventurers going up or down river. Other guests include wildlife enthusiasts, naturalists and, occasionally, missionaries going to save poor naked heathens who do not know Jesus. Some missionaries, it is rumored, have taken to baptizing people in the river, a la John the Baptist in the river Jordan. Considering the bloodthirsty Caiman (cousins of crocodiles) and Machaca (the Central American Piranha), wading in the river requires great faith. Or deadly ignorance.

The narrow street leading to the Elizabeth is a mixture of dismal store fronts and crude stalls made from whitewashed wood planks. Women sell local produce in the stalls. The street is sometimes crowded with shop owners, local shoppers, undernourished horses and wooden carts. Other times it is a listless market. Human and animal wastes sometimes litter the street. The Merchants Association howls at the Mayor in protest. He promises to correct the situation.

Carlos Chibbaro works at the hotel. An ambitious man of 26 years, he is driven by the desire for a better life far from El Castillo. He works mostly in the hotel kitchen and saves all his wages. His father worked at the hotel until he unexpectedly died at the age of 43. His mother works still at the hotel as a chambermaid.

Sometimes Chibbaro tends the hotel bar. Occasionally a foreign guest wants a cool beer, or gin and tonic, after a long day on the river. They are willing to pay the inflated price plus a tip. Chibbaro volunteers at every opportunity to tend bar. He does so for two reasons: first, tips are an important source of additional income and, second, he can listen to spoken English. For more than a year he has studied maps and Basic English phrases. In a country where annual per capita income is about US$2,600, the money is his future. It is the money he needs to escape El Castillo. His journey will take him across Nicaragua, through Guatemala – carefully avoiding Belize – in route to Cuidad Reyes, Mexico. From there he can cross into Texas. There is no fence, no border patrol, and no electronic sensors at the deserted Texas/Mexico line. However, the price of a guide to supply water and lead him safely to a truck inside Texas is US$4,000. He needs to earn only another thousand dollars to make good his escape.

Chibbaro keeps his savings in a quart-size lard tin buried at the base of a matapalo tree at the edge of the jungle. The tree is easily identified because of its size; it is a tree roughly 15 feet in diameter. Locals call it a tree killer because it grows so large it squeezes smaller trees out, and they die. A passive sloth lives in the giant tree. Chibbaro brings leftovers from the kitchen when he makes a deposit.

One warm evening Chibbaro and three other kitchen workers become ill with flu-like symptoms. Rumors spread they have been exposed to a gas leak in the kitchen. Another rumor circulating in town is they have eaten contaminated meat. Everyone is thankful no guests become ill. Bad news travels fast, even in a jungle, and no guests coming to the hotel means no tourists. No tourists translates to no money. No money means more hardships for the local populous. The four workers complain to friends of fever, slurred speech, difficulty swallowing, and double vision. Because there is no doctor in El Castillo, none receive medical attention beyond aspirin, home remedies and community concern.

All die unexpectedly within four days. The town's people are shocked and angry. They blame the Nicaraguan government for not providing health care for the people.

One guest at the hotel is silently pleased. The test has been successful.

Across the river from El Castillo is Costa Rica. Three weeks after the four deaths in El Castillo, Maria Perez, an aspiring 24-year-old newspaper reporter in San Jose, learns of the bizarre event. A former classmate of hers, Alba Leocadia Dorotea, works at the Tiempos Confidencial in Managua. She tells Perez the deaths may be more sinister than publically known. She suspects a government cover-up.

Perez is an attractive and shapely "Tico" (a native of Costa Rica). She believes she is a "stringer" for the Las Cruces News in New Mexico. That's what Alberto Cabeza tells her. He has been "stringing" her along for almost a year. She is romantically involved with Cabeza. He is genuinely nice to her, takes her to dinner a couple times a week, and buys her gifts. Cabeza says he moonlights for the Cruces's Latin American desk. He says he is looking for interesting news items for the Spanish-speaking readership in New Mexico. He pays her US$100 a month for human interest stories; an additional $50 if her story is picked up. Every third story is, he tells her, and provides the $50 bonus. He also claims he may be able to find her a job in North America. Unknown to Perez, Cabeza thinks of her as a source – a source-with-benefits.

Alberto Cabeza is listed in the Embassy Directory as an agricultural economist with the U.S. Agency for International Development. Unknown to all but a few he is an entry-level employee of the Central Intelligence Agency on his first overseas assignment.

Alberto Cabeza is not his real name.

CHAPTER 2

Within an hour Seoul Metropolitan Police inspectors arrive at apartment 1096 in the luxury Medical Towers apartment complex. It is the detectives' lunch hour and they are less than pleased about the call. Across the street in a huge green space, people are enjoying their lunch hour reading on a park bench, walking, or jogging under the smoggy sky.

Two uniformed police officers arrived at the apartment even earlier than the inspectors. The senior officer is stationed inside the apartment protecting the crime scene. A second officer is in the hallway. She recognizes the two police inspectors (detectives) and opens the apartment door. The inspectors enter the apartment and acknowledge the senior policeman with a nod. They expect the worst, and their expectation is confirmed.

"Thank you, officer. You can wait outside," says the Senior Inspector.

Bright sunlight floods the apartment from its many windows. It highlights the semi-nude body of a young woman, duct-taped to a dining room chair. The detectives approach slowly and stop on either side of the body.

"Holy Mother," the Senior Inspector says in a whispering voice. The victim's face has been severely beaten. Dried blood cakes her face and temples and sticks to her black hair. So brutal was the beating, the Senior Inspector suspects her facial bones were broken, and she suffered a fractured skull. He doesn't share his opinion.

"Good looking woman," volunteers the detective. "Once." The woman's blouse is ripped open and her white bra pulled down. There are splattered dried blood spots on the white bra and on her breasts. Numerous puncture marks form an unusual pattern on her breasts. "Nice pair," he says.

The comment disgusts the senior man and his face shows it. "Look at this woman. Someone tortured and murdered her. Show some respect," he snaps, and turns away from the obscene sight.

"Sorry," the detective apologizes, sounding sincere.

The apartment building is in a tony section of Seoul, a mere block from the University Medical Center. The elegant 20-story high-rise has a grand view of the Han River. It is one of the most affluent parts of the city where crime is virtually non-existent. Half a dozen doctors have units in the building because of its proximity to the Medical Center. When details of the murder become known it will send chills through the complex and the Medical Center. For that reason alone, Medical Center officials will bring intense pressure on the police for a speedy resolution to the heinous crime.

"What do you think?" asks the Senior Inspector, looking intently at his subordinate.

"Pretty obvious isn't it?" he answers, trying to reestablish his professionalism. "I mean, somebody was waiting for her when she came home, overpowered her and duct-taped her to this chair."

"Evidently." He is annoyed by the simplicity of his subordinate's response.

A strip of gray duct tape hangs loosely from the woman's right cheek. "They duct-taped her mouth shut when torturing her," continues the detective, "and used the short rope around her neck to strangle her. Those are burn marks on her…ugh…her breasts, probably from a cigarette," he adds, looking for any evidence of a cigarette on the floor.

The Senior Inspector also looks at the floor. There is a bloody fork under the chair. That probably explains the puncture pattern on her breasts. The carpet around the chair is mushy – soaked with something. On the dining room table is a lone empty glass.

"She was abused repeatedly," the Senor Inspector surmises, dipping a finger in the dampness beneath the glass, smelling it, and then touching his finger to his lips. "She probably passed out several times from the pain, and the beating and choking. They threw water on her to revive her."

The detective nods his agreement.

"What are those marks on her face?" the Senior Inspector asks.

"Looks like she was hit repeatedly with a small object." He looks on the table, underneath the chair, and in the immediate area for any physical evidence or clues.

The Senior Inspector says, "Perhaps poked by the blunt end of a dinner knife. Or brutally struck in the face by someone wearing a large ring."

The detective steps closer and studies her face. "A round object that left an impression. Could have been a ring."

No response.

"Why take cigarette butts and leave the fork?"

No response.

Waiting for a reply, he scans the adjoining living room in search of cigarettes or ashtrays or anything else of interest.

"Any guesses about motive?" asks the detective as he looks around. The room has been thoroughly trashed. Books have been pulled from the shelves and rifled exhaustively. The sofa and pillows have been slit open, stuffing scattered everywhere. The detective walks into the bedroom. The situation is the same. Dresser drawers have been emptied and the bottoms checked for anything that might have been taped there. The mattress has been cut open. Clothes in the closet have been searched and linings ripped out. Heels of shoes have been torn off. At the back of the closet is a brown cardboard shipping box. The markings on the box identify a shipper in India. In it are 24 vials of a clear liquid. Each vial contains a 30cc dose of something. He recognizes the writing as French. He leaves the lid open. Retreating from the closet, the detective examines two inexpensive picture frames that have been twisted apart, and the photos destroyed. In the bathroom, the toilet's tank top has been removed and discarded next to the shower. The medicine cabinet over the sink has been trashed. The detective sifts through a few bottles, all over-the-counter meds.

"Not really," calls the senior man from the dining room, in a voice louder than normal. "But you can bet he, or she, or they had something specific in mind. Maybe a diary or love letters. Perhaps a journal of an affair with someone important at the Medical Center, or even a government official."

"Could be hot photos of her with someone," speculates the younger detective, rejoining the Senior Inspector in the dining room.

"I'm not sure you'd torture and murder someone over sex photos."

"Unless they could ruin your reputation, or your marriage, or your career." He hesitates as if considering the most likely motive, then says, "Or all three."

"More likely some confidential memos or financial records," the Senior Inspector says, looking more closely at the victim's hands and arms.

"Like what?"

"Like evidence of sweetheart contracts, fraud, missing funds, kickbacks. Those sorts of things." He turns the victim's left arm to look closely at her veins.

"Yeah, that would be troubling." He takes a few steps closer to the Senior Inspector, who is bending down next to the victim, leans in over him and says, "I'd kill you for that."

"Problem is," the senior man speculates, "none of those things seem likely for a medical doctor."

"You looking for needle tracks?"

"I'm just looking," he answers, squinting. "It's hard to tell."

"Well," says the detective, "what would they want from a doctor?"

"Maybe an illegal operation," suggests the Inspector, "or organs for the black market." He stands up and stretches his back. He remembers he needs to start working out at the Police Gym again.

"Like?"

"Like a kidney. Or maybe a liver. Even a lung."

"What kind of doctor was she?"

"Cardiothoracic surgeon – open heart surgeon," he translates.

"So maybe they wanted a heart," says the detective.

"Maybe. Think about it. When patients die on the table, what becomes of their organs? I hear you can get $50,000 for a liver in Singapore."

"No shit!"

"The organ trafficking rings pay US $1,000 for a donor. Usually less. Sometimes as little as a hundred."

"Still, who would want to do that?"

"Desperately poor people from the favelas in Brazil, barrios in Columbia, slums in Pakistan, China, and the Philippines."

"Still…" the detective says, grimacing.

"Hey, there are tens of thousands of people needing kidneys, and thousands more each year. It's a big money-maker." The Inspector pauses and takes in the scene. "How old was she?"

"34," the detective answers, reading from a note pad he takes from his shirt pocket.

"She looks young for that kind of doctor, if you know what I mean. Makes me feel ancient," he says, bending over the victim's arm again. Any drugs around?"

"Nothing illegal. Think she was using or selling?"

"Unlikely." The inspector continues looking for indications of other injection sites. "You have her medical history?"

"Headquarters is getting the records."

"Good. Better call 'em back and ask for re-enforcements. We'll need to knock on every door in the complex."

The detective wonders aloud. "So, did they get what they wanted and then kill her? Or not get what they were after and still kill her?"

The Inspector gives a non-committal shrug.

The door to the apartment quietly opens. "Forensics here, Inspector," says the policewoman, stepping aside for two men carrying small black bags. They will take blood and body fluid samples, DNA evidence, and test for fingerprints, gather fiber samples, and search for other physical evidence. A medical examiner is in route as forensics goes about their work. The Inspector steps into the living room and calls his immediate superior, the Superintendent.

By late afternoon the Inspector's report has reached the desk of the Superintendent (S). From there it is walked to the Superintendent General (SG), then the Senior Superintendent General (SSG), who personally takes it to the Chief Superintendent General (CSG). The lengthy chain of command is strictly observed.

The Chief Superintendent General opens the blue report jacket. The SSG, who reviewed the report earlier, sits opposite the Chief prepared to answer any questions. The report is comprehensive. The first page is the Report of Investigation by the Chief Medical Examiner. It gives the name of the decedent, age, birthdate, race, sex, home address, location of death, type of premises, and description of body. There are three items at the bottom left of the page:

SIGNIFICANT OBSERVATIONS:

See Autopsy Protocol.

PROBABLE CAUSE OF DEATH:

Severe Blunt Trauma.

MANNER OF DEATH:

There is a check mark by Homicide.

The Chief Superintendent General flips to the autopsy report.

REPORT OF AUTOPSY

Decedent	Age	Birth Date	Sex	Autopsy No	Case No.
MYONG SOON	34	07/05/1977	F	649-05	0904289

Type of Death

Violent, unusual or unnatural: VIOLENT

PATHOLOGICAL DIAGNOSIS

Trauma to the face and head.

- a. Lacerations and abrasions to the face and head.
- b. Fractures to the jaw and contiguous structures.
- c. External ear trauma.
- d. Fractures of the nose (maxilla, orbit. cribriform).
- e. Temporal bone fractures.
- f. Massive axonal damage.
- g. Hemorrhaging in the brain.

CAUSE OF DEATH: SEVERE BLUNT FORCE TRAUMA SUFFICIENT TO CAUSE DEATH.

The facts stated herein are true and correct to the best of my knowledge and belief.

Signed by Dr. Choi (pathologist)

at the location of autopsy, and date stamped.

The Forensic Report is one and a half pages in length and not helpful. There are no fibers, no prints, and no physical evidence such as tissue samples or blood DNA - other than from the victim, and no weapon.

The Chief Superintendent General closes the report and puts it to one side of his desk. "The facial injuries were not life-threatening, if I understand the report. It is the beating to her head that killed her."

"Officially correct, sir. Unofficially, Dr. Choi told me she probably died from an injection of sodium thiopental."

The CSG raises his eyebrows. "Shouldn't that show up in the toxicology summary?"

"Not necessarily. The drug dissipates quickly in the body. It is extremely difficult to detect." He pauses. "Makes for the ideal murder weapon."

The Chief picks up the report for a second time. Licking his index finger each time he turns a page, he reaches the toxicology report. There is no mention of sodium anything, and no mention of any drugs written in the space labeled Comments. He closes the report and looks up. "What do you make of it?"

"At first we thought it a crime of opportunity," he explains. "Perhaps some street gang hoping to rob an easy target. Or some druggies needing some cash."

"Go on."

"The inspectors believe this is not a random or drug-related crime."

The Chief Superintendent General frowns. "Why not?"

"Little things. Intuition born from years of experience, if you like."

"I don't like. Be more specific," the Chief growls, reaching for a cigarette and offering one to the SSG, who declines by holding up his hand in a stop signal. He holds a gold and enamel Dunhill lighter to his filtered cigarette. The lighter is a reward given to him by his wife for 30 years of marriage.

"We think it was a targeted murder. The victim was brutally beaten and sadistically tortured for a reason: to extract information."

The CSG exhales a cloud of smoke through his nose and mouth. "What kind of information?"

"Unfortunately, we don't know. She wasn't molested or robbed, but the apartment has all the indications of a thorough search for something."

"Why beat her to death?" the CSG asks rhetorically, looking out his office window at a darkening sky. "They got, or didn't get, what they wanted and decided to kill her anyway. Probably so she couldn't identify them, don't you think?"

"Perhaps. But I suspect for another reason," he says darkly.

"Regardless, this is an extraordinarily sensitive case. Keep the lid on it. I don't want the medical school people thinking we have some nut loose."

"I'm confident we do not. I think the doctors, medical staff and students are perfectly safe. This was a purposeful crime."

CHAPTER 3

It was an emotional decision as much as anything. Jon London was leaving behind things he wanted to turn away from. Despite some trepidation about living in Bermuda, he decided to try it. He reminded himself that Bermuda has ocean breezes, warm sunshine, great diving, good beer, and no traffic. The casual lifestyle is the tonic he sought.

Jon is surprised to discover the cost of living is much higher than anticipated. Real estate in Bermuda is unexpectedly pricy. He looks at a 1300 sq. ft. condo on St. George's: $745,000. He looks at a two-bedroom one bath cottage built in the late 1940's. It is a 900 sq. ft. cottage with a big price tag: $1.1 million. Residences in Southampton do not come cheaply.

He decides to buy a live-aboard boat. The 37-foot trawler has a brilliant white hull with a thin blue stripe around the deck. It isn't new, but it's in very good condition, reliable and comfortable. The salon is 15 feet wide, with almost seven feet of headroom, and lots of teak. In addition to comfortable furniture, the bookshelf in the corner has space for a computer and an entertainment center with a Sony HD color television. The master stateroom is aft, and the guest cabin is under the foredeck. Both have heads and separate showers.

The pilothouse provides excellent visibility, and a full complement of electronics. Travel is almost unlimited, thanks to GPS, Loran, autopilot, SSB and VHF radios, a weather fax, and the usual depth and speed instruments. Behind the control console is a leather settee with a sit-down chart table. Below deck the engine room is spotless and well organized. There is even a freezer! A long list of standard equipment includes a new generator and a recently overhauled Volvo six-cylinder engine. Other extras range from electric fans to cedar closets. The boat is perfect for island hopping, deep water fishing, scuba diving, and relaxing. He pays $221,975 cash against an asking price of $295,900.

Now, months after the woman he was to marry died in a tragic accident in St. Maarten, Jon has become a man adrift – figuratively and literally.

The ocean is choppy as Jon steers Eagle Ray toward Ireland Island. The island has a history dating back to the 1600s when pirates sailed the island chain. In the year 1618 a tropical storm caused one of the pirates to run his ship aground near Hamilton. The captain of the pirate ship was captured. Instead of the gallows the Governor banished the pirate to an uninhabited island – Ireland Island. Folk lore has it treasures are stashed on the island or in the waters nearby. No one has ever found anything.

A hundred years later Ireland Island was a center for shipbuilding, primarily using labor from islands of the Caribbean. From 1939 to 1949 the island served as a Royal Navy Wireless Station. The Navy built and maintained a dockyard for vessels until 1958, when it sold its facilities to the Government of Bermuda. Because of its proximity to Hamilton, the island today is a tourist attraction.

The darkening skies signal the approaching foul weather, although Eagle Ray's weather radar doesn't indicate any immediate threat. Jon doesn't think there is cause for alarm. On average Bermuda has a hurricane every 10 years and a threat every two years. If the weather changes there will be plenty of time to return to the harbor and safety.

There are more than 250 shipwrecks around the islands. Jon has been in Hamilton for a week to resupply, but he is eager to head out again. The previous week he found several interesting wreck-dive locations. The most interesting is located north of the island in 80 feet of water – near the liner Cristobal Colon. The dive isn't a treasure hunt for pieces of eight; it is just an investigatory dive. Perhaps he might find an artifact from a pirate ship. Stranger things have happened. The power of storms and the shifting sand on the ocean bottom might give up something of interest. If an object were made of metal, it would be encased in coral or shell or sand. It would be corroded and hard to identify. But something made of glass, like a wine bottle, might be recognizable.

Open water brings out the best in Jon. It is exciting and calming at the same time. The smell of the sea, the motion of the waves, the warmth of the sun, all are healing for body and mind.

With the help of the boat's GPS he locates the exact spot from two days earlier. He drops anchor. The sea is up and the sky looks threatening.

Still, there is plenty of time for a dive. He stores his wet suit, gloves, knife, mask, regulators, fins, and other items in front of the wheelhouse on the deck. He takes a seat on a deck bench and gets his dive gear out.

He attaches the aluminum tank of air to his BC and pulls the Velcro straps tightly. Then he checks the regulator/tank connection and the tank/BC connection. He always turns the air to full - then back halfway for safety reasons. He taste-checks the air. It's fine.

It is always a race of sorts to get a wet suit on and in the water before overheating. But he is wearing a "shorty" wet suit and that helps. After suiting up he moves to the boat's ladder. Sitting on the side of the boat he puts on his weight belt and fastens it loosely. Next he pulls on his fins and spits into his face mask. No need for expensive defogger. He carefully goes down three steps. Waist deep at the water's edge Jon pauses and rinses his mask before putting it on. Lastly, he pulls on his gloves, puts the regulator's mouth piece in, and drops into the ocean feet first.

Jon stops at a depth of about ten feet to clear his ears. When they "pop" he's ready to go deeper. Hand-over-hand, headfirst, he follows the anchor chain to the bottom. It's a dark descent. With depth the sunlight disappears, and so does color. Beautiful coral reefs become brownish blue-green and bland. Visibility is nil, which is why he is using the anchor chain as a guide. But once on the bottom the visibility improves substantially because of a white sandy bottom. When he reaches the bottom he does a 360 to get his bearings. Then he attaches a line to the anchor chain and the other end to his wrist.

Scuba diving is therapy for Jon and gives him a sense of peace. Two years earlier he reluctantly agreed to a "walk-in-the-park" covert assignment for the Central Intelligence Agency. Earlier in his life he worked for the Agency after a stint in the Air Force as a pilot. He traded government service for the life of a college professor. And then he fell in love with Kim Lake. Words were inadequate in describing the passion he felt for her. Life was as perfect as it could be. A short time later, he took another agency assignment because of a friend – Bob Wells - and because it paid extremely well. The assignment turned out to be difficult. More difficult still was the tragic and unexpected loss of Kim. She died in an automobile accident before he returned to marry her.

It was difficult for him to get up off the mat after that. He decided to drop out…to take a break…to repair himself…to see if time really did heal all things.

Releasing the anchor chain, he swims freely. In a relatively short time Jon senses a change in the current. It is a tugging sensation. He watches the vegetation sway slightly in the current as if blown by some underwater fan on low speed. He checks his air supply: 900 psi. Normally he doesn't start up until the gauge shows 500 psi. But he decides to go with discretion. He ascends at a rate of 30 feet per minute.

Decompressing for the last time he hangs on the anchor chain 15 feet below the surface. He feels the ocean beginning to heave, and dimly sees the boat above him gently roll. He looks at his watch to time his hovering. Torpedo-shaped gray reef sharks and an oceanic white tip reef shark circle below him, uninterested in the weather. They show no interest in him, either. He focuses his attention on the boat's bobbing ladder to time his exit with the ocean swells.

The time comes soon enough. Several strong kicks of his fins and he breaks the surface. He hurries out of the water. When he is three rungs from the top of the ladder – well above the water - he takes off his fins and throws them on board one at a time. Next, he tosses his rubber and plastic mask on the deck. It bounces several times before coming to a stop near the pilothouse door. Having a dive buddy is helpful when climbing out of the water with a tank, but he has learned to manage. He heaves himself onto the deck in a prone position. Getting to his feet he removes his gloves, weight belt and buoyancy control device with the air cylinder. The tank holds 80 cubic feet of air but is nearly weightless underwater. After he separates his regulator and tank from the BCD, he secures the tank in a rack in front of the pilothouse. He strips off his wet suit and picks up his mask. He will stow his gear after he washes it down.

The darkening skies on the horizon hurry him along. He comes aft and enters the pilothouse, grabbing a towel from the settee and drying his head, face, and hands. With the turn of a key and push of a button the engine starts. Satisfied, he goes forward to retract the anchor. When he returns to the pilothouse, he advances the throttle, spins the wheel and turns the boat into a stiff wind. Sea spray splashes across the prow. It is great fun.

He switches on the weather radar. Conditions have changed. He is wise to head back.

~ ~ ~ ~

On a wall map the city of Heredia is just a punctuation mark northwest of San Jose, the capitol of Costa Rica. Twenty-one-year-old Eduardo Morales teaches 8th grade math at St. Frances' Catholic High School in the city, and coaches the school's football (soccer) team. On weekends he works with livestock at a nearby farm. He is considering becoming a veterinarian because he has a way with animals, and he could use an increase in income if he is to marry and have a family.

Following a hotly contested football game on Saturday, he casually mentions to his girlfriend he is getting a cold. The next day he complains about sore muscles, thinking it is the result of extra physical training with the team. On Monday he decides he has the flu because he is running a fever and has a sore throat; he calls out less he infect the school children. On Tuesday, he feels sick and goes to the Hospital de Heredia San Vicente de Paul – a new and sophisticated public hospital with excellent doctors and nurses. It is the newest medical facility in Costa Rica's national health care system.

But it is too late.

Eduardo Morales, despite excellent medical care, dies unexpectedly on Wednesday of a FUO – fever of unknown origin. The medical staff is concerned and puzzled. When samples taken from Morales are examined under a Transmission Electron Microscope, the squirming and wiggling rod-shaped bacterium are identified as Bacillus anthracis: Anthrax.

It raises alarm.

The authorities contact the Center for Disease Control and Prevention in Atlanta. They request confirmation of the findings and extra doses of Cipro, a powerful antibiotic. Just in case.

CHAPTER 4

Two years after he retires from the CIA Robert Wells is alone. He feels like a frog sitting on a toad stool in the rain: just existing.

Susan and he never expected she would go first. Or, for that matter, considered what life would be like without one another. They planned to travel to as many of the "1,000 Places to See Before You Die" – a morbid title for a book – as they could. But they waited too long. Chemo drained Susan's energy and strength. The drug kills good cells with the same speed as it kills bad ones. The psychological toll weighed heavily on them. In the final week they both knew the end was near, and they were frightened. The night she died in Hospice he struggled to conceal his panic. But it was present in his eyes.

At first Susan was unable to get enough oxygen or morphine to relieve her anxiety and fear. Wells held her hand tightly and then more gently. He whispered words of encouragement. He held back his tears until she lapsed into the arms of "Morpheus."

Minutes later, heavily sedated, she received 6 milligrams of morphine. She died quickly, quietly, and peacefully.

For months afterwards Wells broods over what to do with his life. He finds no solace in hobbies. He has no interests outside of work. He has no need for money. In addition to his pension he sits on a corporate board that pays him $228,058 annually. Friends try unsuccessfully to interest him in outdoor activities. He never clearly sees the sense in fishing or hunting or golf. Hunters are snipers. How sportsmen-like is killing a threatening or non-threatening animal hundreds of yards distant - beyond scent, sight, or hearing - with high powered rifles and telescopic sights? Fishing seems equally senseless. Not only does the fisherman rarely eat the catch, but usually releases it to be caught again and again. That strikes him as cruel and usual – at least for the fish. Golf is expensive, trivial, and time consuming. It is usually played at someone else's expense and rationalized as business. As a form of physical exercise, it has little merit.

And so one morning, in a moment of clarity, he decides to return to work. Work is his real passion. He contacts a corporate attorney/friend and launches Cadbury Metrics International (CMI). Headquartered in an unimpressive medium size office building at Hilton Head, South Carolina, it is hidden among dull office buildings next to a shopping mall. The top two floors of the six-story building comprise 6,000 square feet of office space accessible by a private, swipe-card operated elevator. Office space on the other floors is for lease from Cadbury's real estate division.

The company is named after the well-known British confectioner – Cadbury - because Susan Wells liked chocolate. It is run by Wells and former top officials of the Central Intelligence Agency as a foreign intelligence contractor. Its professionals carry out advanced research, analytics, and special services for the U.S. government. Special Services is a purposefully vague descriptor of the company's function. Its undertakings occur outside the United States - in sometimes volatile areas - in pursuit of the objectives of Central Intelligence Agency. Consequently, Wells keeps up contacts with intelligence services around the world, friends of many years, and in several Middle East countries.

Robert Wells was born in Scottsboro, Alabama. His father was a physician who was forty-five when his son was born. His mother died when he was young, and he had no brothers or sisters. Young Bob was packed off to St. John's Military Academy in Wisconsin by his father, and from there to Harvard. In his junior year, he and his roommate were hired in the summer intern program at the Central Intelligence Agency. After graduating he was hired as an entry-level analyst. Writing reports on political activity in North Africa was interesting, but boring. Two years later the Agency agreed to pay for graduate study in Europe if he agreed to become fluent in Arabic. He spent two years in Berlin at Humboldt University learning Arabic and taking Moroccan history at the University of Berlin. Then he got a major break. His college friend worked in the clandestine section of the Agency and introduced him to the section chief. He never returned to Alabama. And he never lost his southern accent.

Wells quickly learned the world of espionage is a closed one. After training at "The Farm", where he finished top in his class, he went into the field to learn spy craft. Because of his language training in Arabic (Darija), he was posted to Tangier, Morocco. Tangier is where spying became legendary. Wells often took coffee at the El Minzah, a historical hotel where Humphrey Bogart, Barbara Hutton, and many other celebrities once stayed. Winston Churchill, his idol, was a guest there in the 1940s. Moreover, the ancient city is rich in the cultural history of the Phoenicians, Romans, and Carthaginians, and in the mythical history of the Greeks and Berbers. Its international importance is equally fascinating. In 1821, the United States bought its first foreign owned property – the American Legation. In short, for Wells, Tangier is more Casablanca than Casablanca, and more Hollywood than Hollywood.

The political temperature is hot when Wells meets with the head of the Mossad in Tel Aviv. The purpose of his visit is to discuss growing threats in light of developments in Iran. He receives an unofficial update on the overall Middle East "situation." But the Israel/Iran situation dominates the conversation. Iran recovered a downed RQ-170 Sentinel several months earlier. The drone is a tactical operations platform, meaning it provides streaming video in real time, and monitors ground communications from a high altitude. The primary concern for the Agency is whether or not it's possible to reverse engineer its classified technology and sell the secrets to the Russians and Chinese. Wells' intelligence sources suggest the drone was flying over Iran and caught in a powerful electronic cyber trap. The U.S. Air Force was aware the drone was not destroyed when the satellite signal was lost. Because of command failure to act in a critical situation, someone's head will roll. Besides that, sources are confident the sensors are too complex to be reverse engineered.

Wells privately believes a nation's behavior is linked to geography. And geography is linked with identity, and identity is linked to a lot of things, such as economics and history and language. None of these things do Iran and Israel have in common. He expects more violence, and the drawing of the U.S. into a conflict in support of Israel. Reliable peace seems light years away.

The next day, after making his report to the Agency, Wells is on a plane to Casablanca to confer with Moroccan intelligence officials, and unofficial private sources. It is his first trip to Casablanca since suicide bombers killed 45 people in 2003 and 2007. Casablanca is one of his favorite cities, ancient and modern, unchanged and changing. The city has the second largest Mosque in the world – the Hassan II Mosque – which opened in 1993. Thirty-five thousand craftsmen worked years to build it. It is simply magnificent. More than 25,000 believers can pray at the same time in the prayer hall, and part of the roof can be opened to the heavens.

Wells stops at the U.S. Embassy to meet with the C.I.A. Station Chief before going with Abdul Ishak to lunch at Rick's Café. Ishak is an employee of CMI and serves as a "listener" for developments in North Africa. The food is excellent at Rick's, and Wells indulges himself. For starters he orders the Salade de Gambas Tropicana (Prawn salad Tropicana). The main course is Espadon panne au pistou (Breaded swordfish with pesto). And for dessert he breaks his own rules and orders Tarte aux pommes, glace vanilla (Apple tart with vanilla ice cream), and a cup of coffee. Three bites into the apple tart his encoded smart phone vibrates. It's a secure text from Adrian Soperton – Deputy Director of Intelligence at the Agency and his immediate successor – requesting a breakfast meeting in Virginia Beach as soon as possible. Wells still has a few hours before his plane leaves. He and Ishak visit the Hassan II Mosque. It is Wells' third visit.

~ ~ ~ ~

Thomas Forsyth is the Political Section Chief at the U. S. Embassy in Costa Rica. He majored in international affairs and foreign languages at Middlebury College in Vermont. Middlebury is highly regarded in academic circles and has been around for more than 200 years. After four challenging years as a student, Forsyth emerged from college a principled young man, a teetotaler, and an intellectual. He had been a brilliant student – like most of his peers at the college – but oddly obsessive about words. His obsession with words never abated. In his fifteen-year career to date, he takes pains to always find the right words, especially for cables to his superiors in Washington. Because of his love for words and foreign languages, he internalized the Middlebury expression "Life doesn't come with subtitles."

Forsyth has two hobbies: tennis and little theater. Costa Rica is a good posting for Forsyth because it affords him adequate time to indulge both in his off hours. The Embassy's Legal Attaché (FBI special agent in country) is David Turner, his frequent tennis competitor. Turner is well connected with the local and national police, a major part of his job, and sometimes confidentially discusses with Forsyth anything of professional interest. Forsyth is a good listener. One Sunday afternoon, during a brief break at the net on the Embassy's tennis courts, Turner mentions the tragic death of a young man in Heredia, a suburb north of San Jose. Earlier he heard of another case – two, in fact, near the Panama/Costa Rica border, but the police could not make any connections with either. The "Why" was not answered. The "How" was.

"Anthrax?" asks Forsyth, his face dripping with sweat. "You sure?"

"That's what the police report says."

"Just the one case?"

"Uh-huh. Not counting the one on the Caribbean side," he corrects himself, leaning lightly on the net. "Is that unusual?"

"I don't know," Forsyth says, blotting his forehead with wrist bands. He remembers reading a report about anthrax. The important question is: is it respiratory anthrax or ingested anthrax? If the answer is respiratory, that could mean it was spread in an aerosol form. A weaponize form. If it was ingested anthrax, then it could have been caused by bad food. Most likely a meat product. He has another source who has a different idea. He best make mention of it in his next report. "What's the score?"

"Are you kidding me? 40-30." Turner wipes his racket on his shirt and returns to serve game point.

~ ~ ~ ~

The Good Bean in Virginia Beach is a timeless coffee shop undiscovered by tourists. A block from the ocean, it is a favorite of Navy personnel and their families on weekends. However, on weekdays the regulars are a young crowd with their laptops, blackberries, ipads, and smart phones. The young professionals are busy networking and connecting.

The Bean is well known locally for its large mugs of coffee ($2 for the first cup, free refills) and cinnamon rolls. But its masterpieces are the perfectly made omelets, and crumbly-moist browned biscuits. The aroma of the coffee, rolls and biscuits is irresistible.

"Haven't been here in years," Wells says cheerfully, arriving at the table.

The slender, impeccably dressed, man waiting for Wells stands and extends his hand. He is wearing a grey wool suit with a lilac pinstriped cotton shirt and blue silk tie.

"It's good to see you, Mr. Director."

"And good to see you, Adrian," says the bespectacled Wells. He has on a lightweight silk jacket, blue trousers, and an open collar white cotton shirt. "You can drop the 'Director'. I'm just Bob now." They sit at a small window table facing the ocean. There are a dozen other tables in the Bean but only six are occupied. None are close.

"Old habits die hard. Thank you for meeting with me." Soperton unconsciously tightens the knot in his expensive tie.

"It's my pleasure. You're my best client," Wells chuckles, casually looking around, almost expecting to see someone he knows.

"You were my mentor," Soperton reminds Wells, ignoring the "client" comment. "I'm going out on a limb, but I owe you an update about unfinished business."

"Unfinished business?" Wells asks, a puzzled look on his face. He unfolds the white linen napkin and puts it in his lap.

"About the Agency. It's been a challenge since you left. Correction. It is a challenge since you left."

Wells focuses his gaze on Soperton. "More than expected?"

It's a vexing question for Soperton but easily answered. "It's been rough going of late, as I'm sure you're aware. The Administration is taking a lot of heat because of our failures."

"And?"

"And they have imbedded a fractious group of political appointees within the Agency and a political Czar. The old and new have colliding ideas about policies and procedures."

"Sorry to hear that, but it's not unusual. I've followed the torture accusations," he adds quickly, "if that's what you mean."

"It's a political gimmick," Soperton says defensively, sounding ill at ease. "Yet it's more than that. It's everything from the underwear bomber to Guantanamo. Their amateurish and intrusive supervision is hanging our people out to dry."

"So you expect to lose good people?" Wells looks around for a waiter - server - in the new politically correct dictionary.

"You remember George Shanin?"

"Of course. How's he doing?" Wells catches the eye of the server.

"He's one of the smart ones; he separated from the Agency last year. Now he's a "Senior Mentor" to the Pentagon."

"Nice," Wells says, aware of the fire storm brewing over the practice. Privately, he expects the joy ride by some retired generals and admirals to crash and burn soon.

"Really sweet deals." continues Soperton, "He's advising the Air Force on aerospace war games."

Wells says, "George knows his stuff."

"Knocks down $125,000 per in addition to his retirement."

"Guess I should explore a raise," Wells says with a straight face.

"We're already paying Cadbury $2.7 million a year."

"Money well spent," he jokes, then smiles slightly.

The server arrives at the table in somewhat of a hurry. "My name's Jeff," he breaks in. "I'll be serving you this morning. Have you decided what you'd like?" He has his order pad and restaurant logo ballpoint ready. He looks at Soperton.

"A cheese omelet, please. With a mild cheese."

"Sure," says Jeff. "It comes with two sides."

"Bacon and spiced apples," Soperton says, tucking the linen napkin in his waistband.

"Coffee?"

"Regular, please," Soperton answers, returning the menu.

"For you, sir?" Jeff says, turning to Wells.

"Regular coffee and a plain toasted bagel."

"Cream cheese?"

"Plain toasted bagel," Wells patiently repeats, handing the menu to him.

"Certainly."

Jeff pours two cups of coffee and departs.

Wells decides to make chit-chat until breakfast arrives. "What became of Azizi?"

"Amad Azizi was an outstanding operative."

Wells says, "You were always impressed with him. Where is he now?"

"He was killed."

"What happened?"

"He had a team of six contract guys in Afghanistan."

"And?"

Soperton is slow to answer. "Woman informant comes to a meeting wearing 25 pounds of explosives. Vaporizes everyone."

"I'm sorry. Hell of a waste," sighs Wells, shaking his head sadly.

"Azizi's name will be added to the wall later this month."

There is a pause in the conversation. Then, eager to steer the conversation away from Azizi, he says, "What became of Dieter Hetzer?"

"Did you know he was an alcoholic? Threw his career and life away. Sad."

"I'm almost afraid to ask about Zhi Wang?"

Soperton nods his head. "That little prick committed suicide. Threw himself off the Golden Gate. Wish he had done it sooner." He pauses to take a long drink of water.

Wells draws back in surprise. "You never much liked him," he says. "Can you reach the cream?"

"It wasn't a matter of like or dislike," he says, passing the cream, "I didn't trust him. I believe he was the leak." Almost as an afterthought he passes the sugar bowl.

"That's serious," says Wells without facial expression. "What makes you think so?" Wells pours enough cream in the coffee to make it look like hot chocolate. He uses one spoonful of sugar, although he'd prefer two, and stirs. Susan tried to break him of using any sugar.

"After he failed the poly he returned to the Bay Area."

"That was home for him," Wells says matter-of-factly, taking a sip of coffee.

"It was more than that. We discovered – after the fact, unfortunately, - he had a relationship with a Korean language lab instructor at San Francisco State. We now believe she was a 'sleeper' for North Korea."

Raising his eyebrows, Wells asks "Where is she now?"

"She left the country within 24 hours of Wang's termination."

"One step ahead of us. Of the Agency," he corrects himself. He passes the cream and sugar back to Soperton, who moves it to the side of the table.

"Considering Wang was terminated, about to be arrested for treason, and his paramour bailed, suicide may have seemed his best alternative."

Wells nods his understanding. He cups his hands around the hot coffee mug, watching how fidgety Soperton appears. The purpose of this meeting is definitely not just for old time's sake.

"But he hurt us in more ways than one," Soperton explains. "This is why I wanted to meet with you. We have a dilemma."

"What kind of a dilemma?"

"Here we are, gentlemen," interrupts Jeff-the-server, distributing the hot omelet, crisp bacon and spiced apples first, and the toasted bagel last. He tops off the coffee for Soperton and departs with the standard "Enjoy".

Both men ignore him. Wells continues to stir his coffee with his spoon.

Breakfast is excellent. There is no rush and little reason, thinks Wells, that Soperton should seek his advice, other than out of friendship and professional courtesy. After the last bite of his bagel he says, "How can I be helpful?"

Soperton makes eye contact and nods his head almost imperceptibly. He puts his coffee cup down and casually looks around the coffee shop. No one seems to be paying the slightest attention to them. Still, following Agency protocol, he says "Let's continue our discussion in my office after breakfast. I'll get breakfast. You get the tip."

Soperton pays in cash. Wells leaves a 25 percent tip.

Minutes later they are in Soperton's 2010 tricked-out Ford Transit Connect. The smallish white Agency van advertises a non-existent Virginia Beach Army/Navy Surplus store on its side panels. The windows are darkly tinted. They have so many glass laminates that they are as bullet-proof as steel armor. Armoring the vehicle added 1,500 pounds to its weight. The driver and passenger seats turn 180 degrees, facing rearward. Behind the driver's seat is a small table with a keypad, laptop and phone. There is built-in shelving with five cameras providing surveillance on all sides of the vehicle, including one that shows an aerial view of the van.

Once inside the van Soperton locks the doors remotely from the key pad on the table. He stretches his neck in a nervous gesture and feels the knot in his tie. Wells waits for Soperton to speak.

"We're in the most challenging security environment in my lifetime." He leaves the statement hanging in the air.

Wells wonders what the comment means, then breaks the silence. "You didn't invite me here to discuss global security issues."

Soperton replies by apologizing, "No, I didn't. I invited you because I have disturbing information. It's Top Secret."

"On a need-to-know basis?" Wells asks solemnly.

"It's about Project StingRay."

"Really?" reacts a genuinely surprised Wells. Project StingRay was almost three years in the past. He shifts uncomfortably in his seat.

Soperton painstakingly shares some classified information, without alluding to specific details, and plunges ahead to a succinct conclusion: "The Korean doctor who helped London has been murdered."

"Jesus H.!" Wells exclaims. The surprises just keep coming, he thinks. What's next?

"She was beaten to death. At least that's what the official report says. But we think there's more. The actual cause of death may have been a ricin-tipped needle. Or maybe another toxin. It's unclear."

Wells lets out a low whistle. "Murdered or assassinated?"

"She's dead. We have reason to believe it was not random," Soperton answers, "and it involves you professionally and personally."

"Go on."

Soperton exhales like an athlete about to begin a sprint. "I'll give you a few points."

"I'm listening."

"We believe the North Korean Secret Police – the National Security Bureau (NSB) - murdered Dr. Soon. They may have had technical assistance from "The Russian Poison Factory"."

"We know the Soviets have been working with North Korea on bioweapons for years."

"And that they have weaponized a large number of biologicals," agrees Soperton with a nod of his head.

"But why would the North Korean secret police want to murder Soon?" interrupts Wells.

"That's unclear. But there is the new leader - 'The Young General'. Maybe Kim Jong Il wanted to give Kim Jong Un – the 'Great Successor' a clean start."

Wells says nothing.

"Keep in mind," Soperton goes on, "even with Mr. Kim gone, North Korea is still a corrupt and repressive regime."

Wells says, "So you think this is about a clean start?"

"Maybe Kim Jong Il's legacy. Whatever it is, the NSB has been looking worldwide to find and assassinate London."

"Adrian, we protected his identity!" Wells says incredulously. "Why would they want to do that?"

"Names are just names. They know him as Charles Sewell not Jon London. They probably think London is a cover name. Zhi Wang may have betrayed us. Doesn't matter. What matters is they are actively," he says with emphasis, "looking to kill him."

Wells tries to decide whether or not London is really in danger. "You're convinced he is in eminent danger?"

"No question about it. Officially, we are not having this conversation. This is why I have this dilemma…"

"Has anyone tried to contact him? Warn him?"

"Who would he believe? Our asset in North Korea was arrested," continues Soperton. "I want to bring you in to solve some issues. Can I make our discussion official?"

"Go ahead."

"We've got some holes in the picture. First question: What could the North Korean asset have told them about London?"

"Nothing."

"Okay. What could Dr. Soon have told them?"

"Beyond the name Sewell, nothing. How did we get in the loop, anyway?" Wells ask, looking puzzled.

"The South Korean Central Intelligence Agency (KCIA) learned of Dr. Soon's murder and dug around. They are very good."

"Among the best."

"Long story short. North Korea had a low-level informant in our embassy in Seoul. The mole reported to the NSB that a North Korean in the company of an American came to the embassy. The Korean was a doctor, and the American was Charles Sewell. The NSB put the picture together and began a search to find out what the Americans knew."

"They knew what we had?"

"Probably not. But they needed to find out. To do that they needed to find Sewell."

Wells is bewildered. "They are that desperate?"

"Desperate or paranoid or careful," answers Soperton. "The world is still imperfect."

"They have been looking for him for two years?!"

"Apparently. Which brings me to the main point: The North Koreans have not given up on their plans for a bioterror attack on American soil."

"A bleak thought," comments Wells, looking out the tinted windows at a young couple going into The Good Bean. The man is wearing the uniform of a Lieutenant in the Navy. So is the woman. They look incredibly young to Wells.

"North Korea is a rogue state. They terrorize their own people. They starve their own people. They are not going to come to the six party talks with sincerity. Ever. A bioterror attack on a major U. S. city is relatively easy. Within hours we will have a nation of angry patriots! Can you even begin to image what the media would do with that?"

Wells sits motionless, thoughtfully thinking before speaking. "I clearly remember our discussions of such possible scenarios."

"We need to stop them!"

"That's a lofty goal," sighs Wells. "And sobering." He stretches his legs out in front of him. Finally he says, "Let's start at Go and work our ways around to Boardwalk."

"Okay," begins Soperton. "You may know North Korea has befriended several emerging nations, mainly in Africa."

"Emerging nations," interjects Wells, "the politically correct term for what we use to call less developed nations."

"Right. Anyway, the government in Pyongyang provides aid to a number of countries disguised as technical assistance."

"Military assistance?"

"Not all. However, we believe there is a power struggle going on with the army and Mr. Kim's government."

"They have a huge army."

"Fourth-largest in the world. Over a million troops."

"But the Army are the 'capitalists' of North Korea," Wells says.

"Correct. But disgruntled generals are flexing their muscle."

"The shelling of Yeonpyeong Island?"

"Sabre-rattling. The Chinese are not going to allow North Korea to attack South Korea."

"The North Korean military cannot be taken lightly."

"Clearly. But we suspect this was just another diversion. A way of saying 'don't forget about us.'"

"Maybe building his son's military leadership resume?"

"Perhaps. Candidly, Un is incompetent and needs his military handlers."

"What do you think they are up to, Adrian?"

"'Friendship diplomacy' for one thing."

"What's that?"

"North Korea provides advice on how to manufacture certain hard to find items."

"Counterfeit?"

"Legitimate."

Wells shakes his head. His frustration with government bureaucracy never died. "For years they've been expert at counterfeiting pharmaceuticals, currency, and computer parts."

"There are certain advantages," Soperton continues, "to completely disregarding intellectual property rights, patents, copyrights, and trademarks. North Korea has one company with a thousand artists and thousands of workers. All it does is produce sculptures for emerging nations, primarily African countries."

"That seems more symbolic than sinister."

"Perhaps. Even less well known, however, is another company with brilliant scientists. These scientists are highly qualified in chemistry, genetics, physics, biology, microbiology, pathology, physiology…you name it. They provide scientific assistance to countries while disguising their real purpose."

"Which is…?"

"The development of weapons of mass destruction. Mass disruption may be a better term. Bioweapons, biological agents and deadly toxins are my worst nightmare."

"Adrian, we have suspected this for a long time. When London retrieved the North Korean Classified Plan two years ago it was all confirmed. At least in my opinion." He feels his frustration growing, along with his anxiety for London.

"This may explain why they are hot on London's trail."

"I keep telling you he doesn't know what's in the plan!"

"They can't be sure of that, Bob. There are two sides to every story. Regardless, our strategists believe North Korea is now in a more dangerous and threatening phase."

"Go on," he says, cocking his head slightly to one side. He narrows his eyes.

"We believe they are testing on people."

"Whoa, whoa, whoa," he says, shaking his head from side to side. "How do you know that?"

"We had an operator inside."

"Go on."

"Something happened. We don't know what, exactly. But we suspect there was foul play involved. Communication ceased suddenly. The source was probably arrested, or worse, but we have not confirmed what happened."

"So, you're going on limited information and a hunch?" He wrinkles his forehead as he asks the question. Wells knows there will always be gaps, misperceptions, and mistakes in classified data. Intelligence is not always simple and trustworthy. He hopes Soperton's conclusions are well grounded. "There are lots of uncertainties," he says after a moment.

"Doubters tend to focus on uncertainties," Soperton says. "There is always the fog of unknowing. It doesn't mean we're wrong in believing weapon-grade toxins are being produced. And pathogens are easier to package than nuclear materials. It's weaponising them that's tricky. Besides, the N.S.A.'s Signals Intelligence Analysis Group intercepted a lot of cellular and Internet communications. Some of it curled our toes, but it is clear to us we have a serious, serious threat. And we have satellite photos that heighten our concerns. I believe we must act." He angles the monitor toward Wells and strikes a few keys on the laptop. "See for yourself."

O 360714Z JUN 11

FM AMEMBASSY SAN JOSE

TO SECSTATE WASHDC URGENT 4869

INFO SECDEFENSE

C.I.A. WASHINGTON DC

JOINT CHIEFS WASHINGTON DV

DIA WASHINGTON DC

S E C R E T San Jose

SUBJECT: North Korea and Tropical Center for Investigation and Research

CLASSIFIED BY: Political Section Chief Thomas Forsyth

Reasons 1.4 (b/d)

SUMMARY

1. Credible sources insist DPRK scientists in Costa Rica are testing on human subjects.

2. C.I.A. station chief here believes tests on civilians have occurred or are occurring in Costa Rica, Nicaragua, and Panama.

3. Sources suggest chemical and biological WMD are covertly transported from Costa Rica to Nicaragua at night by armed Maras (youth gangs) and mercenaries.

4. End Summary.

"Pretty damning," says Wells, a tone of caution in his voice. From his former position at the Agency, he knows a lot about N.S.A. capabilities. In the intelligence community it is the big enchilada. Thousands of people work on its five-thousand-acre-campus at Ft. Meade in Maryland. Their crypto-mathematicians are the best. With five billion cellphones in the world, and millions of bits of information passing every minute, they have to be. In the last few years, N.S.A.'s sophisticated computers refined its data mining, and perfected the data correlation from Web sites, travel records, G.P.S. equipment, financial transactions, and other sources, and listened in on the plans of the nation's enemies. Which is how Osama bin Laden's hiding place was found.

Soperton nods his agreement. "Here's where you come in."

"You want us to verify your suspicions?"

"Yes and no. Yes we want you to verify. And no, that's not all."

"What's 'all'?"

"If they are producing, and we believe they are, we need to shut 'em down."

"I don't like the idea of doing that. Anyway, I thought producing the bioweapons was only half the calculus."

"The other half being a North Korean delivery system?" guesses Soperton.

"Right."

"We have some theories but no hard evidence. They are pals with Iran, you remember."

"What are the bureaucratic boundaries for this operation?"

"Few. Clearly, we don't want any international incidents. We want to avoid diplomatic and political perils with the Costa Rican government. It's a neutral country."

"The Switzerland of Central America."

"And the oldest democracy in Central or South America," Soperton reminds him.

"I know. Something like 180 years of political stability."

"They are allies of just about everybody. And they certainly are one of our best friends. Those considerations paramount in mind, we still need to disrupt the production and testing. Destroying it would be a homerun."

"We are authorized to…?"

"Do what you have to do. This is off the books," confides Soperton.

"Horse feathers. Give me a hint."

"Horse feathers?" he says, sitting straighter and looking at Wells.

"I'm trying to curse less," he lamely explains.

"How's that working for you?" Soperton jokes.

"Depends on how stressed I am," confesses Wells.

"I'll keep that in mind. But the answer to your question is the Secretary of Defense, the Secretary of State, and the President strongly agreed we have no choice."

"DHS?"

"Homeland Security doesn't know yet."

"Others?"

"N.S.A. is critical. Obviously, they are in. We've had geointel from N.G.A. (National Geospatial-Intelligence Agency) for imagery analysis. As few of the other 16 component intelligence agencies as possible.

"N.S.A. – the old 'No Strings Attached' agency. You know I had a running battle with them over the secret space shuttles and the P-3 screw up."

"The Navy reconnaissance plane colliding with a Chinese jet? Ten years ago?" Soperton remembers it very well because it ultimately led to the creation of the U.S. Cyber Command.

"Eleven years," Wells corrects him. "The Chinese got their hands on the EP-3E's encrypted operating system. N.S.A. said the Chinese couldn't reverse-engineer the system because it had 50-million lines of computer code. Bullshit. Five years later it was apparent they had reverse-engineered the hard drive."

"Which is why both of us believe cyber war is the real threat. But that is not on our plate today."

"Goddamn it to hell!" Wells curses, "Gives me major heart burn."

Judging by Wells' vocabulary, his stress level is going up. But Soperton ignores it and says, "The Director and the SecDef met privately with the President after the regular Wednesday briefing in the Situation Room. We have a Presidential Finding, Bob. That's all we need. And the SecDef wants to protect us and our allies from North Korean aggression as much as we do. We're in agreement bioweapons are a more plausible threat than nuclear ones. He's in. We need the N.S.A. and the military."

"My ass will be way out there," Wells says in an unnerving tone, still agitated. "Will there be any documents for a disgruntled 23-year-old in the Pentagon to leak on You Tube?'

"Absolutely not," Soperton confidently assures him. "No written documentation. No e-mails. No voice mails. No confidential memos or top-secret documents. There may be two million Confidential, Secret, and Top-Secret clearances floating around. But there are only a hundred Ultra One clearances."

Probably closer to three million clearances floating around, guesses Wells without challenging Soperton. "So, I try and pull London back from the edge, recruit my own team, get backing from wherever I need it, verify the situation, and get back to you. How I do this is up to me? Correct?"

"Pretty much." Soperton stretches his neck and does a 180 with his head. It pops a couple of times.

Wells watches the ritual and then says, "A lot has changed since Presidential Order 12.333."

"Reagan's Executive Order barring assassinations was the right thing. But that was then."

"And now is now?"

"Exactly. Clinton took off the gloves after the bombings in Kenya and Tanzania. Our President, I think, was right to authorized taking out the radical American Imam in Yemen. Besides, this is bigger than any one person."

"You're referring to U.N. Resolution 678?"

"Resolution 687," Soperton gently corrects Wells, "classifying chemical and biological agents as weapons of mass destruction."

"Right. I'm sure you recall our debates about Hussein and WMDs." He raises his eyebrows.

Soperton clears his throat and says, "We should have taken the monster out years earlier. It would have saved the lives of thousands of our troops, thousands of civilians, and billions of taxpayer dollars. I lost my only nephew. My sister will never get over it. It will trouble me the rest of my life."

"There will always be a debate about legitimate military action versus Dubai-type assassinations."

"The Mossad took the heat for Dubai, but a lot of countries were glad someone got him. Personally, I hope Israel will assist us in this world."

"Inshallah," Wells says in fluent Moroccan Arabic, meaning "if God wishes" (or, in the alternative, "I hope so").

Soperton nods his head and then puts the question: "How fast can you pull assets together?"

"How much time do we have?"

"Should have done it yesterday."

"Figures. Some things never change. What about support?"

"Whatever you need."

"Funding?"

"Not a problem."

"Can't do it without DOD and State," Wells says flatly.

"I realize that. We'll have their full cooperation."

"How fast can they move?"

"They can mobilize in a hurry," he assures Wells. "How about you?"

Wells sits quietly for a moment, running what he knows through his internal check list. He tugs on his ear lob. "I'll need London."

"From his last assignment, I'd say his courage is never in doubt." Soperton emits a small grin as he says this.

"Sheer guts and a total lack of self-doubt helps," responds Wells.

"Think he's in good shape?"

"I'd say his physical abilities are tip-top. Anyway, to answer your question, if I can get London and another person I have in mind - a week to get it in gear. Three more days with briefings, logistics, probably ten to fourteen days total."

"I hope you have that much time," warns Soperton.

Wells nods.

That's it.

CHAPTER 5

Bob Wells returns to Hilton Head Island later that day. He attempts to contact Jon London on his boat, and on his cell. Neither have voice mail. He silently curses CPO people – Cell Phone Only people. That night he sleeps hardly at all.

Early the next morning the sun is a faint glow on the horizon when he arrives at his office. A steady light rain blurs the view from his office window overlooking the ocean; the Atlantic is waking up. He looks at his watch and times the waves. Five waves break on the beach in one minute. The wind is picking up. The stronger the wind the fewer number of waves per minute. The weather has been gloomy for days. He chides himself for not calling the ONR's Ocean Battlespace Sensing Department. Their meteorological predictions are spot on.

Wells forces himself to concentrate on his huge workload, much of it he brought upon himself to compensate for the loss of Susan. But yesterday's meeting with Soperton has changed his priorities. It's still too early to get a cup of coffee - an oversight he plans to correct when he has a moment. Instead, he sits down at his Brazilian Jacaranda desk and tries to reach Jon London. Again, he is unsuccessful.

His desk is well organized but cluttered. He picks up the nearest and thinnest political report. Gas prices in Libya have dropped back to $.40 a gallon. Waiting lines for petrol have returned to normal. The slightest rumor of oil shortages causes the price of Brent crude shoots up $5 or more a barrel. He makes a mental note to fill up his gas tank after work. He reads on: Tunisia's leader toppled, Egypt's still in chaos, Yemen's in turmoil, Bahrain is struggling, Pakistan, Iran, Afghanistan, and Indonesia, all with issues. Worst of all, from a Western perspective, Israel and Iran are at a crossroad. A terribly busy Arab Spring.

He picks up another confidential report that details the Pakistani situation. When he was Deputy Director at the Agency there was ample evidence the Pakistani military was protecting OBL, and their intelligence service was leaking U.S. intentions to the Osama bin Laden camp. After locating Osama bin Laden in Khost, Afghanistan, the Clinton

Administration launched 75 tomahawk missiles at the camp. OBL had left a few hours before the attack. The Agency believed then he was tipped off by the Pakistan intelligence service. Eleven more years of futility followed before the military finally got their man. Now, with minimal success in Afghanistan, the nation is rushing to the exit. He privately predicts it will prove unwise.

"Not in my lane," he thinks, and puts the reports neatly to one side of his desk. Reaching into the center desk drawer he takes out a cloth and cleans his glasses. Then he replaces the cloth and closes the drawer. He opens the jacketed folder Soperton gave him and focuses again on the task at hand. The secret report is six pages, excluding photos. He devours each word, looking for anything that will be helpful. The three clear images are low orbits satellite photographs. The first one is of the institute campus. The second photograph is of the suspected target building. Photograph three is of the same building three months later. It shows a substantial addition. Refrigeration? Testing? Production? When he finishes studying the photographs he spins around and unlocks a file drawer in the cadenza behind him. Sensitive data and top-secret reports are sequestered in the drawer under a faux bronze bust of Winston Churchill. Wells liked political and military history as a college student. There are parallels in Churchill's and his life, he believes. Churchill was considered a failure when he was five years older than Wells is now. He didn't become prime minister until he was 65. One historian's assessment: "Churchill was a man who was called on, late in life, to do the one thing he was uniquely able to do, and he did it." Or something like that. Perhaps the same can be said of him. Anyway, 60 is the new 50. Carefully watching his weight, his diet, and exercising four days a week, Wells considers himself not older than 45.

He retrieves his private phone directory from the cadenza. He will make a series of phone calls, starting with Irwin Emanuel, C.I.A. Station Chief in Hamilton, Bermuda. With no U.S. Embassy in Bermuda, the Agency's presence is a closely guarded secret. For Emanuel, Bermuda is a small and quiet posting. He answers the phone on the second ring.

"Video Photographers."

"Do you recognize my voice?" says Wells quietly.

"Can't say I do. Talk a little more."

"Soperton called you."

"He beat you by a good thirty minutes," he laughs. "You're slowing down, Bob." His is an easy voice, very relaxed.

"In your dreams. Is this a secure line?"

"Ah, it had better be. Why do you care? I thought you retired."

"Never retire, Irwin. Work as long as you can. Your life depends on it."

"Hope you're wrong about that." Emanuel has six months remaining on his last two year overseas tour before retirement. Most of his career has been in exotic and dangerous locations, but courage never failed him anywhere. The Bermuda assignment is his retirement gift from a grateful C.I.A.

Emanuel is one of the Agency's old schoolers - a Yale man, married for 37 years to his college sweetheart. He is father of two adult children, and grandfather of four girls. Thoroughly dependable, he is excellent at managing risk. Bermuda, fortunately, is a no-risk slam dunk for a delightful and decent guy.

"Soperton told you what I need - we need?" asks Wells.

"Generally. He said you would call with details. I'm all ears."

For the next hour, Wells details what he knows, what to expect in the next 24 to 48 hours, and what he wishes for him to do. At the conclusion of the mini-brief, Emanuel asks, "for the record, what are you calling this operation?"

"There is no record. This never happens."

"Soperton is going to have to okay that, Bob," he warns.

"We may have a plumbing problem that needs to get fixed. Until we do let's not help anyone."

"I'll play along as long as I can. Give me a name anyway?"

"MNEMOSYNE?"

"Operation Mnemosyne?"

"What do you think?"

"I can't spell it – n-e-m…" he begins, scribbling on his note pad.

"No, no. It's M-n-e-m-o-s-y-n-e."

"Greek?" Emanuel asks.

"Of course."

"Meaning?"

"I think 'remembrance'," answers Wells. "She was the goddess of memory. I'm

taking some literary license here."

"Operation M. Does that memory thing mean something to you?"

"I'm hoping it means something to one of our people."

Emanuel watches the rough ocean from the office window. He is trying to think of anything more he needs to know. "For what it's worth," he tells Wells, "the weather outside is turning nasty. This time of year, it could mean a storm is brewing." As quickly as he finishes the sentence, the sunlight is snuffed out by a thick cloud, darkening his office. A strong gust of wind pushes at two palm trees in his field of vision.

"It's looking none too good here, either. We'll get going ASAP," responds Wells.

When he hangs up he is pleased the call went well.

Disregarding operational procedure, Emanuel plugs his digital voice recorder into his PC and uploads an audio file. The voice recognition software will enable him to create a written document for his files. Just in case.

Wells flips a few pages in his private phone directory. The third entry under the R tab is Regor. Regor is Roger spelled backwards. Not exactly a complex brain twister for the curious. Wells developed his secret code in the fifth grade to guard his journal from his mother's prying eyes. He permits himself a childish grin as he remembers how silly it was then. Even more so now. The Freud thing: the child is father of the adult.

"Regor" is an acquaintance of many years, and the United States Under Secretary of the Air Force from 1989 to 1993. Following government service, he joined a private equity investment firm in New York. He found a small aircraft manufacturer in Georgia that was struggling to survive and bought controlling interest in the company. He installed himself as president and C.E.O. and pushed to develop a new top-of-the-line private jet for the general aviation market. He was in the one percent.

He answers the phone on the first ring. "Appling," the voice says in a deep monotone.

"Roger, this is Wells."

"I knew it was you, Wells. You're the only son-of-a-bitch that gets to work as early as I."

"Be nice, Roger. I need a favor."

"Oh, I'm shocked. I thought you were calling because you missed me," he chuckles.

Thirty minutes later, a deal cut with Appling and a cup of self-made coffee firmly in hand, Wells studies a photo sent by Soperton. It is of Lieutenant Colonel Katherine Breeden as she approaches the iris scanner and facial-recognition devices to her classified office in the Pentagon. She has a youthful face: high forehead, dark eyes, and medium lips. Her unblemished face is smooth. She looks 10 years younger than her actual age. Maybe 15 years younger. Clearly she is blessed with good genes. Staying in peak physical condition keeps age at bay. She vaguely reminds him of someone else, but he can't recall whom. He punches in the classified direct dial number for the Office of the Secretary of the Air Force. Breeden answers on the first ring.

Breeden is a 1994 graduate of the U.S. Air Force Academy. As an officer she is described by her superiors as dedicated, bright, talented, and capable. She is on the five-percent list for Colonel. To her peers she is often described as highly intelligent, goal-oriented, good-natured, a careful listener, athletic and upbeat. For those who don't know her, and/or never will know her but have seen her, she is usually described with one word: hot.

On page one of the Breeden File is a handwritten marginal note: "competitive and disciplined. Worked well with London."

Breeden was born and raised in rural Kansas. Soldier, Kansas, to be precise. Soldier is located in the Township of Grant in Jackson County. It took its name from a creek that flows southeasterly towards Topeka, where it joins the Kansas River. Legend has it the town was named by government surveyors who came across two soldiers camped along the creek bank. That was in the 1850's when there were thousands of acres of wild land available. Breeden's great, great, great grandmother was born in Soldier in 1854, the first recorded birth of a non-American Indian in that state. The endless prairie of her birthplace provided land for grazing and agriculture, and nearby deposits of magnesia and limestone contained the necessary materials for building purposes. The future looked bright for Soldier.

It never quite panned out.

When Breeden was growing up in Soldier, population 122, she thought of the community as a "space" on the forever frontier rather than a town. There were only two churches in Soldier. Her family belonged to the Methodist one. There were only two businesses, one a café. The café doubled as town hall. The other business was a general store. It was a two room brick building. One room had wide doors and stocked farm supplies such as feed and seed, fertilizer, ropes and wire, ammunition, buckets and pales, and tools. The other room was a general store and sold basic food items such salt, sugar, candy, and limited clothing. There was no future in Soldier for a young person with ambition.

After much handwringing, her mother, Alma Breeden, sent her to live with Aunt Haley and Uncle Howard in Holton so she could attend high school during the week.

Holton High School is located on New York Avenue. To Breeden it could have been in the real New York City. While she participated in the usual extracurricular clubs, her passion was running. And she was good. So good, in fact, she won the Kansas Cross Country Championship as a high school senior. That December, during a winter storm, she received a visit from the Head Coach of the track team at the U.S. Air Force Academy. The Academy was her ticket out of Kansas, and she got on the bus.

At the Academy she continued to run track. In her junior year she was selected Western Athletic Conference Woman Athlete of the Year. Her classmates gave her a nickname: The Hammer. By the end of her fourth year she had earned a degree in aeronautical engineering. Her first assignment was as a student at the Air Force Institute of Technology, Graduate School of Engineering and Management, at Wright-Patterson Air Force Base. She finished in the top ten percent.

Breeden is physically unchanged from two years earlier when Wells recruited her: a well proportioned 5' 8" and 114 pounds. To Wells' way of thinking, the Breeden recruitment is mission essential. The chat he has with her is brief, but covers all that needs to be covered. They will go face-to-face over specifics within 24 hours.

Before 9 a.m. Wells informs Soperton of the offer and acceptance and asks him to have a conversation with the Secretary of Defense to make the necessary arrangements for annual leave, not TDY. Breeden will be a private contractor with Cadbury, not a member of the U.S. Military.

Wells' last call goes to "Rusty" Burke in Miami, Florida. Burke is Commander of SOUTHCOM – the U.S. Southern Command. Not surprisingly, he is unavailable.

To fill the time, Wells scribbles an outline of things he wants to consider. In vertical order he writes:

* PRIORITY – get London out

* Objective: covert observation and report

* Personnel: London/Breeden/Agency/State and military support

* Tactics: covert entry, land travel, exit

* Timing and deadlines: a.s.a.p., flexible

* Technology: equipment, weapons, air

* Flexibility: depends on above

* Logistics: military/air/equipment

* Special requirements: TBD

* ROE: None. Ruthlessness

Ballpoint in hand, he begins to flesh out the skeleton outline. He ponders Technology, Special requirement, and Rules of Engagement. He twists possibilities around, arranges and rearranges requirements. It is an hour before Burke returns Wells' call on a secure line.

"Bob, sorry I have taken so long to get back," says a courteous and confident voice.

"I understand. Life at the top can be trying," Wells deadpans.

"You should know," counters Burke. "Tell me whom I owe for this flattering call?"

"National security." Wells summarizes events leading up to the call. He purposely leaves out a number of details that might cloud the operation. "You'll get a call from the Pentagon today. They can answer most of your questions."

"Anybody I know?"

"I'm not sure. Maybe the Army Chief of Staff. Or the Chairman of the Joint Chiefs. Maybe even the SecDef."

"Must be important."

"Life and death, Rusty."

"Any idea what they have in mind?"

"Only that it is important we work together, and that a personal meeting is critical."

"Oh?"

"They are likely to say your cooperation will be expected and appreciated."

Burke is not fazed. He is a four-star general. A native of Ocala, Florida, Burke is a Distinguished Military Graduate of Florida Southern College's ROTC unit in Lakeland, Florida, class of 1975. He earned a master's degree from the Sloan School at M.I.T.

Burke is a quiet man, not a proud one, and a man with few peculiarities. He wears his uniform with pride but has always thought wearing his resume on his uniform was not for him. He never felt he had to prove anything to anyone other than himself. Maybe his mother. So he decided to wear only the decorations that meant something to him: Combat Infantryman Badge, Ranger Tab, 82nd Airborne Patch, Pathfinder Badge and Master Parachutist Badge. He earned, but does not wear, a Silver Star, Bronze Star, Combat SCUBA Diver, Purple Heart (3 awards), and 10 other awards and decorations plus five unit citations. With his decorations reduced to a minimum, he jokes, he weighs a lot less.

"Thanks for the heads-up."

"Call me after you talk with whomever," says Wells, and hangs up.

On the Caribbean Sea the border between Costa Rica and Panama is unmarked. There are no customs officials or border guards from either country. The road south from Costa Rica just runs out. A wood planks shack sells local beer at end of the road. Panamanians occasionally cross the border via the sandy beach to enjoy the topless beach. Theresa Silva is a 19-year-old Panamanian who loves the outdoors. When she jogs along the beach men stare in fascination. Her tan breasts seem alive. Her father, a municipal judge in Panama, would not approve of her exposing herself. So Silva keeps her secret to herself. It will reflect poorly on him if people think his daughter is an exhibitionist.

When Silva comes down with severe flu-like symptoms on Monday, following a weekend of total body tanning at the beach with a friend, it is not cause for undue concern. The "friend" is a young man from Costa

Rica, a secret kept from her parents. Her mother takes very good care of her young daughter and namesake. Unknown to anyone are the millions of bacilli that are attacking her lungs and brain. The bacilli multiply with incredible speed from millions to billions. By Wednesday trillions of the parasitic microbes are destroying her body. She dies an excruciatingly painful and horrible death on Thursday. Death comes not as a thief in the night, but as a welcomed friend. Silva's death is as shocking to her parents and friends as it is incomprehensible.

Because of her father's lofty position in the community, samples are taken by car to the Medical Center in Panama City. They are carefully examined. Other samples are sent by air to the CDC in Atlanta. The CDC sends a portion of their samples to USAMRIID – the Army's Medical Research Institute of Infectious Diseases, and to UCLA's Infectious Diseases Division.

All agree: Anthrax.

CHAPTER 6

There are thousands of landing fields suitable for small airplanes in the continental United States. Some are little more than a cleared field. Others are a grass strip or a dirt road. A very few others have short asphalt runways for single or twin-engine aircraft. Most fields, however, are not long enough to accommodate the take-off requirements of a corporate jet.

On the edge of the Francis Marion National Forest is a long forgotten and isolated airfield. It is ten miles north/northeast of Jamestown, South Carolina. Surrounded by barren fields it is mostly hidden by tall pines. Vegetation hides the strip from passers-by. The low scrub surrounding the airfield is full of sandspurs, copperheads and rattlesnakes. The savanna-like grass never gets very high because of coastal winds and miserable weather. Twice a year a farmer brings in a tractor and gives the field a haircut.

A seldom used rural road leads to the abandoned airfield. The single strip of aging and cracking pavement is 4,500 feet long and 50 feet wide. In consideration of prevailing winds the runway is aligned East/West - runway 9 and runway 27. Weeds and brownish sand fill cracks in the concrete runway. The airstrip was constructed in 1943 by the Navy on 50 acres of land that had been worked-out. Farmers didn't rotate crops much in those days. After generations of planting the same cotton crop year in and year out the topsoil was ruined. The government bought the land cheaply.

The newly constructed airstrip was designated an auxiliary field. Its primary purpose was to provide a practice field for student pilots preparing for war. And it provided an emergency landing site. There were two sod strips in addition to the paved one just in case. Student pilots would shoot touch-and-goes hour after hour on long and humid summer days.

Gary Fannin was barely 17 in 1945 when he lied about his age and enlisted in the Navy. He liked it from the first day. Basic training was at Great Lakes, Illinois. Then Seaman Fannin was sent to the Repair Base in San Diego. He was barracked on Coronado Island and ferried to class each day. In due course the lad from Union, South Carolina, was assigned to the airfield as an aircraft mechanic.

Only one building still stands on the property: a brick and metal hut – a Quonset hut to be precise - originally used as an aircraft hanger. Named for the place the huts were first manufactured – Quonset Point, Rhode Island – the arch-shaped structures filled a variety of military needs for cheap and quickly produced buildings. There had been a dozen or more on the base when it was active, but after World War II the Navy declared the huts surplus and sold them for $1,000 each. All but one, that is. The remaining Quonset hut is different. It had been built on a concrete foundation to raise the height of the ceiling to 15 feet to accommodate an aircraft. It was one of the bigger models; it was 100 feet long 40 feet wide, insulated, and had corrugated steel sides. There is a side door that leads to an interior office/maintenance/supply room, but otherwise the Quonset is just a big open bay. In its prime, the interior was well lit but now only half the overhead lights work. The wooden doors on each end of the hanger were replaced with galvanized steel ones.

It was only a matter of time before the Navy "decommissioned" the field but finally, in 1959, it was closed. Locals found it odd, but not unnatural, when retired Senior Chief Petty Officer Fannin bought the abandoned airfield from the government for pennies on the dollar. He painted Navy Supply Facility Jamestown on the side of the Quonset hut. For several years into the 1960s Fannin rented the hanger to a local crop duster. The pilot of the red and white bi-plane was his sole tenant. He never made any demands on Fannin for anything.

Over a period of 18 months Fannin thought about the pesticides being sprayed on crops in the area. Maybe he was ahead of his time as an environmentalist, but he decided chemical fertilizers and sprays carried into streams, near-by lakes, and the Atlantic Ocean. He was convinced toxic chemicals found their way into the food chain through fish and birds that ate fish. Heck, he didn't need the meager rent from the crop-duster to live on; he had his Navy pension. Anyway, he didn't want poisoning the land he loved on his conscience.

So he ran the crop-duster off.

Now a thin 83 years old, he has a full head of gray hair pulled back in a ponytail. "Chief" Fannin is still in the Navy and C.O. of the deserted airfield. He has no living relatives, rarely has visitors, and most of his Navy buddies had died, or are in a VA hospital in Charleston, Columbia, Aiken, or Myrtle Beach.

Fannin has seen too much of life to be much intrigued when a dark blue sedan bumps its way down the sandy road to the hanger. Wearing faded Levi's and a camo vest of many pockets, he is leaning against his Ford pick-up sucking on the end of a Camel. From age and sun exposure he has a deeply lined face. He has thin forearms and tobacco-stained teeth. He doesn't move when the car stops a dozen feet in front of him.

"Chief," calls the driver, energetically jumping out of the car and approaching him. "I'm A.T. Banks. This here is my partner, Tommy Taliaferro." He turns to Taliaferro, who walks over to shake hands. Both men have on khakis and open collar shirts. Fannin looks at their shoes. He measures men by their shoes.

"What brings you fellows out here?" says Fannin, barely moving to shake one hand and then the other. His half-smoked cigarette hangs loosely between the thumb and index finger of his left hand. He wonders how these guys know his name.

"Well, sir, we'd like to talk to you about renting your hanger."

"Did that once," Fannin says, taking a drag off his cigarette and exhaling a cloud of gray smoke. "Not really interested." Fannin looks directly at Banks, his clear blue eyes unblinking. He hasn't shaved for two days and has white stubble on his face.

"We thought you might feel like that, Chief. Any chance we could talk you into reconsidering?"

"Can't hurt to listen, I suppose. As long as you understand I'm not inclined to change my mind," he says bluntly, taking another deep drag from the cigarette.

"Could we talk inside?" asks Taliaferro, wiping sweat from his forehead with two fingers. "It can't be any hotter in there than it is out here." He grins as he says this.

"You'd be surprised," Fannin answers, stubbing out the cigarette on the heel of his shoe. Field-striping the cigarette, he scatters the tobacco in the ocean breeze and flicks the tiny ball of rolled up cigarette paper in the direction of the visitor's car. "Come on in," he says, leading the way.

Fannin was right. The inside of the hanger is as hot and dry as the Yuma Desert without any breeze. "What do you think about opening one or both of the hanger doors?" suggests Taliaferro, taking off his sunglasses.

"Help yourself," replies Fannin, standing his ground.

Taliaferro enlists Banks to get first one door moving, and then the other. It is apparent the doors are not used on a regular basis and they complain loudly. The temperature drops 10 degrees with the doors open. But it is still hot. Probably 90 degrees or more. The inside of the hanger is not in too bad of shape. It could use a good cleaning, but that doesn't present any major problems. The office/maintenance shop will be more than adequate. The three men enter the office and Fannin takes the chair behind the used, dented, gray metal desk. Banks sits near him in a collapsible gray metal chair. Taliaferro stands nearby.

Fannin takes another unfiltered Camel from his shirt pocket and lights up. Exhaling through his nose he says, "Okay, so what do you boys have in mind?"

"You're retired Navy so you know about classified," says Banks, looking very serious. "Your country needs your help."

Fannin's expression is one of skepticism. "How am I supposed to know you guys are on the level? You could be anybody."

Banks looks at Taliaferro, who reaches into a side pants pocket and takes out his wallet. He removes a lamented card and hands it to Banks, who has already retrieved a card from his wallet. Banks hands both green-tinted cards to Fannin. The cards are IDs with photos, and the seal, stamp, and illegible signature of the Department of Defense. They are fakes, but damn impressive ones. They have the desired effect on Fannin, who hands them back after studying them - front and back - for a few moments.

He sits up ramrod straight, and in salty language says, "Ah, fuck, what you want from me?"

"Well, chief, we just need your cooperation for a short time."

A week later Banks and Taliaferro return. With them is a newer pick-up truck with two aircraft mechanics. In the bed of their truck are a dozen metal boxes. A third vehicle – a dirty white panel truck - completes the three-vehicle convoy. While the mechanics set up in the maintenance shop, the four guys with the panel truck check electrical power sources and install a portable air conditioner in the office. Then they set about cleaning up the hanger, replacing overhead lights, and installing electronic openers on the hanger doors. By afternoon, the hanger had taken on a new life. Fannin is as pleased as a new Dad.

At 4 p.m., a Ford Bronco drives up and parks next to the door. An armed security guard gets out. The patch on his uniform says Cadbury Security. Banks and Fannin greet him, give him the tour, show him the head and the hanger office, and explain his duties. He will be relieved at midnight.

At 7:00 the next morning the panel truck returns. The four men are stopped and checked by the security guard on the midnight to eight shift. Banks and Taliaferro arrived 45 minutes later in time for the security shift change. They bring a cup of black coffee for Chief Fannin. Then they brief the men about completing preparations.

By late afternoon the panel truck team has completed patch work on the airstrip. The rain doesn't help. There are no working runway lights, and no time to repair the old ones. In lieu of this the panel truck team strings a series of low intensity lights across both ends of the runway. That should be sufficient for a good military pilot. An hour later a fuel truck arrives from Shaw AFB in Sumter, South Carolina. It carries standard jet fuel. It is parked outside the hanger on the tarmac. An auxiliary power unit (APU) and two fire extinguishers are brought inside the hanger. Then they wait.

It is nearly 7 p.m. when they hear the whine of a jet engine. It takes a moment to visually locate the plane in the reduced visibility of the rain. There is no radio communication between the ground and the aircraft, an oversight easily handled had they thought of it. No matter now. The V-tailed, single engine, dark blue jet is on a bouncy final approach to the runway.

Banks, Taliaferro, Fannin and the security guard stand together to watch the landing.

"What the hell is that?" asks Fannin to no one in particular but beginning to feel like one of the team.

"It's a personal jet," answers Banks, remembering what Wells called it.

"The engine," offers Taliaferro "sits atop the cockpit!"

"Looks like the hump on a Goddamn camel," says Fannin, who has only seen pictures of camels in books.

"I hear it's pretty fast and has a parachute."

"You're making that shit up – a plane with a parachute?!"

"That's what I hear," says Taliaferro, cocking his head to one side. "And airbags."

"I'd like to look inside that sumbitch," Fannin says, reaching for another Camel cigarette and his Zippo. The lighter is old and battered. Engraved on one side is NAVY. On the reverse side:

This is my Zippo lighter

There are many like it.

But this one is mine.

Fannin.

"We all would like to check it out," chips in Banks. "But work before pleasure, boys."

~ ~ ~ ~

The original plan was for a mid-morning departure the next day. And for a time it looked like the tropical disturbance might move inland. So they waited. When the rain came in waves, the plan was aborted.

Cheerios-size raindrops pound the metal roof of the Quonset hanger; sweep across the runway and into the pine forest. Hours pass. Everyone does what the military often does: wait. Finally, Banks' cell phone rings. The decision is made to chance it. Dressed in a sage green flight suit void of any identifying marks, the pilot thanks Banks and Taliaferro for their help and nods to the two aircraft mechanics. The three leave the maintenance office and go to the plane. They conduct a meticulous preflight inspection. The pilot planned to file an IFR flight plan and cancel it nearer the destination. On second thought, the decision is made to not file a flight plan after all.

Banks, Taliaferro, Fannin and the security guard watch the preparations from the office window. Satisfied with the walk-around the pilot thanks the mechanics a second time and gets in the jet. One mechanic positions himself with a fire extinguisher at the left wingtip. The other remotely opens the hanger's sliding door and starts the APU.

This is an experimental airplane – on loan from Roger – and represents what his company hopes will be the next generation general aviation aircraft. It has an all-glass cockpit and the look and feel of an expensive sports car. In the center consol, where a car's gear shift would be, is a gray and chrome throttle. The pilot adjusts the Clark H10-76 headset (standard military issue for the U.S. Air Force and NATO) over a dark green baseball cap. The microphone is on a boom attached to the left earpiece. It is pulled down and positioned directly in front of the lips. A casual observer might miss the very small grooves in the plane's wings, the result of research by a Chinese professor studying scorpions. Irregular surfaces are projected to increase the life of the wings by a fifth. The pilot turns the Master Switch to the on position, and the computer comes to life. With the touch of a finger the screen displays the Engine Start Procedures. There is a slight tension because the pilot is relatively unfamiliar with the airplane. The checklist and procedures begin: check switches for various on/off positions, trim tabs and flap settings, oil, fuel, and a half dozen other things require careful attention. After a few minutes, the pilot looks out the window and points a finger at the man with the fire extinguisher. He makes a circling motion with the index finger of his right hand. The engine starts with a low whine, building into the swishing sound of a jet. The APU is disconnected. All graphics are "in the green." No red anywhere. With a slight advance of power, the aircraft moves easily and slowly out of the hanger, guided to the end of the rain-slick runway with the skilled use of throttle, brakes and rudder. The hanger door closes automatically as the plane exits.

At the end of the runway the pilot checks the Electronic Flight Information System (EFIS) directly in front of the yoke. The high-resolution 12 inch x 12 inch display, with a multi-color moving terrain map, stands out in contrast to the cobalt-colored instrument panel. The plane is equipped with XM weather, dual GPS receivers and redundant electronics with a QUERY keypad. There are two 6 inch x 8 inch color liquid crystal multi-function displays. Completing the package is a digital 16-watt VHF and a private channel – an Extremely High Frequency (EHF) radio - for secure voice communication with Cadbury. The pilot scans the tower and military radio frequencies of nearby facilities, listening for aircraft traffic. Nothing of concern is heard.

At the end of the runway the pilot lines up the nose of the jet on the nearly invisible center line. Releasing the toe breaks, the pilot advances the throttle. The spool-up from idle to full power is smooth. With zero payload the plane eats up 3,500 feet of runway and leaps into the sky. There is the comforting thump of the wheels retracting. The pilot breaths easier.

Painted on the plane's tail is the number N5172J. The pilot ignores the plane's official numbers, and keys the mike from a button on the yoke: "Cadbury, Caramel. Wheels up at one-four-four-zero."

"Caramel this is Cadbury. Good luck. Cadbury Out."

The plane makes a bumpy right-hand turn, climbing at a rate of 1,500 feet a minute through heavy turbulence and puffy cumulus clouds. The gloved right hand remains on the throttle during climb-out. When the plane reaches 5,000 feet the pilot punches in the GPS destination. With a full fuel load the plane has a range of 1,100 nautical (1,265 statute) miles.

Flying almost directly east the plane heads out to sea over the unseen, steadily deepening water of the Continental Shelf. The moving terrain map displays in color the blue of the Atlantic, with a darker blue strip indicating an underwater trench. Nearer Bermuda the map shows dark blue pebble-like steppingstones running northwestward from the islands, to a point halfway between New York and Boston.

Before long the jet will fly over the very deep waters of the Hatteras Abyssal Plain. The eerie underwater mountain range of the Plain, thousands of feet below the surface of the Western North Atlantic was formed millions of years earlier when molten magma from volcanic formations cooled. Near the tops of the undersea mountains, 893 statute miles east of Charleston, are the 138 islands collectively called Bermuda – more accurately, the Bermuda Islands. Hundreds of miles to the south of Bermuda is the Puerto Rico Trench. Measured by satellite it is the Atlantic Ocean's deepest point – 28,232 feet below the waves.

Within an hour the weather turns nasty; the dark swirling clouds and strong winds cause concern. The pilot turns the rotating beacon and strobe lights off. Heavy rain beats loudly on the cockpit roof like a handful of rocks hurled against glass. The plane seems to creak as if rebelling against the storm. The engine sounds a note of anxiety. The autopilot keeps the plane on course, but the pilot is keenly alert none the less. Flight Service (weather forecast and flight plans) and SX weather are accurate. Because of a tropical disturbance southwest of the destination the pilot thinks about the potentially dangerous conditions en route, and at the destination. It will be a race of sorts. Hopefully the storm is not transitioning into a hurricane and won't arrive before the plane does. The Bermuda Islands are not strangers to hurricanes and dangerous storms.

The pilot powers back to 80 percent to minimize stress on the airframe. The cabin's interior lights are turned to full bright. The electric pilot's seat is lowered to its lowest point. The pilot continues to fly co-pilot to the autopilot.

At 240 knots (275 miles an hour), it's a three-and-a-half-hour flight, more or less, depending on winds and weather. Thoughts of the legend of the Bermuda Triangle creep into the pilot's thoughts but are quickly dismissed.

Flying into a possible hurricane is something else.

Hurricanes and big storms begin in Africa. Somewhere over the Sahara a potential thunderstorm is born when it captures hot air rising from the dessert floor. The storm moves westward toward the Atlantic Ocean, absorbing cooler upper atmosphere air as it moves. By the time it reaches the mid-Atlantic, hundreds of miles distant from its birthplace, the air mass collides with high pressures and begins a slow counterclockwise motion. As the storm grows in strength it becomes a tropical depression and sometimes a hurricane. Eighty-five percent of Atlantic hurricanes originate in Africa.

Forty-four years earlier, in 1968, a lumbering U.S. bomber was on final approach – five miles from touchdown - in hurricane-like weather. Crew members were tightly strapped in their uncomfortable seats, jiggling, vibrating, and bouncing around. The bomber protested loudly. On the flight deck the pilots did what all experienced military pilots do: trust the crew, trust the plane, and trust the instruments. Never trust instincts. What happened next was a rare event because something went terribly wrong. Perhaps it was the instruments or the pilots or something else. In the soup, on instruments, with zero visibility, they flew the B-52 bomber into the ocean, killing all aboard. The four thermonuclear bombs were destroyed, and plutonium silently sank thousands of feet below the waves.

Accident investigators from the Air Force arrived within hours. They had theories about the crash. However, it quickly proved easier to identify contributing factors to the crash than a definitive cause. Was it catastrophic mechanical failure? Was it metal fatigue on an old airframe? Was it weather related? Perhaps it was a sudden microburst? Were the pilots so focused on the landing they didn't recognize the aircraft shudder that precedes a stall? Did they stall into the ocean? Pilot error?

The accident was never publicly disclosed. But it leaked out. As a result, 6,000 feet of the 12,000 foot runway was purposefully destroyed. The airfield would be unsuitable for landing any BUFFs (Big Ugly Fat Fuckers) ever again. Existing buildings at the airfield were shuttered. Personnel were relocated. Months later the U.S. Government announced it was moving its nine P-3C Orion aircraft (anti-submarine patrol aircraft) from the base on St. David's Island to another location.

Two years later, in 1970, the highly classified Navy research submarine - NR-1 - was able to dive to a depth of 3,600 feet to recover the bombs. The existence of this unique submarine was never publicly acknowledged. In 1995 the base was officially closed because of environmental factors, said a spokesperson for the government. The U.S. returned base land to the Government of Bermuda in 2002.

In the years since the B-52 accident the northern end of St. David's Island enjoyed modest development. Because the Bermuda Islands sit on an underwater volcano the land has little agricultural value. The earth is mostly limestone, coral and sand. Fresh water is minimal. Residents collect rain water on the roofs of buildings and homes. Economic development mostly comes from the 500,000 tourists annually, and the sale of condos with beautiful views of the ocean and pink sand beaches.

There remains still, however, the desolate but useable airfield on St. David's Island. There is only one passable road to the former base. In the middle of the road is a billboard-size rectangular sign.

ROAD CLOSED! (black letters)

DO NOT PASS THIS POINT!

Two hundred yards further along the blacktop is another sign. Same size. It has a yellow background. Its greeting reads:

DANGEROUS OPERATIONS!! (yellow letters)

The last sign in the middle of the road issues the final warning:

TRESPASSERS

WILL BE ARRESTED! (red letters)

~ ~ ~ ~

The flight to St. David's from South Carolina is anything but boring.

"Cadbury, this is Caramel. Over."

"Caramel this is Cadbury. Over."

"Roger Cadbury. Caramel is fifteen minutes out. Over."

"Roger. Understand one-five minutes out. Suggest you use runway one-niner. Wind is two-zero-zero at one-zero, gusting to three-zero, in heavy rain. Visibility one mile. Over."

"Roger Cadbury. Runway one-niner." The pilot wonders where Cadbury is. Physically, that is. Certainly not in Bermuda. Is the Navy relaying weather and landing information to Cadbury? Does the Agency have a covert controller at the field?

Breaking out of the dark clouds and dangerous winds the pilot is relieved to make a visual on the faded runway; runway 19 looks like a misty mirage. The pilot punches Landing Checklist into the computer and scans the instrument panel. Making the last turn, into a stiff headwind, the pilot touches the computer screen icon for Final Approach.

"Bitchin'Betty", a computerized female voice, advises the pilot from the cockpit communication box:

You are now on final approach. Suggest you adjust aircraft to final approach speed. Make final flap settings. Re-check gear down and locked. Check, check, check.

Speed-bleed into the wind is substantial and the plane experiences severe buffeting. The pilot manually overrides the system to kick in a little right rudder. Seconds later there is the comforting jerk of the landing gear extending. No need for flaps. The aircraft crosses the runway threshold with air speed up and power on.

Considering the weather, the pilot is pleased to achieve a wobbly one-hopper landing. With the tires safely on the pavement, the pilot pulls the power and pushes the yoke full forward, insuring the plane stays earth-bound, and then keys the mike:

"Cadbury, Caramel. Touchdown at one-eight-zero-five."

"Roger, Caramel. One-eight-zero-five. Cadbury out."

The pilot turns the airplane 180 degrees and heads for what once was base operations. The now trailing wind pushes on the aircraft as it taxies down the center of the runway. At the first taxiway a figure in a yellow slicker waits. With bright orange light-sticks the figure directs the pilot toward a hanger 50 yards away. As the aircraft passes, the figure runs to a junker-car beside the taxiway, jumps in, and races to the hanger ahead of the plane. Jumping out of the car at the side of the hanger, the yellow figure hurries to get inside ahead of the plane. Like some kind of mechanical monster on remote control the plane follows. The figure scurries to the far end of the hanger, turns and crosses both arms to indicate stop. When the plane comes to a halt, the figure makes a slashing motion across the neck with one light-stick. The pilot shuts the engine down and secures the aircraft.

There is no logbook and no need for one. Malfunctions and mechanical history are automatically recorded on the plane's internal computer. A man in dress slacks and a linen jacket appears from the side of the hanger and chocks the wheels. A third figure watches and waits for the pilot to step out of the craft.

It is not a long wait.

"I'm Irwin Emanuel," the older man says as the pilot gets out of the airplane. Emanuel is a stocky man of medium height and build. His dark hair has no hint of gray and is closely cropped. He has thin lips and intense eyes. He doesn't smile a lot, but he has a good sense of humor. He has been with the Agency since college, following a 3-year hitch in the Army. The last 18 months of his life have been in Bermuda.

The pilot says, "I'm Katherine Breeden. Mr. Wells told me to expect you."

Emanuel turns to his right. "This is Larry Stephens, my deputy."

Breeden notes he isn't surprised to see her. Wells obviously told him to expect a woman pilot. She looks at Stephens, the man who chocked the wheels. Stephens nods a welcome but doesn't speak. She nods back at Stephens thinking he has arrogant eyes. Men like him think they are superior to everyone else. Especially women. The dislike is instant; the reason is instinctive. She would wager he is an outstandingly nasty man.

"You can get out of your flight suit over there," Emanuel says, pointing to a side office, "but there is no working restroom. Sorry."

"That's fine."

They walk together toward the office. The rain is hammering loudly on the thin roof of the hanger. In a louder than normal voice Emanuel says, "I've got an extra raincoat. Is your plane okay?"

"Yes. Why?"

"We can't do any maintenance. Harris will get your plane refueled but that's all we can do. Other than an APC to get you started again. Larry will keep an eye on things."

"That's fine. When will it be ready?"

"Couple of hours. When do you need it?"

"I'm not sure."

"Well, no matter. Stephens and Harris will be here. If the weather doesn't let up I doubt you're going anywhere."

"Looks that way," Kate says. "I'll just be a minute. Do we have far to go?"

"No. In this weather everybody with a brain is inside. Anyway, the road is officially closed."

After Kate goes into the office to change, Harris gets out of his rain gear and hangs it over the APU to dry. Stephens says to Emanuel "What can I do to be helpful, Irwin?"

"You're in charge, Larry. If you have any problems call me."

"Right. But, Irwin, I'm concerned about our cell phones. There are reports of power outages everywhere. Contrary to the phone company's pronouncements, cell towers don't hold up well in these high winds. Just so we're on the same page, what's the immediate plan?"

"We're going to the Black Dog and hopefully hook up with London. After that I'm not in the loop. But at some point we'll come back here.

Tonight? Tomorrow? Probably tomorrow. I'll call if there is any change. But nobody is going anywhere in this weather."

"It ain't looking good," agrees Stephens in a good-natured but anxious voice. He has a lot on his mind.

"No kidding. We're in for some overtime."

"Abby is use to that. Besides, we can always use the extra money."

After shedding the flight suit in favor of light gray tailored slacks and a light windbreaker, Kate grabs a leather-trim cotton twill overnight bag. She puts on the pro-offered raincoat at the hanger door.

Stephens holds the door open as the two dash through the rain – hopping over a few puddles - and jump into a battered car with peeling green paint. Despite its appearance the car starts immediately. The engine sounds strong, although the windshield wipers are having a hard time keeping up with the downpour. Emanuel cautiously pulls away from the hanger in search of the main road.

"What kind of car is this?" asks Kate, peering out the window.

"Peugeot 306," answers Emanuel, leaning over the steering wheel to better see. "It's a 2001 example of what happens when a government runs the car company."

"So, we can expect cars like this from Chrysler?" There are rubber mats on the floor, and the seats are worn, but otherwise the interior has been well kept. The dash is clean.

"Fiat you mean," Emanuel laughs. He projects a casual down-to-earth demeanor. "They have controlling interest in Chrysler now. Anyway, mechanically the car's fine," he says. "Maybe even excellent. It leaks oil like an underwater rig in the Gulf of Mexico. And the engine management light stays on all the time. Would you believe we paid $23,000 for this Gallic masterpiece?" He takes a quick look sideways at his passenger.

"Seems expensive."

"This is Bermuda. If you have money it's paradise. I can get you a 1991 Mercedes for $45,000."

"I'll pass. Thanks all the same." The car glides onto the main road heading south at 35 mph.

After the car pulls away Harris and Stephens secure the hanger door and return to the airplane. Standing at its wing, Harris says "It sure is a strange looking bird."

"Why don't you check it out?" suggests Stephens. "I'll be right back."

"Take your time," kids Harris, "I'm not going to steal it."

"No shit," he says, and heads to the office.

Harris is older than Stephens by ten years. An ordinary man, he has worked for Video Photographers for over a year. He has an acne-scarred complexion and slight frame. He never married but is unsure why. A high school drop-out, his work history includes years of menial jobs. Most recently he worked four years as a lazy janitor. Before that he was an inept insurance salesman. Before that, he was an uninspired cat shelter worker and, finally, he was a failed used-car salesman. Success never found Harris, probably because he lacked ambition and mental toughness. But he is honest and mostly dependable. Video Photographers is the best job he ever had.

Although he never mentions it, Harris suspects Emanuel and Stephens are private investigators. They seem to always be following people and snooping around. Maybe the videos and photographs they take are used in divorce cases. He has seen Stephens and Emanuel with a gun before. He figures they were ex-cops that became PIs. Emanuel is a stand-up kind of guy. Stephens is an asshole. There is just something not right about that guy. But he can't quite put his finger on it. Besides, Harris is not a boat rocker. He likes being told what to do. The pay is good, and they mostly treat him with respect.

Stephens goes to the office and watches Harris disappears into the plane's cabin; he takes out his cell phone and punches in a number. The screen reads "call failed." Great. The storm must be playing hell with the cell towers again. If the phone company wasn't so damn cheap they would have put in fiber optic cables instead of unreliable microwave towers. Frustrated, he punches in the number again. This time the phone connects. It rings for a long time. Finally, an accented voice answers. "Yes."

"Black Dog. Probably within the hour."

The call disconnects. Stephens snaps his phone shut and inwardly smiles. He's hit the lottery. About time. He considers himself a complex man rather than a misguided one. Life's been good to him, and he feels he has earned and/or deserves all it has to offer. At his core, Stephen is a man unburdened by ethical constraints.

Prior to joining the Agency, Stephens was an up-and-coming certified public accountant. He worked on the Hill as a staffer to the Senate Committee on Foreign Relations. The Committee staff director was a middle-age guy named Stan Billington. They hit it off right away, probably because both were deviously ambitious. After a few months of working together, Billington introduces him to a Dr. Lisa Jinping – a Washington psychotherapist of Chinese descent. She is a well-connected supporter of senators and congressmen on both sides of the aisle. She is also drop-dead gorgeous and has great legs. Stephens suspects she and Billington have a thing going so he keeps his distance. Several more months go by. Billington calls him one day and says they will accompany senators on the Foreign Relations Committee for a week-long investigatory trip – junket – to Bangkok. As it turns out, Jinping arranges an after-hours dinner for him and Billington with some stunningly attractive local women. It is the beginning of a fascination and obsession with Asian women. To him the young women seem totally uninhibited and eager to satisfy every whim and fantasy. He is trapped in an insatiable appetite for all Asian women. Whenever someone says the word Bangkok, he and Billington coyly smile thinking about the double-entendre.

Washington is well-known as the Eye Candy Capitol of the U.S. If a guy can't get laid in Washington, he can't get laid. Young and attractive women are everywhere; in the Library of Congress, the halls of Congress, the parks, jogging along Pennsylvania Avenue, biking, on the streets, and in the shops. Everywhere. Through Billington and Dr. Jinping, Stephens meets a new and exciting circle of friends and attends elegant parties on Embassy Row. This leads to sexual excesses, and a series of torrid affairs with pretty young Asian women: Korean, Japanese, Filipino, Thai, Chinese, and Vietnamese. After many encounters Stephens decides he prefers stunningly lovely Korean women to all the rest.

After Stephens joins the Central Intelligence Agency, he continues his friendship with Billington. Despite frequent polygraph examinations, his indiscretions go undiscovered by the Agency. Had his affairs been discovered, they would have constituted a major security breach and his dismissal would have been immediate. But they were not discovered. This is because Stephens is a practiced liar, and polygraphs can be fooled. The affairs with the women are always brief. When Abby marries him she does what the Agency couldn't, and puts a stop to his philandering. However, about a year later, when he is on home leave, his old friend Billington calls and asks him to meet and assist an Asian friend of Dr. Jinping's. He is more than excited to do so. When he meets Chung Yoo Cha a few days later over wine, it is lust at first sight. Not only does she fulfill his every desire but she offers to hire him as a consultant. She agrees to pay him $25,000 for some benign information when he returns to Bermuda. It doesn't occur to him that she may be as deceitful and cunning as he. His brain is parked somewhere else that day.

~ ~ ~ ~

The Peugeot hits an unseen pothole with enough water to fill a swimming pool. Good suspension. Emanuel steers toward the center of the road.

"For a minute there I thought we were a submarine," Kate wisecracks.

"Yeah, me too. Think I'll stay away from the shoulder."

"I assume you have been fully briefed."

"Briefed, yes. How fully I'm not sure. You know Wells." He cast a brief look at his passenger.

"He has a lot of nice things to say about you. He didn't mention Stephens."

"Understandable. Stephens backs me up. Langley probably thinks I need someone younger to look after me. This is my last tour before the pasture."

"Wells told me. You look more than capable to me," flatters Kate.

"Stephens has been real helpful. Especially since we got the word on such short notice."

"I'm sure he has."

"He's had surveillance for the last few days," he continues. "That's not exactly exciting stuff."

After a moment Kate says, "What did he find out, if anything?" Water is dripping off her raincoat onto the car's worn cloth seats.

"London just does his thing. Pretty predictable. Jogging, taking his boat out, dinner every other evening at a local pub when he's here. That's where we hope he is now. Clearly he has no clue anyone has any interest in him."

"No reason he should, I guess."

"But the target subjects have arrived," Emanuel reports. "At least we have observed an Asian couple that appears interested in London. They've been watching him for at least three days."

"Is it unusual to have a couple as a team?"

"Nothing is unusual anymore. Stephens took some digitals and we sent them to Langley for identification."

"Where are they now?" Kate's side of the windshield is beginning to fog up.

"The photos?"

"The Asian couple."

"Can't say. We dropped surveillance to meet you. But Stephens says they located London's boat at the Marina. They know where to find him."

"But they haven't taken any action."

"Not that we know of."

The conversation stops. The wind and rain do not. An old car in front of them is splashing along at less than minimum speed, almost as if on water skis. Emanuel makes sure his headlights are on but decides against honking the horn or distracting the driver. The windshield wipers clap back and forth with a steady hypnotizing beat.

After another brief pause Kate asks, "What do you know about Stephens?"

"Larry Stephens," he says, stalling as if preparing an answer. "Why?"

"Just curious."

"Well, his mother was a Stevens who married a Stephens. How weird is that?"

"Not as weird as being named Army Brown or Dean Dean or Major Deal. Parents who name children like that must have a drinking problem," she jokes.

"Well, anyway, Larry's a solid guy. A likeable guy. Serious, high-minded, guy. Raised somewhere in middle Georgia. I forget where, but top of his class in business school. Took his degree in accounting. Passed all parts of his CPA exam on the first try. Joined one of those big accounting firms."

"What happened?" Kate examines the air conditioning controls looking for the defroster button.

"Nothing really. Just got bored, I guess. Accounting isn't the most thrilling line of work in the world." He allows himself a tight grin as he says this.

Kate nods agreement. "Did he join the Agency after that?"

"Oh, no," Emanuel answers, taking the hint and switching on the front window defroster. "He told me he was always interested in international affairs. With the support of his senator he got a job on the Hill with the Senate Committee on Foreign Relations. Said he was inspired by the Committee's idealism." "Really?"

"He apparently did a good job. He was there three or four years before hooking up with us."

"How about his efficiency ratings?"

"I looked at his DA 67 dash 9 before he was assigned here."

"Your OER?"

"Yeah," Emanuel answers, "same thing as the Officer Evaluation Report. The guy is smart. Quick thinking. Spends a lot of hours on the job. Passed the background check and polys with flying colors and finished second in his class at the Farm."

Kate nods. She remembers seeing a list of humorous definitions for terms used in Fitness Reports. "Quick thinking" means offering plausible excuses for errors. "Extra hours" on the job translated to a miserable home life. "You trust him?"

"Sure." Pause. "I'd trust him with my life."

"Am I missing something? Is there a 'but' there?" She turns her head to look directly at Emanuel.

"Why do you ask?" He looks at her for a second, then back at the road.

"No reason. It was just a look. He seems to have a chilly persona. Know what I mean? Or is that just me?"

Emanuel hesitates. "Confidentially, his last review mentioned something about lacking the 'human touch,' whatever that means. He likes to keep to himself; you know?" "I know."

"Anyway, you can trust him. He'll take good care of your plane until we get back."

Out of the corner of his eye Emanuel sees a nod of silent agreement. It is plain she has already formed an opinion of Stephens. Interesting, he thinks, and returns his focus to the flooding road. Maybe he should not have said anything even remotely negative.

Changing the topic, Emanuel asks "Considering the weather, when do you think you will get out?"

"I'm not sure. Depends on how this goes. Hopefully as soon as possible."

"But not today," he prods. "It's not looking like it. Wells made me a reservation at The Edwardian House. Do you know it?"

"Sure. Classy place, and it is close to where we're going,"

"I won't be long. Just want to drop off my gear and wash my face."

CHAPTER 7

Jon London has a busy day. As much as possible he tries to maintain his usual regimen, meaning a light breakfast and a five-mile run. The weather, however, has taken center stage. Dressed in foul weather gear against the lashing rain, he admonishes himself for not moving Eagle Ray to the other side of the islands the day before. It's too late to do much about that now. The marine weather report is predicting a tropical storm or possible a Category 1 Hurricane. While a Cat 1 is classified as the smallest hurricane, it is still capable of 75 mile an hour winds. Equally bad, the hurricane can produce a storm surge of 10-15 feet. He'll check the weather reports frequently, tighten the moorings on his boat, gather up some essentials for later, and hope for the best. Rooms on shore may be at a premium, but he is sure he can find a place for the night.

He finishes his external inspection of the rocking boat when he notices a solitary figure hurrying down the dock in his direction. The figure is wearing bright orange rain gear, head hidden inside the tightly pulled hood, leaning into the wind and rain. There are only a few remaining boats dockside, all straining at their lines. Certainly, thinks Jon, this person is not going to try moving a boat in this weather! Probably just checking the lines.

As Jon is about to disappear inside the salon, the person cups his hands around his mouth and shouts: "Jon!"

In an instant Jon recognized the voice. Doug Clayton, a colleague from the University in Sint Maarten. Jon moves to the side of the boat, grabbing the handrail to steady himself. "My God, Doug, come aboard before you drown!" Clayton jumps, slipping slightly, and Jon pulls him aboard by the elbow.

"What are you doing here? How did you find me?" he says, leading Clayton inside.

"I came looking for you," Clayton says with a grin, taking his rain gear off, shaking it, and looking around for a place to park it.

"Here," Jon says, "let me take that." He opens a nearby narrow coat closet and stows the gear inside. Over his shoulder he says, "I'm surprised. I really am. It's good to see you!"

"It's mutual," Clayton says, looking around the salon. "Nice boat. Bet it's really nice when it's not in a hurricane." He mock punches Jon on the shoulder.

"Let me get you something to drink."

"You wouldn't have any coffee, would you?"

"I can brew it up in a minute," Jon says, stepping behind the bar in the salon to find the coffee and mugs. "You can fill me in on the University since I last saw you. How did you find me, anyway?"

Clayton pulls up a stool, leaning his elbows on the countertop. "You left so suddenly a lot of the faculty and staff didn't get to say good-bye."

"I'm not much at goodbyes." Jon puts the filter in the coffee maker and starts to spoon coffee into it. "Strong, medium, or weak?"

"Medium's fine. A drop of brandy might be nice, considering the weather," Clayton adds.

"Medium it is. Not sure about Brandy, but I think there is some port around here. Can you add port to coffee?"

"Let's find out."

As Jon pours bottled water into the coffee maker, he says, "Look in the liquor cabinet to the left of the TV."

Clayton gets up and goes to the liquor cabinet. He doesn't see any brandy, but on the second shelf he finds a bottle of C. da Silva Dalva Porto from Portugal. "This is 30-year-old stuff," he says, turning around holding the bottle.

"Bring it over. It's good."

Back on the stool Clayton says, "The President thought you would be coming back to the University."

"Well," – Jon pauses – "that chapter is closed."

"Everyone was devastated by the accident. We all loved Kim."

Not wanting to dwell on the accident and its aftermath, Jon veers the conversation in another direction. "So how did you find me, Dick Tracy?"

"Van Note – the student body - said her last contact with you was from here."

"Now, now, no lusting over my student assistant. Christine was an excellent student and a sweet kid. What became of her?"

"You should know. She told me you were a grad school reference. Oh, I almost forgot," he says, reaching into his jacket, "before Christine left, she gave me this envelope for you. Love notes?" He holds out an envelope.

"You mistake me for a politician, Clayton," Jon says, briefly glancing at the thin envelope, and putting it in his rear pocket without further comment. "Yes, I recommended her at three universities, but I don't know how it worked out." The coffee begins to loudly perk.

"I'm not absolutely sure myself, but I think she was accepted at Michigan State. She mumbled something about it having an outstanding graduate school of education, and cool weather. She was tired of hot and humid."

Jon pours two mugs of coffee, placing one in front of Clayton. "Cream? Sugar?"

"Half and half is fine, if you have it. Do you have any Equal?"

"How about one percent and Splenda?"

Smiling, Clayton says, "That's what I meant. One percent and Splenda." He adds a splash of port to his coffee, unsure what to expect. Thirty minutes later Clayton has brought Jon up to date on the faculty developments and mutual friends at the University, and life in general in St. Maartin.

"I feel terrible to mention this," Jon says, finishing his coffee, "but I really need to meet a department chair from Bermuda College about an adjunct position. I'm getting bored with the life of leisure. The meeting has probably been called off, but my cell phone isn't working."

"I understand," Clayton says getting up. "We can catch up later. Maybe tomorrow."

"No, no. I won't hear of it," Jon says, motioning for him to sit back down. "The storm isn't getting better, but it isn't getting worse, either."

"I don't want to be an inconvenience. Or drown on your boat!"

"I insist you stay. Really, you are no problem. There is plenty of coffee and brandy. Lots of reading material, and I won't be gone too long."

"Well…"

"If the storm gets worse before I get back, and you decide you really must leave, where are you staying?"

"The Manchester. It's not the Fairmont, but it's okay."

"A block off the harbor? I've been there."

"I'm on per diem," he explains. "The less expensive the hotel, the more coins in my pocket."

"Sure I can't get you to stay with me on the boat, and pocket all per diem?"

"Maybe next time."

CHAPTER 8

The Black Dog Pub on Front Street is a popular tourist attraction. The mahogany bar with carved columns is stocked with a wide variety of spirits and every brand of Irish whiskey. It looks like an antique bar removed from a gone-out-of-business pub. It isn't. It could have been disassembled in the UK and reassembled in Bermuda. It wasn't.

The front entrance to the pub has a heavy wooden door with a stained glass insert. It is flanked by two large windows and three smaller windows running up to the gold leaf sign that announces BLACK DOG PUB. Above the sign are four brass flood lights highlighting the pub's name.

The Black Dog is owned by a red-faced Irishman, Nigel Effingham, C.B.E. The Commander of the British Empire is the eldest of ten children born to his Irish father and English mother. He has the upper torso of a bodybuilder, the raw grit of all Royal Marines trained at Lympstone, and the dry wit of George Bernard Shaw. The pub is more than a business to him; it is a reminder of the comforts of home away from home, a dim and comfortable place where all conditions of people meet with no questions asked. In some ways pubs provide a perfect setting for a secret plot. Or maybe some mystery drama.

The Black Dog's downstairs seating is comprised of fixed booths with stained glass dividers. On the walls are brass portholes, ships lamps, fish nets, and seafaring memorabilia from a century earlier. Near the entrance are several dart boards – not often used but useable nonetheless - acquired from several of the more than 6,000 pubs that have closed in the UK since 2005. Tourists frequently crowd the first floor.

Upstairs is less noisy and usually preferred by locals. It has white linen covered tables, brass fixtures, an expansive bar, and oil paintings with a nautical theme. On nice days there is a small veranda off the upstairs dining room with five tables overlooking the harbor. On stormy days, the awnings are rolled up.

The upstairs bar of the Black Dog is dominated by a gold-framed portrait of the acclaimed British actor David Niven, in a British Officer's uniform. Niven graduated from Sandhurst and was a commando who took part in the invasion of Normandy. In somewhat similar fashion, in 1982, then Major Nigel Effingham led a company of Her Majesty's Royal Marines in the amphibious landing of the Falkland Islands in the South Atlantic. He wondered if those who sent young men to the cold, rainy, and desolate islands 8,000 miles from Britain had ever been there. The only usefulness of the place must have been as a way station. Ships sailing to and from the end of the world stopped at Port Stanley for provisions and shelter. During the brief Falkland War, England and Argentina agreed to not fight past a certain street in Port Stanley; that was a civilized thing to do.

The uncivilized thing was the 260 British combat deaths during the campaign. Twelve of the men were under Major Effingham's command. He knew each of them personally. Their names and faces are forever embedded in his memory, and he took their deaths personally. They trusted him to get them through any situation. Many times, over the years, he wished he had died with the 12. Instead, he carries in his heart the pain of letting the men down. The military awards no decoration for emotional scars; there is no purple heart for a wounded heart.

Effingham's military career of twenty-five years is successful and fame enough for him. But the price is high. He is often absent from his home in Ireland and distanced from his wife and son. Finally, the marriage fails - but on good terms, if there is such a thing. He and his ex still think of themselves as good friends that the realities of life divided.

When Effingham returns to Ireland for his once-a-year visit he goes to see his son and former wife. They live on a lovely 5,000 acre estate not far from Aghadoe, deeded to his family by Charles II in 1669. For generations, the family lived close to the earth. His deceased father was a successful cattleman and farmer who bequeathed his estate, with the handsome manor, to him. He rents out the vast farmland to raise barley and oats and sometimes crops of potatoes, and to raise sheep and cattle. His son, Brian Effingham, was influenced in his youth by a doting maternal grandfather who instilled in him a respect for the land, and animals. In time Brian became a large animal veterinarian. He lives on the estate, not far from his mother. This provides a measure of comfort for Effingham. Visiting Ireland is always a reflective time. In his lifetime he traveled to many places in the world, but Ireland…Ireland…Ireland is home.

David Niven and Nigel Effingham never met, of course, but there existed still the unspoken bond all veterans share. Niven died in 1983. It was a disappointment for Effingham, who had hoped to meet him one day. Still, life goes on. The Black Dog is a huge financial success, and Effingham enjoys living in Bermuda and owning the pub. He also enjoys Jon London, who has become his best friend in the islands.

Effingham spots Jon as he reaches the top of the stairs and goes to greet him. "I was wondering if you'd chance this beastly weather for fish and chips," he teases in the good-natured way of the Irish.

"It's the Wild Hogg beer that brings me out, Major."

"Get the Eagle Ray moved?" Effingham asks as he leads Jon to his favorite table near the veranda. "This could be a bruiser of a storm."

"But not enough of a storm to overcome your profit motive, I see."

"Something like that."

"Anyway, I waited too long. I hope to meet someone here for dinner at 6:30." He slides the sleeve of his shirt up to check his watch. "Plus, I have a guest aboard."

Tilting his head slightly, Effingham say, "You're a popular chap."

"One guest does not a popular chap make," counters Jon. He eases himself into his usual chair and looks up at Effingham. There is no need for a menu. His usual fare of fish and chips and a beer is unchanged.

As he makes himself comfortable, Effingham says, "I am referring to the couple at the table behind me - against the wall." He consults his wristwatch. "They've been here since six – about 30 minutes."

"Oh?" Jon twists his head to one side to see around Effingham.

"Do try and not be so obvious, old bean. When I move you can see them."

'Old bean' is just one of several terms of endearment Effingham uses when playfully addressing Jon. When displaying his keen sense of humor, and obvious pleasure of being an Irishman, he is often jovial.

"I don't know any couples - old bean," Jon replies.

"The barkeep told me they came in a few days ago and asked about you. Said they were old friends. Probably the same folks unless, as I said, you've suddenly become unnervingly popular. Not making mischief, are you?"

"Hardly," Jon answers, curious about the couple.

"Well, I'll just carry on then," he says with a twinkle in his eye. With Effingham moving away from the table, Jon cast a peripheral glance in the direction of the table. He doesn't recognize the man, and the women's back is to him. All he can see of her is long black hair. So much for that, he thinks. Tommy-the-waiter arrives with the Wild Hogg beer. "The Major says it's on the house." He departs as rapidly as he arrived.

Meanwhile, the man in question gets up from his table without so much as a glance at Jon, and heads to the bar. So much for that. Jon turns his attention first to the weather outside, and then to the television over the bar. The local weatherman is reporting live from the southern tip of the islands. High winds and heavy rains are expected, he forecasts, with the storm probably passing between 2 and 4 a.m. The television cuts to the Premier of Bermuda. He advises everyone to stay inside. The man returns to the table by the wall with a tall drink in his hand. Dark hair, Asian features.

Six thirty comes and goes. His dinner guest and potential employer is a no show. Jon doesn't blame him. What idiot, other than the few already in the Dog and himself, would be out with a hurricane approaching? Then he remembers the envelope in his pocket and takes it out. It's a cream-colored envelope of good quality. He recognizes the handwriting. Carefully, as if handling something dangerous, he removes one thin sheet. It reads: Where are you? L, Kim. He takes a deep breath, remembering her playfully running into the surf and calling for him to follow. He thinks of her in intimate tender moments, uninhibited minutes, falling asleep in his arms, sleeping late, and laughing so hard it was difficult for either to catch their breath. How could he have overlooked this note? He searches his memory. There is no date on it. Why the note? She could have called. Well, maybe not. He did not like to spend time talking on a phone. She frequently reminded him of that and threatened to stop calling if he wasn't going to answer. He takes a long draw on the beer.

Without turning in his chair he is aware of a person approaching the table from behind his left shoulder. His sixth sense. It is his secret survival tool. Probably someone else heading to the bar, he thinks.

"May I join you?" a woman says.

Jon instantly recognizes the voice. "Kate!" He quickly turns, gets up and hugs her. He gently guides her to the seat next to him, stuffing the envelope into his pocket. "What a wonderful surprise!"

She smiles as she sits down, pleased Jon is excited to see her.

"You are a welcome sight," he says, studying her beautiful complexion, dark brown hair, and slender neck. "With all due respect," he teases, "you are even lovelier out of uniform."

"Oh? I'll take that as a compliment," she says. "I think you look better in uniform." Her lips curl up at the corners of her mouth in an elusive smile.

"And I'll take that as a compliment," he laughs. "What are you doing here? How did you get here? When did you get here?" he uncharacteristically gushes with questions.

Kate is pleased Jon is happy to see her and full of questions. She is more than a little happy to see him as well. "I'm here looking for you!"

"I should be so lucky."

"I didn't swim to get here if that's what you're asking. Although that might have been easier. And I got here a short while ago."

Her expressive brown eyes lock onto Jon's. It is difficult not to look at her.

"I thought the international airport was closed," he says, unable to divert his attention.

"It is. Apparently, the airport causeway is also closed. I went into a private field," she says, her gaze steady, her eyes unblinking.

Instinctively, the private field comment raises Jon's antennae. "You said you're looking for me?" His face is one of puzzlement.

"If you let me order something," she says, tilting her head, "I'll fill you in. I'm starving."

"Of course. I am sorry. Forgive me, I'm just surprised to see you," he says, breaking his trance and motioning to Tommy-the-waiter, who has been observing the reunion. He is standing next to Effingham, who is a curious onlooker. He catches Jon's eye and gives him a subtle approving nod. Effingham decides to play a member of the wait staff.

"It's been a long time since I last saw you," she says. Less her comment be taken too personally, too soon, she quickly adds "Do you come here often?"

"Not often enough. Particularly if you've been coming here!" His eyes say he is serious, but his mind is struggling because of the note in his pocket.

"This is my first time. As I am sure you know."

"I'm still in shock. It's really good to see you." He moves his hand closer to hers but resists the urge to touch her. They look at each other for a long moment. She excels at picking up meaning in a face. People from Kansas are good like that. She recalls the words of something she read: 'the marks of battle are all over his face.' It's an attractive face, lightly tanned, with a day-old stubble. He has a fair complexion, hazel eyes, and light brown/dirty blond hair.

"You've come in the middle of a hurricane, I'm afraid…" Jon says, interrupting her musings. "But I'm pleased you're here," he adds in a stumbling sort of way, feeling like a 7th grader for the first time asking a girl to dance with him.

"I'm sorry we lost touch. I wondered what became of you."

"I'm sorry, too," he says, in an uncharacteristic display of vulnerability.

A menu arrives, personally delivered by the curious Effingham. Handing her the menu he says, "Any friend of this gentleman is a valued friend of our humble establishment. We are at your service." He winks at Jon, who rolls his eyes upward.

Kate laughs lightly. "I'll just have what he has, but I'd rather have a glass of cider."

"Not much of a drinker, are we?" Effingham says in the cheerful manner of the Irish. "It breaks me heart. But I can tell you're a lady of refinement," he kids. "I'll attend to it personally." He does a slight bow and departs, feeling clever, indeed, for seeing Jon's mysterious friend up-close.

"That was very nice," says Kate, taking in the room, and then returning her gaze to Jon.

Leaning forward across the table - perhaps psychologically to get closer to her – he says, "Yes. He's very nice. Now tell me what brings you here. Really."

"Wells sent me." There, she thinks, the shoe is dropped.

Jon knew there had to be a catch 22. This was too good to be coincidental, coming at a time in his life when he needed someone. "Oh, no. I thought he was retired," he sighs.

"Was is the operational word. I guess you know his wife died."

"I did. She was a wonderful woman. I never met her, but he would talk about her sometimes," he says in a soft voice, then takes a swig of beer.

Effingham breaks in with the fish and chips and cider. He winks at Kate when he puts it down. "Thank you," she says. Jon rolls his eyes at Effingham, again.

Kate takes a small sip of the cool cider and continues. "He apparently was at loose ends. Retirement wasn't working for him. He tried all the usual diversions and hobbies."

"It must have been difficult," sympathizes Jon, recalling his own loss more than two years earlier.

"In the end, all he knew was the Agency. It was natural for him to return to what he knew." She lifts the glass of cider to her lips. As she does so, she studies Jon's face and recalls her initial attraction to him. He is as handsome as ever, un-aged in the two years since she last saw him. Still, his face seems different. It seems…gentler. That's the word: gentler. She wonders why. She also notices a plump couple at a nearby table.

"There is a man at the table behind you. He keeps staring at me." Her eyes dart from Jon to the man and back.

"Oh? Do you know him?"

"Never seen him before," she says, reaching inside her jacket as if looking for keys, cell phone or something in her pocket. She keeps her hands beneath the tablecloth.

"I'll take care of it." He turns to look.

"No, no. He's not dangerous. But I think he knows me, or thinks he does. He'll come over here before we leave." As she finishes her sentence the man gets up, leaving his napkin on the table. He says something to the woman with him. Then he heads for Jon and Kate's table.

A dozen steps later he stops at their table. "Excuse me," he says, "I don't mean to interrupt your dinner. I'm an American, and you look very much like a celebrity back in the States." He smiles and looks at Jon, then back at Kate. "You wouldn't be Cote de Pablo would you?"

"That's very flattering, but no I'm not."

"I'm sorry," he says. "It was just a shot in the dark." He looks back at his table. "I told my wife I wasn't sure, but you could be, you know? Like I said, I'm sorry for the interruption."

"It's quite all right," Kate says and smiles. The man leaves the table. "See, it was a harmless case of mistaken identity. Anyway, her hair is darker than mine. Where were we?"

"People often come up to you like that?"

"Every once in a while, but not often."

Jon nods and reaches for his beer without further comment.

Kate cocks her head slightly and smiles broadly. "You don't know who Cote de Pablo is, do you?"

"Should I?" he asks, slightly irritated.

"Not necessarily. But it might indicate you have a life." she jokes.

"Now you know my secret. I'm just wasting away in Bermudaville."

They both laugh. "That's another subject, but I don't believe you. Anyway, about Wells…"

"He's back in the game," Jon quickly says, making a mental note to Google de Pablo.

"He and a few hand-picked others," Kate continues, wondering what became of Jon after he left Colorado Springs. And why he is now living in Hamilton.

"I've heard the Agency is being hounded by critics," he says.

"It's all politics. And it is going to get worse before it gets better."

"The former Director's predictions were spot on according to Wells. And you work for?"

"Wells."

"I suspected as much." He stiffens slightly in his chair. "You're out of the service?"

"No. I'm on annual leave."

"For vacation?"

"For a change of pace."

"For Wells?"

"For a special project."

"And when you've completed the 'Special Project' what then?"

"That depends on a lot of things. I can continue working for Wells. Or I can return to the Air Force."

"I would think you would have a lot of opportunities."

"Maybe. Unglamorous ones I'm sure. On the other hand I am confidentially promised – in writing – that I can return to active duty as a full Colonel when I finish this assignment."

"Must be a very special, special assignment," Jon says, raising his eyebrows. He is suspicious.

"Making 0-6 at 37- 38 years old is pretty cool. Only 20 percent of the Air Force is women. A lot less are women officers at the 0-6 rank."

"I'm a little rusty, but that would be way 'below-the zone' because you wouldn't have enough time in service."

"What can I say? All things are possible under the right circumstances."

"Would those circumstances include politics?"

"I'm not saying that. All I'm saying is that one day you might pin on my star. You do remember what you said to me at Peterson?"

"I remember," he answers, vividly remembering. She had dropped him off at Peterson AFB Flight Ops. "Do you think you will be back?" she had asked. "Probably not," he answered. For some reason he kissed her on the cheek. "I hope this does not constitute sexual harassment," he said. "It's only sexual harassment if I protest," she answered. Half-teasing, he added, "I want to pin your stars on someday. Don't forget me."

He remembered her nose turning pink in the morning chill. "I won't forget you," she said, teasing not at all.

"Should I assume it is just my plain dumb luck that you are here?" he asks her.

"I don't know about the luck part, but it would be plain dumb to assume it."

"I'm not getting a good feeling."

"You may want to order another beer," she says. "You're not going to like what I have to tell you."

Most of the people in the pub are glued to the television watching the weather station's meteorologist and listening to his weather warnings. The man who mistook Kate for Pablo steals an occasional look at Kate; he is still unconvinced he has not seen a TV star.

"I'm not a big drinker. Besides, Wells may have mentioned I'm an expert in dealing with things I don't like."

"Wells is pretty tight lipped." Her voice is hushed but her eyes are alert. Jon stares at her. She reminds him of the girl from Ipanema – tall and slender with warm olive skin coloring. She is making him feel alive again. But he feels a tinge of guilt. He realizes he has been lonely for a long time. Maybe it's time to move forward. "Want to start at the beginning?" he asks, trying to focus on what she is saying, but also casting a glance at the television and the weather outside.

"You remember when Wells first got in touch with me?"

"At the Air Force Academy." He sips his beer, nursing it.

"Yes." Kate empties her glass. "I have to tell you something."

"No, you don't."

"Yes, I do." She hesitates, and then drops the shock and awe bomb. "Wells believes you are in imminent danger."

"Aren't we all," Jon says, trying to keep the conversation light, but secretly tensing inside.

"I'm serious. I'm here to bring you back."

"You can't be serious. Bring me back?! From what? Why didn't Wells call me?" He leans back in his chair, distancing himself from this revelation. He reaches into his pocket and takes out his cell phone. It's turned off. He turns it on and slips it back into his jacket.

"You don't tend to respond to cell phone calls," she says watching him put his cell phone in his pocket.

He protests. "I have a radiophone on the boat. He has the frequency!"

"Apparently you don't turn that on a great deal, either." Kate's iPhone vibrates. She takes it out of her jacket and looks at the text message.

GO NOW!

"Jon," she says tersely, "we have to leave now."

Jon starts to argue but thinks better of it. He begins to thinks this is all a ruse. A darn good joke! It's probably a surprise birthday party for Effingham. And that devil invited Kate. He has talked to Effingham about Kate. Okay, he'll play along. He gets up from the table and follows her.

Emanuel is waiting at the bar, still wearing a wet raincoat. His eyes are focused beyond them, on the couple at the table against the wall.

"Hi," Emanuel says to Jon. "I'm on your team. So is your friend Mr. Effingham. I'll explain later. We need to get out of here pronto. Follow me."

The three enter the upstairs kitchen behind the bar through an "Employees Only" door. Effingham is on the other side of the door, having been enlisted earlier by Emanuel. "I've got your back, Jon," he says. The Major is actually enjoying whatever game they are playing.

Jon hesitates, wondering if this surprise birthday party is here or somewhere else. He will kill Effingham for this joke. Kate takes his arm. "Come on. I'll tell you more later."

"What about our raincoats?"

"Later," she says as they hurry out the back door - actually a fire exit - and scurry down the slippery metal steps. It is raining hard and the daylight is nearly gone. No sooner have they cleared the last steps when the Asian couple bursts into the kitchen. Effingham steps in front of them to block their way. In his most dignified and commanding voice he says to the woman. "I'm dreadfully sorry, madam, but this area is for employees only."

"Back the fuck away," threatens the woman. She steps closer to him.

Effingham leans back against a stainless steel table, a large kitchen knife in his right hand. He was warned the couple could be dangerous.

Suddenly, the woman pulls a pistol from under her jacket and fires two shots into Effingham's chest. He crashes backward against the table and slides to the floor. His mouth and eyes are open in surprise. Blood quickly pools beneath his body. The couple step around him and hurry to the exit.

At the bottom of the steps Emanuel discovers the tires on his car have been slashed. He, Jon and Kate hear the muffled report from the pistol.

"I'll hold them off," Emanuel shouts into the wind and rain "Get out of here!" He takes a .38 revolver from beneath his rain coat.

Jon hesitates. "Come on!" Kate yells.

"What the hell is going on!?"

"These people are here to kill you!" she shouts.

The couple explodes onto the second floor landing and look down. Emanuel raises his weapon and hollers, "Hold it right there!"

The woman confidently raises her pistol. With the help of an illuminator she fires twice. The first bullet strikes Emanuel in center chest. As he falls backward the second round hits below his Adam's apple. Death comes quickly. His blood flows from his wounds, mixes with the rain, and is washed down the street.

Kate and Jon hear the gun shots and are in full flight. They race down the slick street, turn left and slow to a fast walk. Moments later they hear the couple behind them in a dead run, puddles splashing with each step.

"Turn it on." shouts Kate, watching the rapidly approaching couple.

"Jesus!"

Jon and Kate are good runners in excellent physical condition. So are the two behind them. But running into the strong wind is like running with someone holding your shirttail. They turn at the next corner and speed up on the slippery street. The pursuers turn seconds later. The woman slows, raises her arm and squeezes off a round. Her shot is wide, missing Jon, who is trailing Kate. He doesn't know how near the bullet came to him. But he is sure the situation has taken a deadly serious turn.

After turning yet another corner the pursuing woman quickly comes to a stop. She takes a more steadied aim and fires again. This time she is almost on target. She misses Jon by mere inches, but takes out a piece of cornerstone from a store front.

Kate slows and looks back at Jon. "Come on!" she yells.

Twenty-five yards further they hear another muffled shot. Bullets don't "whiz by" or make ricochet sounds. They either hit something or they don't. The exception is a bullet traveling at supersonic velocity. It makes a lot of noise in flight. Jon doesn't know where this bullet hits, but it isn't either of them. Still, it's time for a change of strategy.

What happens next is a blur. When they turn the next corner Jon calls to Kate, "Wait up!"

She stops. Jon catches up and pulls her into a narrow side alley. He can't tell if it's a dead end. But it's narrow and dark. "Tell me you have a weapon," he says in short breaths. She nods yes and pulls a Beretta 8000 Cougar from under her jacket.

"Okay. The first person around the corner we let go. I'll stop the second one. You cover me. Got it?"

She nods her head.

They flatten themselves against the wet, grimy alley wall and listen for the splashing steps of the people racing towards them. The wait is short.

The first figure around the corner is the woman. She holds her pistol skyward at shoulder height as she runs. She passes them as quickly as a person can in a downpour. The man behind her is slightly slower. Jon blind-sides him with a shoulder block, sending him sprawling onto the street, and hitting the pavement with a loud grunt. Jon is instantly on top of him.

The man's companion hears the collision and turns, pistol at the ready. Kate fires a shot from her Beretta in the woman's general direction. It is not anywhere close to hitting the woman. But it has the desired effect. The woman knows they are armed. She takes off, bobbing and weaving, and disappears into the fading light. In thirty minutes it will be dark.

Kate turns and trains her pistol on the man Jon pulls to his feet. He pushes him into the alley and throws him against the wall.

"On your knees," Kate commands.

The man either doesn't understand her or pretends he doesn't understand her. Jon delivers a swift kick to the back of the man's left knee, and drops him like a brick to the wet pavement. The man groans. Jon pulls him upright on his knees by the back of his jacket.

The man is dazed and disoriented. His face is streaked with rain, but even in the dim light he shows no sign of intimidation or fear. His cheek is scraped where he made contact with the street. Jon reaches inside the man's suit jacket and retrieves a rather large pistol from a shoulder holster. He also removes a passport from the inside coat pocket. He hands the pistol to Kate in return for her Beretta. He is sure her weapon is "good to go" but unsure about the man's pistol. Then he leafs through the wet pages of the man's passport. It is a diplomatic passport issued by the Government of South Korea in the name Joo Lee Kim. Jon suspects a forgery, but it could be real. The man has been in Hamilton for seven days. He hands the passport to Kate.

"Who are you?" says Jon tersely.

"I am a diplomat," the man answers, head down against the wind and rain.

"A South Korean diplomat?"

The man doesn't answer.

Switching to Korean, Jon asks again. "You're a South Korean diplomat?"

The man looks up at Jon, blinking as the rain strikes his eyes. He obviously is not expecting Jon to speak Korean. "Yes," he grumbles in Korean, "and my government will see you are severely punished for this criminal act."

"You don't sound South Korean," snaps Jon, ignoring the fringed indignation. "I am familiar with the differences between spoken North and South Korean."

The man is uncomfortable with his physical situation. He squirms on his knees on the hard wet concrete. "I am a representative of the Government of South Korea," he insists, blinking.

Jon and Kate exchange glances. He presses the muzzle to the man's forehead. The man looks at Jon but his face shows no fear.

In English Jon says, "Do South Korean diplomats normally carry weapons?"

"If the situation demands it," he answers smugly in perfect English.

"I see," Jon replies. "Tell you what I'm going to do Mr. Diplomat. I have a few questions. If you answer them to my satisfaction, I may let you go."

The man stares back angrily, the rain and water from his wet hair dripping into his eyes, his face contorted.

"If you don't answer them to my satisfaction, I'm going to hurt you," he says menacingly.

The man furrows his forehead, wiggles on his knees, and takes a breath. Kate keeps watching the deserted street for signs of the woman.

"Are you from South Korea?"

"Yes," he says, "I am a representative of the Government of South Korea."

Jon pushes the pistol deeper into his forehead. He is no mood to be generous.

"Last chance Ajo-shi (uncle)."

There is a momentary pause as the man considers whether or not Jon will kill him. He doesn't think so, but…

"No."

"No, what?"

"I am not from the South Korean government."

Jon eases the pressure of the pistol on his forehead. "Okay. Who do you work for?"

"The Democratic People's Republic of Korea."

"The DPRK?"

"Yes."

"Why are you following me?"

"It is my duty. You are a criminal."

"What crime have I committed?"

"I am not privileged with that information. All I know is that you are a threat."

"To what? To whom?" Jon fumes.

"I don't know that. Neither of us knows that."

"And when you found me, what were your instructions?" Jon demands.

"To question you."

"Just question me?" Jon asks.

"Yes."

"You're lying." A pause. "I'm wet. I didn't get to finish my beer. I don't like you or your girlfriend. One more lie and I'm going to blow your fucking head off." It is not the words, but the tone of Jon's voice that convinces the man of the seriousness of his circumstances.

"We were to interrogate you about certain matters, and then take the appropriate action."

"What matters?"

"My partner has a list of questions. They are about something stolen from my country."

"You mean the North Korean government?"

"Yes."

"So your government – the DPRK – thinks I have stolen information it is interesting in. And when I provide it to you, or you retrieve it from me, I will have no further usefulness. Is that it?"

"Yes."

"How did you find me?"

"I do not know. We were given your name. But you have assumed another name. It was hard to find you. Our government has been searching for you for a very long time. I swear that's all I know."

Jon looks at Kate. "What do you think?"

She shrugs. "I think he is holding something back."

There is a pause in everything but the rain.

"You have screwed up Mr. Diplomat turned Foreign Agent. I think your government will deal harshly with you for your failure. Nevertheless, I want to leave you with a token of our meeting."

Neither the man nor Kate has a clue of Jon's meaning. Unexpectedly Jon quickly grabs the man's right hand by the wrist. He thumbs the safety off the pistol. He aims left of a large signet ring on the man's hand. From inches away he fires one round. The man screams in pain. Blood spurs in all directions.

"I'll call an ambulance for you. They will be here in minutes."

Turning to Kate he says, "Let's get out of here." After he takes a dozen steps, Jon drops the passport on the street for the police to find. "This way," he says, re-orientating himself, and running toward the Anglican Cathedral.

The quiet of the approaching night returns, except for the howling wind, driving rain, and the one gunshot. The assassin hears the gunshot from her hiding place in the alcove of a store one street away. She waits a few minutes and then cautiously makes her way back to her partner and the foreigners. She finds him moaning and cursing. He is bleeding heavily and trying to rip a piece of his shirt with his uninjured hand, and teeth, to make a bandage.

"Help me!" he commands in Korean. "That animal shot me!"

"What did he want from you? What did you tell him?" she asks, seemingly unconcerned with his wound.

"Sahangnyun, I'm in pain! Rip this shirt and bind me!"

She steps closer and leans over, tearing his shirt. "What did you tell him?"

"Nothing. This hurts like hell!"

"Stop whining!" she says, putting the shirt bandage over the wound. She pulls it tightly.

"He said he'd call an ambulance."

"Considerate," she says sarcastically. "Does he know you are North Korean?"

"He speaks Korean. He detected it from my accent."

"So you compromised our mission." She straightens up and steps back.

"He looked at my passport," he explains, nodding with him head to the spot where it was dropped. "He knew it was a forgery."

"Give me the vial," she orders.

"It was smashed when I was knocked down."

"Broken?" she asks, astonished. "Gone?"

He answers, grimacing in pain, "That is the usual result when glass meets concrete."

She turns away from her partner, boiling with anger. When she turns back towards him he is pulling himself up against the rain slick wall. He is holding his blood soaked hand.

"Shibsek!" she curses in Korean, extending her arm and shooting him in the side of the head. He collapses like a puppet when the strings have been cut. His eyes are frozen open and blank.

She calmly retrieves the passport from the wet pavement. There is still time to carry out her duty.

CHAPTER 9

"Thank God you were armed," Jon says, looking over his shoulder as they slow to a jog. The pistol in his hand is pointed downward. "Nice weapon."

"Maybe now you believe this is serious," Kate says, catching her breath.

"I'm worried about Effingham and Emanuel." He stops. "We should double back and see what we can do."

"I don't think that's a good idea." She looks left and right as if crossing a busy intersection. Then, with blinking eyes, directly at Jon.

"Why not?" he asks, ducking into a dark storefront and gently pulling Kate with him. The rain is unrelenting and both are soaked to the skin.

"First, we don't know where that woman is. Second, the police are probably there by now. We'd just get in the way. Or get ourselves arrested."

"I see your point. But I need to go by my boat. I have a friend who's there."

"Do you think it's safe?" She wipes her face with a wet hand, and pulls her hair back. "Your friend has probably left the boat by now. The weather is really rotten."

"You may be right …"

"Besides," she interrupts, "these people are worse than bad. And they know you live on your boat."

"What makes you so sure of that?" he asks, standing to her side so he can watch the street. It is deserted.

"Emanuel told me they had been watching you for a several days."

The revelation gives Jon pause. But he remains concerned for his friend. "I should try to contact him."

"He can't stay on your boat tonight - not in this storm, with a hurricane on the way. He's probably left you a note," she says, to appease him.

"You're probably right. I'll get you back to your hotel, and then I'll find a place.

Where are you staying?"

"The Edwardian House."

While Jon and Kate make their desperate escape, the North Korean assassin – ChungYoo Cha - makes her way to the Harbor Marina. In the downpour, she sees only two moving vehicles. Both are police cars. The storm is getting worse. She is totally drenched. Her slacks stick to her legs, making her seem naked from the waist down. Undeterred by personal discomfort she walks quickly and purposefully. The overcast skies and heavy rain help to hide her in the dim light. She hugs to the blackness of the boarded-up store fronts that have lost electrical power and are now dark. In less than twenty minutes she arrives at the Marina entrance. The docks are deserted. Pier lights flicker on and off, creating a Charlie Chaplin silent film effect. She is still angry the initial plan turned into an operational disaster. It could hardly have gone worse. Her partner drew up the plan and he was the team leader. She is the skilled assassin. Jong-Cheol is – correction - was a miserable failure. The clumsy fool put the entire operation at risk! Now it's up to her to complete the assignment.

Chung Yoo Cha watches the pier and Main Street for several minutes. The rain comes in sheets, reducing visibility to fifty feet. She doesn't see anyone. Walking slowly down the concrete pier, she stays to one side to reduce her profile. The few boats at the pier strain at their moorings, fighting rising water.

Doug Clayton has waited long enough for Jon. It's past 7:30 and night has arrived. The weather isn't getting any better. As a matter of fact, the boat is rocking considerably more. The television has gone out. His cell phone doesn't work. Staying on the boat is crazy. He gathers his rain gear at the salon door and puts it on. As he is about to leave he decides to leave a note for Jon. He quickly goes to the bar, bends over the counter with pen and paper in hand, back to the door, and begins a short note.

The howling wind and rain are so loud he doesn't hear the saloon door open behind him. Chung Yoo Cha is in luck. It appears to her London is preparing to leave the boat. Obviously, he is aware he is hunted. She takes one step inside the saloon and fires the standard two round sequence into the back of Clayton's head. He pitches forward, hitting his forehead on the counter top, then slumps forward, the hood of his rain jacket flopping over his head and covering his face.

Chung Yoo Cha looks at him but doesn't bother on checking her victim. His brains are scattered everywhere. She looks at the piece of paper near his hand. She reads it: "It is after 7:30 and I have..." She leaves it untouched. From her jacket pocket she removes a small C4 packet, places it next to the body and sets the timer. Next she locates the butane gas tank under the stove. She places another charge and sets the timer. Lastly, she looks forward and aft for the ladder to the engine room. When she finds it, she descends holding the ladder tightly because the boat is pitching violently. The light switch is at the bottom of the short ladder. Moments later she finds the fuel tanks. They are well marked. She places the third C4 charge between the twin tanks and stabs the putty-like plastic explosive with the timing donator. She sets it for 20 minutes. Satisfied she has completed the assignment, and is destroying all evidence, she is ready to depart. Her initiative in difficult circumstances will be well rewarded. The mission has been successfully completed. Before ascending the ladder to the main deck Chung Yoo Cha turns out the engine room light. Habit. Again on the main deck, she peers out the saloon window for possible witnesses. Visibility is almost nothing. Confident the coast is clear, she exits the saloon and easily jumps from the boat to the pier.

One last piece of business.

CHAPTER 10

The Edwardian House was built in 1851 when Hamilton was a small village. Originally it was a ship captain's home. The Captain lived in it for nearly 38 years, long after his sea-faring days were over. It was said he made a fortune trading African human cargo in the Caribbean for gold. He made more than enough money to build his home and acquire waterfront property.

The house has an impressive sandstone façade, its own walled garden, planted borders and gravel pathways. It is reminiscent of a Victorian-era hotel on Regent Street in London. Not far from the Edwardian House - enclosed by a wrought-iron fence - is the Anglican Cathedral, begun in 1886. The Captain donated much of his money, and all of his soul, to its construction. By the end of the 1800s the Edwardian House was in a fashionable residential neighborhood. Successive owners were shippers, importers and exporters, traders, merchants, and finally a boutique hotel owner.

The Edwardian has been faithfully maintained over the years. It was last renovated in 2001. From its quiet perch on Church Street it overlooks the Dockyard, Marina, and Hamilton's Inner Harbor. Except for the howling wind and the rain drumming on the roof, the Edwardian House is an intimate and quiet retreat for the well-heeled.

The quiet is suddenly interrupted when the lobby door is abruptly flung opened. Gale-force winds threaten to tear it off its hinges. Jon struggles to slam it closed. The night clerk looks up at the loud racket as Jon and Kate step inside. They look like sailors plucked from the sea. The clerk recognizes Kate from earlier in the day. He reaches behind the counter and takes a room key from a key cupboard. He holds the key in his hand as she approaches the registration desk.

"Appallingly damp out tonight, wouldn't you say?" he deadpans with a slight British accent.

Kate steps to the counter and takes the key from his outstretched hand. "Yes. I'm looking forward to a hot shower and a change of clothes," she politely answers.

The clerk looks past her at Jon and curls his lips up in a smile. Jon narrows his eyes in return but says nothing. Jon can read the clerk's unsavory thoughts. Kate and Jon exit the lobby leaving wet footprints on the carpet.

The room is on the second floor. It is one of three rooms with a four poster bed. Draped in fine fabrics and replica period furniture, it is quite grand. A fire is dying in the fireplace, probably because Kate was expected earlier and not later. However, there are eight or nine pieces of wood in a polished brass coal shuttle next to the fireplace. Jon carefully places two small logs on the fire. The rain pounds loudly overhead. The popping and crackling of the fire dispels the dampness and creates a sense of shelter from the storm.

Kate goes to the windows and closes the heavy drapes. Jon sits on the edge of one of two large wingback chairs in front of the fire. He dials his boat's landline number. It doesn't ring. He tries his cell phone. The screen reads: "service unavailable." He pulls off his soaked shoes and socks while Kate picks up her overnight bag and quietly retreats into the bathroom. Seconds later she returns with a large fluffy towel. "This will help," she says, throwing it to Jon. "I'm going to take a shower. Then it's all yours."

Jon strips off his wet clothes and dries off. He stokes the fire until the flames capture the logs. Then he carefully lays his pants and shirt on the back of one of the chairs. He hopes they will be dry by morning. When he gets in the bathroom he'll roll his shorts and socks in a hand towel to help dry them.

He reminds himself he should have gone by his boat. He tries his cell phone again to no avail. With the towel securely wrapped around him, and his hair standing almost straight up, he goes to the armoire in search of a hanger for his pants and jacket. In countries that build houses without closets, the armoire is essential. This one looks like an antique, but he suspects it is a reproduction. It is tall and dark. Darker than Cherry or

Mahogany. In it are half a dozen dark wooden hangers, and two bathrobes with an embroidered Edwardian crest. Discarding his towel he puts on a robe and hangs his pants. He goes to the bathroom door and knocks loudly.

"What?" she answers over the sound of the shower.

"May I open the door to leave a bathrobe for you?"

"Yes, thank you."

Jon cracks the door and puts the robe on the vanity. The bathroom is like a sauna, with a cloud of steam fogging everything. If he could see it, he feels certain the mirror is completed fogged. He rapidly closes the door and returns to the fireplace. He turns his back to the heat, feeling the warmth spreading throughout his body. Occasionally the logs hurl a flaming ember against the fire screen as if the Fire God is angry.

After a few pensive moments he retrieves the Korean's pistol from Kate's coat. Sitting in the Wingback he studies the heavy black 9mm. It has a threaded barrel to screw on a suppressor. On the left side of the barrel is the name Jericho 941. Beneath the name are the letters IMI: Israel Military Industries. Jon remembers the manufacturer use to be IWI, Israel Weapons Industries. And before that another name he can't recall. He does remember it is the company that manufactured the legendary Uzi. On the left side of the frame is a safety. He makes sure it is on, and ejects the magazine. He removes the round in the chamber. Its ammo is hollow point, 9 millimeter Parabellum. It looks different from other hollow points he has seen. He puts the round ejected back into the magazine. Then he reinserts the clip and jacks a round into the chamber. Satisfied, he puts the weapon on the table beside the chair.

Things are beginning to unravel. Everything was fine a few days ago, except for nearly being run over by some dumb ass tourist when he was jogging. Or maybe not tourists. Maybe would-be assassins. He tries to match the faces in the car with the Koreans in the pub.

Nigel Effingham. The shots they heard must have been intended for him. That woman doesn't miss stationary targets at point-blank range. And she doesn't shoot to wound. Effingham is probably dead. Maybe the second gunshot was a coup de grace. No, the shots were in rapid succession. Two shot sequence. Professional. What were the other gun shots?

The last few hours have been bad. Things could hardly get worse. Perhaps he feels the paranoia of the hunted. In any case, he doesn't like it. Still, he and Kate should be safe for now. The Koreans don't know about her so they won't know where to find them. The police will be able to discover the identity of the one Korean – probably have already identified him - and arrest both of them. They can stay out of sight till the coast is clear and then resurface. Tomorrow he will scan the The Royal Gazette Early Edition and the Bermuda Sun in the afternoon for any police reports. He'll make a few calls to make sure the coast is clear.

He picks up his cell phone and again tries to reach Clayton. The phone indicates no signal. Nothing. He considers how to get a message to his friend. He fears the weather has worsened in the last few hours. If Clayton has the TV on he'll see the weather warnings and leave the boat for the Manchester. Maybe the phone will work then. He will keep trying.

~ ~ ~ ~

When Stephens' cell rings he expects Emanuel. The voice, to his delight, is his new Asian friend. He's glad for something to break the monotony; he can only take so many of Harris's Secrets-Of- A-Used-Car-Salesman stories.

"Hey, how are you?" he says.

"Fine."

"Everything okay?"

"Yes. It's been one of those days, as you say. I was hoping we might get together," she says in a low intimate voice, "and get our minds on something other than the storm. If you get my meaning."

Stephen's lustful heart begins to pump additional blood in anticipation of meeting with her. It also races in anticipation of receiving a promised $25,000 finder's fee. "Well, sure. I've got to take care of some business, so let's say as soon as I can. Forty minutes? An hour at most."

"I'll just have to wait. Same place?"

"Sure. Give me an hour." He hangs up and goes in search of Harris, who has wandered off. Where can that guy be? he wonders. In short order he finds Harris asleep in the aircraft. He bangs loudly on the composite wing with his hand. Harris jumps like he has been shot and opens the door.

"This is a really neat plane, Larry. I was just checking it out, you know?"

"Whatever. Listen, Emanuel just called and needs me. You need to get down here and stay awake until I get back."

"Hey, I am awake!" he protests, climbing out of the cockpit.

"Jesus, Harris, don't be an asshole. Just stay alert. I'll be back in a couple of hours. If you need me or anybody shows up – anybody – call me on my cell. Got that?"

"Sure. Where can you go in weather like this?" he says, raising his eyebrows.

"You've been with us long enough to know people are crazy. We have to be ready at any time in any weather. You know that." He uses his parent-to-child voice.

"Yea, you're right, Larry. I understand. Sorry I asked. I'll take care of everything."

CHAPTER 11

"The bathroom is yours," Kate announces. Even dressed in a bathrobe, with a towel wrapped around her head, she has a sensuous appeal.

"Thanks." He tries to not think about her. Jon takes a long shower. When he emerges from the bathroom, Kate is sitting in the wingback closest to the bathroom. Her legs are curled up beneath her, and the bathrobe pulled tightly. Jon pulls the other chair nearer to her – throwing his still damp shirt on the bed. "You okay?"

"No," she says in a quiet voice. "Are you?" She turns to look at him.

"I've had better days, and I've had worse. I prefer better."

Looking away she stares into the fire. Silent for a moment. "Some time ago I dreamed we'd meet again."

"Hopefully it was under better circumstances." He turns to look at her.

"In my dream it was at the Broadmoor," she says softly, poignantly, returning her gaze to the fireplace.

"That's a beautiful place," he says, trying to forget his last visit to the grand hotel in Colorado Springs. "You really liked your time at the Academy…" The sentence just dies.

"I value it more with every passing year. Sometimes it's like that with lots of things. What was that old movie line, 'In my experience, it's best to remember the happier times.'?"

"Got me."

"You're not trying."

Jon nods his head slowly in agreement, his mind a long way from old movies. "What is going on? Why hasn't Wells gotten in touch with me directly? Couldn't we have avoided all this?"

"You're going to have to ask Wells."

"He just calls you out of the blue and says go get London?"

"That pretty much sums it up."

"What else did he say?"

"How dependable you are. Said you always bring your 'A game' to an assignment, and are aggressive and courageous. Also mentioned you had no reluctance to do whatever was required." Pause. "Would you have killed that man tonight?"

"If it had been necessary. It wasn't. Anything else?" Jon answers harshly.

"Wells said you received a National Intelligence Achievement Medal for…"

Cutting her off in mid-sentence, Jon raises his eyebrows and says, "Thought you said he was tight-lipped, not glib."

"Maybe he was trying to impress me."

"I was recalled to active duty. What I did, I did it for a friend. Less you misjudge me, I'm a mercenary."

"He didn't mention mercenary. Actually, he said he holds you in high regard."

"Wells is an optimistic pragmatist who believes in meritocracy. You've got to be good to work for him. That's what should impress you. You should take his wanting you to work with him as a compliment."

"I do. Apparently that works for you, too."

"Working for Wells reduces ethical conflicts and moral consequences."

Kate feels she is talking to another person. Or another personality. Or, maybe the dark side. "Does anyone really know you?" she asks, looking concerned.

"No one really knows anyone. People only let you see what they want you to see."

"Maybe one day I'll get to know you."

Jon shakes his head, but doesn't comment. He doesn't need intimacy.

"Well," she says when she gets no response, "I'm worn out."

"Me, too. I'm sorry if I sounded grouchy. Probably the stress. I'd like to get some sleep, but it may be hours before I can." He gets up and goes to the bed, grabs a pillow and pulls the comforter off. "I'll sleep here, next to the fire."

"If you'll behave you can have half of the bed."

"I like sleeping on the floor. Use to do it all the time as a kid." There is a short pause and then he says, "On second thought, I'm probably too tired to be naughty. I like to sleep on my side, so if you don't mind I'll take the right side."

"Do you snore?"

"I've never heard it."

"Has anyone else?" She raises her eyebrows.

"Not playing that game," he answers and gets in the bed.

With his back turned, she turns out the light and takes off her bathrobe. She gets in bed wearing only her thong. They lie back to back but neither is asleep. Jon is wide awake, heart beating faster than normal from the evening's excitement. Or maybe Kate. He feels the softness and warmth of her backside. She is keyed up as well. She tosses and then turns on her side facing Jon's back. He turns over to look at her in the darkness. She sighs and leans toward him.

"Kate," Jon begins, but is interrupted when she kisses him. He returns her kiss, gently at first, and then more passionately. They embrace and moments turn to minutes, and minutes to a loss of time. After the final frenzy both are as drenched as if they had run a record-setting 10K - bodies wet with perspiration. Jon withdraws from Kate as she pleads for him to stay where he is. He rolls to his side, gently pulling a willing Kate into his arms. The stress of the last few hours takes a toll. He cannot stop himself from falling into a heavy sleep.

Hours later he slowly awakens, feeling guilty and selfish. It was an unanticipated moment of intimacy. He wonders what time it is, but doesn't want to wake her by moving his arm to look at his watch. It's dark in the room but he can dimly see the outline of her face. What in God's name is she doing here with me? he thinks. What in the world am I doing here with her? Last night was a nightmare! And wonderful! I must be losing my mind!

The wind and rain continue to batter the room's windows and roof. But the storm seems to be lessening. Kate stirs and her breathing changes; she opens her eyes and slides off Jon. Pulling the sheet up around her chin, she whispers "Hi."

"Hi." He turns to face her and checks his watch. He has been awake for at least an hour.

"What time is it?"

Jon looks again at the brightly illuminated watch face. "Almost five."

"Are you hungry?"

"I don't know what to say," he answers, wrestling with his emotions.

"Yes you're hungry, or no, you are not hungry."

"You know that's not what I mean."

"I know," she says in a whispering sleepy voice, and snuggles closer.

"No, you don't know," he quietly but gently insists.

"Jon, its morning and I still respect you," she teases. "You did not seduce me. At least not in the traditional sense."

"And what is 'in the traditional sense?'"

"You know… money, power, position."

"Are you saying I seduced you in a non-traditional sense?"

"Not exactly," she sighs. "You seduced me with your intellect, your wit, your gentleness. Your feminine side."

"I don't have a feminine side. And I didn't mean to take advantage of you in any sense."

"We're consenting adults. You did not take advantage of an underage girl or a subordinate officer."

"Kate, I don't do one-night stands."

"I don't recall anyone talking about one-night stands."

"It's more complicated than that…" he stutters.

"May I ask," she says, "if you are married?"

"You know I'm not."

"Engaged?"

"Don't be silly."

"In love with someone?"

"Not in the usual sense."

"What does that mean?" she asks, drawing back to look at him.

"It just means…I don't know what it means. I have to sort things out, and this isn't the time or place to do that."

They look at each other through the darkness with searching eyes. Then Kate says, "Let me tell you how I feel. Ever since we met I felt attracted to you. Maybe it was because up to then I was focused on my career, or had been living in an artificial world where men are men, and women officers are expected to be men, too. There was no romance in my life. There was no time for me."

"Kate…" he groans.

"Let me finish. I felt some chemistry but ignored it. You were hell-bent on your assignment – whatever it was - and never let me in. But I could sense - I could feel - something. I believe things might have been different, if circumstances had been different," she says, her eyes glistening with emotion. "You know that's true."

Jon feels trapped by memories and emotions. He doesn't want to hash his personal life. Not now. Not here. Not ever. Wrestling with the past has gripped him for two years. He wants to let it go, but it's not easy. Time does not heal all wounds; time merely dulls the pain.

"Tell me how you feel," Kate says.

He exhales loudly. "I am not into recreational sex. I don't go to bed with people I am not committed to. That's first. Second, I do have deep feelings for you. It's difficult for me to say that. I feel guilty about it. Third, I have some personal issues to deal with and I haven't. I hope you know last night was not just ah, for me…ah screw. And lastly, I know what I want for breakfast." He smiles at her and lightly kisses her forehead.

"Maybe we have been ships passing in the night?" she says in a genuinely hopeful voice.

"Maybe."

"Or maybe I'm just a good screw!" she giggles, recovering her playfulness.

"Officers do not use that kind of language."

"Oh? You've been out of uniform too long." Kate comes out from under the sheets, exposing her small but firm breasts. She embraces Jon, and then pulls the sheet up over both. "Let's do it again, or go back to sleep."

"We've been through too much to go back to sleep. Let's make a plan and get on with it. Can you share some toothpaste?"

She does, and Jon goes to the bathroom and brushes his teeth with his finger. He hops in the shower and turns the water jet on his forehead.

Kate cracks the bedroom door and picks up the early edition of the newspaper. The headline reads:

HURRICANE MISSES BERMUDA. AGAIN!

ONLY A TROPICAL STORM

Kate scans the front page. There are the usual post-storm reports: trees falling on houses; roofs and signs being blown away in the high wind; roads closed; damage to a cell tower; and flooding in coastal and residential areas. Considering the islands rest atop a submerged volcano this is to be expected. Further down on the bottom right of the front page she reads:

In a freak accident a powerboat in the inner harbor exploded during the storm, killing the local owner, Mr. Jon London, and totally destroying the boat. The police investigation is continuing. An unnamed source speculates a rare lighting strike ignited the petrol tanks causing the explosion. The boat sank at its berth in the Marina. The body has not been recovered.

"Oh my God!" exclaims Kate under her breath. She hurriedly turns to the newspaper's second front. Her eyes widen when she reads:

Hamilton business owner murdered. Police reported the fatal shooting of Mr. Nigel Effingham, owner of the Black Dog Pub. A second man, whose identify has not been released pending notification of the next of kin, was found fatally wounded behind the Black Dog. While the investigation is on-going, police speculate a person or persons was attempting to rob Mr. Effingham, who resisted and was shot in the ensuing struggle. Mr. Effingham was a highly respected member of the business community, a much beloved member of Saint Theresa Church, and a decorated member of the Royal Marines. No suspects have been identified, nor arrests made.

At the bottom of the page she sees another local news item:

Unidentified man fatally shot. Crime continues to increase in Hamilton. An unidentified man was shot near The Comer House last night. No details were available at press time, but the police are investigating.

There is no mention in the article of Emanuel. Kate hurries to the bathroom door. "Jon!" she shouts. "Come out!"

"Give me a minute," he answers loudly.

"This is urgent. Come now!"

Jon rushes wide-eyed out of the bathroom, with a wet towel wrapped around him, expecting another unanticipated misfortune to add to a day of misfortunes. "What?" he says, not seeing any cause for alarm.

Kate has the newspaper in her hand and waves Jon to the corner of the bed, where she sits down. When he sits beside her, she hands him the front page.

"I can believe it!" he says, as he reads rapidly.

"There's more," she says, handing him the second front. Jon devourers the words and shakes his head. "Doug and Nigel. Poor bastards!"

"They are withholding the name of Emanuel. At least for the time being."

"And I'm dead." He puts the paper down and looks at her.

"They also have not identified the North Korean. You didn't kill him!"

"They should have been able to I.D. him from the passport."

"Unless it was picked up."

"You thinking what I'm thinking?"

"She's one thorough killer. Let's not give her a second chance," Kate said. "Let's get out of here."

"And go where? This is as safe a place as we have until we come up with a plan," said Jon, racking his brain. "Any plan."

"I think we can fly in this weather. Let's get to the airfield."

"How far away?" Jon wonders if they can jog to it.

"Not far. But too far to just run out there," she answered, reading his mind.

"We can get a plane there?"

"Sure."

"How about a pilot? Or do you know where we can get one at this hour?" "Not a problem."

"Thank goodness Wells thinks of some things."

"How do we get out there? Should we call Emanuel's office?" she asks.

"Absolutely not. And we can't call a taxi. Let's try and "borrow" a car?" "And how do we "borrow" a car?"

"Leave that to me." He looks around the bedroom, and then walks into the bathroom, continuing to look around. Kate sits on the corner of the bed and waits.

"Call housekeeping or maintenance. Tell them you think something's wrong with the air conditioning and it smells funny. Sound concerned."

Kate leans over and pulls the phone onto the bed. She touches 31 for house services. Moments later, in her best panic voice, she convinces maintenance she is frightened her room might catch fire or explode. Ten minutes later there is a quiet knock on the door. The maintenance man comes in carrying a metal tool box. While he inspects the vents, Kate leans over his shoulder to provide a diversion for Jon. He takes a medium-size flathead screw driver from the tool box. As Kate keeps up her conversation, Jon also quietly takes a small cordless drill and small drill bit. Both fit comfortably in his hand.

"Lady," says the sleepy maintenance man, "I don't think you have anything to worry about. Maybe the condenser froze a little but everything is okay now. If you smell something in the morning just call me."

"That's good news. I was worried. Thank you for coming at this dreadful time."

"No problem," he says closing up his tool box without looking. Kate walks him to the door.

Jon waits for the maintenance man to leave the hotel floor. Turning to Kate he says, "Grab your things. Let's get out of here."

CHAPTER 12

The ocean is crashing over the causeway. Half a mile from the international airport, the causeway is near a modest hotel. Hotel customers are travelers leaving the island or over-nighting. Because of the advancing hurricane, many tourists to Bermuda left the previous day. The causeway is closed, so there are no police or barriers to block vehicles. In fact, there are no cars of any description in sight. The hotel is a standard one, surrounded by a pink sea wall that is taking a pounding. It is a clean, but otherwise unremarkable, hotel. It appears empty.

The rain sweeps across the narrow street leading to the hotel, as yet still passable. He parks his car on the second level of the hotel parking deck. The deck is deserted. Stephens races into the wind to the protection of the tattered and flapping awning over the brightly lit hotel side door. He is a driven man. On the drive to the hotel he plans his exotic adventure.

Stephens makes his way via the stairs to the second floor. The room he is seeking is at the far end of the deserted hall. He walks quickly to it, and knocks once on the door. Chung Yoo Cha opens the door immediately. Her hair is wet and she has a large towel wrapped around her. After he steps inside she looks up and down the hallway before closing and locking the door. The hall is empty.

"You got here fast," she says in accented English. "I was just taking a shower. Give me a minute to get something on."

Stephens grabs her and kisses her hungrily. He breaks off the kiss and stares at the wet towel covering her breasts. "No need to get dressed," he says with a smirk on his face. He kisses her again, forcefully, and rips the towel from her body.

Chung Yoo Cha sucks in her breath as he roughly grabs both breasts, pinching her nipples. "Ouch," she said, "you're hurting me!"

"You'll get over it," he says in a coarse voice, pulling her to the bed. He throws her on the bed and falls on top of her. His left hand curls around her neck in a choke hold. She surrenders to him as he jams his tongue down her throat and roughly parts her legs.

"You're hungry." She breaths her words as she reaches to unzip his trousers.

"I'm hungry for you, bitch. I've got just what you need."

Their lustful session goes on for forty minutes, climaxing with Chung Yoo Cha on top of Stephens. "This is heaven," he says, now relaxed and noticing, for the first time, the spider tattoo on her left shoulder. "If I got to die, this is the way to go!"

She wiggles to get off of him. She is anything but relaxed, but hides it well. Inside her rage is building. "Why don't you turn over," she purrs, "and I'll massage your neck and shoulders."

"Oh, yeah. You are one great piece of ass," he says, and flops onto his stomach. With strong hands and fingers she kneads his neck and shoulders. He groans with pleasure. Abruptly, she stops.

He lifts his head slightly and half turns. "Hey,' he questions, "what are you doing?"

"I'm just getting some baby oil," she says. "Relax."

She gets up and heads into the bathroom.

"Oh, okay," he calls after her. "That's a good idea." He collapses again, face down on the pillow.

Chung Yoo Cha quietly returns. In a hand towel she conceals a Korean folding knife. Its razor sharp blade is made of ballistic steel. She again straddles Stephens' back.

"Where did you learn to fuck like that?" he asks in a vulgar voice, but meaning it as a compliment.

"From fucking people like you," she replies, a slight change in the tone of her voice. He detects the change, with some alarm, and starts to tense up.

With her left hand Chung Yoo Cha forces his head into the pillow. With her right hand she draws the knife blade deeply and expertly across the base of his skull, three fingers higher than the bone notch at the base of his neck. The spinal cord is severed in the C-1 - C-3 area. Stephens is paralyzed immediately. He instantaneously loses control of his arms and legs and respiration. He is suffocating, but his whimpers are deadened by the pillow. He dies within a minute, long enough for him to know what has happened, and that he is dying. Had he lived he would have been a quadriplegic. But she enjoyed killing him. His kind did not deserve to live.

Chung Yoo Cha showers. She washes and carefully dries the knife. Then she takes the shower curtain, returns to the bed and rolls Stephens' body in it. She considers what to do with it as she dresses. She removes his wedding ring and watch and puts them in her jacket. She takes the credit cards and $87 from his wallet and pockets them. She throws the empty wallet on the bed. She plans to scatter the watch, ring, and credit cards in three different locations. She is confident the room is registered to someone other than him. It should take the police a day or so to learn his real identify, well after she has left the island. The hotel is nearly deserted and few, if any, people will be out in this weather or at this hour. She could take the body to the ocean – probably unseen. Authorities wouldn't find it for a day, maybe more. By then the crabs would have done their work, making identification even more difficult. But she knows successful professionals don't take chances. There is no reason for her to take additional risks, she decides. The hotel won't find the body for another 24 hours anyway. She wipes everything she touched with a hand towel, and hangs the Do Not Disturb sign on the door knob. Stepping into the deserted hall she looks for other guests or staff. There are no trays, dinner or breakfast, in front of any hotel room door. She silently enters the stairwell, and exits on the ground floor into the stormy night.

Behind the hotel is a dimly lit narrow alley. Delivery trucks bring fresh food daily for the hotel restaurant. Several times a week trucks deliver supplies for the hotel gift shop, its fitness center and the indoor pool. Spaced roughly 30 feet apart in the alley are three metal dumpsters. The garbage dumpster is easily identified by smell. Chung Yoo Cha stuffs the knife and her pistol into a plastic bag of rotting food. She looks around to confirm no one has seen her. Then she walks to the second dumpster further down the alley. After a few moments of shuffling around in it, she finds an empty cardboard box. She stashes her passport in it, and pushes it under other boxes.

CHAPTER 13

"What are we looking for?" ask Kate as the stinging rain hits them.

"An unlocked car. You take that side of the street. I'll check this side."

Minutes pass as they go from car to car. Two blocks from the hotel Kate waves her hand. Jon scurries across the street to join her.

"This one is unlocked," she says, looking around to satisfy her they are unnoticed.

"It's a BMW," Jon says in a disappointing voice. "Did I mention I have limited mechanical skills?"

"I have the feeling you haven't mentioned a lot of things."

The distance between them is less than a foot. She's lovely even when peeved, Jon notices. "High price car like Bimmers and Mercedes are safe from me. I need an older car. Preferably an American one. Keep looking," he says in his best encouraging voice and hurries back across the wet street. A block further Jon spots a beat-up 1995 Olds Cutlass. It's locked, but the window is open enough for the rain and Kate to get in. She slips her slender hand in the window and pulls the lock up, then hurries to the passenger side.

"Jump in," Jon says as he slides behind the wheel on well-worn cloth seats. They sit for a moment to make sure they haven't been seen. The interior of the car is a trash bin, with litter everywhere. No one rushes out of a building yelling "Thief!"

Satisfied they are unnoticed, Jon takes the screwdriver and drill from his jacket. He puts the drill bit into the ignition and drills the length of a key. This destroys the lock pins. He repeats the process. As he does, small pieces of metal from the ignition lock fall out. "So far, so good," he says.

Kate continues to keep watch. The streets are deserted. No one in sight and no cars moving.

Jon hands Kate the drill. He inserts the screwdriver into the steering wheel ignition cavity and turns it. The engine starts.

"And that is how you hotwire a car," he says proudly.

"Looks to me like its how to screwdriver a car," she kibitz.

"Same thing." He puts the car in D and slowly pulls away from the curb. She turns the defroster to max. Thirty minutes later they arrive at the deserted airfield. It is still raining heavily.

"The plane is in the hanger," Kate says as she motions him to a parking place next to the hanger door. She frowns.

"What's the matter?'

"There should be at least another car here."

The last hours have made Jon cautious. He takes the Israeli pistol from his waistband and checks the magazine. Full. He racks the slide and thumbs the safety off. "Who's inside?"

"I don't know. Emanuel told me he was leaving two people here."

"You met 'em?"

"Yeah."

"So you go in and call for them. I'll follow behind just in case."

They get out of the car leaving the doors slightly ajar. More rain will not depress the value of the wreck, and they don't want to alert anyone inside. Kate opens the hanger door as gently as she can and steps inside. Jon closes it quietly. All is silent. Half of the hanger's overhead lights are on. The airplane is the only object in the hanger bay, turned around for departure, with the APU positioned near the nose. They stop and listen. Nothing. All the lights are on in the maintenance office. Jon motions with his pistol for Kate to check it out. He remains in the shadows. Kate sees Harris through the office window reading a magazine. She can't see the cover fully, but she can read Girls of. She looks for Stephens but doesn't see him in the office. She wonders where he is. Quietly she retraces her steps to Jon. "Only one guy here," she whispers.

Jon tucks the pistol in his waistband and says, "Let's see what's going on."

~ ~ ~ ~

Only the most experienced – or most foolish – pilots would take off in the dismal and dangerous weather. As they taxi toward the runway, Kate keys the mike.

"Cadbury, this is Caramel for takeoff instructions. Over." Through the headset her voice has a mild echo and crackle.

Unknown to Kate, Cadbury makes contact with the BWS (Bermuda Weather Service), located at the southern end of St. David's island. It is manned 24/7. After what seems a long wait Kate get a response. "Caramel, this is Cadbury. Runway one-niner. Wind is two-zero-zero at one-six, gusting to two-five. Visibility one half mile. Reported two-zero-zero foot ceiling. Over."

"Cadbury this is Caramel. Runway one-niner."

"Caramel cleared for takeoff. Use discretion. Out."

Two clicks.

Hurricane Alley. FAA requires one mile visibility and a 500 foot ceiling for civilian pilots. The military has its own requirements. Kate doesn't consider herself a civilian pilot or a military one. She makes her own rules. This attitude of boldness is one Well's observed and valued.

They are eager to leave, and Kate is a competent instrument pilot. Jon, while not current, is still experienced enough to be a good co-pilot to the auto-pilot. Some basic things you plain don't forget; it's the bicycle rule. At the end of the runway Jon types into the computer LF Wade Intl. When it pops up he selects Airport/FBO info. From there he looks for radio frequencies. There is one for Dept. ATIS, another for Arr. ATIS, a frequency for Ground Control, and another frequency for Tower. He punches in 124.5 for Ground Control and listens.

Nothing.

He changes to channel to 118.1 – the Tower – and listens until they are lined up at the end of runway 19. The rain pounds the windshield. Low grass alongside the runway is bent horizontal in the wind.

Nothing, again.

Jon says: "I'd say not even geese are flying."

"That should make it safe for us to take off," she says, and advances the power without waiting for Jon's response. The aircraft bucks like a bronco heading into the wind, almost like it wants to break free of its riders. The ground disappears quickly as the plane climbs through the low lying clouds. It's a bouncing, bumpy ride. Jon watches the radar altimeter. Height is safety. He remembers a placard hanging in Flight Ops when he was an Air Force pilot:

Less thou maintain adequate separation

The earth will surly rise up and smite thee.

"Cadbury this is Caramel." Kate broadcast on the discrete EHF channel. Jon adjusts his headset so he can listen through the static.

Fifteen seconds later she repeats her transmission. "Cadbury this is Caramel. Over."

What seems like a long time is another 10 seconds. Then: "Caramel this is Cadbury. Go ahead."

"Roger, Cadbury. This is Caramel. Wheels up at one-two-three-zero Zulu (7:30 a.m.). ETA one-six-zero-zero Zulu (11:00 a.m.). Problems at the station. Lion captured. Do you copy? Over." She looks over at Jon. He winces.

"Roger Caramel. Copy problems at the station. Lion captured. ETA one-six hundred Zulu."

"Read back is correct. Cadbury out."

Business handled, Kate changes channels to intercom. "Let me know when you want to strap on this little filly."

"The lion is perfectly happy as it. Wells is not going to be happy with the mess we left behind."

"Hopefully Emanuel's deputy has reported to Washington."

"If he knows." Jon turns the volume down. "When were you going to tell me about getting your wings?"

"Actually, I never got my wings."

"Should I be worried now?"

"We're out of there, are we not?"

The conversation on the intercom is almost like being on the phone, neither looking at one another. Kate is watching the instruments. So is Jon.

"You told me you were not PQ (pilot qualified) as a cadet." The plane climbs steadily through the overcast, the ocean beneath invisible.

"I wasn't. But that didn't mean I couldn't fly. Only that I couldn't fly for the Air Force. I earned my licenses and ratings on my dime, and my own time. Every opportunity I'd be in the air. I've logged more than 3,000 hours."

"So could you fly for the Air Force now?"

"Probably not. I don't plan on asking." She eases back on the power.

"But Wells knew." Jon scans the instruments.

Kate nods. "He knows a lot – or knows how to find out what he wants to know." She trims the plane up. The conversation dies. Almost four hours later they touch down at the deserted airstrip in South Carolina. The weather is much improved from when she left. But a steady rain is still falling. Kate taxies the aircraft to the hanger and shuts the engine down. Wells is waiting nearby when they de-plane. In his retirement he has taken to wearing dark jackets and open collars. It is a look different from his previous 20 years.

There are two doors on the plane. Kate and Jon exit at the same time, but on opposite sides of the craft. Banks, Taliaferro and the security guard respectfully stand behind Wells as they approach.

"I'm glad to see you, Jon," Wells says, warmly shaking his hand. "Kate," he nods his greeting to her. They stand together, unmoving. Jon's face is all business. "Jesus, Bob, what the hell is going on?"

"I got your message about problems. I'm eager to get the details. Obviously, there were some unexpected events." He looks back and forth between Jon and Kate.

"Unexpected? You have no fucking idea," Jon says, looking at Kate for support after he speaks.

Kate returns his look, and then says, respectfully, to Wells, "It's been a challenge."

"I want to know all about it. But first things first. Let's get you out of here."

Banks and Taliaferro led the way to a waiting SUV. On the way out the door, Banks stops briefly to give Fannin instructions: "No visitors. I'll see you later." Then he catches up with the others.

Jon climbs into the rearmost seat of the SUV. Wells and Kate take the seats side-by-side behind the driver. Taleforro drives with Banks riding shotgun.

Wells says, "I know you must be tired."

"Tired is the last thing I am," interrupts Jon.

Wells tries to not look perplexed. He wonders if things have gone worse than expected. His face shows his curiosity - and his anxiety.

"Things went pretty well until Mr. Emanuel and I found Colonel London," Kate begins.

"Stop with the titles," reminds Jon in a weary voice.

"What went wrong?" asks Wells.

"It turned out we were only minutes – literally – ahead of the Koreans. When they were preparing to…to confront Jon. I don't know. Maybe we forced their hand."

"What happened?" says an anxious Wells, now looking at Jon for answers.

"Kate hurried us out of the place," Jon explains. "They were close behind."

"Emanuel was killed," Kate says suddenly. She looks at Jon to continue. Wells starts to speak but Jon beats him to it.

"He's not the only one. A good friend of mine was murdered trying to slow them down. Another friend was accidently killed in the hurricane."

"What happened to the assassin?" Wells asks in an even, controlled voice.

"Assassins," corrects Jon.

"There were two. One woman and one man," explains Kate.

"They tried to kill us," says Jon. "But we caught one. He confirmed they were sanctioned by North Korean authorities. The woman got away."

"What happened to the man?"

"We let him go," said Jon, stealing a sideway glance at Kate. "He had no value."

"We suspect the man was the spotter and the woman the assassin," Kate suggests.

Wells is stunned, not only because the hastily constructed plan misfired but because his friend Emanuel is dead. He dreads telling the family, but better he than anyone else. This bungle will reach Soperton quickly, if it hasn't already. This does not bode well for the operation so far.

"I'm truly sorry. But I'm glad both of you are okay." Wells says.

"Okay is a relative term," offers Jon.

"Jon lost his boat in the hurricane," volunteers Kate.

"Home," Jon corrects.

Wells turns his head and body completely around to look at Jon. He shakes his hed.

"Guess I'll need to borrow some toothpaste and old clothes, Bob," Jon says unemotionally.

"We'll take care of everything, Jon. Kate. We've got rooms for both of you, and we'll get whatever you guys need."

The big SUV turns off the main road and enters a Marriott vacation property. At 2:00 p.m. Kate and Jon are brought by Banks to Bob Wells' office at Cadbury. The late brunch is catered and consists of light and healthful fare. It is followed by a detailed debrief conducted by two Cadbury staff.

Ninety minutes into the afternoon debriefing, during a break, Wells casually motions to Jon to step out. They walk to an empty conference room down the hall.

"How's it going so far?" Wells asks.

"Should be about finished," answers Jon. He waits for any shoes to drop.

"I'm truly sorry about events in Bermuda. I've talked to Langley. They believe Emanuel's number two is also dead. They have a team on the way."

"I hope they are sending someone to whack that Korean assassin."

"I'm particularly sorry about your and my friends, and the loss of your boat and personal possessions," Wells says as he takes a seat.

"Me, too." Jon sits across from Wells and folds his arms across his chest. "Is Kate going back to D.C. or working with you here?"

"That depends." Wells sits back. "She told you about her opportunity?"

"It wasn't a long conversation."

Wells nods. "Do you know what we want you to do?"

Jon has known Wells for a long time and knew there was something else on his mind. "Me? You gotta be kidding." he says, unfolding his arms and pushing back from the table literally and figuratively.

"There is some unfinished business that involves you. I'd like your help in finishing it."

"I have a lot of loose ends to tie up."

"I know."

"You'll be getting a good person in Kate. She saved my bacon in Hamilton in more ways than I'd like to admit. I'm beginning to think I may have underestimated her."

"She's signed on. Still, she needs a partner for what I have in mind. I've considered several people, but was thinking you two would make a good team. I thought the chemistry was good last time around."

"Give me your one best reason," challenging Wells to convince him.

"Kate is an outstanding individual. She's an Air Force Academy grad, you know."

Jon opens his eyes widely as he says, "That's your best reason?"

"I'm coming to it," Wells answers. "Like many military academy grads she is analytical, objective, and data-driven. Classic left-brain."

"So…"

"And you are a creative, out-of-the-box, kind of person. Classic right-brain."

"I know you're coming to the punch line."

"Going with just Kate I get a left-brain operative. Going with you I get a right-brain operative. Either way with just one of you, I get half a brain. But together, I get a whole brain." He grins broadly, unable to conceal how pleased he is with his analysis.

"Hell of a salesman, Bob," Jon says, and both break out laughing. After they recover from their brief lightheartedness, Jon gives Wells a serious look. "How many did you consider?"

"Let's just say you're the final finalist. But always my first choice," he hastens to add.

"Interesting. Except my brain isn't looking for work. I'm definitely not looking for the kind of chicanery you engage in –whatever it might be this time." He permits himself an equally wide grin after the word chicanery. "And, I don't like the sound of final finalist. Nice try." He holds up his hand and starts to get up.

"Dr. Myong Soon was murdered," Wells blurts out. "Probably because of you."

Jon stops instantly and sits again. He glares at Wells. "I don't believe you."

Wells face freezes in seriousness. "Do you believe the North Koreans that just tried to kill you are unconnected to Soon's murder?"

"No." Then quickly, "I mean I don't know."

"Do you want me to connect the dots?" He raises his eyebrows as he asks the question.

~ ~ ~ ~

Jon doesn't return to the debrief. He waits with Wells in the conference room, feeling trapped and saddened about Soon. Worse, he feels himself being drawn into something very serious. The price of poker has just gone up.

Wells and Jon sit quietly for what seems a long time, locked in thought, until one of the Cadbury staff enters. The debrief is over. Wells asks Colonel Breeden be invited to join them. "And, Richard," he adds, "would you mind asking someone to please have some coffee brought in?"

"Certainly," Richard replies and exits.

Minutes later Kate Breeden enters the room. She is prepared for whatever is coming. She is a steady performer. Jon witnessed her talents several times in the last 24-hours and thinks she is a remarkable woman. And that may be an understatement.

"Yes sir," she says to Wells, as if reporting. She looks to Jon for clues. His face reveals nothing. But his mind is racing.

"Please, Kate," says Wells, gesturing to a seat to his left. She sits opposite Jon. Glancing sideways Wells says, "I'm trying to recruit Jon to be the other half of the team."

She looks at Jon for a reaction. He meets her gaze but says nothing. He leans back in the chair looking only mildly interested in the conversation.

"Starting now," Wells says to both of them in his deepest baritone voice, "everything is ultra-secret." He looks at Kate first, and then Jon. "Shall I continue?" Both nod very slightly.

Jon feels the gloves are off. "This better be good, Bob. There is a lot on the line. You hear what I'm saying?" His tone sounds more like a challenge than a comment.

Wells cuts Jon a lot of slack because of their years of friendship, previous assignments, what has occurred in the last 24 hours, and because of what he has just revealed about the Soon murder.

"Understood." Wells would like to stand up and walk around, but decides to keep the anxiety level as low as he can by staying seated.

Kate feels the tension between the two men. Interpersonal dynamics have always fascinated her, particularly as it relates to leadership. But the exchange is troubling.

"Our government – and others – is rightly focused on the Iranian nuclear program, North Korea's saber rattling, Yemen, shifts of power in

Egypt, Libya, Syria, and a half-dozen other threats. The Middle East and Africa have plenty of unstable governments and terrorist organizations. This operation – to a considerable extent - is lost in the bigger picture."

"And how 'lost in the bigger picture' are we?" interjects Jon, clearly irritated.

"We're off the radar. However, the sheer relentlessness of the North Koreans is a major concern. Personally, I think electronic intrusions from China – cyberwar if you like – is a larger danger than nuclear war," answers Wells, "but that's not in my lane."

"I haven't been keeping up with current issues," admits Jon.

Kate joins in. She has a current Pentagon perspective. "There are targeted intrusions aimed at defense engineering data and military operational data. Daily."

It occurs to Jon that Kate is probably a lot more knowledgeable on such issues. He says, in a less hostile sounding voice, "Not a happy thought. This brings me to my next question."

Before Jon can ask the question, Wells answers it. "This is strictly a recon operation. You're not going into hostile territory – exactly."

"Meaning we're not vulnerable?" asks Kate, almost as a reflex.

"The question is what level of risk is acceptable. Money is the reward for risk."

Jon rubs his forehead as if thinking. "We'd had this kind of discussion before. Do you expect us to outrun the coverage?"

"I'm just saying the most hostile factor may be the environment. It's an uninhabited rainforest. But there isn't any threat from a foreign government. So, my guess is medium risk."

"Medium risk," repeats Jon. "I have a hunch there is more to it."

"The only bad guys will be us. Not that we're – or you – are bad guys. You know what I mean." He tugs on his right ear lobe.

Jon says, "Okay, what are we looking for?"

"We believe a research institution is producing biomaterial – toxins, pathogens. We need to confirm production."

"In Central America?" asks an astounded Jon. "That's crazy!"

In the next hour Wells and Jon go toe-to-toe and belly-to-belly on details large and small. Finally, Jon says, "Okay. Since we're not going into a hostile environment – except for your 'uninhabited rainforest' and - you forgot to mention - deadly bioweapons, why don't we just fly in? Or parachute in? Or send in the Rangers?"

"I'm going to give you an answer," Wells says in his because-I'm-paying-the-bills voice, "but you really should leave the heavy lifting to me."

"Just asking," says Jon, turning up the palm of his left hand.

"Bottom line. The SecDef put the kibosh on military action."

Kate watches the continuing banner back and forth. Sometimes it's light. Sometimes it's heavy. She decides they have an all-weather friendship, and it's just how they communicate. She graciously lets it pass.

"Let me try to make this as simple as I can," says Wells bluntly, finally sounding impatient. "The price of poker went up in '04 when Qaddafi sent a hit squad to assassinate a Saudi Crown Prince. After that, security went into a higher, high-tech gear. The assassination of a Hamas commander in Dubai provided ample evidence of the power of surveillance cameras. All to say, there is excellent security at the San Jose airport. They have modern security cameras that record a person's facial bone structure that is interpreted by algorithms. False identities are easily cracked using biometric passports - such as yours would be - and allies government data bases. They are within a knat's hair," he says, holding his index finger and thumb extremely close to each other, "from retina scans. We don't need that."

Jon feels a bit scolded, but gets the gist of Wells' concerns.

"And just to put the parachute idea to rest, about five years ago we parachuted three of our people into a hostile environment. We never saw them again. For years we parachuted operatives into places like North Korea and Albania and Chile. Every agent disappeared. Every agent. On this operation I will not lose sight of you. I'll get you in, and I damn well sure will get you out."

There are a few more operational questions about everything from contacts, inoculations, equipment and provisions to entry and exit plans. In the end, the air clears, hurt feelings are put aside, and all arrive at a sort of mutual agreement.

"North Korea will continue on a reckless path unless we do something," Wells concludes.

No one speaks.

"Well then, that's it," Wells says. "Banks will take you back to the hotel. Get some rest. Tomorrow will be busy."

Kate and Jon head to the door.

"Jon," says Wells, "a word please."

Kate stops and turns.

"I'll be right behind you," Jon assures her. "Meet me in Wells' office."

When she leaves, Jon quietly closes the door. He turns and walks back to the conference table and sits down. "I'm on board only out of concern for Kate."

"What's that mean?"

"I don't know."

"Did you think I was drawing a line in the sand?"

"Forget it. I'm in," Jon says. "Besides, what else is there for me to do right now?"

135

"You apparently know the deal I cut with Breeden. But we haven't discussed your fee," says Wells, dismissing his question.

"I don't need the paycheck."

"I know that. Nevertheless…"

"If this all works out, I don't want anything." Jon pauses. "On second thought, your guys can handle dealing with the insurance company about my boat. I'll give you power-of-attorney."

"We'll handle everything."

"While you're at it, how about a couple of divers to salvage any personal belongings?"

"Will do."

"I appreciate that."

"I'll deposit $500,000 to your account at that Swiss bank in Geneva. You still bank there?"

"No. I'll giver you a number for my bank in Montevideo."

"Uruguay? Never been there."

"You should visit. Outstanding private bankers."

"Anything else?" asks Wells.

"If things don't work out give half of my fee to the Association of Graduates at the Air Force Academy. Restrict it to the Academy's Mock Trial Team. We're going to need some good Air Force lawyers." He permits himself a small grin.

"And the other half?" Wells asks, scribbling notes on a small piece of paper from his jacket.

"Endow a scholarship in the name of Dr. Kim Lake at Sint Maarten's University. Restrict it to B students. They're the ones who do something in this world."

Wells writes it down. "Consider it done."

"If that's all," Jon says as he gets up from the table, "I'll catch up on the briefing, and brace myself for whatever shots I have to take. I hate needles."

"I know. They still have your photo in sick bay on the USS Ford."

"Very funny," Jon groans.

"I hope you realize having some real weapons on this operation might be helpful."

"You were right last time. If I hadn't been so bone-headed I would have carried something. As it turned out a man lost his life because I was powerless to help him. That won't happen again."

"One last thing. Any reason you and Breeden can't work together?" he asks, almost shyly.

Jon looks surprised. "Is there a problem?"

"Just want to make sure you're comfortable."

"Why do you think I can't do this alone?"

"You aren't fluent in Spanish for one thing."

"I didn't know I'd be talking to the locals."

"Hopefully you won't. But it's possible. Spanish and Korean capability might come in handy."

"Okay." Jon shrugs, opens the door, and walks out. Medium risk assignments pay well.

Early the next morning the medical briefing and needles begin. The briefer is an expert on tropical diseases. He gives an overview of the worst of the diseases and goes over the usual DOD and State advisories. Of particular importance are leptospirosis, dengue fever, vivax malaria (high risk in Central America), chagas disease, and tick-borne fever. Cholera and polio present so low a threat as to warrant little more than a brief mention.

Because Kate is active duty military, recently on an overseas deployment, her immunizations are current. But she will still need country-specific immunizations. Jon anticipates with dread the idea of becoming a pin cushion. The doctor explains the first injection is for Hepatitis A. It should have been given two weeks earlier. The next shot is for Typhoid. Then there's the Hepatitis B vaccine. There is an immunization to guard against Tetanus-diphtheria, another for measles, and another for chickenpox. He informs them that a small supply of antibiotic drugs, including Cipro, will be supplied at a later time. A self-explanatory first aid kit will be included with their provisions.

An hour later Jon's arms are sore at several injection sites, and he feels he is developing a slight fever. Kate says she feel fine. Jon suspects she is not telling the truth. She thinks he is kidding. He isn't.

Banks brings the SUV around and takes them to a nearby Wal-Mart to pick up a few personal items. And two cheap suitcases. To fill the suitcases Banks has a specific list of items. Several make little sense to Jon.

After breakfast the next day they return to Cadbury's headquarters for more mission briefings. Wells is there, the nearly constant coffee in hand, with a sinful supply of local pastries. Then they get down to work.

Wells introduces the first mission briefer: Dr. T. Sawyer, a prominent professor of geography at the University of Wisconsin is a private consultant to Cadbury Metrics International (CMI). He has a confidential security clearance, which is sufficient for briefing purposes. Thomas is his first name. He never uses it. He'd prefer others not use it, either. He's heard all the Tom Sawyer jokes.

Dressed in rumpled khaki trousers and a smart polo shirt, Sawyer is a handsome tan-skinned, middle-age man with thick salt and pepper hair, and a charming smile. The only child of two medical missionaries, Sawyer was educated in missionary schools for years. It was natural enough for him to become religious at an early age and, by the time he was eight, he could recite the names of the 27 books in the New Testament backwards and forwards. As a young adult, however, he lost faith when he decided a loving God wouldn't send people to Hell. He felt his life was empty. During his undergraduate years at Chicago, he was convinced Christianity was oppressive puritanism. But by the time he completed his doctorate, he decided his reasoning about God was flawed and regained his faith. At the same time, he found God in nature and the wonders of the planet. He decided God's purpose for him was found in higher education.

Wells introduces Sawyer as a friend of many years, and describes him as a man of contradictions. Sawyer, he says, is the world's preeminent expert on the Southern Patagonia Ice Field, and Chile's labyrinth of fjords, inlets, and twisting peninsulas. Less well known is Sawyer's zeal for Central American butterflies, German poetry, British libraries, the Spanish language, and Aramaic. His secret passion is exotic snakes. He emphasizes to Kate and Jon the habits and whereabouts of the most dangerous creatures they might encounter on their journey. Oddly, unlike many academics, Sawyer never complains about university administrators. Tenured full professors with many publications are safe from all threats. He has written scores of articles and several acclaimed books about life in the Caribbean islands; his most widely acclaimed books include: The Banana Plantations of Honduras, Nicaragua, Guatemala and Costa Rica; Costa Rica: Legacy of Land Tenure; and The Seven Central American Republics. Sawyer's primary purpose at the briefings is to discuss the planned route through Costa Rica's Central Highland Zone. He goes into great detail describing the mountains, sparsely populated jungle, wild rivers, the volatile Nicaragua border near their route of travel, and geographical obstacles they will encounter. When he speaks he tends to go on in long sentences.

Jon has only mild interest in Sawyer's brief. It's not like the mission will be cancelled because of any of the mentioned hardships. He can't tell what Kate thinks. But he is glad when they break for Java. He wonders if the coffee is Costa Rican.

While Kate looks over maps of northern Costa Rica with Sawyer, Jon talks privately with Wells about his late wife Susan. Wells struggles to hide the deep emotion he feels, but his eyes betray his sorrow. Jon understands. Wells knows he understands. Life is frequently a bitch.

Coffee break over, the next member of the briefing team is introduced by Wells. Colonel (Dr.) Mike Screven is a senior member of the Army's biodefense team. Colonel Screven is bland. He has no distinguishing features, unless male pattern baldness is one. A twitch in his left eye may be another. His contribution is to describe what Kate and Jon might encounter in a bioscience/bioproduction laboratory. The brief focuses on how to identify various deadly viruses, and laboratory safety issues they might encounter. In summary, he shows a short video on recognizing symptoms of exposure to various toxins. It reminds Jon of the VD videos the military use to show the troops. The films always showed the afflicted at an advanced stage of venereal disease. Several recruits always threw up. Jon avoided meat products for a week. Kate pays close attention to Screven. Wells briefly joins in during the Q&A.

After the next coffee and restroom break, Air Force Lieutenant Colonel Stan Pulaski opens his briefing folder. He spreads out a half dozen sheets of notes, maps, and satellite photos. He spreads his hands palm down on them as if to control them. Which he does. Clearing his throat, he nods to Kate. Jon pays rapt attention to Pulaski, and Kate listens intently. For nearly forty-five minutes, Pulaski describes entry and exit plans, timelines and waypoints. He provides names, photographs and physical descriptions of contacts. He details supplies, weapons, technology utilization, call signs, communication, and military back-up support. Wells has a lot to contribute during the Q&A session.

The last coffee break is short. Jon eats the last cinnamon donut.

CHAPTER 14

For many years the National Reconnaissance Office (NRO) was so secret a spysat agency its name could not be published. Beginning in 1961, and housed in the Central Intelligence Agency Headquarters in Langley, Virginia, NRO worked with the Agency, and the Department of Defense (the Air Force), and NASA, to put secret satellites in orbit from Vandenberg Air Force Base in California. Over a period of 15 years, 20 spy satellites were launched.

STS-1 – code named ONYX – was the first billion dollar secret satellite. The satellites were huge, 60 feet long and 15-tons, and made possible the precise creation of world maps and imagery. Photographs were particularly helpful in monitoring weather and geographical changes. Classified payloads included advanced technologies such as an Ultraviolet Horizon Scanner (UHS) to detect missile launches from space, imaging satellites, and eavesdropping for signal intelligence on ground communications and telemetry. Over the years "black" budgets funded as many as a hundred secret missions.

Unknown to the public, mission specialists were not school teachers taking seventh grade science experiments and ant colonies into space. In fact, mission specialists were highly educated scientists, at least one with a Ph.D. They were tasked with the maintenance and/or upgrade of the satellite's ability to observe ground and underground targets anywhere on earth, in any kind of weather, day or night.

On June 5, 2010, STS-96 – code named OPAL – placed the most up-to-date sensors and scanners in orbit. When OPAL calls home from space it is to a highly secure area in the United States Southern Command. SOUTHCOM, as it is commonly known, is located in Miami (technically the City of Doral), Florida. Its mission is the "efficient command oversight of U.S. Military operations and partnership-building activities in Latin America, and the Caribbean." SOUTHCOM's $400-million four-story complex was officially opened in February, 2010. It houses more than 2,000 employees – civilian and military – in a 630,000 square foot building that is modern, efficient and secure. Its pleasing and impressive architectural style more closely resembles the corporate headquarters of a large multinational company than a military facility. There are no old barracks, training fields and troops jogging along blacktop roads. Most of the employees and service members have no memory of the days when the U.S. Army was America's the largest slum lord.

SOUTHCOM is a 21st century garrison, a fortress of the latest technology and brightest minds. Each branch of the military establishment is represented. Federal government tenants include the Drug Enforcement Agency, A.T.F., Secret Service, C.I.A., U.S.A.I.D., F.B.I., Homeland Security, and five other agencies. The National Security Agency (N.S.A.) maintains a bank of powerful Narus computers for signal intelligence at this location in addition to Ft. Meade.

Behind the impressive facade of the main entrance is a restricted Blue Card Only area. Unofficially, this is a "smart power" area. Officially, it is the Classified Flight Operations Center (CFOC). There are three rooms in the CFOC. Room One (R1) is a 14,500-square-foot room with five rows of tables rimmed around eight large screens. Each screen is half the size of the typical movie theater screen. The screens focus on specific geographical areas 24/7. SOUTHCOM's screens monitor Central and South America from space.

Screen 1 monitors Venezuela, Guyana, French Guyana and Suriname one half of the time. Satellite surveillance of Columbia commands the other half time.

Screen 2: Bolivia and Paraguay.

Screen 3: Argentina, Chile, Uruguay and Paraguay.

Screen 4: Ecuador and Peru

Screen 5: Brazil

Screen 6: Mexico

Screen 7: Nicaragua, Costa Rica, and Panama.

Screen 8: Guatemala, Honduras, El Salvador, and Belize.

Each of the tables has sophisticated computer stations with highly complex software. Government-issued (meaning lowest bidder) fabric arm chairs, a headset, one to three computer screens, and an equal number of phones, are at each station. Uniformed military personnel wear headsets. They alternate their attention between the computer monitors in front, and the large country screens around the room. At any given time there are 40 military personnel in the room, and another dozen milling around. At the end of each row is a low-tech metal trash can. All paper, from candy bar wrappers to classified print-outs, is placed in the trash cans. The trash is secured and destroyed at the end of each shift by security personnel. Oddly, every other row has a red fire extinguisher sitting on the floor next to the trash receptacle. It is the only old tech thing in the room.

Next door to R1 is Room Two (R2). It is a single purpose room that houses the cockpit and flight deck of the Hummingbird drone. Unmanned aerial vehicles (UAV) are a high priority for the heavily funded Defense Advanced Research Projects Agency (DARPA). The holy grail of UAVs is a drone that can fly into the stratosphere and stay there for 30 days or longer, and ultimately a year or more. Hummingbird is an evolutionary step on that road into the future. A giant wrap-around screen provides a 180 degree external view from the drone's cockpit. A picture-in-picture monitor (PIPM) on the big screen provides the pilot with real-time aircraft performance information such as air speed, altitude, engine performance, angles of bank, and rate of climb or descent. An additional screen between the pilot and co-pilot monitors sensors, cameras, and receives and transmits IF images. The room is designated for highly classified operations (HCOPS).

Room Three (R3) is reached via a connecting door from R2, and is guarded by a face and fingerprint biometric scanner lock. It has stacks of computers that provide the software to keep the drone flying. The required air conditioning for the computers earned R3 the nickname "ice box."

Hummingbird is a docile name for an aircraft in the company of Strike Eagles, Hornets, Wart Hogs, Raptors, Falcons, and Cobras. That's because it is not primarily a strike (or offensive) drone. Thus,

Hummingbird is a better classified as a Liaison aircraft, like the L-2s, L-3s and L-4s, of years long gone. For military purpose, however, Hummingbird is officially designated a Monitor and Assist craft. The politically incorrect prefer the shorter designation of MoAss. The actual name was suggested by the manufacturer, and approved by the Air Force.

When in operation R2 is dimly lit to enhance screen visibility for the flight crew. Flying the expensive drone is serious business. F-16s are fly-by-wire (FBW) aircraft. The Hummingbird is a fly-by-keyboard (FBK) aircraft. The flight crew sits side-by-side, pilot on the left and co-pilot/systems engineer on the right. The joystick can be passed from pilot to co-pilot and vice-versa as circumstances require. Both have a fold down arm on their seats with an attached microphone. There is a smaller backlighted keyboard in front of both crew, and a backlighted mouse. The drone's engine commands are located on the keyboard between them, easily accessible by pilot or co-pilot. The engine auto-start is the E key. Power (increase, decrease, or emergency), prop (maximum, minimum or incrementally), and fuel mixture (lean, enrich, full, idle) are controlled by a specific key. The B key is for brakes. Fly-by-wire technology essentially eliminated the need for rudder pedals. When the Esc key (protected by a clear plastic shield) is pressed three times it will destroy the drone. There are other automated computer systems designed to reduce pilot error by letting the computers take control in the event of an emergency.

Hummingbird's back-up flight control commands are on the Num Pad. Unlike the usual PC keyboard, the crew Num Pad is enlarged to avoid mistakenly hitting the wrong key. Typical commands are elevator trim up – Num Pad 1; elevator down – Num Pad 7; pitch up – Num Pad 2; pitch down – Num Pad 8; bank left (ailerons) – Num Pad 4; bank right – Num Pad 6; center ailerons and rudder – Num Pad 5. And so on. There is no landing gear command because the drone has fixed landing gear. Flying the drone is complex and takes skill and practice. This is why all drone pilots have earned pilot wings.

The co-pilot/systems and sensors engineer has a second computer controlling the drone's cameras and sensors, providing enhanced tactical views for the crew. Many of these commands use both the keyboard and the Num Lock, when it is in the ON position.

Hummingbird's only self-defense weapon is activated by pressing the F1 key four times. Tapping the space bar will fire long or short burst from a single .50 caliber machine gun located in the nose of the drone.

Like an actual Hummingbird, the drone is small and seems to floats in the air. From a distance, in the daytime, at low altitude, it appears to hover because of its slow speed. It rarely flies, however, in the daytime or at low altitude. And small is relative. The drone has an 18 foot long fuselage with a 43-foot wingspan, roughly half the size of the Predator, and dramatically smaller than Boeing's Phantom Eye. It has real-time data and voice communication, and a wireless data link. Sensor pods in the wings give it surveillance capabilities. There is adequate room for optical sensors, synthetic-aperture radar and a forward-looking, heat seeking infra-red camera. And the one .50-calibre machine gun. Unlike a real Hummingbird it can sting the unsuspecting.

Hummingbird is powered by a 150 horsepower truck engine that runs on hydrogen fuel. Boeing's drone is powered by two truck engines that run on hydrogen fuel and can stay aloft for a week. By contrast, Hummingbird can stay airborne continuously for four days.

The drone flies via satellite link. It is based and usually flown out of Davis-Monthan AFB, five miles from Tucson, Arizona. But for this mission, its senior pilot is Major Julie "Boilermaker" Berrien, is in Room 2 at SOUTHCOM. She has flown drone missions from as far away as 7,000 miles.

For Major Berrien, a military career was always in the cards. An Air Force brat, never very long in one place, she attended six different elementary schools before graduating high school in Spain. While a college student at Purdue University, majoring in mechanical engineering, she was a member of AFROTC Detachment 220. One of the top 4 Air Force ROTC programs in the country, Berrien was one of the stars of the Detach 220. In fact, she performed so well she was selected for 1 of 12 rated positions for a pilot slot. However, because of the needs of the service, pilot training was 18 months distant. In the interim, the Air

Force permitted her to attend Massachusetts Institute of Technology in the double E program. Before she completed her electrical engineering degree, her pilot training program started. M.I.T. was put on hold. She finished her degree three years later while on active duty.

Berrien was born to fly. When the opportunity to transition from the right seat of a C-130J to drones was presented, she eagerly accepted. Her selection was extremely competitive. She honed her skills by flying drones that took off from a base in Northern Pakistan against the Taliban. She piloted the drone from U.S. soil, and successfully completed 26 strikes in two years. In C.I.A. jargon, each successful hit was known as a "bugsplat". Her experience convinced her the future of military aviation was in unmanned – but human piloted none the less – drones. The Pentagon's 2010 request to increase funding for drones proved her correct.

Behind the flight crew are three theater-like seats arranged in a tight semi-circle. Sometimes the seats are occupied by a relief crew. For this mission there are four 2-person flight crews. They work four hours on, eight hours off, until the mission is completed. Other times the seats are occupied by intelligence officers, image analysts and/or the brass. Wells will be in one seat for sure. Lastly, there are four more seats in a tight semicircle behind these seats.

~ ~ ~ ~

It is a humid early afternoon when the small civilian jet – on loan from "Roger" – squeaks onto a private runway on the outskirts of Colon, north of Panama City. The jet departs as quickly as it arrived, its tires still hot from the landing. A worn looking, dull-colored, green and yellow taxi picks Kate and Jon up on the runway, and drives them to the cruise ship dock at Colon, 40 minutes distant. The cabbie is Martin Catoosa, a Native American and C.I.A. operative. He provides them with their stateroom number, keycard and cruise ship IDs. He also provides the combination to the stateroom safe. He doesn't do small talk. On the fantail of the cruise ship is it name:

SANTOS DUMONT Rio de Janeiro

Registered in Brazil, the Dumont honors a Brazilian pioneer aviator and national hero. For a cruise ship, however, the Dumont is small. The 180 passengers are mostly Spanish/Portuguese speaking. The cruise itinerary is confined to the northern tip of South America, the Amazon and the Caribbean. The Dumont arrived in Colon, Panama at 6 a.m. and will depart at 4 p.m. Colon is a port of call with several interesting attractions, and an opportunity to fish for the famed Peacock Bass. The trip from Colon to Puerto Limon, Costa Rica is 250 miles as the purple martins fly. The ship is scheduled to dock there at 8 a.m. the following morning. Already on board is A.T. Banks. He occupies a spacious stateroom, with an adjoining room for his bedroom. Kate and Jon will share stateroom 1061 as Mr. and Mrs. Echols. They are on the opposite side of the ship from Banks.

The ship identification cards for Kate and Jon are real. They were not terribly difficult to come by. Bribery makes most things possible in the developing world, particularly when dealing with people as poorly paid as crew on a cruise ship. The price was US$10,000 cash – more than the average crew member sends home in two years.

The noon boarding is uneventful. No one gives them a second look. They find their stateroom in minutes. As they enter the stateroom the bedside phone pulses a bright red. Kate puts her small suitcase in the closet to the left of the stateroom door. Jon throws his bag on the bed and picks up the phone. Kate opens the sliding glass door and steps out on the balcony. Jon expected a message from Wells. Instead, it is a familiar man's voice. The voice reminds them a light lunch is served on the top deck until 3 p.m., and invites them for a glass of wine in stateroom 1048 at six-o-clock.

On the top deck, lunch can be taken outside around the pool or inside the café in the air conditioning. They decide on the pool area as a preconditioning to the heat and humidity that awaits them. Jon finds the hamburgers and fries at the beginning of a cafeteria-style line, and Kate locates the salads further along the line. She finds a table on the starboard side of the ship. The passengers around the pool are mostly in the thirty something age group, and well-conditioned and tan. Members of the crew circulate among the guests. Servers are mostly young women, happy to re-fill glasses with coke or bring guests other refreshments. Kate has a bottled water, and Jon a light beer. The atmosphere is pleasant and relaxed. Without looking at Jon, Kate says "I feel like we're on a secret passage."

"Really."

"Is what we're doing now something like what you did before? I mean, when you were at the Academy?"

"Can't really say," Jon says, troubled by the thought. Thinking about it makes him feel emotionally weary and a prisoner of his memories.

Kate realizes this is off limits. "I'm sorry. I shouldn't have mentioned it." She turns to look at him. He looks sideways at her, eyes hidden behind dark sunglasses.

"No harm. No foul." He smiles and takes a swig of his beer. End of discussion.

Thirty minutes later, back in the stateroom, Kate says she feels sticky and wants to take a shower. "Don't you want to get out of those clothes?" she asks, taking off her shoes and unbuttoning her blouse.

"I'll wait until you finish."

"We can save water," she says, raising one eye brow and lifting her chin.

"We're at work," Jon reminds her. And himself.

She sticks her tongue out. "You know what all work and no play did to Jack." It's a statement, not a question.

Jon takes a deep breath and exhales. She is irresistible, but he is working hard to resist.

"I'll warm the shower and you can join me."

CHAPTER 15

They have been waiting for ten minutes in the SOUTHCOM Conference Room. A door unceremoniously opens, and a 30-year old Army Captain, followed by a 34-year old Army Major, and a 40-year old Army Lieutenant Colonel, all aides-de-camp to General Burke, enter single-file. An Air Force Colonel follows. The Army officers wear immaculately tailored uniforms. The Air Force Colonel's uniform, by comparison, looks less gung-ho and more "off the rack." Following the Colonel is General Burke. Generals rarely go anywhere by themselves. R.I.P. (rank has its privileges).

Everyone in the room stands.

"Sit down, Gentlemen," Burke quickly says.

All sit.

Moments later Wells and Soperton quietly enter the room from the same door, and take their seats near Burke. The Army Lieutenant Colonel, Major and Captain sit in the cheap seats surrounding the wall behind Burke. They join the other aides-de-camp lining the wall. Insiders refer to these seats as the First Aid Station. The Air Force Colonel sits next to Wells.

The conference room is large in order to accommodate an unusually long and wide conference table. Eight computer monitors are built into the table and can be raised or lowered as desired. Walnut paneled walls match the conference table. The ceiling contains a large recessed monitor, recessed lights, and overhead spots directed in front of 20 swivel chairs. Each place has secured power connections. Most of the chairs are occupied by men in uniform. Not all chairs are occupied.

Burke sits at the head of the table, meaning in the middle, equal distance from both ends. This is more a Navy interpretation of head of the table, as opposed to a corporate or Army one. Seating is not casual or accidental. It follows military protocol as defined by rank. Admiral Jake Lamar sits to the immediate left of Burke. Lamar is responsible for Navy special-operations (i.e. SEAL teams) activity. A year earlier Lamar and the C.I.A. Director signed a secret agreement for joint military/C.I.A. operations. It was a historical shift in the relationship and effectively militarized spy operations. The agreement is still a secret, although Burke has been fully briefed. The new relationship between the C.I.A. and the military was the key to the bin Laden strike.

Lamar is of medium height and weight, with thinning gray hair, thin lips, and an unsettling expression. Famously uncharismatic, the Admiral rarely appears in public. The last time he did was at graduation ceremonies for newly commissioned Coast Guard officers. He has an erect bearing, is obsessive about secrecy, and has an unwavering belief in his own judgment. When he speaks he expects everyone to listen.

To the left of Lamar is Soperton, with an equivalent rank of a 3-star general. To his left is Wells, with an equivalent rank of a 2 ½-star, if there were such a thing. Which, of course, in the Army, Marines and Air Force, there isn't. On Burke's right is an Air Force 3-star, and to his right a civilian with an equivalent rank of a Major General.

"Gentlemen," says Burke, with a sober expression, "this meeting is Ultra Secret. Let's keep it in the room. A very short while ago several of you received advanced briefings due to the nature of this mission. Thank you for your assistance. Others of you have valuable expertise and/or mission support capability that will be needed. That's why we have assembled this specific group." He then introduces, in a minimal way because he doesn't have much information to go on, Adrian Soperton.

Soperton gets to his feet and adjust his silk tie. "Thank you, General. Gentlemen. We have reason to believe a rogue state is producing deadly toxins in a clandestine program in violation of United Nations Resolution 687." He pauses to take a breath. "The decision has been made to stop it. And with your help, we shall." He purposefully pauses, again – this time for effect. Wells is pleased to see how much Soperton has matured in his role at the Agency.

Soperton continues. "If you are vague about U.N. Resolution 687, let me summarize. It classifies chemical and biological agents as weapons of mass destruction." Everyone in the room is aware of what constitutes WMDs, but didn't necessarily associate them with any specific UN resolution. Soperton unconsciously rechecks the knot in his tie and continues in a cautious tone of voice. "We have reason to believe preparations for a biological attack on the U.S. are underway. If we obtain indisputable proof our suspicions are correct, we will make a preemptive strike on such a facility to discourage, disrupt, delay or destroy it. We need to do this covertly. Our Commander-in-Chief – POTUS -has authorized this covert action. He is mindful of our nation's security issues, and of our international responsibilities. Some of you have already participated in planning this bold and decisive step. But this is not, I stress, strictly a military operation. Mr. Wells will fill you in and answer any questions." Soperton sits.

Wells says, "Thank you, General Burke and Mr. Soperton, for your assistance on such short notice." Turning to Burke he asks, "Do you mind if I remain seated?"

The general shakes his head. Wells prefers to remain seated by design. He believes it is perceived to be less condescending to those seated, and creates a better sense of team.

He begins. "I appreciate you and your staff, General, working around the clock on such short notice." Burke nods almost imperceptibly. Wells looks at the faces around the table. "Our people are now on the way. They will be in country by 8:00 a.m. tomorrow. By mid-afternoon they will be in the field. In the next 24 to 48 hours we expect to be faced with a critical decision. If our worst fears are realized, we will need your operational assistance." He pauses. "Please feel free to interrupt me at any point."

No one interrupts. He continues. "We are here because this is a joint effort."

Silence. Admiral Lamar nods, looking a bit distressed. Wells briefly introduces Air Force Colonel Stanley Treutlen with the 509th Bomb Wing. Treutlen preceded Burke when entering the conference room. He walks around the table to an open space across from Burke. Obviously, this space was planned for individuals making reports.

"Good morning General Burke and gentlemen. With your permission, General, Mr. Wells has asked me to make a few comments."

Burke says, "Please continue." Burke has excellent posture and sits up straight, hands folded calmly on the table in front of him. No one would suspect his career has been chaotic, but salvaged time and again by brilliant managerial skills and a charismatic personality. A high level of adrenaline didn't hurt, either.

"Should the initial and preliminary information prove accurate, the target will be subterranean. If we wish to destroy it, we should consider a direct hard target strike weapon."

Everyone is attentive. And silent. They look at Treutlen with a steady gaze. There is no note taking and no distractions. Laptops, ipads, smartphones, and cells are turned off. Each man seems to be mentally calculating Treutlen's words. Wells can almost guess their thoughts. He understands professional military men. All would prefer to spend their time in responding to current and future military conflicts, not cooped up in a conference room.

"Such as?" speaks up Vice Admiral Woody Haralson in a skeptical tone of voice. He is commander of the U.S. Naval Forces Southern Command, based at Mayport, Florida. Sitting next to him is Admiral Thomas Wilcox, Commandant of the Coast Guard, who just flew in from Anacostia. Haralson is tall, completely bald and wears wire-frame glasses that look like they may just hold his ears on. He has a long slender nose and a look of grave concern. Other than that he looks like everyone's favorite grandfather. Admiral Wilcox, in contrast, is short and rather plump. A Mormon, originally from Salt Lake, he is a graduate of the Coast Guard Academy in New London, Connecticut. He could more easily pass for the corner butcher than an Admiral. Wells thinks Wilcox suffers from low self-esteem because as good as the Coast Guard is, and it is, it doesn't have the statue of the Army, Navy, Marines, and Air Force. Distractors refer to the Coast Guard as The Privileged-Kids-from-New England Sailing Club.

"Well, Admiral Haralson, Israel has an UAV called 'Eitan.' They have had good success with it. It drops the Greek made 2,000 pound Perseus bomb that can crash through to a basement."

An unconvinced moment passes. No one speaks.

"Other options?" quizzes Major General Clay McIntosh, commanding the U.S. Marine Corps Forces, South – based in the Miami area. Sitting quietly, he idly snaps and unsnaps a government-issued ballpoint pen. On his left hand he wears an Annapolis class ring. It's no secret McIntosh is a tough guy. Promoted to 2-star rank in 2010, he has large military ambitions; his straight-talking, outside-the-box style is his worst enemy. He doesn't mince words. He openly opposed and deeply resented any change in the "Don't Ask – Don't Tell" policy, a position expressed by his superiors at the time, but overturned by the President. His distractors consider him an "unguided missile."

McIntosh has the thick neck of a wrestler, which he was at the Naval Academy. He dislocated both shoulders while wrestling. Most of the time it is no big deal. The exception is when doing push-ups or some other strenuous activities. Then they hurt like hell. To dull the pain he began taking Oxycodone. He has been using the drug for ten years. The dependency torments him.

Treutlen says, "Yes sir, General. The MPR-500 can hammer through two concrete stories of a building and explodes at an exact time."

"Impressive to be sure," comments Major General John Randolph. "Is that a big enough bomb to do the job and not destroy everything else?" Randolph is Commander of the U.S. Army South, headquartered at Fort Sam Houston. He wears Airborne/Ranger insignia on his uniform. A man of reason and calculation, he is also a "ring knocker." Of all the services, West Pointers have the best chance to make general – something on the order of 50 percent. To a large extent, it's a number game. Air Force Academy grads have the smallest chance of making general, in the range of 30 percent. Wells expects Randolph to retire soon and become an analysis/commentator for a major news network. Then he, like most of the other TV generals, will be despised by the general officer corps.

"Boeing's KHDAM system guarantees the bomb within a yard of its target," replies Treutlen.

"Reducing collateral damage," Burke reminds everyone.

There is a collective nod of understanding from everyone at the table.

Wells interrupts to add, "And it incinerates everything in the area. It may be the best way to destroy and sterilize bioweapons laboratories."

"May I ask about delivery?," says Lieutenant General Lucas Whitfield, Commander of Air Force South, Twelfth Air Force at Davis-Monthan, near Tucson, Arizona. Lauded by the Air Force Chief of Staff as a near-genius, he could be from central casting: tall, trim, and handsome with piercing blue-gray eyes. In his thirty-two years in the Air Force he has acquired enough silvery hair to lend an air of authority and wisdom. As an Air Force Academy graduate he tends to be persuaded by logic and mathematics because, at his core, he is an engineer. Classmates at the Academy joked he was so smart he could factor in his head the products of large prime numbers as fast as a computer. On his right hand he wears an Air Force Academy ring with a brilliant blue stone. On his blouse he wears sterling silver Command Pilot wing. A gift from his daughter.

Whitfield is influential and smooth, and a student of military history. In speeches to civic clubs – always in an immaculate uniform – he refers to his wings. In the early days of military aviation, he likes to tell his audiences, earning wings required a pilot to fly to an altitude of 2,500 feet, fly into a wind of 15 mph for 5 minutes, carry a passenger to an altitude of 500 feet, make a dead stick landing within 150 feet of a designated area, and make a reconnaissance flight of 20 miles, at an average altitude of 1,500 feet. It brings a lot of chuckles and smiles from the audience. Considering pilots flew airplanes of wood and paper – more akin to kites than modern aircraft – they probably should have been awarded medals for valor rather than wings.

"As you know, General," Treutlen goes on, "if it's a smart bomb the 509th bomb wing can deliver it."

"Fly a B-2 from Whiteman?" questions the Commandant of the Coast Guard.

"Not out of the question, sir. We fly from Missouri to the Middle East. With a ground speed of, say, 560 mph, it doesn't take long. And we can drop from 50,000 feet," Treutlen boasts. "But we recognize there are other weapon alternatives."

"For example?" asks Admiral Sam Bibb. Bibb heads up the Special Operations Command, headquartered at MacDill AFB, in Tampa.

"We have a medium altitude, long endurance surveillance craft named Excalibur. We can fly it out of Panama and modify it to carry a 2,900 pound bomb, Hellfire missiles and GBU-38 bombs. It has optical surveillance cameras and flies in excess of 500 mph. It's powered by JP-8 and lithium-polymer batteries."

"That seems like overkill, don't you think, Colonel?"

"Well, sir, there is the GBU-39. That's a small-diameter guided bomb. It has a GPS inertial system. It's accurate. And it only weighs 250 pounds."

"Thank you," McIntosh says, sounding somewhat irritable, "I'm familiar with it."

"We have the GBU currently integrated on the F-15E Strike Eagle," comments Whitfield. "Outstanding weapon."

"Interesting," says Soperton to no one in particular. "What do you think, Mr. Wells?"

"I think this discussion is helpful. Certainly there are a lot of options to consider. I also think we should not rule out any of them at this point. Let's not be premature. Lastly, I think the Air Force can better answer this question at an appropriate time. " As he speaks he scribbles a note and passes it to Soperton. It reads "unit cost for GBU GPS version is $70-$90k."

The assembled seem to think that makes sense judging by the grunts and head nodding.

"This is helpful," says Burke. "Thank you, Colonel Treutlen." He looks around the table, briefly pauses, and says, "If there are no further questions at this time, we'll stand adjourned." Burke stands up, and so does everyone else, and exits the room.

After Burke leaves the room, followed by Soperton, Wells, Treutlen, and the three aides, those remaining mill around talking with each other and their aides. Lieutenant General Whitfield is the ranking general in the room. Army Major General John Randolph says, "Certainly we'll get solid intelligence."

"We assume so," says Admiral Bibb. "Is that a concern, John?"

"No, I'm not saying that, Sam. But experience tells us it is sometimes easier to find what you want to find, as opposed to what is really there. You know what I mean. I hope this is not the result of wishful thinking." The comment strikes a nerve with everyone.

"Thank you, John," says Lieutenant General Whitfield, effectively curbing further discussion. "I assume those discussions have preceded this meeting."

"I hope we have a good handle on the most plausible scenario. And that we are not being myopic," adds Marine General Clay McIntosh. "We're only as good as our Intel."

Whitfield says, "They will have a team in the field gathering first-hand, real-time, intelligence. We'll have situational awareness, and a live feed to see what they see. In any event, our job is to carry out POTUS's instructions."

No question about that.

CHAPTER 16

Alberto Cabeza is in charge of in-country preparatory logistics. He arrives shortly after dawn from San Jose in a titanium-colored 2007 Toyota 4runner. It has 37,438 hard off road miles on it. It's beginning to show. There is a pronounced dent in the right front fender, and a long scrape beneath the fuel cap. It's starting to rattle, and it pulls to the left.

The task at hand includes setting up the tent, and unloading the mission gear from the trunk. He will meet his contact at the Tortuguero National Park. Shortly afterwards he will drive to Limon to meet the "decoys" and pick up the operatives. After making the exchange, he will bring the operatives to the Park. If all goes well he will take the operatives to the drop off point later in the day. He will again return to the park before driving back to San Jose.

Playing the part of Cabeza's girlfriend is Victoria Coweta. She grew up a semi-romantic on a small farm outside of Beatrice, Nebraska. Once or twice a month the family would load up the faded red truck and drive 40 miles north to Lincoln. Lincoln had everything. It was a good life in Beatrice, but Victoria wanted more. Everyone seemed to be related to everyone in Beatrice. Farming was the same year in and year out; it was just plain hard work. Some years Mother Nature reminded everyone who was really in charge. Her two brothers were better suited by temperament to carry on after her father passed. Coweta longed for travel and adventure, like half the young people who sign up for the Marines. So, considering her options, she too decided to join the Marines. Probably because her father served in the Corps.

"Gunny" Coweta is a trim 5' 4", 110 fat-free pounds of diamond-hard Marine. But a Marine with curves. And a light brown pony tail. A year earlier she finished second in the 26.2 mile Marine Corps Marathon. If it hadn't been for a twisted knee she would have broken 3 hours and 2 minutes easily.

As part of a secret special ops team – Marine Special Operations Team 3 (MSOT3) – she is the first and only woman Marine to graduate from the Marine Special Ops School. It doesn't get any more elite than that. As one of the hand-picked, she received advanced training in special reconnaissance at Camp Lejeune, North Carolina. Fluent in Spanish, she is a rated expert with small arms. In hand-to-hand combat she can defeat men twice her size. She is on TDY to the U.S. Embassy in Panama when she receives a three page packet marked SECRET. The first page is the Operational Order. It is specific, describing in detail what is to be accomplished, where it will be accomplished, and when. It is straight forward and leaves nothing to guesswork. Her mission is to brief and assist the people on page three.

The second page identifies a man named Alberto Cabeza. He is the initial contact, and a member of the U.S. Embassy in San Jose. She studies the photo of him. He has a soft round face. She doesn't like men with soft round faces. But it doesn't matter. She is a mission-focused Marine. Hoorah!

The third page has a photo of a woman and a man. Coweta studies the photos. The woman is young. Early to mid-thirties. Attractive. Looks vaguely familiar. No name. The man looks to be in his mid to late thirties. Maybe early forties. Hard to tell. His eyes seem to burn through the camera lens. Interesting face. Looks used. Unlined and unsmiling. Short hair. Light skinned. No name.

The following morning, before Alberto Cabeza begins his drive from the capitol to the coast, Coweta is riding a 1974 Honda CB 100 from Chanquinola, Panama to the rendezvous point. Wide open, with a strong tailwind, the bike won't hit 70 mph. Underneath Coweta's shorts and tank top is a white spandex bikini. If stopped coming into Costa Rica, she plans to say she is merely coming northward to swim and sun. The bikini can be a helpful distraction, if needed. She knows Latin men. As it turns out she crosses the invisible border between Panama and Costa Rica unnoticed. Even after the early morning sun comes up there is no traffic along the road. There is no one on the chocolate-color sands of the beach, either.

Coweta rides the Honda to a point approximately 33 miles north of Puerto Lemon. For a mile or so there is a small truck in front of her. Then it turns off. When there is no one in either direction she pulls off the road into the thick undergrowth. She lays the bike down on its side, removes the license tag and puts it in her backpack. She expects the bike to be there when she returns. If not, without the license tag, it won't be traceable. The VIN numbers – such as they were in 1974 – were removed prior to her trip. Satisfied the bike is concealed from passer-by and is not a fire threat, she begins a seven mile jog to Tortuguero National Park. Jogging to her is like a leisurely stroll to most people.

When she arrives at the campsite she slows to a walk and searches for a grayish-colored Toyota with CD plates (Corps Diplomatic) and a red and blue "La Sele" sticker on the back window. La Sele is the nickname of the Costa Rican football team. Shortly before 8:00 a.m. she approaches a Toyota fitting the description. A man is sitting in a beach chair next to the vehicle, wearing tan cargo shorts but no shirt. In his hand is the local Imperial beer. Coweta stops in front of him.

"Que hora es?" she asks, thinking the man has an undeveloped chest.

"Ten," he answers in Spanish. It is the recognition signal. By his watch it's really three minutes to eight. Because the photo of her was face only, he is impressed with her physique.

Coweta steps closer to Cabeza. "You're not really drinking beer at this hour are you?" She is not smiling.

"Nah," he says. "The cerveza is just a prop. But later…" He gets up and offers his hand. She shakes it. She has a firm grip. She isn't even sweating.

"You filled the list?" she asks, without so much as a "how do you do." She takes in a large forest green tent behind Cabeza.

"Everything they gave me," he assures her.

"Did they give you a towel I can use? And some water?"

"Sure." He turns and goes to the Toyota. She follows. He takes a towel off the backseat and grabs two bottles of mineral water. He hands them to her.

"Thanks," she says, tossing her hair out of her face. She guzzles one bottle and starts on the second one. "What's the drill?"

"I pick up the team," he says, looking at his watch, "in about an hour. We go to the market immediately after and wait. I should be back here not later than ten or ten thirty. Eleven at the latest. Depends on how quickly they find me."

"I'll check this stuff out while you're gone. They can decide what they need when they see it." Coweta walks over to the tent, followed by Cabeza. "Nice tent," she observes.

"Yeah. Enough room for four people. Five-foot ceiling and nearly 60 square feet of space."

"Where did all this stuff come from?" she says, clearly impressed with the mound of equipment and supplies, but not expecting an answer. She turns to Cabeza who stops short. "They didn't ask for all this did they?"

"I don't know what they asked for. I'm just the delivery boy. As they say, I'm the last to know and the first to go."

"Come on, you're not going to whine on me are you?" Cabeza is a bit portly, and definitely unthreatening. In a confrontation with Coweta he'd last five seconds. Maybe less. She knows it. So does he.

"No," he answers, thinking he'd like to punch her in the face. But that could backfire.

"Where's the hardware?"

"The rucksack frames?"

"The weapons," she says slowly, thinking him an idiot. Her hands hang loosely at her side like coiled steel. She is aware she is not making friends with Cabeza. She couldn't care less.

"In the water cooler," he says, pointing to the rear of the tent.

Coweta nods and steps over the supplies. She opens the cooler and looks up.

"Under the ice in a separate bottom."

She empties the ice and water toward the tent wall. Pulling up a second panel, she retrieves the weapons. "This is really top of the line," she comments.

Cabeza is an Intel guy and a lover, not a fighter. He became phobic about guns at an early age, and is uncomfortable around people who like guns. He abhors violence. He just wants her to put the stuff down.

Coweta picks up one of the silencers. "First class."

"I wouldn't know."

"You don't know jack shit do you?"

Cabeza doesn't say anything. Just goes to the Toyota and gets in. He jams the gear selector in reverse. The wheels spin in the sand, then catch. He centers the steering wheel and pulls away from the campsite. He glances at his watch. Plenty of time to get to the Port of Limon. Driving always calms Cabeza's nerves and focuses his mind. Damn Marines think they are hot shit, he thinks. In a few miles he refocuses his energy on the mission, and not Coweta. He forms a mental picture of the contacts, and mentally reviews the "meet" arrangements.

As it turns out, there are no glitches and picking up the contacts is a breeze. Ninety minutes later the Toyota enters the port town and slows to a crawl. Traffic is rarely a problem. Except when a ship comes in. There is the usual amount of locals in town. But when a ship comes in, the sidewalks and the street are packed with hundreds of tourists. A big cruise ship is scheduled to dock minutes before "the team" and that will mean thousands of people crawling over the port city like ants. Most will walk from the ship to the market in the center of town. It's a short walk.

The Toyota creeps pass the market, already filling with people, and goes two blocks further south. Cabeza parks on the street, puts the windows down, and gets out. He walks to the back seat side window. "No way to know how long I'll be gone," he advises his passengers. "With luck not more than 30 minutes."

"We'll be here," says the guy. The woman just looks at him.

The market is typical of many Latin countries. The market building is square, with an old façade and filthy-looking stone walls. It helps create the mystique and adventure of a dark, dirty, and crowded place tourist love to photograph. The structure could be a hundred years old. It may have been some kind of fort or fortification in the distant past. Hard to tell. But it is a tourist trap designed to make "gringos" feel they have visited an underdeveloped country. That is far from the truth. Greed makes American tourists think they are getting real bargains for their dollars. There are no health inspectors or fire marshals to be sure. That would leave a too "developed" world impression. Vendors outside the market hawk local crafts. Inside there are even more crafts, natural products of Costa Rica, cheap jewelry, knock-off Calvin Klein jeans and Gucci handbags, fake Rolex watches, various food items being cooked, and colorful T-shirts.

As instructed, Cabeza stations himself outside the market. He is hoping to be anonymous among the hundreds of tourists flooding inside the market building. Or at least becoming indistinguishable from them. He pretends to be a tourist interested in Cuban cigars. Keeping an eye out for the contacts in the approaching crowds, he eliminates the older tourists, the single tourists, and tourists that look Latin. There are younger couples – probably honeymooners – that command his attention. He eliminates couples if the woman is a blond. He focuses on couples that may be looking for him, or looking like they are looking for him. He knows what they are supposed to be wearing.

Kate and Jon leave the ship in the second wave and join the tourists walking down the dock. Street vendors intercept the throng as they leave the cruise ship area. Several times Kate and Jon step around vendors to avoid them, with a smile and a "no, thank you," in English. They turn left at the second street, following the crowd and strolling toward the local market center. There are no vehicles parked on either side of the street. Many tourist walk in the middle of the street.

"Titanium Toyota SUV," Jon says out of the corner of his mouth. The humidity is already causing his shirt to stick to his back.

"Hmm," Kate says. "I've heard that before. Suppose to be south of the market – east side." She is wearing tan cargo pants with a "Sparkey Buckle" brown belt, blue tank shirt with pocket, running shoes, and pair of sunglasses. No hat.

"Right. I think I can make the guy. Unless he is really, really good." As instructed, Jon has on Khaki pants and a blue cotton shirt, with roll-up sleeve tabs. He is wearing a Bud Lite ball cap. They stop in front of a Pharmacia and appear to be looking in the window. The window is a good mirror. After a few minutes Jon says, "Either that guy looking at cigars is counting how many are in a box over and over, or he's our man. He hasn't moved since we stopped."

"Why don't you go find out?"

"He'll be looking for both of us so I might surprise him."

She shrugs her shoulders.

Jon crosses the street. Kate watches him in the reflection of the drug store window. He walks to the market behind a slow walking older couple. The man doesn't make him. At the entrance he peels off from the couple, and walks up beside the man. "Does it rain here at night, friend?" he says to the man, who is startled.

"Only in November," the man answers with the countersign, looking like the proverbial deer caught in the headlights. "I didn't see you."

"I know."

Where is the other one?"

Kate was already waking toward them.

"Oh yeah, I see her now. The belt buckle."

"What next?' asks Jon.

"I'm going to walk to the SUV. Just follow me."

Cabeza puts down the cigar box he is holding and walks away. Steps later Kate joins Jon.

"Let's just follow him down the street," Jon says. "We'll give him a head start."

"That guy is lucky we weren't trying to kill him."

"Yeah. I think he is new to the game."

They walk casually down the street for two blocks. The further they get from the market, the fewer people but more traffic. Obviously, parking is prohibited nearer the market. In the distance they see the Toyota. As they get closer they also see two people sitting in the back.

Cabeza is in the driver's seat, with his window down. He speaks to Jon when they are close. "Why don't you get in front?"

Jon walks to the other side and gets in. The back door on the driver's side opens and Kate slides in beside a woman. The woman says, "Hi." And moves to the center, against the man. She is wearing tan cargo pants with a Sparkey belt buckle. The man in Khaki pants and a blue shirt leans forward and says, "Hello."

Jon and Cabeza turn around. Cabeza says "Okay, that was a breeze."

The short conversation that follows is all business and no chit-chat. Jon and Kate give the look-alike couple their cruise and stateroom cards. They have left all personal identification in the stateroom safe. Kate and Jon are wearing the same clothes in the ship ID car photos as they are wearing now – and as the other couple are also wearing. The woman looks generally like Kate – dark hair, dark eyes, and same clothes. The man generally resembles Jon. Unless carefully inspected they should easily pass security. It is unlikely the ship's security will look at their faces so long as the cruise cards "ding" when they re-board.

In the Toyota, on the road heading south, the talk is more of an operational nature than casual conversation. "We should be at our initial point in 30 or 40 minutes," Cabeza says. "After you pick up your supplies I'll drive you to the drop off point. Then you're on your own."

Kate, from the back seat, says, "Have you been in-country long?"

"About a year," he answers. "It's really been interesting. This is a plush assignment for me. I love the people."

"You been in this business long?" Jon asks.

"Not long at all," he says quickly. "Spent most of my time in prep and language training. This is my first operational assignment. How about you?" He looks in the rear view mirror at Kate.

"Just lucky to have a job," says Kate, thinking this guy doesn't really think we're going to talk about ourselves - or our assignment – does he?

"Oh, yeah, I know what you mean."

The conversation dies and Jon looks through the window at the passing scenery. It's quiet. After a few minutes Kate tries to salvage the awkward silence with small noninvasive talk. The time goes slowly.

Back at the national park grounds Coweta recognizes the sound of the approaching Toyota. She gets to her feet in front of the supply tent, and faces the vehicle. It pulls in and stops only feet from her. Jon gets out first. Coweta ignores Cabeza. "Welcome to your Mobile Quartermasters Corps – Sustainment Unit," she says lightly. "Beans and Bullets. I'm Gunny Victoria Coweta, USMC, at your service, sir."

"Glad to meet you, Gunny," says Jon, stepping closer to shake hands. He recalls his dad using the beans and bullets expression. It's an old Army expression. Means supplies.

"We're the Echols," Kate says, coming around the Toyota and shaking hands.

Coweta shrugs her shoulders at the introduction as if to say, "whatever." She studies Jon. This guy, she thinks, I could like. "The credit goes to Mr. Cabeza, sir. I'm just here to offer advice and assistance."

"Thank you both," Kate says, her eyes darting behind Coweta at the tent floor. In her judgment both Cabeza and Coweta fit their data profiles and photographs.

Coweta steps toward Kate and says. "I'm going to assume you're familiar with this stuff."

"Excuse me," blurts out Cabeza, "but we don't have a lot of time. There is a timeline."

"Hey, numb nuts, don't cut in line," Coweta says, narrowing her eyes as she speaks.

Cabeza doesn't know what she means, exactly, but he doesn't like how she said it.

"We're eager to have your advice, Gunny," Jon says, trying to smooth things over. "We asked for the 72-hour survival package. It weights a lot less than the packs the troops are carrying around."

"Right. They have 120 – 130 pounds on their backs. The Brits carry more. It's hell on the knees and ankles, sir. Excuse my language."

"Of course. I'm glad we're going into a rainforest. We don't need a lot of weight."

"There's a lot of stuff here. Did you specifically request it all, sir?"

"Some of it," Kate volunteers. "We pretty much left it up to higher powers."

"Right," she says. "With 'Brass Creep' being what it is these days, there are a lot of higher powers." No sooner have the words escaped Coweta's lips than she recognizes the inappropriateness of her comment. She apologizes. Again.

"We understand," comforts Kate.

"Thanks. Sometimes I say too much. Where do you want to start?"

Jon says, "We'll take the standard 72-hour packs. With modifications."

"We've already modified the Tactical Combat Assault Rucksack."

"How's that?"

"Well, sir, we went with a mountain rucksack. It has the hyper-adjustable suspension system, waterproof ziplock and zippered internal compartment, shoulder pads, and a two-piece hip belt that has lots of padding where you need it. It's pretty comfortable."

"And it has the standard 72-hour load?"

"Yes, sir."

"Outstanding. Let's do the add-ons."

"I assume you were sized?" questions Coweta. She pulls two sets of clothing out of the stack and hands them to Jon. "This is the latest stuff - 2006, I think. MARPAT fatigues in woodland pattern to match the rucksack. The pants have calf storage pockets. They come in handy."

Coweta picks up and hands two pairs of jungle boots to Kate. "Great boots," she says. "Panama sole pattern. They come broken-in. These here" she adds, passing two fabric soft hats, "are wide-brim Bonnie hats in digital camo." Kate takes them from her.

Jon looks at them. "They're treated to reflect infrared wave lengths?"

"Yes, sir," Coweta answers, thinking he knows a lot more than he's letting on. "Here are the parkas. You're nearly invisible in woodland fatigues."

Jon studies the digital camos. They are irregular patterns of tan, brown, green and black. He agrees Kate and he will be well concealed in the jungle, and in the woods.

"They're made out of water-repellent silk and they are as light as feathers," Coweta goes on. "They are warm when it's cool, and cool when it's warm. The insect netting is attached to the hood."

"Certainly light," comments Kate, balancing them in her hands.

"Yes ma'am. They have Gore-Tex lining and everything is impregnated with large amounts of permethrin. That stuff keeps the creepy/crawlies out real good."

"This parka is especially for you, sir," Coweta says, "and this one is for you, ma'am."

The parkas were briefed in South Carolina. Jon's parka has an inside pocket with an encrypted single channel transceiver for voice and data contact. The drone's FLIR images are linked to what looks like a large diver's watch on his wrist. The watch is actually a miniature video monitor. Hidden in the parka's lining are conduits that keep wires out of sight and tangle-free. Power is in his rucksack, with a range of about a thousand yards. A button on the watch allows voice communication with airborne support. A second button allows intercom communication with Kate. For Kate's wrist there is a micro GPS receiver with four communication buttons. The antenna in her parka runs from shoulder to shoulder and down her neck to her waist. Hidden conduits in her parka keep the wire to her ear bud tangle-free. She studies the GPS watch, remembering a day trip she took as a cadet at the Air Force Academy to Schriever Air Force Base in Colorado – home of the 50th Space Wing, and military GPS.

"Might want to try this out before too long," says Coweta.

"Good idea," Kate agrees.

"Wish I could beat you out of this artillery," Coweta continues, bending down and picking up the weapons. She hands Jon two PDWs – personal defense weapons. The HK MP7A1 is manufactured by the German company Heckler & Koch. It weighs 2 lbs and fires a 4.6 x30 mm armor-piercing round that can penetrate Kevlar. The coal black weapon has a short 7-inch barrel. Jon hands the second MP7 to Kate.

Coweta says to Jon, "Ever fire one, sir?"

"Once."

"Well, you know it can be fired as a handgun or a rifle. I prefer the rifle myself."

"Ma'am?" Coweta says turning to Kate.

"Didn't know our military issued these," she answers, inspecting the PDW from side to side. On the right side, behind the trigger guard, is a sort of international sign language selector switch for firing the weapon. It has three positions. The top position points to a white rectangle: safety. The middle position has a red rectangle with one bullet shape symbol: semiautomatic. The bottom position has a red rectangle with four bullet shapes in it: full automatic. The latest model has a "Glock" style trigger.

Coweta answers Kate, "Definitely not standard issue, Ma'am. But Naval Special Warfare Development Group has 'em – Bundeswehr, naturally, and the UK, and Ireland, and a couple of other countries."

"I take it you are familiar with it?" Kate asks.

"A little," allows Coweta.

Kate continues to look at the futuristic-looking weapon. At the base of the grip where the magazine is inserted is a stylized HK followed by MP7A1.

Coweta continues. "It has very little recoil so it's easy to fire a tight pattern. You have three 30 round magazines with small high velocity rounds."

Jon looks in the supply stack and picks up a round metal tube. "These are nice suppressers."

"Light weight and absolute minimum signature and muzzle-flash."

"What's the rate of fire?"

"Nine hundred and fifty rounds a minute. Nothing beats it for firepower. Firing 30 rounds on full automatic takes about 1.5 seconds. A short burst is just a tap of the trigger. You got three clips each."

"Impressive," Jon says, attaching the light-weight suppressers.

"You might want to squeeze off a round or two when you get a chance," suggests Coweta.

Cabeza looks irritated. "I wouldn't do it anywhere around the military. They are sensitive."

Jon looks at him with an expression of mild surprise. "I thought Costa Rica didn't have an Army."

Cabeza says, "Don't fool yourself, sir. They don't have a standing army. That was abolished in 1949 in favor of a civil guard. Nowadays it's the National Guard. But there are plenty of them. They are highly trained. All of 'em in army fatigues and armed with M16s."

"Okay. Thanks for the heads up, Mr. Cabeza," Jon says.

Continuing his search through the supplies and equipment he turns to Coweta. "Extra socks in the sack?"

"Yes, sir. There's also NVG (night vision goggles) and binoculars."

Kate steps over some body armor. "How much does this armor weigh, Gunny?"

"Twenty pounds, ma'am."

"Guess that's off the list," remarks Kate, looking at Jon.

He nods his head in agreement.

"Is there anything you want that you don't see?' asks Gunny Coweta.

"I'd like a couple of Army Rangers," he jokes.

Coweta is mildly amused. "Would SEALS do?"

"They're heavy duty. Talking about heavy, what's the basic sustainment and survivability kit come in at?"

"Fifty-seven pounds, sir. Throw in a weapons kit, that's another 57 pounds. Then you got your basic surveillance and target acquisition equipment. That's about 6 pounds. Body armors another 20 pounds. Pretty soon you're heavier than a tank with a boat on it."

Jon nods. "Glad we aren't taking all that with us. Thirty pounds is enough."

"What's this?" ask Kate, holding up a small object.

"UVL pen. It kills bacteria, viruses, and protozoa in water."

"Wouldn't hurt to throw in two."

"Water?" asks Jon.

"Five liters of Datrex in the pack. There are some MRE flameless heating packs, four 3,600 calorie high energy bars, combat first aid kit, and the standard spoon, toothbrushes, and toilet paper. These here are the protectors you requested," she says, holding out two railroad spike-shaped objects. Into the rucksack goes a flashlight half the size of his thumb, with a red lens. It weighs less than two quarters. There is also a bionic ear.

The rucksacks are filling up fast. Kate closes her pack and hands the objects to Jon.

"Oh, yea," Coweta says, "I almost forgot. There is some face paint in mud brown, green, and black. All in about 35 items, sir. Plus whatever you've added. All U.S. labels and identification marks have been removed. Where there are instructions or writing, it's in Korean. Don't ask me why." She shakes her head.

Jon is still rummaging through the Korean labeled MREs. He tosses out the grilled chicken breast and beef stew. He checks dates on the MREs. Most have a 2011 date. But he finds Maple Oatmeal with a 2012 date, and a few other MREs. He puts them in his pack.

"I think we're pretty much loaded up," says Jon. Turning to Kate he asks, "Have I forgotten anything?"

"Robobees?" Kate asks.

Jon turns to Coweta with a questioning look.

"There are two biomimetic robobees, sir, ma 'am." The robbers were developed for the agency by M.I.T. They are about the size of an actual bee but contain ultrasensors. What they "see" is fed back to Jon on his wrist monitor.

"Thanks, Gunny. Anything else?" Jon asks, looking at Coweta and Cabeza.

Looking around he asks "Walther?"

Coweta turns and heads to the back of the tent. Coming out again she says, "Yes, sir. Sorry about that. It's on the other side of the cooler." She quickly retrieves the weapon and a black folding knife. She hands both, and a tactical holster to him.

The Walther is the .40 caliber model P99. It's an ugly looking weapon. Jon prefers it to the Glock. The knife is a light weight folding knife with a four inch ceramic blade of Titanium coated 420 stainless steel. Its cutting edge is 10 times stronger than a steel one. It's sharp as a razor and rust proof.

Referring to the MP7 ammunition, Gunny Coweta says, "Thirty round clips, sir. First clip is Hollow point. Second clip is armor-piercing, and the third clip is mixed. Flat-bottom butt plate. Three-dot sights. All of Mrs. Echols' clips are hollow points."

Jon looks over the equipment and supplies. "Philippines Jungle Knife?"

"To your left, sir," Coweta says.

Jon takes three steps to his left and picks it up. He says, "Thank you both. We're as ready as we're going to be."

"Wish I could come along, sir."

Jon makes steady eye contact. "I wish you could."

~ ~ ~ ~

The Toyota pulls out of the park and turns westward. The main road is well maintained. In 45 minutes it will cross the Chirripo river and turn in the direction of Muelle. Cabeza will drop off his passengers a few miles after reaching Muelle.

Coweta stays behind as the Toyota rolls out. She will guard the tent and remaining equipment until Cabeza returns. In addition to guard duty she will continue the tourist charade. She strips down to her bikini to get some rays.

Meanwhile, in the back of the Toyota, Jon is cat napping. Kate stares at the passing scenery, banana trees in neat rows as far as she can see. "I've never seen bananas growing," she comments.

Cabeza glances left and then right. "Most the banana plantations have moved to the Pacific side," he says. "But there are a few subsistence farmers on this side. They grow the Giant Cavendish banana because it's disease resistant. Bananas like a lot of sunshine and a lot of rain. But not frost."

Kate says, "I had no idea they grew so tall. And there are a lot of bananas. What are the white plastic bags covering the bananas?"

"Banana trees are easily 10 feet tall. Sometimes taller. Usually there are – oh, 120 or more bananas on each stalk," he lectures. "Some growers are planting another type of banana tree that is shorter. Less likely to be blown over in strong winds than the tall ones. The bags seal the bananas from insects – and Tarantulas – until harvest."

"Tarantulas?"

"They love bananas. They're bigger than your fist. Maybe 6 inches. Hairy legs add another 6 inches."

"Charming."

Cabeza grins. He is enjoying himself now that Coweta is out of the way. Mile after mile there are only banana trees. Then he says, "The history of bananas is fascinating. At least to me."

"I haven't really thought a lot about that."

"I can give you a brief summary – if you'd like – just to pass the time." He hopes for a positive response.

Kate says, "Yes, that would be interesting." What she really thinks is what history can a fruit have?

"For starters, Alexander the Great brought bananas out of the jungles of China and India about 300 B.C."

"That really is interesting." She means it.

"Yes, and they were brought to the U.S. in the late 19th century – 1870, 1880, somewhere along in there – from Jamaica. The man who did that started what was to become United Fruit. The company was so successful that Latinos called it El Pulpo."

"The Octopus."

"Right," he says, more than mildly surprised she translates the word. "They owned hundreds of millions of acres of land."

"Did United Fruit later become Dole?"

"No. Standard Fruit became Dole. But here's the incredible thing. The fields of bananas we're passing don't have seeds. Did you ever think about that?" Cabeza steals a glance at Kate.

"I've never thought about it."

"That's because bananas are triploids."

"Meaning?"

"They have three sets of chromosomes – so domesticated plants produce bananas without fertilization." Cabeza slows for a string of traffic in front of them. Jon snoozes on.

"You know a lot about bananas," Kate says after a few minutes.

"The most interesting thing about bananas is the political intrigue behind the corporate leadership. It's like an Agatha Christie novel." Kate doesn't take the bait.

The passing scenery changes abruptly. "Looks like we're about to run out of banana trees. What are those trees on the left?"

"Cocoa trees. Look at how colorful the leaves are. They are an old crop brought here by the Spanish. There's a lot of sugar cane further up the road but we'll turn before we get to those fields."

"Interesting," she says.

The traffic thins as they speed from the hot Caribbean lowlands. Most vehicles are headed east toward the coast. Kate is aware of their westward track. Jon seems to be sound asleep. It starts to rain. In another mile, she says "If you don't mind, I think I'll take a nap before we arrive."

"Not a problem. We've got another forty-five minutes before we get where we're going."

Kate leans her head against the jiggling window, listening – almost feeling – the

rain striking the cool glass. She is asleep in 20 seconds.

More than an hour later, Cabeza slows and pulls to the shoulder of the road to let a

trailing car pass. After it does, and there are no other cars in the rearview mirror, he turns onto a narrow tan and clay colored road. It is wet from the afternoon rain. There are muddy potholes and ruts every few feet. Kate and Jon are jarred awake when the Toyota hits the first one.

"This is it," announces Cabeza in a loud voice, easing over the next pothole in the uneven road. Lining both sides of the narrow plantation road are more banana trees. They travel a quarter of a mile seeing no one. Cabeza senses Jon's curiosity.

"Because of the heat and rain the workers usually finish up around two," he volunteers. "I don't think we'll likely to see anyone."

Jon looks at his watch. Almost 4:00.

A hundred yards further Cabeza stops and engages the four wheel drive. Then he heads across the hip-high grass to the edge of a row of bananas trees parallel to the road.

He stops in another 20 yards. Everyone gets out. Cabeza goes to the rear of the Toyota and opens the tailgate. Jon and Kate join him. He takes the rucksack out and hands Kate her rucksack and clothing. She takes both, walks to the front seat of the Toyota, nearest the bananas trees, and changes clothes. Jon and Cabeza go around to the side facing the road.

Cabeza walks away from the vehicle, stealing a look in Kate's direction, while Jon changes into his camos.

"As soon as I get in these boots," Jon calls to Kate, "I'm going to try our communications."

"I'm ready when you are!" she shouts back. She quickly changes into the camouflage shirt and pants, and drops her other clothes on the floor of the Toyota. She's puts on her parka and rucksack and adjusts the straps. Jon puts in his ear bud and motions he is going across the road. As he walks she watches him. She slings her MP7 over her right shoulder.

Jon continues walking. He stops 50 yards distant. "Can you hear me?" he says, barely above a whisper, and purposefully turned away from her.

"Affirmative," Kate answers. "Just like you're standing next to me."

"Okay. I'm going to call the all-seeing-eye-in-the-sky."

Cabeza watches.

"Hummingbird this is Firefly. Over."

"Firefly this is Hummingbird. Over."

"Hummingbird, how do you read? Over."

With the drone and Jon in contact, the drone's green screen transmits the image to R2 in SOUTHCOM. The thermal image of the three standing beside the vehicle is clear. Jon can also see the image on his wrist screen, but that image is in ghostly gray and bright white, not green and red. Cabeza, Kate and Jon are easily identifiable. All three figures project a vivid white image because of their body heat. The Toyota is whitest because its engine is much hotter.

"Five-by-five," comes the standard response for loud and clear. "Over."

"Hummingbird tell Navigator we are about to push off. Over."

"Firefly, Navigator is on this channel. Over." Hummingbird pilot Berrien looks over her right shoulder to verify Wells is on channel. He is.

"Navigator, Firefly. We're about to get started. This is the low risk walk in the park you promised. Right? Over."

"Firefly," says Wells in his familiar baritone voice, "More like a walk in the woods. Over."

"Roger. Just keep an eye on us. I'm not a ranger…no pun intended. Over."

"We've got your back. Over."

"Can we shorten Hummingbird to H-Bird? Over."

"Firefly, consider it done. Anything else? Over"

"Navigator, our ETD was later than expected. I'll give you a call when we clock out. Firefly out."

Jon hears two clicks in his ear bud. It's a normal sign off, meaning "I understand." It replaces the "roger" and "out."

The trio meets for the last time at the side of the Toyota.

"Thanks again," Jon says to Cabeza. He shakes his hand.

Kate steps around Jon and also shakes Cabeza's hand. "Please thank Gunny for her help."

"Certainly," Cabeza says. "My pleasure. Good luck."

The start out later than Jon wanted, in an uneven row of tall banana trees, and stumble along in single file. Kate checks her GPS and indicates, with a chop of her hand, the correct direction. A four foot deep trench between rows of the banana trees makes crossing a pain. Despite this the trees are aligned in the direction they want to travel, and the ground starts to level out soon enough. They walk at a slow pace for about ninety minutes, saying little. There is no communication with Hummingbird. That's a good sign.

"How far have we gone?" Jon asks, pausing to scrape mud off his boots on a leaning banana stalk.

"2.2 miles," Kate answers, consulting the GPS on her wrist.

"Not exactly route-march speed," he says with frustration, adjusting his rucksack.

"I'd say we are not going to get up to four miles an hour anytime soon."

"How much further from here?"

"Twenty-seven." She looks around, clearly impressed by the sheer number of banana trees. "Did they say this was a 2,000 acre plantation?"

"20,000 acres." Jon's thoughts are a long way from the briefings at Hilton Head.

"Incredible."

"Yeah. We're running out of day. We can only go another 20 or 30 minutes. We need to make Point A before dark."

Kate looks at her GPS again. "Not much further."

Not much further turns out to be almost 40 minutes. The sun is getting lower on the horizon. From the banana field they cautiously approach a clearing: Point A. It is the initial waypoint. In the center of the clearing, at the edge of the jungle, is a long one story concrete structure with a metal roof. It is open on three sides. Inside the building are five waist-high tables running the length of the building. It looks deserted.

The unremarkable structure is a collection point for bananas, and a work shed. After workers harvest the bananas, the fruit is brought to the shed to be inspected, sorted, and prepared for shipment by truck to the wholesale market in San Jose, or to the docks in Limon for export. The shed doubles as a shelter for workers in bad weather.

"H-bird this is Firefly. Over."

"Go Firefly," answers pilot Berrien's familiar lower-register voice. It is a smoothing and calming voice.

"Firefly is at Point A. How's it looking? Over."

"Ah, Firefly – looks clear. Over."

"Thanks H-bird. Firefly out."

Despite the favorable report, they approach the building cautiously. It is always the overlooked details that get a person killed. Jon does not like surprises. Rather than separate they go around the shed together in single file. Kate takes the lead. Jon is ten feet behind her. It's easy enough to see through the length of the structure. It is less easy to scan the nearby jungle at the edge of the clearing. Ten minutes later they are satisfied they are alone. That's good news.

The bad news is they are behind schedule, and still have another day in the jungle before reaching their destination. Standing several feet from Kate, Jon adjusted his ear bud. Then he pressed the upper button on his watch monitor.

"H-bird. Firefly. Over."

Instantly, "This is H-bird. Over."

"Roger. Patch me to Navigator. Over."

"Firefly, stand by one."

Wells says, "This is Navigator. Over."

"Navigator, we're going to run out of daylight. Over."

"Roger that. Over."

"You have our location. Let's start again at 0530 tomorrow. Over."

"Roger. Over."

"Okay, Navigator. I'll keep my cell phone on just in case," Jon jokes.

"That would be a first. Don't forget your prayers. Over."

"You can bet I won't. Firefly out."

Kate and Jon decide to hold up at the northern end of the shed, backs literally against the wall. Kate considers sleeping on top of one of the long tables but decides she would be too exposed. Rather she and Jon stay together. He decides to sleep sitting up, on semi-guard duty. They drop their packs and stretch. Darkness is only minutes away. In the fading light

Kate spots a 55-gallon steel drum at the opposite end of the shed. She goes to investigate. Apparently workers have a fire in the drum during the day. Maybe to cook or for early morning warmth. Whatever. She rounds up sticks and small branches and trash and fires it up. Once it's going she returns to her rucksack and brings it back to the table nearest the drum. Jon gathers a few pieces of wood from broken packing crates and tosses them in the drum.

"I'm glad to make dinner," she says lightly as she rifles through her rucksack. She

pulls out two MREs. "Beef Ravioli or Spaghetti with meat sauce?"

"Ravioli is fine." Jon removes the small but powerful flashlight, and the night vision goggles (NVG) from his rucksack.

"Side dish can be noodles or rice," Kate says.

"Rice." He loosens his boots but doesn't take them off. He doesn't think he will need to inspect his feet or change socks this soon. His feet are dry. Then again, it will only take a minute. Army "ground-pounders" are obsessive about keeping their feet in good walking order. He was Air Force. After a moment, he reconsiders and pulls his boots off to check his feet.

"And as a special treat," Kate continues, "we have pound cake or oatmeal cookies."

"I'll go with the cookies." He stops to look at her. Everything else aside, he likes her positive attitude and playfulness. She looks like the last person in the world who would kill another person. But he has no illusions. She most assuredly can finish the drill. Obviously, Wells shares that view. It is not difficult to think she ought to be back at the Pentagon, or getting ready for a night out in Georgetown. Instead, she is in the middle of a banana field in Central America.

"Coffee, water or me?" she teases, striking a seductive pose.

Jon meets her gaze but pretends not to notice her poise.

The MRE heating packs get as hot as 200 degrees. The heat is produced by a chemical reaction when as little as an ounce of water is added. Just fill to the black line. Boiling furiously it takes only minutes to get a hot meal. In short order the 1,250 calory MREs are ready.

Jon pulls on his boots. Kate sits cross-legged next to him under the table near the middle of the shed. "Ravioli's good," he says, spooning up a hot mouthful. He hates it.

"Not bad," she says. "It's pretty hard to screw up the rice."

"Thanks for everything."

"No big deal. That's why they call 'em Meals Ready to Eat."

"I mean for everything in the last couple of days." His tone is soft.

She nods. They turn to look at each other. Her eyes find his. He thinks she is most beautiful when she doesn't smile. "Well," he quickly says, turning away, and standing up. "I've got KP tonight. You've got it tomorrow." They both laugh. "Because the His and Her bathroom is 30 feet away, keep your ear bud in."

"What?"

"You know what I mean. The wooded area." He feels instantly stupid for saying anything. She doesn't need to be coddled. She is a graduate of a demanding military academy and capable of taking care of herself – and him if need be.

Kate steps off the slab of the shed and disappears into the jungle. He moves to the northern end of the shed and waits for her. She returns in a few minutes and sits down next to him, stretching her legs out. She leans the MP7 across her thighs, pointing in the direction of the jungle.

"Okay, Tarzan," she says, getting comfortable, "What is the first law of the jungle?"

He looks at her. "I prefer to be addressed as Lion."

"Stop stalling. You either know it or you don't."

"Is this a trick question?"

"Serious question."

"Okay," Jon says. "Eat or be eaten."

"No."

"Know your enemy?"

"Good answer, but wrong."

"Really? How about survival of the fittest?"

"You don't seem to get any better with multiple guesses," she teases.

"Okay, Jane, what?"

"The first law of the jungle is the Law of the Three Ss: Watch where you Step, watch where you Stand, and watch where you Sit."

"That seems like three laws, not one. But I'll try to keep that in mind." He gives her a playful shove. She fakes being pushed too hard, and then settles back.

Night is fast upon them. They sit back to back, leaning into the wall with one shoulder, each covering a field of fire of 90 degrees. She stretches her neck to the right, looking over her shoulder at Jon.

He appears to be studying his watch.

"What are you doing now?"

"Shhhh." Seconds pass. "Okay," he says and twists his neck to look at her.

"What are you doing?" she repeats, almost in a whisper.

"Checking the temperature."

"By looking at your watch?"

"By counting cricket chirps."

"You're making this up."

"No, I'm not. I'll show you. When I say go, count the chirps." He looks at his watch again. "Go."

Fifteen seconds later he says, "What did you get?"

"Thirty five."

"Close enough. I got thirty six. So you take thirty five or thirty six and add 48. That tells you the temperature." He smiles and cocks his head with an air of superiority.

Instantly she says, "You're telling me its 83 degrees?"

"I'm not. The crickets are. It's proven science."

"I've never heard of such a thing."

"Maybe they don't have crickets in Colorado."

"I wouldn't know a cricket if …what do they look like?

"I'd guess that depends on where you are. Geographically, I mean. In the southeastern U.S. they are brown and look like a small grasshopper. I don't know what they look like here. Or in Kansas or Colorado."

Kate gives him the do-I-look-that-stupid stare and turns away. "Well, they are certainly loud."

"That not the crickets," he says. "That's cicadas. They are the noisiest insects in the world."

"Where did you learn that?"

"Jungle school," he says smugly.

Kate quickly spins around when they hear something at the far end of the building. Jon holds up his hand, takes out the NVG, turns them on, and slips them over his head. She picks up the MP7 and switches the safety off. He scans the area in the direction of the sound. The shimmering greenish picture shows the heat signature of cat-sized rats surrounding the steel drum looking for something to eat. Kate looks at him for a report.

"Nothing," he says, not wanted to spook her more than he has already.

"As long as it isn't tarantulas. I hate big hairy spiders." She leans back and stretches out using her rucksack as a pillow and cradling the

MP7. She pulls her boonie hat down and zips up her parka. She leans into him. He pats her shoulder, removes the NVG and turns them off.

"Let me know when you want me to relieve you," she says.

He has the bionic ear in his right ear. The "ear" is battery powered and is seven times more powerful than human hearing. With his left ear he listens for alerts from Hummingbird. He looks at his watch: 10:52. He likes watches, especially this one. It's a Special Ops watch issued to the CIA. This one he wore on the North Korea assignment. The time is easy to read in total darkness because the hands are illuminated by a radioactive isotope of hydrogen. The manufacturer refers to the remarkable light as "Tritium Illumination." It will glow for 20 years. Hopefully he won't.

Kate is restless. She pulls the insect netting in her hat down, and slips into a light sleep.

Jon feels exposed in the work shed. It is not a good defensive position even if they aren't in hostile territory. Were it not for Kate he would be digging in and sleeping in the jungle. Another reason he doesn't like having a partner. He is more comfortable looking out for Number One. The Korean assignment was stressful enough for one person. With Soon it was doubly so. And here he is again with more than just the mission and himself to be worried about. It is inconceivable how in the space of a few days his world has crashed. Over and over he replays events in Bermuda. Mere days ago he was racing through the rain with crazy people trying to kill him. Two of his friends died, this boat was lost, and his quiet life turned upside down. The intimacy with Kate greatly bothers him. His mind is racing. Sleep comes and goes in spurts. He sleeps with his eyes closed and his ears awake.

The next morning, seemly only minutes after he dozed off, he hears: "Firefly, this is H-bird with your wake up call. Over." The voice is a male. Must have changed drone drivers.

Jon looks at the watch – 5:30 and dark. It's an hour before the sun comes up, but there is a hazy moon casting a dim glow in the darkness. "H-bird, this is Firefly. Thanks. Out." Jon gently nudges Kate, awakening her. Actually, when Hummingbird woke him, she was awake. He pops a glow stick to provide light. She gets to her feet, and takes a deep breath. A little stiff from sleeping sitting up and lying on the cement floor, they head off, one at a time, with the small flashlight, into the jungle. When he returns to the shed they do a modified 'daily dozen' of exercises to limber up and shake off the night. There is a cool crisp mist in the dark air. The parkas are a comfort.

With light from another glow stick Jon rummages through his rucksack for MREs. He finds two hash browns with bacon, dated 2011. And a fig bar. After they finish eating, he judges the MRE decent. He makes a cup of coffee. She thinks the hash browns remind her of high quality cardboard. The bacon is microwave-limp. She mixes water with the Raspberry Electrolyte beverage power and pronounces it good. They take a few pills – for malaria among other things – and gather up their trash for later disposal in the jungle. In another 20 to 30 minutes it will be light. It will take that long to get out of the banana field and find their way. They shoulder their rucksack, adjust the straps, check the MP7s, and move out.

"H-bird, Firefly. We're on the move," he reports.

"That's a rog, Firefly. H-bird standing by."

Kate checks her GPS and takes the lead. The full moon casts a pale and eerie light among the banana stalks. The ground is uneven and both stumble several times. Shortly, however, they find the secondary back road from the banana plantation. Forty minutes later, after sunup, they cut across a large estancia that grows coffee on the gentle slopes. There are hundreds of thousands of plants. Further on they walk among mature coffee bushes, seven or eight feet tall. In the distance they see workers spilling onto the fields. The coffee bushes are heavy with beans, mostly dark brown but some red. To avoid being seen they move up the slopes in a northwestward direction. Pausing near the top of the slope they stop and look back.

"Coffee plants as far as the eye can see," says Kate. "This can't belong to one person."

"Probably a corporation. Maybe a cooperative."

"Maybe Starbucks."

"I suppose. They could change their motto: Starbucks – coffee barons."

Within an hour they approach the edge of the rainforest. Time for a check with Hummingbird.

"H-bird, Firefly. Over"

"This is H-bird. Go."

"H-bird, how is it looking?"

"Firefly, negative contacts. Over."

"That's good news, H-bird. We're about to enter phase two. Over."

"Firefly, this is Navigator. Hope you had a good night's sleep."

"Not as good as yours, Navigator. But I had a great breakfast. Over."

"Firefly, phase two is in the danger zone. Rough terrain. Do you copy?"

"Copy that. Stay in touch. Out."

Two clicks.

CHAPTER 17

The Costa Rica rainforest is a lush ecological menagerie. Like the colors in a kaleidoscope, sunlight filtering through the canopy produces every imaginable shade of green and gold and orange, and yellow and brown. The dense foliage conceals a treasure-house of millions of species of trees, plants, monkeys, birds, insects, snakes and frogs of every conceivable description. But the jungle is also an inhospitable place. Deadly snakes, parasites, ants, mosquitoes, ticks, leeches and raging rivers challenge all but the most determined adventurers.

By definition a rainforest has a lot of precipitation. Giant trees are numerous and impressive, partially the result of twenty years of all but outlawing deforestation by the Government of Costa Rica. Trees increase rainfall. On the Caribbean Slope the rainy season lasts from April to November. Because of the daily rains the soil is soft. It is easier to walk quietly because nothing underfoot is completely dry. Mornings are usually sunny, but afternoons bring rain showers. High humidity is a remainder of the chemical process turning water and hydrogen and carbon dioxide into air. Kate fills her lungs with the clean air. She can almost smell the plants giving up oxygen. It's wonderful air! Reminds her of the air in Colorado Springs. She misses the Springs, but doesn't dwell on it.

They begin their trek into a strange region. It is like stepping into another world. Because of giant trees and overgrown vegetation, the jungle is a windless place. It is still, but not quiet. And it is noisy when they first enter. Monkeys and birds and other creatures register their displeasure with the uninvited visitors. Or perhaps their squawking and screeches serve to alert others of the approaching strangers. Birds large and small take flight.

The dirt and grass path leading from the coffee fields into the thickening jungle is well worn. Sharp needles on shoulder-high bushes tear at their fatigues as they pass. Jon's left hand bleeds slightly from the scratches. Still, without the primitive path the jungle would be impenetrable. Wide enough for two people side-by-side when they begin, it becomes narrower and darker the further they go. In the space of twenty yards they disappear completely in the dense foliage. Within an hour the path ends abruptly. Two smaller paths are born, one to the left and the other to the right. From this point on progress is going to be slower.

"Stay close," advises Jon. "We'll just have to work our way through. Hopefully it will get easier in the woods of the mountain ridge." He pushed the upper button on his watch.

"H-bird this is Firefly."

The reply is instantaneous.

"This is H-bird. Go."

"We've at a dead end. How do things look?"

"There is activity behind you. Analytics advises probably laborers headed to work. No threat. Clear in front. Except for the river. Nothing heading in your direction. Over."

"Roger that. Thanks."

"H-bird standing by."

Jon pauses and pushes the lower button for the intercom mode. "No news is good news." He looks back at Kate.

She nods and looks at her wrist GPS "We should take the left. It parallels the river." She does a hand chop to indicate the direction.

Weaving their way down the diminishing path Jon uses his jungle knife to clear overhanging wrist-thick vines and small limbs. Even on the path, greenery is often waist high with large bushes, tropical ferns, and green plants of all kinds. Frequently, the jungle floor is not visible because of the dense jungle. They brush limbs and leaves aside as they pass. It is impossible to walk in a straight line because of the undergrowth. Zigzagging is a time and energy killer.

Unexpectedly, Jon stops. In three steps Kate is beside him.

"Let's try these things out," he says, referring to the MP7s. "There can't be anyone around for miles." Finding a clear target presents a problem. After turning around in a circle, he says, "See that big tree about 25 feet away? To your left?" He points.

"Got it."

"Six rounds each. Whoever is closest to the vine about midway up wins an all expense trip to Disneyland." He unslings his weapon and turns to her. "Ladies first."

"'Ladies first'," she repeats, narrowing her eyes. "I'd be careful with that kind of sexist talk. Particularly when "the lady" in question has a high performance weapon in her hands." She mock smiles, showing her teeth.

Kate configures the MP7 as a rifle. Safety off, feet firmly planted, she relaxes her muscles and brings the weapon up to take aim. There is adequate light to establish a good sight picture on the target. She takes a breath, holds it, and slowly squeezes the trigger. When the weapon fires it is almost a surprise. Perfect. She quickly re-acquires the target and rapidly fires five more times. It's a tight pattern. She's a darn good shot. She puts the safety on, points the weapon down and turns to look at him.

"Okay," he says, secretly impressed, "this is your last chance. I don't want to embarrass you. What happens in the jungle stays in the jungle. Concede now and it will stay between us." He grins like a kid.

"Are you familiar with the expression 'fat chance'?" She returns his grin.

He, too, configures his weapon as a rifle, takes aim and leans into the weapon. He fires one shot. It's on target. He moves the selector switch to automatic and fires a burst of 10 rounds. The vine is cut in half and falls to the ground. "Looks like I still have my mojo," he says.

"Even a blind pig in the woods…." She shakes her head.

"Okay, truthfully, I didn't mean to fire so many rounds. I guess I cheated. But now I know we can empty a magazine in a heartbeat." For a split second he realizes he is having fun. Maybe it's being with her.

Both take a moment to make minor adjustments to their packs and start off again. They pick up the pace. An hour and a half later she pauses. "Want to take five for water?"

'Sure." He stops and scrapes a small area with his boot and drops to one knee, careful to make sure he doesn't drop on an ant colony. Or something worse.

She walks behind him and retrieves two containers of water from his rucksack. She re-zips his pack and moves around in front of him. She hands him one container.

The snake might have escaped unnoticed if it had not moved. But it's hard to miss a ten foot snake as big around as an adult's thigh slithering near the trunk of a large tree behind Jon.

"Did they say 87 percent of snakes in Costa Rica were not harmful?" she calmly asks, her focus slightly left of his right shoulder.

"Were not dangerous," he corrects her. "Why?"

"I think I see one of the other 13 percent."

Jon jerks his head around and jumps to his feet. "Wow. That is one big boa constrictor. It would ruin my entire day to walk under a tree limb and have it drop on me." He draws the Walther from its holster.

"Does it look hungry?" Her gaze is steady and unblinking.

"I don't see any bulges. I don't think it has eaten recently."

"Funny. Not what I wanted to hear." She slides her MP7 off her shoulder and takes a firm grip. Her finger is alongside the trigger guard.

The snake stops slithering under the leaves. It's brown, with inverted black and

yellow triangles. It blends perfectly with the forest floor. The head is the size of two softballs.

It gives Kate the shivers.

The snake doesn't move.

Neither do they.

After a moment Jon says "Maybe it's sizing us up. I hope it thinks we're too big to

eat. Maybe it just wants to give you a love squeeze."

"I don't think it thinks," she says quietly. "It's a snake." She clicks the MP7 safety to the off position.

"You don't have to whisper. Snakes don't have ears. Let's just ease around it – give it a lot of room." Kate bobs her head in an "I know that" gesture.

Slowly they step further off the path deeper into the underbrush, putting 30 feet between the boa and themselves as quickly as they can. The snake's beady eyes seem to follow them the entire time, like an Uncle Sam Wants You poster.

"Do they follow their prey?" she asks, looking back and pushing Jon on the shoulder.

"I don't know. Guess we'll find out."

"Are they fast?"

"I hope not." He smiles and turns to take her arm. The snake continues to watch but doesn't move. It's another twenty tense yards before she is comfortable enough to put the safety on. Maybe the snake has better things to do. She slings MP7 on her shoulder. Jon holsters the Walther.

"It's official," she says.

"What is?"

"I've over large snakes."

They continue along the narrow jungle path for two hours, stopping twice for a water break. She wonders who uses the path. It's small and narrow, but well worn. The jungle on both sides of the path has heavy underbrush. They have not seen or heard anyone. They walk on for another hour. They are making good time, relatively.

By midafternoon the air is crisp, and the jungle darkens. There is the smell of moisture. Then they hear it: deep claps of thunder and the sound of rain seeping through the thick jungle canopy. The rain becomes louder before reaching them. They pull the parka hoods over their boonies. Seeking shelter under a large tree, they are careful to scan the limbs above them for anything that "doesn't look right." They don't say it, but the earlier encounter with the boa has left an impression.

She says, "What are you thinking?"

"I'm thinking I love the rain. Growing up in south Florida we had a lot of afternoon showers. It's a great smell, like it's cleaning the earth. Know what I mean?" The parkas perform well. Much better than the old Army ponchos. The temperature drops five degrees.

"Yes. I meant, what do you think about how much further we can get today?"

"Right," he says, realizing he misunderstood her. "Depends on the rain. Going to be dark soon."

"I hate to stray too far from this path."

"Let's push on a little further. The rain is just a shower. It will be over soon."

It isn't over soon. The thunder gets louder. The shower becomes a torrent, crashing down and flooding the jungle floor. Their boots becomes sluggish. Their footsteps fill instantly with water. Rain runs off giant exposed tree roots creating large ruts in the soil. The temperature drops another five degrees. They push on another hour, their pace slowed almost to a stop because of the soft ground. Ankle deep in mud, they stop again.

Kate checks the GPS. "We should dead end at the river. Couple hundred yards. After that it's uphill into the mountains."

"Then how far?"

"Maybe four hours."

"Should be there by late morning tomorrow?"

"Probably," she shrugs. In these conditions it could be eight hours, she thinks.

They move out. The rain has lessened but shows no sign of stopping.

Kate says, "Have you been noticing the path?" She looks down as she speaks.

"You mean the swamp path?"

"Notice anything?"

"It's heavily traveled. Is that what you mean?"

"Why would that be? It isn't used by workers going to or coming back from any banana or coffee fields. We're too far away for that." She looks in all directions as if scanning the jungle for an answer.

"Indigenous people? Animals? Other foot traffic?" Jon asks.

"You think so?"

"Not really," he admits.

"I've been watching for any animal tracks. Haven't seen any," she says. "Besides, animals don't usually use trails or paths." She has a puzzled look on her face. Perhaps the paths are used by the shy and elusive – and dangerous - people of the forest.

Jon says, "You're thinking it may be the bad guys?"

"I'm thinking we're carrying weapons for a reason."

Ten steps later, Jon says, "Hopefully, we won't need to use them. But if you're right, and I'm not saying you are, we just need to stay alert. Let's keep moving."

She doesn't say anything. But she is thinking a lot of things. The rain slows to a drizzle. The air cools.

Jon is thinking, too. He respects her observations and opinions. He knows the unknown is always frightening. But in his experience, fear is a motivator. When he is not afraid he is less alert.

They slog along the muddy and slippery path protected by still dry boots and parkas. Jon looks at his watch: 5:15. Daylight is already fading. The sun will set by 6:00 p.m. The rain has slows to a drip. "Let's make camp at the base of that tree up ahead."

That tree is a Guanacaste tree, the national tree of Costa Rica. It is probably three feet in diameter and as tall as a ten-story building. There are no low lying branches, which suits both of them just fine. The snake incident unnerved them. With the trenching tool from his rucksack he scrapes an area between the tree's giant above-ground roots. Then he digs a shallow hole three feet in front of that. Kate picks up a few pieces of wood close to the tree and drops them near the hole. The jungle is thick on both sides of the path. She isn't about to go far.

"They're soaked," she reports as she dumps the sticks and twigs near the shallow hole. "I don't think a fire is in our immediate future." She squats near the pit.

"We'll get it going," he says. "It's just for mood lighting anyway." He smiles, and she feels more relaxed. She reminds herself if she had wanted to play in the woods she would have joined the Army.

Jon rummages through his rucksack for one of the MRE heaters. "The special for tonight," he says, mimicking her the previous night, "is chili macaroni spaghetti with meat sauce - or grilled chicken breast."

"Is chili macaroni spaghetti one entrée or three?"

"I think it's one."

"Grilled chicken breast."

"Excellent."

"Chocolate or vanilla shake?"

She smiles, feeling more relaxed. "Yummy chocolate."

"And for dessert we have pound cake or marble cake."

"Which do you want?"

"Maybe the pound cake?"

"The marble cake will be fine."

After a day of dodging the hazards of the jungle, Jon silently evaluates their progress. It wasn't what he had hoped for. He still hopes this assignment will be merely troublesome and not difficult. Either way, here he is on a rainy evening in a jungle. The good news is there have been no equipment or communication failures. More good news is they have not encountered any dangerous situations – other than the snake – or mission-jeopardizing problems.

"Do you have plans for when we're finished here?" Kate asks, policing her trash and throwing it on the skimpy fire.

"I'm just trying to stay focused on finishing." He shakes his head like a dog trying to shake off water. "You?"

"I'd like to have tea and cucumber sandwiches at the Ritz in London."

"I'd prefer something stronger at the Berkeley in Knightsbridge. I'm not one for tea and crumpets."

"London with London has a nice ring, don't you think?" She looks at him.

Jon ignores her. "Let's try out these Protectors." He then places one to the right of where he plans to sit, and the other to the left of where Kate will sit. It's easy to tap them into the ground with the butt of his Walther. The Protectors, at least in theory, provide protection from predator snakes. Battery powered, they creates a vibration that mimics a very large creature, and deters other snakes from coming closer. When he finishes, he asks, "You want the first or second watch?"

CHAPTER 18

Sunrise is 5:30. It has been a miserable night. He rolls his shoulders to get the kinks out. The MRE heat packs make the Maple Pork Sausage Patty, Cheese Omelet (dated 2011), and coffee decent. They bury their breakfast trash eight inches into the soft soil and move out. An hour and a half later they leave the level forest floor and begin an incline to the mountain ridge. It is a steepening path, transitioning them from jungle-like to woods-like surroundings. Jon is unwrapping one of the 3,600 calorie energy bars when Hummingbird calls.

"Firefly, H-bird. Over."

"This is firefly. Go."

"Yo u ot mpany."

"H-bird, you're breaking up. Say again."

"Lo a li ve feed."

"Roger." A second passes.

"Whiskey Tango Foxtrot?!"

The transmission unexpectedly clears up. "Looks like three people carrying weapons, and three more with boxes on their backs," H-bird broadcast.

Kate and Jon were briefed the drug trade is difficult to control in Central America. Columbian drug lords are inventive and creative when it comes to moving the finest coke in the world. Youth gangs see big paydays in running drugs, and they have no remorse about violence or even murder. Jungle dealers make Paco – a poor person's cocane - and sell it to city drug dealers, who can make $30 to $50 day.

"Standby Firefly."

Jon motions Kate to come to his side. He holds his arm out so both can look at the image. "We're on a collision course," she says, looking at the screen, and readies her MP7.

"Firefly, H-bird. Company is definitely heading your way. Over."

"Roger that."

Kate and Jon move off the narrow path. Twenty steps later, lying prone, they are swallowed by the jungle and no longer visible. They roll out of their rucksacks waiting further word. Jon moves 15 yards away from Kate, but on the same side of the path. "Don't shoot me," he whispers as he moves away. They check the MP7s. Safeties off.

"H-bird," Jon says after a few moments, "what's the word? Over."

"Firefly, analytics are scanning. Standby."

Back in R2 at SOUTHCOM, the image is forwarded to the Analytics Team in R1 as well as to the conference room display. The teams confer and study the feed from Hummingbird. Their considered opinion is communicated to Wells in R2.

Jon is impatient. He hopes the jungle floor is not concealing some snakes or killer frogs or attacking ants. It has been at least five minutes. As he is about to call Hummingbird, they call.

"Firefly, H-bird. Over."

"Go H-bird."

"Firefly, this is Navigator. Your company presents only moderate danger. Over."

"Navigator, moderate danger? Over."

"Firefly, we don't think they are running drugs or guns. Over."

"Navigator, Bravo Sierra! Those objects in their hands don't look like walking sticks. Over."

"Roger. Those are AK-47s. Maybe a M16, too. But we think your company is wildlife trafficking. Over."

"Ah, say again Navigator."

"Firefly, we believe your company is involved in the illegal animal trade. Look at the boxes. We think they are poaching small animals. Parrots, parakeets, wild birds. Over."

"Navigator. Doesn't mean they won't use those weapons. Over"

"So be careful. Over."

"Kilo Mike Alpha. Out."

CHAPTER 19

Because of the nasty weather, flights had not left Hamilton for two days. By the third day, the terminal was overcrowded with exhausted vacationers and honeymooners eager to get home. Conditions were less crowded in the departure lounge because the hurdle to rebook a flight had been cleared. In the VIP lounges free beverages and snacks made waiting tolerable for the business elite.

At a window overlooking the tarmac a woman with shoulder-length black hair is sitting alone drinking a 2008 Portuguese "pale yellow" glass of wine. She detects a hint of lime in the wine but still considers it very nice, and refreshing for an inexpensive wine. Probably cost the airline $10 a bottle. Maybe less. She prefers white wines because red wines give her headaches. Shortly after 3:00 p.m. her flight is called. The attractive woman with the slim face, wearing a dark business suit and dark frame glasses, casually goes to the gate, pulling a small carry-on bag with nothing of interest in it. Her Business Class seat assignment is a window. The plane is packed. She speaks to no one, and falls into a light sleep for the duration of the flight.

When the flight arrives at JFK at 5:00 p.m., 90 minutes after leaving Bermuda, Dr. Lisa Jinping is waiting in the arrival area. After clearing Passport Control and Customs, Masuyo Yosano, a Japanese national, and Jinping embrace like sisters.

Yosano says, "I hope it was not inconvenient to meet me."

"No, not at all. It gives me an excuse to shop at all the exclusive places." They walk closely together, through baggage claim, and step outside as a chauffeur-driven black Mercedes pulls to the curb. The uniformed chauffeur gets out, takes the carry-on bag, and opens the passenger side door. He returns to the front seat, watches for taxis and buses behind the car, and pulls into the traffic flow without a word.

Traffic into Manhattan is always terrible. Several times the Mercedes slows to a complete stop, causing a chorus of New Yorkers to lean on their horns. Yellow cabs dart in and out at dangerously fast speeds, causing more horns and raised arms with an extended middle finger. The women talk softly in standard Chinese (Mandarin) about the Bermuda assignment.

"The General eagerly awaits your report," Jinping says. She looks at the passing urban scene.

"Will others be there?"

"Absolutely," Jinping says, looking directly at Yasano. "This is a very important meeting."

"I would value your advice, doctor."

"These are powerful old men. The dreams of their youth flatter them. You would do well to remember you can flatter them, too. The more dangerous and daring your assignment, the more exciting it will be for them. Your success is their success."

"So I might be permitted to stray from total objectivity?"

"You must always be truthful. To deceive them will work against you. But you may embellish some details."

"Would you?"

"If your drama excites them as much as I think it will, and if they are taken with you, your career will definitely be enhanced."

"I have excited men before. It is not a difficult task."

Jinping smiles knowingly and nods her head. Both return to their private thoughts.

The Mercedes winds its way through darkening streets in lower Manhattan. Cars are illegally parked on both sides of the street, two wheels in the street and two wheels on the sidewalk. Traffic cops pretend they aren't there. The Mercedes stops at the entrance to the Ritz-Carlton New York, Battery Park. The chauffeur gets out and hurries to assist the women exiting the car. The hotel doorman removes the carry-on from the trunk, and precedes the women inside. The women graciously thank the doorman, and immediately go to the top floor of the hotel. They are met at the door by a moderately tall man with polished manners. He relieves Yosano of her carry-on as they enter. The host promptly appears.

"Welcome," he says, without introductions. "Please come in and refresh yourself." He guides Yosano by the arm to the dining room, and Jinping follows.

The suite is a huge. Twenty-five hundred square feet, with the finest furnishings. From the living room window they pass briefly a magnificent view of the Statue of Liberty. The dining room table is large and filled with foods of every description on silver trays. There are desserts for the sweetest tooth. All manner of beverages are available. The extravagance is stunning. Yosano looks over the collection of wines. She nods at a bottle of Italian Vernaccia. It is a dry white wine with a delicate fruit taste. A second young man fills a crystal glass and hands it to her. Jinping has limited appreciation for white wines – because they are not aged – and selects a glass of 1990 Chateau LaTour Pauillac. She likes its chocolate and cherry flavor. She particularly enjoys knowing the bottle cost at least $700.

The women follow the host to a conference table in the living room. Four middle aged men await them. The young man at the door, and the one serving the wine, position themselves away from the table but close at hand. Clearly they are bodyguards, not servers.

The host speaks to the women. "We are pleased you are here. Dr. Jinping is a friend of long and valued standing." When he smiles a gold tooth is visible.

Jinping bows her head slightly and smiles at everyone around the table. "It is I, General," she says, "that thank you for all your help." No surname is attached to General; however, everyone in the room except Yosano (Chang Yoo Cha) knows the General represents Marshall Kye-Ong-nam, North Korea's Chief of the Armed Forces.

The General acknowledges Jinping's comment with a slight dip of his head. Then he says, "Masuyo Yosano is a woman of many names. But she is Chang Yoo Cha to us. She has successfully completed her assignment – overcoming demanding challenges – and we eagerly await her report."

There are several tonal sounds from around the table as the men settle into their chairs to get comfortable. "You may remain seated as you give us your report," the General says.

"Thank you, Comrade General," she begins, standing at her seat. She stands for two reasons: first, she wants to show respect for her superiors and, secondly, she wants to keep their interest by providing them the opportunity to look at her stunning figure.

For Chang Yoo Cha, events began in Seoul when she was selected for her assignment, along with her team leader. She assumes they are aware of this meeting. But she retells of her travel to Washington for support and critical briefings by Dr. Lisa Jinping. She picks up the pace when she talks of events rapidly unfolding once she arrived in Bermuda. She watches the eyes of the men, and from time to time shifts from one leg to the other. The questions begin after her description of locating the man named Charles Sewell.

"He was in the company of a bodyguard and they attempted to elude us," she says.

"Us?" asks a well dressed man at the end of the table. His name is not mentioned, but Jinping knows he is with the Korean National Security Agency – North Korea's secret police.

"Excuse me. I meant to say my team leader, Joo Lee Kim, and I." Her voice is neutral but her eyes are not.

"Yes, of course." He nods and smiles subtley. "Please continue."

"We pursued Sewell and his bodyguard. Another person, perhaps another of his guards, attempted to stop us and I had no choice but to take action."

"How did you know he was a bodyguard and not an innocent person?"

"I could tell. He was a large, well-built man. Intimidating."

"You killed him?"

"I shot him."

"Go on," says the General, his voice soft but commanding.

"We raced to catch up with Sewell as he left the building. He had another guard outside who was armed. He drew his pistol to stop us."

"And you shot him?" says Yi Jong Shik. He sits next to the man at the end of the table.

"I did."

"Did not all the shooting cause alarm? Bring the police?"

"I can not say. Joo Lee Kim and I were pursuing Sewell and his other bodyguard in the rain and fading light. I was intent on capturing him."

"And did you accomplish that? Did you capture him?"

"Sadly, no. As events developed, because of the approaching night and the heavy rain, he captured Joo Lee Kim…it's complicated…but I will describe it if you wish…" Her voice trails off. She casts her eyes downward.

The faces of two of the men at the table show subtle expressions of concern. One opens his mouth to speak but the General speaks first. "No, perhaps later. Go on, please."

"I did not want to leave Joo Lee Kim, but Sewell's bodyguard fired several shots, narrowly missing me more than once, and I had no alternative but to seek cover."

"You were lucky to have escaped."

"Yes, I believe so. But I never lost focus and planned to rescue Joo Lee Kim."

"You are a comrade of exceptional courage," adds Kyoung Yi Park, speaking for the first time. He is the personal representative of Pang Yong Song, North Korea's head of internal national security.

"Thank you, but it is Joo Lee Kim that is a hero. As I began to retrace my steps to my captured comrade I heard a single pistol shot. I raced forward, prepared to die if need be…but I was too late to attack Sewell, who was running away...and I found Joo Lee Kim lying on the street. I rushed to him. He was shot in the head, execution style," she lies.

"What did you do then?" Park asks.

"I vowed to complete my assignment no matter the costs. I retrieved Joo Lee Kim's weapon, his passport, and all identification, money and jewelry, so it would look like a robbery."

"Very clever," suggests the man at the end of the table.

"We had learned of Sewell's residence earlier and, in spite of the hurricane, I hurried there to confront him. It was a terrible night." She pauses as if recalling the difficult circumstances. "I was just in time because he was in the process of fleeing."

The men around the table are spellbound by the tale of daring. They lean inward in anticipation of the unfolding drama.

"When I broke into his capitalistic yacht, he was waiting for me. He fired twice. The second shot missed my head by inches," she says, her deceit unabated. "I am well trained and lucky. My first shot killed him. Naturally, after identifying him and making sure he was dead, I searched the yacht for any documents that might implicate us or reveal secret information. I found nothing. But he could have hidden information anywhere. Time was running out. Someone may have heard the shots in spite of the wind and rain. The storm was worsening by the minute. I decided to set explosives to conceal my acts, and destroy any evidence that would be hurtful to our great country."

She exhales heavily, pauses again, and takes a sip of wine. Her spectators' eyes reveal their intense interest, but their faces remain fixed.

"Incredible! Remarkable! Certainly worthy of our praise," says the General. "I am recommending your immediate promotion to Chungjwa (Lieutenant Colonel).

"Unfortunately, our deepest personal gratitude for your heroic actions can only be expressed in secret," adds Kyoung-Yi Park, looking at others around the table.

"I do not seek rewards or recognition, only the personal satisfaction of serving our people. But there is one final action I must report."

It is a shock to think there could be anything more. The faces remain stoic.

"Dr. Jinping providing us with an American contact who was willing – for a price – to assist Joo Lee Kim and myself in finding Sewell. Someone with contacts on the island."

"How much?"

"$25,000 U.S."

"Where did you get the money?"

"It was not required. We never planned to pay the greedy and corrupt American."

"You were able to resolve the matter quietly?" asks the General, his eyes narrowing.

"Yes. Hopefully you will agree the last link had to be deleted."

"Without question," says Park.

"No other choice," agrees the General.

"Clearly required," says the man at the end of the table.

Chang Yoo Cha bows her head to signal completion of her report, and sits quietly. The General says, "Extraordinary. An impressive success, showing your great talent and courage. Thank you, on behalf of all our people."

Later, after more wine, and before retiring for the night, Jinping goes into a guest bedroom with Chang Yoo Cha. Sitting comfortably on the bed she says, "Impressive report. You hand them eating out of your hand. All true, no doubt."

"Almost all."

"Oh?"

"The American – as you must know – was a sexist pig. In addition to money he wanted to be paid in sex."

"And you paid?" Jinping asks nonchallentely, raising one eyebrow.

"I was successful in carrying out my duty. It is he who paid for sex. With his life."

"I suppose it was necessary," she says, yawning.

"Yes. But I tell you honestly, I enjoyed killing him."

Jinping observes Chang Yoo Cha's unblinking eyes. The eyes, she thinks, of a cold-blooded murderess.

While the women chat in the bedroom, Kyoung-Yi Park lingers with the general and the others. It is time to enjoy expensive drinks and cigars in the living room. Park says, "That is a remarkable women."

"Yes, remarkable," agrees the general.

"It is difficult even for me to believe she is so capable. She is such a lovely and delicate flower."

The general makes eye contact for a long moment. Unsmiling, he says, "She is the most beautiful and perfect sociopath you will ever meet. You are safer sleeping with a rattlesnake than her."

~ ~ ~ ~

"Chang Yoo Cha – if that is her real name – flew from Bermuda to JFK on a Japanese passport as Masuyo Yosano. With a change of clothing, another wig, and temporary facial make-up, she flew from JFK to San Francisco as Martha Chow, a Chinese- American. Changing identities and nationalities is effortless with authentic passports. Dr. Lisa Jinping secured the passport blanks in exchange for information stolen from a defense contractor. Then the passports are expertly filled in, with numerous stamps and the required photo. Holographs are not difficult to forge for a government with considerable resources. It is all a bit confusing, which is the point.

In San Francisco, now traveling under the alias Yang Al-ling, a Chinese national, Chang Yoo Cha, aka Masuyo Yosano, aka Martha Chow, was booked First Class on Korean Air. The 747K, with the new Kosmo sleeper seat, was outbound for Gimbo International airport in Seoul. Yang Ai-ling is in seat 2J. The steady hum of the engines encourages relaxation and reflection. Chang Yoo Cha is not by nature a reflective person. She doesn't count assassinations or keep reminders. She rarely thinks about her work, except to critique how she might perform better. She was raised in a government world, a secular world, an amoral world, and doesn't believe in right and wrong in any traditional sense of good and evil. She thinks good and evil should really be good and hope. Hope is an evil because it is unrealistic and deceives people. She adjusts the headset and selects a classical music channel. She closes her eyes and reviews her professional record: five or six dissents and trouble-makers in North Korea eliminated; a black-marketer in Hamhung; a man and his wife in Kanggye; two men in Sariwon …that's ten. Four North Koreans that escaped to Dalian, China, and were helping to smuggle others out of North Korea (a capital offense), three more in South Korea (one a woman, all enemies of the state), and now one, two, three, four, five in Bermuda. Five in one day! That's makes 22 kills in all! Certainly she has earned a Gold Hero medal for punishing enemies of the state.

CHAPTER 20

Centro Tropical de Investigacion y Ensenanza (CTIE) lies in a sheltered valley, in a natural bowl, in the mountainous highlands of northern Costa Rica. The Center is the leading international agricultural graduate research institution in the world. Because research is its primary function, CTIE has a limited enrollment of 150 doctoral students, most from Central and South America. The results from its teaching, research and publications are critical to agriculture in developing nations and countries with crops such as sugar cane, bananas and coffee. Its core activities are funded primarily by contributions from Central and South American countries, although members of the European Union are also helpful. Officially, its multinational faculties of about 150 members are experts in such areas as tissue culture, plant genetics, and the development of disease resistant plant materials. Support staff brings the total number of faculty, students, and staff to about 500.

CTIE's Genetic Resource Center is funded by the French government. The German Technical Cooperation Agency established the Plant Germplasm Center. Honduras maintains refrigerated seed storage chambers of more than 1,200 cultivars of Arabica coffees, and 4,000 varieties of seeds. Brazil runs the Plant Biology Laboratory, Costa Rica the Latin American Forest Seed Bank, and the Swiss the Natural Resources Center. Peru funds the Tubers Research Laboratory. It conducts research on 5,000 varieties of Andean potatoes. Panama established the Infectious Tropical Disease Research Center. The United Kingdom built and maintains the Center's Research Library, and the European Union provided the funding for construction of graduate student housing. Each center and/or laboratory is staffed by experts from its respective sponsor-nation. Every year CTIE sends seed samples to the "Doomsday Vault" deep beneath the permafrost in Norway's artic region. The vault stores hundreds of thousands of seeds to preserve agricultural biodiversity in the event of disaster.

Less well known is the Cellular and Molecular Laboratory established by North Korea. Local operatives report the Koreans may have secondary rudimentary biology, hematology, and parasitological labs. And, perhaps, much more.

To prevent distractions from its teaching and research mission, CTIE is closed to visitors. The main entrance to the institute, and the back service entrance, are manned by armed guards twenty-four hours a day. Coffee plantations, medium-size farms, cane fields, and the rainforest provide yet another layer of isolation from curious outsiders. Further east – toward the Caribbean – are several foreign-owned commercial banana plantations. There are two large national rainforest parks in the same general area.

Just after 9:00 in the morning Jon and Kate leave the jungle. In the wooded forest there is less noise and animal chatter. Nothing seems out of place or threatening. Visibility is good. Two hundred yards after transitioning from the jungle they begin a steeper incline. Five hundred yards further the incline increases to 40 degrees. For the next two hours they increase their pace, seldom speaking. Their legs feel the incline.

Finally, a little after 11:00, they stop to rest and listen. It's quiet. A slight breeze gently moves through the trees. Grey clouds gather overhead. Jon kneels down and slips out of his rucksack. Kate does the same. While their pause for water, Kate verifies their position on her GPS. Jon takes the waterproof binoculars from his rucksack.

Kate says, "It should be dead ahead. How do you want to do this?"

"I'll have a look see," he answers, putting his rucksack and MP7 next to her pack.

"Stay in sight," she says.

They are 50 yards below the crest of the mountain. Maybe 75 yards. Jon covers the distance slowly and carefully in less than three minutes. Kate watches his progress. She loses sight of him in 30 yards because of the trees. Nearing the top of the mountain, he stays low to the ground. The sky is darkening for the usual afternoon showers. He stops to observe and listen. He looks behind him. He sees nothing. Then he starts out again, avoiding any sudden movements that might attract attention.

The mountain top is nearly flat and a 100 yards wide. He crawls to the other side of the mountain, staying low, and drops to the prone position. Spread out below him like a toy train village is the Institute. Leaning on his elbows he adjusts the binoculars under his boonie hat. He pushes the lower button on his left wrist. "Come on up," he says. "When you reach the top, I'm a hundred yards straight ahead. You can walk it. The coast is clear."

Kate picks up both packs and weapons and moves slowly, but still faster than Jon did.

"What do you think?" she says in a low voice, taking a deep breath, and flattening herself next to him. She had a heavy load to carry. Through the trees the Institute looks exactly like the images they previewed from the C.I.A. satellite recon photos. Jon has the fleeting thought that it is nice to have Kate near him. She has no such thoughts. She is all business.

Jon says, "The layouts the same. Oval track with buildings around it. Grass recreation fields in the center. Probably for soccer. Main gate at 9 o'clock. Service road behind buildings." He passes the binoculars.

She pushes the bonnie hat up on her forehead and adjusts the binoculars to her eyes. "Doesn't look too difficult." The white guardhouse is made of cement block, with large windows on four sides. There are two uniformed security guards visible inside, and one outside, but no barrier to entry or exit as in a physical gate. Two white security trucks are parked behind the guardhouse. On the trucks side panel is a large circular logo spelling out Centro Tropical de Investigacion y Ensenanza in green and white.

"Kalashnikovs," she says, studying the guards.

"Seems everybody in the world has AK-47s. Look down a little. Seven o'clock." She moves the binoculars slightly. After a moment Jon says, "See the pool? Probably the faculty club."

"Most likely," she agrees. She sweeps the binoculars back to her right. "Can't be sure of where the classrooms and laboratories are. I think the main dining facility is the building at the far end, 3 o'clock, halfway around the circle. Looks like people are on the way to an early lunch. Take a look."

She passes the binoculars. He readjusts them for width. "Looks like the labs are on the far side, directly across from us. People are coming out. Apparently headed to the dining hall, too. The two story building on the near side looks like the graduate dorm."

"What next?"

"Let's take turns observing. Then make a plan."

Kate says, "I'll go first."

"Fine," he says and passes the binoculars. "I'll take a nap. Then we can change places."

~ ~ ~ ~

An hour later the rain starts.

Suddenly jerking awake, Jon says, "Were you going to wake me or let me drown?" he rolls from his back to his side, wiping rain from his eyes.

"I was just waiting to see if you had the sense to come in out of the rain." The binoculars are fixed to her eyes. She holds a steady gaze.

Jon shields his eyes from the rain with his hand and looks up at her. "You're having way too much fun. What have you learned?"

"A lot."

"As in …?"

"The service road running from the guard station goes behind the buildings to the dining facility. On this side of the faculty club is a small circle of houses. Probably visiting faculty, or maybe full-time senior faculty."

"Significance?"

"I'll tell you in a minute." She put the glasses down and turns to him. "I think you are correct about classrooms or laboratories. Whether or not the target building has the laboratories we're interested in remains to be seen. Literally."

"What else?"

"I think you're right about the grad dorm."

"Is there more?"

"Yes, but that's pretty good for an hour. Don't you think?"

"What have you concluded?"

"Several things. I've observed people hurrying from one building to another, or to lunch. It's easy to distinguish faculty from students and vice versa."

"Faculty have umbrellas."

"Apparently. Here is my idea."

Jon moves closer and looks at her.

"Neither of us can get near that place dressed like this."

He says, "I don't think we ever planned to walk in there during the day, and meet people."

"That is precisely what we will need to do," she says.

"What are you suggesting?"

"I'm suggesting I go down there and locate the laboratory." She tilts her head slightly as she says this.

"And then what? Our mission is to locate the building, confirm the laboratory beneath it, and have H-bird paint it."

"Yes, but confirm we have the correct laboratory. And to verify they are making nasty stuff, we've got to see it."

"Go on."

"You remember the houses I mentioned?"

"Of course."

My observation of women students is that some wear jeans, some slacks, and a few all kinds of stuff. I can get away with wearing camo fatigue pants, but not the rest of this wardrobe. If the rain stops in time, I can slip down to the houses and borrow a top…a blouse, something to wear over the fatigues."

"Break into a house?"

"No, borrow something off a clothes line. Take a look," she says and hands him the binoculars.

"Even if you could do that, then what?" he says, focusing the binoculars on the houses. There are eight facing each other across a narrow blacktop road, and separated by chest-high hedges on three sides. All the houses have clothes lines in the back yard. Two houses have lines with clothes on them.

"Then I drop by the faculty club or pool or dorm and borrow a few books. I'll walk into that classroom building, hopefully locate the laboratory, and see what I can see."

Jon thinks about it. Pretty bold. Might work. "Think you can fit in?"

"Don't insult me. I don't look that old!" she protests.

"No, you don't," he admits.

"And I'm fluent in Spanish. Actually, my Argentine Spanish is flawless. Everyone knows Argentines speak the best Spanish."

"It might work," he says, warming to the idea. "With luck we could turn loose one of the robobees."

"Sounds like a plan to me." She grins and takes a robobee from her pack.

~ ~ ~ ~

Shortly after 3:00 the rain stops. The recreational fields are filling with people, both faculty and students. Jon watches. "Looks like everybody on the campus turns out for soccer in the afternoon."

"Let me see," Kate says. It looks like a regular event. There are hundreds of people on the fields. Maybe as many as 250. Four or five faculty/student teams are preparing to start. There is no common thread in the clothing of spectators. Women wear shorts, jeans, slacks, lab coats, and dresses. The men are more casual than the women, and many of them are going to play soccer at some point in the afternoon.

Kate and Jon start down the mountain, moving slowly. Frequently on their butts. When they are halfway down they stop. The rain helps with the humidity. But it is still high and both are feeling sweaty and sticky. While Kate strips off her parka, Jon rigs a battery for her ear bud. They are unsure how far it will carry not attached to the parka. She lays the parka and fatigue shirt on her pack. Beneath the shirt she wears a black T-shirt.

"I'll be watching," he says. "I'll try and call to make sure we can communicate."

She says, "I don't expect any problems. Unless I get caught swiping a top."

Jon ignores her comment. "This could be a good time. Looks like most of the campus are heading to the rec fields."

"After I find a top I'll look for some books. Then I'll head over to the classrooms. Maybe this robobee will come in handy." She stands up, hidden behind a large tree at her back, looking at Jon.

"Depending on how this works out, a good time to return may be after the soccer games when everybody heads to dinner."

"Maybe." As Kate turns and slowly heads down the mountainside, Jon keeps the binoculars next to him. It's probably 200 yards to the bottom, then a100 yards to the nearest house with a clothes line.

"Hey," he says, "can you hear?"

"I haven't moved very far."

"I can see that. I'm just checking."

Jon hates just sitting on his hands. Kate is moving agonizingly slowly. He decides to check in with Hummingbird and Navigator.

"H-bird, Firefly. Over."

"Go ahead Firefly. H-bird. Over."

"H-bird, what's your position. Over."

"A heck of a lot higher and further north. Over."

"Patch me into Navigator. Over."

Three seconds pass.

"Firefly, this is Navigator."

"Ah, we're in the make-it-up-as-you-go mode, Navigator. Can you see us? Over."

"Roger, Firefly. Looks like we will be of minimum help at the moment. Over."

"Roger that. Just wanted to give you a status report. Hang around. Firefly out."

Jon picks up the binoculars and searches for Kate. She is nearing the bottom. "Hey, can you hear me?"

"Weaker, but I can hear you."

"I don't see anyone. Nobody in the back yards."

"Okay."

The 100-yard buffer between the forest and the campus grounds is mostly waist-high grass and small brush. It is cut closer to yard height for the last 50-yards before reaching the first house.

"Stop!" Jon suddenly says. "Someone's coming out."

"I see them. Probably checking the clothes. You're fading."

A woman with a basket is inspecting the clothes line, feeling several articles of clothing on the line. The rain has soaked most things, but they are beginning to dry as the sun comes out again. The woman takes a few small items, but leaves others. She may have just gathered lingerie. She goes back inside the house.

Kate waits for five minutes to see if the woman will reappear. When she doesn't, Kate stands up and walks casually in the direction of the house. She is prepared to veer off if anyone comes out again.

No one does.

Kate stops near the rear of the first house, sheltered by the thick shoulder-high hedge. There are several possibilities on the clothes line, including three different button blouses, and a half dozen T-shirts. She had no clue about sizes. The blouses seem casual, but too formal for students. Something you'd wear with a skirt. Several of the T-shirts are white with a logo or graphic design on them. Not necessarily a good match-up for camo pants. There is a blue T-shirt and a dark green one. Green is the target. She kneels on one knee so her head is well below the hedge. She watches the house through breaks in hedge.

"Hey," she said to Jon, "see any movement in the house?"

"Negative."

"Here we go," she says. She stands up, squeezes through the hedge and walks to the clothes line. Quickly she takes the green shirt and returns to her position on the other side of the hedge and kneels down. She holds her breath. No one comes rushing out. Jon doesn't say anything. There is a small stand of trees behind her, 30 yards from the sidewalk that rings the campus. She waits for a few minutes and examines the steal. The front is plain. On the back is a graphic of an oil rig with the words Cidade de Angra dos Reis. Kate recognized the words as Portuguese and not Spanish. She pulls it over her head. It's too small and too tight. She takes it off. Looking around to make sure she is alone, she takes her bra and black T-shirt off. Then she put the green shirt back on. Still tight, but better. It is somewhat revealing, and still damp. She feels she has been in a wet T-shirt contest. But she reminds herself she is a university student in a Latin country. It will have to do.

She wraps her bra in the black t-shirt and stuffs the shirt in the hedge. Then she stands up, looks around, and heads for the stand of trees and nearby sidewalk.

"What's going on?" says an anxious Jon. He spots her walking on the other side of the hedge toward the inner campus.

"Everything's fine," she responds. "except we're going to lose communication soon. You're pretty weak."

"What?"

"Nothing."

The campus day is winding down. Classes and labs have concluded, and a large crowd is gathering on the soccer fields. She decides to go to the event with the flow of faculty, students and staff. Several male students give her unabashed looks and say "Hi." She smiles, says "Hi," and keeps moving. Some students cradle their books in their arms or carry them at their side. Others put their books in a backpack. Most backpacks are dropped on the thick grass, damp from the humidity and rain.

When the several teams take to the fields, the student crowd pushes closer to the sidelines and packs tightly in. Kate lingers behind. At kickoff, she bends down and picks up one thick textbook from an open backpack. She wipes it off on her T-shirt, and holds it to one side pretending to be interested in the game. She screams and yells with the crowd and then slowly eases away.

CHAPTER 21

The two story white concrete building is halfway around the circle, on the opposite side of the field from her. Kate slowly walks around the north end of the fields and back again to pass the building. She stops, pretending to look in the text book. No one pays any attention to her, or apparently thinks she is out of place. Next to the front entrance to the building is a small brass plate in Spanish and English: Cellular and Molecular Building. She skips up the several entrance stairs and pushes open the glass front door. A uniformed guard, sitting idly at the guard desk, looks blankly at her but doesn't speak. She smiles at him. He nods politely. She walks pass him as if looking for a classroom. All are empty. Everyone is on the recreation fields. There is an elevator at the end of a long corridor. Above the elevator door is B, 1, and 2. She reverses herself and briskly walks pass the guard again with a shrug, as if she just remembered something she needs to do. The guard is disinterested. She exits the building, and walks around the circular drive in route to the graduate dorms.

While Kate is carrying out her charade, Jon hides their gear behind a large tree facing uphill, away from the campus, and covers it with Kate's parka, fatigue shirt, and twigs and leafs. He sticks the Walther pistol in his waistband. Carefully he half walks and half slides downward through the wooded area. He hopes to reestablishing voice communications when he reaches the bottom. Unexpectedly, he hears her say: "Jon, if you can hear me, meet me behind the dorm. I've five minutes from there."

Jon works his way along the tree line to a point 20 yards behind the grad dorms, but still in the woods. He sees a female form walking midway between the dorm and the wooded area. As he gets nearer he recognized Kate. When her back is turned he closes to ten yards. "Hey," he says into his headset, "I'm in the bushes behind you." She looks around and, seeing no one, steps into the woods and follows his voice.

"Were you worried about me?" she asks, sitting down in front of him.

"Of course not. Why would I be?"

"I thought you were beginning to like me," she teases.

"I'm at work. What did you find out?"

She shakes her head. "I think the cellular and molecular building is our target."

"Good. Does it have a basement?"

"It has a basement, but I couldn't go there."

"Then how do you know?"

"The elevator has a B button."

"You don't sound like you're absolutely sure."

"Okay," she sighs, "I'm absolutely sure there is a basement level button on the elevator. Besides, I walked past a couple of other buildings, and none seemed to be a better candidate."

"We're going to have to do better than that," Jon says, sounding a tone of frustration.

"So we make a visit to be sure," she says confidently.

"If you're right, that's great. If you're wrong, we've got to find out tonight. So why don't you go back and walk around. Make the circle. I'll wait here. Now that we have communication again, if you run into any problems you can call me."

The soccer games are nearly over. Bystanders are beginning to gravitate toward the dining facility for the evening meal, filling the circular campus road with loud laughter and shouting. Kate approaches the woods 30 minutes later. Jon has moved. He emits a low whistle into his headset. She drifts into the wooded area and takes a knee. "I'm kind of hungry," she says as Jon joins her.

"Our supplies are stashed up the mountain. Sorry."

"You could have retrieved it while I was out walking."

"I didn't want to risk losing contact with you again."

"Let's get something to eat and wait for dark."

~ ~ ~ ~

Like most good plans, theirs is a simple one. Shortly after midnight they start down the mountain in darkness, moving slowly and carefully until they reach the graduate dorm. Only a few lights are on in the dorm; however, the major buildings around the campus circular road are well lighted.

Kate says, "Wait here. I want to retrieve my bra and T-shirt."

"I was just getting use to the braless thing," he jokes.

"Shut up," she hisses. "You're starting to sound like a chauvinist. It does not become you."

In ten minutes she is back. "What did you do with the green shirt?" Jon asks.

"What do you think? I put it back on the clothes line." Jon shakes his head.

They pause at the road, looking for late night students or security vehicles on patrol. After a few minutes they decide to walk directly across the fields. Should headlights appear they plan to drop to the ground and hope they have not been seen. If things really go south, they will pretend to be students making out. Latinos will understand.

The 11 p.m. to 7 a.m. guard is Luis Alejos. He is a skinny 22 years old, and looks all of 12. His uniform is ill fitting for his 5' 4" height and 115 pounds. The pistol on his belt seemly hangs from his waist to his knee. He is sitting at his desk reading a pulp fiction paperback. Kate knocks on the glass door. Alejos looks up, shakes his head from side to side and returns to his book. Kate knocks more urgently, and gives her best facial impression of please. He nods "no" again and ignores her. Kate continues knocking loudly and insistently. Giving up, Alejos puts the paperback down and leisurely walks to the door.

"Please," she says in a voice loud enough to be heard through the thick glass, "I left my notebook. I've got an exam tomorrow!" She places both hands over her heart as if pleading.

Alejos hesitates. It is absolutely against the rules to open the door after hours except for another guard. But what harm can come from helping a student? He's not guarding the national treasury. His mother would remind him to be respectful to women. So would his wife. He slowly nods his head, and reaches for the keys on his belt. The door is unlocked and Alejos opens it a few inches. Unexpectedly, Kate jerks it from his grasp. Jon flies through the door and tackles the stumbling guard, driving him to the floor on his back. He straddles the guard's chest and sticks the ugly Walther pistol in his face. Alejos is terrified and paralyzed. Jon hopes the guard doesn't wet his pants.

Kate quickly closes the door and relocks it. No one is outside or in sight. She walks over to the guard, who is disoriented, frightened and blinking his eyes rapidly. Quietly she says in fluent Spanish, "Try and be calm. Do what I tell you and everything will be fine. You understand?"

Alejos looks at her but doesn't speak.

She repeats slowly. "Do you understand?"

"Si," he says feebly, lips twitching. He is obviously frightened.

"Good. We're going to let you up now. Where are the security tapes?"

Alejos nods toward a door to the left of his guard desk. Jon holds his hand out. The guard sits up, finds the key on his key ring, and hands it to him. Jon walks to the guard desk and sits down. There are two chairs behind the desk. A clipboard and paperback novel are the only things on top of the desk. The clipboard has an hourly check list. Guards initials each hour of a shift. It occurs to Jon that a guard could initial all spaces at the end of a shift, not hourly. He opens the file drawers on both sides of the desk. He finds a dirty dust rag, a small flashlight, a few magazines, two paperbacks, black shoe polish and a shoe rag. No weapons. He gets up and walks the six steps to the door behind the desk and opens it. The room is no bigger than a hall closet. Two stacked rows of monitors line the wall; four monitors on the top shelf and four on the bottom one. Jon looks at the blinking lights on the control panel. He ejects the security tape and puts it in the small of his back. He'll dispose of it later. Then he throws four switches to turn the system off. He closes the door and returns to Kate and the guard. The three walk toward the far end of the hall, past classrooms, toward the elevator. It is controlled by a swipe card. The guard has one.

Kate pushes the button labeled "B". The elevator starts down. It is agonizingly slow. The guard stares at the floor. When the door smoothly opens, it is to a wide and brightly lighted corridor. Everything is glaring white. The floors, the walls, and the ceiling focus light on anyone getting out of the elevator. The security camera – were it working – would have clear photos of anyone exiting the elevator. There are several rooms on both side of the corridor, and a single door at the end of the hall. They slowly walk down the hall looking left and right. The only sound is the guard's squeaking shoes. As they walk, Kate translates in a whisper, so the guard cannot hear, the signs on each door: Molecular Diagnostic, Microbiology, Gene Amplification, and Histological Analysis.

All the laboratories have double pane windows. All are deserted. Dead security cameras follow the three as they walk slowly down the hallway. Each laboratory has a thick glass door with cypher locks and push button keypads. Looking thought the doors they see white lab coats hanging neatly along the wall. Nothing terribly unusual. At the end of the hall is a solid yellow door with a plaque on it. As they get closer, large black lettering stands out against the yellow background.

Jon pronounces aloud the top word: "we hum." Luis thinks he has heard some of the professor sound like that – not Spanish sounding words.

"What is that?" Kate whispers.

"Danger."

The second line is: JIN-EEP-GUHM-GI. "And this?" she asks nodding her head toward the words.

"'Do Not Enter.'"

"Korean?" she questions and looks at Jon.

"Uh-huh."

"Bingo," she says.

"Let's hope."

"Open it up," she loudly commands the guard in perfect Spanish.

Eyes wide, still struggling to cope, he softly says "I don't know the code."

Jon doesn't understand the words, but he understands the shrugged shoulders. He steps closer to the guard, and forcefully jams the pistol in his ear. He remembers the same scene from a few days earlier. It is a heavy weapon and probably painful to have pressed into an ear. But it is effective.

Stepping in front of the guard, Kate calmly and kindly says, "My friend has killed many men. Do you wish to be next?"

The guard's knees begin to instantly quiver and shake. A panic attack or worse is near. She worries he will collapse from a heart attack. "I swear I don't know the code – to any rooms!"

Kate speaks to Jon in Spanish. Of course he doesn't understand a word. But he knows the script. "Give him one minute," she sighs sadly, "to say a few Hail Mary's before you kill him." She nods her head in a yes motion. He follows her lead and nods "yes." Standing motionlessly, his eyes narrow, he focuses his glare like a laser on Luis. He looks outraged and evil and about to pounce. It has the desired chilling effect.

Tears are forming in the guard's eyes. "I don't know the code," he lamely repeats. "I have a family!" he pleads. "Mother of God!" he cries.

"I'm sorry." Kate says, shrugging. She turns the palms of both hands up as if to say there is nothing else I can do."

"Wait! Please!" Luis begs, finding his voice out of desperation. "The locks are weak…I know that…the striker plates are old and worn! We've had problems before. The rain. The humidity. There is a crowbar in the storage and shipping closet next to the elevator. I have a key to that room," he adds, hopefully.

"Give it to me," demands Kate.

The guard is so frightened he fumbles with the key ring, different from the one upstairs, spilling several keys. He removes a large master key and hands it to Kate. She hands it to Jon. "Opens the storage closet next to the elevator," she says in Spanish, pointing to the storage closet. Jon can figure out what she is saying. "He says there is a small prybar or crowbar (she says the word crowbar in English) in there that will break this lock."

Jon quickly goes to the closet and unlocks the door. He finds the light switch inside the door and turns the light on. Inside the cramped space are two metal boxes in the middle of the floor, and four stacked shelves. Various shaped containers are on the shelves. Probably cleaners and chemicals, supplies of all kinds, and replacement light bulbs. Mops lean against the wall. On the floor is a water hose, a pair of rubber boots, and what appears to be a tool box. On the second shelf is a hammer, large screwdriver and a small crowbar. He grabs the crowbar and hurries back to Kate and the guard. It is a simple task to jimmy the lock from the door frame and open the door.

There is a popping sound when the door opens. The laboratory is pressurized. It is also noticeably chilly in the lab. Probably 10 to 15 degrees cooler than outside or in the hallway. Fluorescent lights flood the laboratory. There are no shadows anywhere. And no windows. Hazmat-like "space" suits and hoods hang inside the door on metal pegs. Each suit has a self-contained air supply. Further along the wall are white lab coats on pegs. Long tables with electronic microscopes dominate what is obviously a clean room. Every table has at least two built-in stainless steel sinks. Several have three sinks. At the end of each table is a large box of green latex gloves. A second box contains white face masks. Kate and Jon's eyes adjust to the bright light quickly.

There are two chambers branching off the restricted laboratory room. Both have large glass windows. The chamber at the left contains two giant metal chambers. They have no clue as to its purpose. A large white metal chamber looms in the second chamber. The three approach the second chamber with caution. Massive rubber seals and airlocks guard against leaks. The box is probably 15 feet long, 15 feet wide and 10 feet high. Next to its airlock door is an enclosed shower with glass panels and door.

"Refrigerated environmental vault," Jon says in a low voice, his back to the guard. He walks to it.

Kate motions the guard to the far side of the room, has him kneel down and cross his ankles. He is too panicked to present a problem. As she does so, she looks at the chamber and comments to Jon, "Locking pins on the door." She stops at the side of the chamber and reads safety instructions, printed in Spanish and Korean. Jon peers through the multi-pane viewing window. "All the control circuits are here," she softly calls out. "Dials and switches control temperature, air circulation, and humidity. It's a Level 3 chamber."

"Is that good?"

"Actually, no. The number is an international biosafety rating. The most secure and highest rating is Level 4. You remember that from our brief, right?"

"Yeah. But Level 3 was okay."

"Depends on what's in there. What's this warning sign in Korean say?"

Jon goes to her side. "Two scientists must be present at all times."

Kate nods. "The door to our right. Bet it leads to another lab where whatever is here is worked on."

"Worked on?"

"Maybe experimented with. Let's look."

Motioning the guard to come with them, they enter the adjoining laboratory. It resembles other laboratories, with large stainless steel sinks and biohazard suits. But it also contains laboratory equipment unfamiliar to them, except for several centrifuges. "How about those big pots or kettles?" Jon asks.

"Fermenters. To incubate bacteria. I'm absolutely positive."

They return to refrigerated vault.

"What do you think is in the vault" Jon asks.

"I'd bet freeze-dried bad stuff."

"Like freeze-dried anthrax spores?"

"Wouldn't surprise me."

"Then this is what we're looking for," Jon says, unmoving from the window. He studies what he can see, attempting to make sense of it. Inside the chamber are four large rectangular-shaped glass containers. The containers are constructed so two pairs of hands in thick rubber gloves can work remotely. It is a hint of a disciplined and risky science.

Kate joins him at the viewing window. "How can we tell?"

"One of us could suit up and go inside." They look at each other trying to think of an alternative, remembering their pre-mission contamination briefing.

"Not an exciting thought. Anyway, what's to see?" she asks. Moments pass. "But how do we tell what's inside the containers if we don't go in?"

"Look," he says tapping the window with his index finger, "the vials in the container on the left side of the room have labels. In the metal trays. See what I'm talking about?"

"Yeah. L1, L2 in that one, and L3 and L4 in the second container." The tall glass vials labeled L1 and L2 have a red cap. L3 and L4 are green capped vials. Four columns and ten red-capped vials in each column. Forty. Four columns and ten green-capped vials are forty more.

The two rectangular containers on the right side of the room are labeled with the prefix N: N1, N2, N3, N4, N5, and N6. There are thirty yellow capped N1-N3 vials, and thirty N4-N6 blue capped ones. Sixty in all.

They give a puzzled look to each other. "Could be anything," she whispers, watching the guard for any reaction. He is mute. Frozen by fear. "But freeze-dried spores, refrigerated, is the most likely answer," she says.

"Whatever it is, there's a lot of it." Jon keeps his back to the guard and half-mouths, half-whispers, his words. "But we can't verify anything. The numbers are meaningless."

Time is suspended as they rack their brains. Things only go as planned until the plan gets going. Then the nature of the unanticipated, the unseen, and the unknown kicks in. Surgeons often say to patients "we'll know more once we get in." Not always an encouraging perspective. Jon's life experience leads him to believe that many of the good things he experienced have needed a lot of luck. Maybe on the order of 20 percent. Sometimes more. He forces himself to relax, putting his mind in search mode.

Kate interrupts Jon's thinking. "Look at the last container on the right. The "N" container."

"Okay," he says, shifting his focus back through the glass. "What?"

"Look on the other side of the blue vials."

"What am I looking for?"

"Do you see the VX?"

Jon strains to see past the blue vials. "Yeah, blacks caps. I didn't see them before."

"Why would they be out of sequence? And why the Roman Numerals?"

"I don't have a clue. Did you take Latin?"

"Two years in high school. You?"

"One year in college. Is that 50 plus 10? Sixty? Or maybe 5 plus 10 for 15?"

"No. Fifteen is XV."

"Okay, so I made a "C" in Latin I."

This is going no place, and not very fast. Time freezes. Kate and Jon freeze. A minute passes. Then Jon leans close to Kate's ear and whispers. "Okay, forget the Latin. Ask the guard what the metal boxes on the shipping room floor are for." Jon turns to look at the guard, who is thinking a decision on his fate has been made, and the worse is about to happen. His eyes blink rapidly and his hands tremble slightly.

Kate closes the distance between herself and the guard. "What are the metal boxes in the storage closet used for?" she asks in Spanish.

"I don't know," he nervously assures her. "I'm just a guard. Mother of God, don't let him kill me!" he prays aloud.

She bends down, putting her eyes directly in front of his, her nose four inches away. Quietly she says, "Luis, I'm trying to help you. I don't want him to kill you. But I promise he will if you don't help me!"

She hears the guard swallows hard. It is loud enough for Jon to hear. "All I know – I swear it on my mother's grave – is the doctors put things in them and they are carried away." He closes his eyes and breaths heavily.

Kate knows there is little to be gained from further terrorizing the guard. "Carried away by whom?" she softly asks, thinking she should have said by who so she didn't seem too educated.

"They are bad people," he says, opening his eyes and beginning to hyperventilate. "I know that. I don't know what is in the boxes, but I know bad people come for them."

"How do you know they are bad?"

"There is talk. They have been seen before. They are desperate men."

"Why do you think so?"

"I have heard them talk. They are from Guatemala. The leader is a sicario."

Kate turns to Jon, who has been listening but not understanding. Her voice is barely a murmur. "The guard says the pick-up people are from Guatemala, and their leader is a hit man."

Jon raises his eyebrows. "The plot thickens," he says.

"You can bet they are taking this stuff across the river to Nicaragua."

Jon cuts his eyes to look at the guard. "Did he say that?"

"No. You have to understand, Costa Rica and Panama are pretty stable. Guatemala is a murderous place, and Nicaragua is right up there with them in terms of corruption. The people moving this stuff probably think they are transporting drugs."

"And thanks to U.S. consumers," comments Jon, "the drug business out of Central America is booming."

"The wholesale price of cocaine is climbing."

"Probably $12,000 a kilo."

Luis can't hear what is being said, but he hopes it is in his favor. His heart is racing – he can count the beats in his throat – and he has started to sweat again.

Kate turns back toward the guard. "How often do they come?"

"Not much. I forget," he stammers. "Every few weeks. Maybe once a month. I'm not sure."

"Do you know when they are coming again?"

"Tonight. I mean this morning." He slurs his words. "I am to put the boxes outside the delivery door at 2 a.m."

Kate turns and steps closer to Jon. She translates in hushed tones. They both look at their watches. Thirty minutes.

"Guess we need to look inside the boxes," Jon says.

Kate motions for the guard to walk out of the room in front of them. Jon takes the video security tape from behind the back of his pants and throws it on the floor. The door to the laboratory he closes out of habit. It doesn't close completely, so the air lock will leak. No matter. That is the least of his concerns. Jon quickly walks to the closet door near the elevator. It was self-locking. Jon fishes around in his pocket for the key and opens it.

In Spanish, Kate says to the guard, "On your knees. Cross your ankles, put your hands behind your head. Do not move."

Jon slides the first box out of the closet without difficulty. It slides easily enough on the basement tile floor. He guesses it weighs 50 pounds. It is secured by a pin like a bolt and nut. No lock, just unscrew the nut. It is screwed tightly and requires substantial effort to loosen and remove. He pauses as he considered whether or not he needs to put on gloves. Or a mask.

"What are you waiting for?" she asks.

"Maybe you want to step back a little," he suggests.

She does. The guard stays where he is.

Jon frees the pin and flips three hinges – not unlike on a trunk – and slowly opens the lid. A cloud of smoke pours out, causing Jon to step back. Dry ice. Carefully padded in dry ice are several dozen frozen vials with blue and green caps. They are separated by heavy packing partitions. Blue capped vials on the left and green capped vials on the right. L4 (green) and N2 (blue).

Jon slides the second box into the corridor. It is secured in the same manner as the first. The vials are packed and padded in dry ice the same way, but have yellow and red caps. And the black capped vials of VX. Closing and relocking the containers, Jon says to Kate, "Tell the guard to take these to the delivery door."

The two trips to and from the delivery door – with Jon as guard – take nearly 20 minutes. Luis is sweating heavily, probably as much from fear as exhaustion. Accompanying the guard provides Jon plenty of time to think.

Jon says, "I'll call Wells."

~ ~ ~ ~

Thirty minutes before the scheduled pick-up Wells and Jon connect. Luis is lying face down on the cool floor. Kate holds the pistol on him. "We've got a situation," Jon says. "We think we have found the bioweapons laboratory, but we can't verify what it contains, and we're running out of time."

"Why not?" Wells doesn't sound pleased. "What's the problem?"

"The stuff is in a refrigerated environmental chamber – a fortified area in the basement– and we can't tell what it is?"

"Someone knows what's in the chamber," Wells says, sounding irritated. "Aren't there indications of what's inside? Names of things in Spanish or Korean?"

"There are lots of frozen vials of something. They are labeled, but no names. Maybe it means something to you."

"Tell me what you have."

"Just numbers and letters. Lima 1, Lima 2, Lima 3, and Lima 4."

"Lima 1 through Lima 4," Wells repeats.

"November 1 through November 6."

"Copy."

"And Victor X-ray."

"Just Victor X-ray? No number?"

"Affirmative. The vials are like fat glass test tubes. And they are refrigerated. There is a lot of the stuff packed in dried ice, and time is short."

"What do you mean, 'time is short?'"

"There is a scheduled pick-up for all the above."

"What time?

"About thirty minutes from now."

231

"We're on it."

Jon has never been good at waiting. "The timing is bad," he says to Kate.

"What do you want to do about it?"

~ ~ ~ ~

The use of poisons and toxins for bio warfare has been around for thousands of years. Armies in ancient times contaminated drinking water or dipped their weapons in some kind of filth or plant poison. Historians suspected Cleopatra of using toxic potions on her prisoners. In the late 1930s until the mid-1940s Japan produced biological weapons. Some of their tests were on prisoners of war. The U.S. was interested in biological warfare since the early 1940s. In 1944 the Army established a plant in Indiana to produce anthrax spore flurry for potential use in bombs. Winston Churchill, fearful the Germans might use germ warfare, requested 500,000 anthrax munitions from the United States. For roughly 20 years - 1949 to 1969 - Dugway Proving Ground in Utah was the U.S.'s center for biological warfare testing. More recently, the Iraqi used Mustard and Nerve gas against Iran and the Kurdish civilians. It was widely known Libya stockpiled chemical weapons for decades. And Amazon Indians still dip their arrows in plant and animal poisons to bring down a prey.

Years after World War II ended, the Russians and the U.S. were in a race to build offensive weapons of a biological nature. It was President Nixon who stopped the U. S. program. Several years later the Biological and Toxin Weapons Convention was signed. The Convention prohibited the production of germs of war. Unknown to the U.S., the Soviet Union secretly continued its research and production. Much of the work was performed in the name of science at the Institute of Molecular Biology in Siberia. In fact, Russia has a long history of developing and deploying chemical and biological weapons. Surrounded by secrecy, Soviet scientists developed codes for research with pathogens. And it was the Russians who covertly provided North Korea with knowledge of deadly bioweapons.

Wells goes to work, with the help of Soperton, and every person in the SOUTHCOM conference room. All seats are filled, and every person is in direct contact via secure drop lines to their offices and sources. They can also monitor intercom conversation between the drone and the operatives in the field. All data bases – military and civilian, public, private, foreign, domestic, and classified – from every source – are interrogated. Wells calls Cadbury's chief of the World Geopolitical Analytics section. The answer is found in less than 11 minutes. Six other sources report within 20 minutes, corroborating the information.

The Russians secret code identified bacteria with the prefix "L". L1 is the plague. L2 is tularemia. L3 is brucellosis and L4 is anthrax. The "N" prefix was used to identify viruses. N1 is smallpox. N2 is Ebola and N3 is Marburg; all are Hemorrhagic fevers. VX has a double meaning. The V in microbiology means transferring DNA fragments from one cell to another. But the V in VX is the code for nerve gas. Currently, U.S. troops in the Middle East are trained and equipped to deal with a nerve gas attack.

"Firefly, Navigator."

"Firefly. Go."

Wells yanks his tie off and drops his coat on the floor. "It's a nightmare," he begins, looking at the sheet of paper in his hands, and abruptly dispensing with standard operating radio procedures.

Kate is cheek to cheek with Jon, leaning against him to hear what is being said.

Wells continues. "No time for a microbiology lessons. We think you have the most hazardous and dangerous chemical and biological agents known."

Kate hears Wells. She looks at Jon. All that comes to Jon's mind is a time-delaying question. "Like what?"

Wells answers. "Like viruses and bacteria and nerve agents."

"So VX is…?"

"Nerve gas," answers Wells. "We think you have uncovered a pit of deadly agents like Smallpox, Ebola, Marburg, Botulism, and Anthrax."

"Suggestions?" says Jon.

"We're going hot immediately. Acknowledge."

"We've got a few details to handle first. Over." Jon reverts to standard radio procedure.

"Be more specific."

"There is a scheduled pickup of the supplies anytime now."

In difficult circumstances there always comes a moment – commonly referred to by business types as the "tipping point" – when the right decision can save the day, and a poor decision can cause events to spiral out of control. The stomach-churning tipping point had arrived.

"You've got to stop it," Wells says, as calmly and firmly as he can.

"We've got a problem," Jon says. He looks at his watch. He looks at Kate and the guard. He looks at his watch again. "What's your ETA for the Calvary?"

Wells leans sideways and huddles with Burke, who in turn looks to Whitfield. Whitfield heard the question and has already put the question to his people. Burke says, "What do you think, Lucas?"

"One plus 15. More likely 1 plus 30."

Wells considers his words carefully, watching for a reaction from Burke and Whitfield. Then he keys his mike and says, "Ninety minutes."

"Standby, Navigator," replies Jon. "What do you think?" he says to Kate.

"I think Level 3 wasn't enough."

Jon is not amused. "Try and be a little more helpful."

"Three obvious points. One: what level of risk are we willing to accept? Two: if we engage the bad guys we are badly outgunned – and outmanned. Three: we would have a better change if we had our MP7s."

"Okay, here's the deal," says Jon. "We can't stop the pickup, so we won't. And we've got to accept the risk of being here when our troops get here. That's that."

"And the guard?"

"Wells doesn't like to leave fingerprints or take prisoners, but I'm not of the mind to make the guard collateral damage. And just to refresh your memory, killing civilians in any conflict is a war crime."

"So…"

"So the guard will give us away at the pickup. Maybe not intentionality, but his nerves are shot. He's on the verge of a breakdown. The pick-up guys will instantly know something is amiss."

"We have to meet them?"

"Not we. You. You have to be the guard."

"What?" Her face shows instant skepticism.

"You and the guard are about the same size. You speak Spanish. Make up a story and open the door. You can pull it off."

Luis Alejos lies as flat against the concrete floor as possible. If he could, he'd crawl into it. He is not shivering, but he is mentally blank with fear. Jon taps him on the head with the barrel of his pistol and motions for him to get up. Together they return to the supply room. Using hand gestures and pointing with the weapon, Jon successfully communicates to Luis to remove his uniform. He then motions for the guard to sit on the floor. He holds the gun momentarily to his lips to indicate silence. Luis understands.

As Kate changes clothes, Jon judges the results. "The pants look okay. Shirts a little snug."

"I can't wear his shoes."

"Your boots are fine. Here, put the gun belt on." She pulls the belt as tightly around her waist as she can.

Jon thinks she can pull it off. Should things go badly, he will be close by and at least get a few shots off. As Kate buttons up the shirt, Jon calls Wells. "Navigator, Firefly. Over."

"Go Firefly."

"We've got a plan. Is H-bird going to paint the target? Over."

In the drone overhead, Major Berrien cuts in. "Firefly, this is H-bird. Can do. Suggestions?"

"H-bird, let me get back to you. Just hang around. Over."

"Roger. H-bird standing by," says the pilot. Jon thinks she has a calm voice. That helps to keep everything on an even keel. Lower register voice. Not excited. Flat. Sounds mid-western. Chicago. He's like to meet her after this adventure.

~ ~ ~ ~

In R2, Wells, Soperton, Burke and Whitfield huddle. The rest of the core team is in the SOUTHCOM Conference Room. Admiral Jake Lamar is the ranking person present, and has followed events minute by minute. Wells drains his fourth cup of coffee. "Admiral," he says, "General Burke and General Whitfield agree with Mr. Soperton and me to proceed. Do you agree?"

"I agree we should proceed at quickly as possible."

General Burke says, "Jake, I think we have no choice. I think the ball is in General Whitfield's court, but it is important we all agree."

"Certainly, General," replies the Admiral. "What do you recommend, Lucas?"

"I have alerted the strike crew, Admiral. Armament is being loaded as we speak."

"What have you and your team decided?"

"We are modifying and loading two GBU-39/Bs. The 39/B is the weapon of choice for hardened structures. The bombs can penetrate six feet of reinforced concrete, so should easily reach the basement. Usually each bomb weighs 285 pounds, but we are modifying each to carry 300 pounds. The first bomb is loaded with 150 pounds of explosives and 135 pounds of phosphorus as an incendiary. The second has a reverse loading, that is, 135 pounds of explosive and 150 pounds of phosphorus. The incendiary will destroy everything in the building."

"What your ETD?"

"Within the hour, Admiral."

~ ~ ~ ~

The pick-up is scheduled at 2 a.m., in about fifteen minutes. Even if the launch of the aircraft is done quickly, and all goes well, it can't deliver until an hour after the shipment leaves. Most likely 3:30 a.m. or later. Time is the most pressing concern.

Luis is sitting on the floor in his undershirt and shorts, legs crossed, silent. He doesn't understand what is going on, but fear has nonetheless sharpened he senses. He begins to make deals with God in exchange for his life. He stares at the floor. Jon is standing nearby with his Walther in hand, pointed at the floor.

Two a.m. comes and goes. Nothing.

CHAPTER 22

Twenty-nine year old Captain James Newton wasn't born when the F-15 went into service. But he was a focused kid, and never lost sight of his goal to fly. In time, after college and a great deal of military training, he realized his dream of becoming a fighter pilot. It took more years of study and training, but he eventually mastered the F-15C Strike Eagle. One reason he liked the aircraft so much was because it was just him and the plane. He was master of his own fate. No crew to worry about. No one to be responsible for other than himself. No back-seater to judge or comment on his flying skill.

Following more training and more flight time, Newton transitioned to the F-15Es. The E series had dozens of improvement over the earlier models, but C pilots loved the Fighter Data Link – Fiddle – best of all. It provided them with a graphic picture on the Fiddle display.

At 1:35 a.m. the call came. Thirty minutes later, Newton straps on the sleek $100-million, two-person, F-15SE Silent Eagle. The canopy is closed and locked. He sits awaiting clearances and listening to his own breathing inside his helmet. It is slow and measured. For some reason he didn't expect to get the call for a flight. Or, for that matter, any flight out of the continental United States with a bombing mission. He scans the glowing instrument panel for the hundredth time. He compares the plane's clock with his wristwatch: 0207 local. He is tired because the day has been long.

Riding behind Newton is thirty-four year old Major Franklin Gilmer ("Bama"), the GIB (Guy in the back). As the weapon systems operator, he is very much focused on the aircraft's sensors and systems. There is no world outside his world or external to his seat in the rear cockpit. Strictly speaking the flight is not a combat operation. Nevertheless, Gilmer is comforted by the special radar-absorbent coating that makes the craft stealthy and safer from an enemy. Gilmer grew up in Ozark, Alabama, fell in love with Sandra from Mountain Brook, and graduated from the University of Ala-by-god-bama. He was a second string wide receiver on a team with 14 national championships. The University produced 40 general officers and he hoped, one day, to be another one. As a student in AFROTC, he decided early a flying career was his goal. Unfortunately, he couldn't pass the rigid eye exam for pilots. So he rides in back, the next best thing. There was never any question in his mind about flying. He loves it. Sex runs a distant second compared to being in the air. Snug in the womb of the cramped backseat gives him a warm and protected feeling. He particularly likes flying at night, the glow of the instruments, and the feeling of power at his fingertips. He doesn't anticipate missing the target.

Pre-flight mission planning takes longer than usual. The weather en route and at the target looks good. Round trip is 2,389.243 miles. Estimated time to target is 41 minutes, at a speed of Mach 2.5+ (1,650 mph). Conformed fuel tanks and external fuel tanks give the F-15SE - Silent Eagle - a range of approximately 2,400 miles. That presents a problem. So, instead of external tanks, the aircraft will rely on in-flight refueling on the return leg. That's always a bit dicey in the middle of the night. Total payload consists of three SDBs (Small Diameter Bombs). The Silent Eagle could carry up to eight GBU-39 SDBs, but the brass thinks two will be enough, with one in reserve.

Even with the aid of computers, Newton and Gilmer like to hand check the math on all aspects of the flight. The Silent Eagle has a rate of climb of 50,000 feet per minute. They plan to bomb from that height if everything works out. The Silent Eagle will be like a Ghost Eagle to anyone on the ground. To conserve fuel Newton won't "light the fires" until he has take-off clearance.

Newton is ready to go, and has been since he got the phone call. As a fighter-pilot with exceptional flying ability, waiting on the ground is not his long suit. He tries to divert his attention from the waiting by various games. He closes his eyes and points to or touches every instrument and every control. Then he checks to make sure he is correct. He always is. Lowering his heart rate is another game, and a matter of concentration. He guesses what his pulse is and then checks it. He is rarely wrong because he can hear his pulse in his ears. He doesn't particularly like night flight, although he is equally competent day or night. The worse part of night flight is the absence of visual landmarks. And night in-flight refueling. There is nothing to see, anyway, because his head is "in the cockpit" all the time – or "in the helmet" all the time. He hates training in flight simulators and wearing a virtual reality helmet. It makes him nauseous about 10 percent of the time. In many ways modern flying only resembles flying when taking off or landing. Most of all he hates waiting for a clearance.

"What's the hold up?" questions an equally impatient Gilmer on the interphone. Gilmer always experiences an eerie and uneasy calm waiting for a clearance. It's like nerves before a kick-off is how he describes it.

Gilmer's unexpected voice stirs Newton's consciousness. "Got me."

It is quiet again. Then: "How many astronauts do you think we have?" says Gilmer.

"What?"

"Take a guess."

"Jesus H. Christ. From the beginning of the program?"

"Sure."

"Hundreds I suppose. Why?"

"How many actually got in space?"

"What's your point?"

"I'm just thinking we're going the way of the astronauts. Know what I mean?"

"Not exactly." Gilmer sounds slightly annoyed.

"They trained hundreds of astronauts. Maybe five percent got in space after years and years of study and training."

"Okay."

"I'm just saying we have hundreds – thousands – of pilots, and the future is pilotless drones. Combat pilots are going to be like astronauts. Not much future demand."

"I'm not thinking about it."

"Well, think about the structural changes drones will have on the Air Force. I mean we wouldn't have need for Search and Rescue missions anymore. A drone goes down, just push a button and it's destroyed. No pilot to rescue."

"Make your point," Newton says, not in the mood for idle chatter.

"I'm just saying do you have any idea of the impact of drones on our future?"

"Last time I heard, we're buying 2,400 F-35s, for God's sake. They are going to need by pilots for the rest of my career. And yours."

"Bet you a Bud that number will be cut," he responds.

The time-killing banter is interrupted by a soft crackle in their earphones: "SAM One Two, MacDill." The call sign SAM stands for Special Air Mission. One Two may or may not signify it is the twelfth such mission in a specific period of time.

"SAM One Two," responds an eager-to-go Newton. He and Gilmer have their game-faces on.

"Sam One-Two cleared to runway two-two. Wind one eight zero at four. Altimeter two niner, niner four. Flight pattern restrictions lifted. You are cleared for immediate takeoff. Over."

"Sam One Two. Roger." Newton gives a thumb's up to the ground crew and starts the engines. The chocks are pulled. The airman on the tarmac points with his light sticks to the taxiway, and Newton nudges the throttle forward. In minutes the aircraft is at the end of the active runway, and ready for immediate takeoff. As Newton lines up on the runway centerline he says, "Ready to roll, Bama?"

"Roll Tide, Villanova." For the next 41 minutes there will be no chit-chat.

The F-15SE blasts down the runway, roaring into the night sky at a steep angle. It's a smooth climbout. Newton keys the mike: "Sam One-Two, wheels up at zero two, two one."

"Roger Sam One-Two. MacDill out."

~ ~ ~ ~

General Burke, General Whitfield, Adrian Soperton, and Bob Wells return to the SOUTHCOM Conference Room. Everyone is present and fully awake. Some are standing and others sitting. They are in agreement about the plan of action, but will remain in or close to the conference room until the operation is complete. Gallons of coffee and dozens of sandwiches are consumed. Alternative courses of action are discussed should tactical situations change.

General Whitfield quietly makes an announcement: "Airborne at 0221."

Burke asks, "What's the ETA?"

"0302, General."

Wells steps away from the table and keys the microphone on his headset. "Firefly, Navigator."

"Go ahead Navigator."

"Calvary ETA is 0302."

"Roger. 0302."

"H-bird," says Wells, "did you copy?"

"Roger that. 0302," says the mid-western sounding voice from R2.

~ ~ ~ ~

The delivery door buzzer sounds shortly after 2:15 a.m. Kate and Jon freeze in place. They wait. The buzzer sounds three more times, each time longer and impatiently. Jon nods at Kate, and takes the safety off the Walter pistol. Kate goes to the door and slowly unlocks it, saying in Spanish as she does, "Hold on." Then she pushes it open.

"Who are you?" says a gruff voice when the door is fully opened. "Where is Luis?" He stares at Kate, looks quickly at those behind him. He peers around Kate as if expecting Luis to appear.

Jon can't see the voice, but imagines the speaker as a violent mercenary with an untrimmed beard and stringy dirty hair. He hears feet shuffling.

"Luis got sick. I'm the relief," Kate says, her voice flat and under control. "I was told to expect a pick-up at two. If that's you, you're late."

"Why haven't I seen you before or been told about you?" he asks suspiciously.

"Are you here on the weekends?"

"What does that mean?"

"I'm work at the pool Sunday afternoons. And at the library on Saturdays. You ever been in a library?"

"You making fun of me, bitch?"

"I'm telling you when and where I work. That's all. If you want to see me, that's where I am. Unless I'm called to fill in. Like tonight." She puts her hands on her hips.

The hit man looks hard at her for a moment, evaluating her and the situation. "Maybe I'll just do that. Get out of the way." He waves his hand and three equally unkempt rogues push past Kate to get the metal boxes. The containers are a mere half-dozen steps from Jon's position. If he steps out from behind the wall, the men will be ten feet from him – targets at point blank range. He is confident he can take out the voice and a couple more, although he doesn't know the number of men. Kate should be able to get another one, he thinks. Two men, their weapons left outside the door, secure the first box to the back of the third man, and then the sicario and the other man lash the second box to the second man. "Let's go," he says to the three. As the men file out, the leader stops in front of Kate. "Maybe I'll come to the pool. I'll bet you turn a lot of heads," he says with a smug grin on his face.

"I'm not swimming," she says defiantly. "I'm a guard." She puts her right hand on the holstered pistol. He grins when she does.

"When I come back, you better be on guard." He slaps her on the butt and laughs as he goes out the door.

When Jon hears the door slam and the bolt secure the lock, he steps out. "Good job," he says to Kate. She is taking Luis' shirt off as she goes to retrieve her clothes.

"They're a motley bunch of Macho jerks," she says. "There was another one, or maybe two, outside the door. I couldn't tell." She struggles to get the pants off over her boots.

Jon looks at his watch: 2:27. He pushes the top button on his watch. Nothing. Kate pulls on her one leg of her fatigues, and hops toward Jon pulling on the other pants leg. He goes to the back of the building and carefully opens the door. The men are gone. The coast is clear. "H-bird. Firefly."

"Firefly, H-bird. Go."

"H-bird. How many bodies left this location?"

"Firefly, on your screen. Looks like six."

"H-bird. Let's keep an eye on 'em. Over."

"Roger that, Firefly."

"H-bird, patch me to Navigator."

"Navigator here."

"We're out of here in five minutes. Did I tell you the building is two stories, and the stuff is in the basement?"

"We got it."

Twenty-two minutes! "H-bird standing by for your signal to "paint" the target?"

"Roger that," says Wells. "What is your estimate of collateral damage? Do you have any hostages? Over."

"Zero collateral damage. The area is deserted. We're out of here. Acknowledge."

"Roger, Firefly. I got your back," says Wells.

"Watch my front, too," replies Jon.

"Navigator and H-bird standing by."

Back inside the building, Jon sees Kate has given the guard his clothes and is waiting for him to finish dressing. "Give me his shirt," Jon says. "And his gun and holster belt. And one shoe. Does he have any matches?"

"What?"

"We need to hurry up, Kate. The train has left the station." Jon drops the gun belt and shoe to the floor. Kate gets a cigarette lighter from Luis – thankfully he smokes - and hands it to Jon. He sets the shirt tail on fire, and then stamps it out on the floor. He picks it up and tucks it, the shoe, and holster belt with gun beneath his arm.

"Let's get out of here," he says, as they head for the basement delivery door.

Once outside they stop on the darken service road. Jon calls Wells again to say they are clear of the building. He says they will find a place to observe the strike and confirm when the building is destroyed. He tells Kate to take Luis behind the dining facility and wait for him there. "If you have any problems," he tells her, "shoot him. This is not the time to screw up. I'll join up with you after I get our stuff."

As soon as they head off, Jon hears Wells call H-bird with instructions to "paint the target". Good. He carefully creeps to the side of the building, clinging to the shadows, and drops Luis' shoe. Twenty feet further he drops Luis' gun belt and pistol. Another ten feet further, and closer to the building, he drops Luis' partly burned shirt. Near the front of the building he drops into the grass to watch for security cars, foot patrols, or anything else moving. All is quiet. No patrol cars. Nobody on foot. He jumps up and sprints across the recreation fields toward the graduate dorm.

Kate and Luis walk at an accelerated pace on the service road. In ten minutes they arrive near the front of a dimly lit dining facility. The few lights on inside the building indicate cooks are doing what cooks do a couple of hours before breakfast. Kate and the guard leave the blacktop road and cautiously sneak behind the building. They stop in the woods adjacent to the loading dock and wait.

Meanwhile, Jon encounters no one as he sprints across the campus. A lone light spills onto the grass from two student windows in the graduate dorm, both on the second floor. He hurries up the mountain to retrieve the rucksack and weapons. So far, so good. He puts on his pack and slings the weapons and other pack over his left shoulder. He doesn't want to push his luck so he stays in the woods as he heads toward the dining facility.

Kate has her back to Luis watching for Jon. He had been subdued by fear. Unknown to Kate, Luis has now recovered slightly from the rigors of the night. He is a new father of two young children, and trying to muster the courage to atone for his cowardly inactions. He worries what his superiors will think of him, and how he will be remembered by his family. He convinces himself that everyone has to die eventually, and he must die honorably. In this frame of mind he rushes Kate from behind.

The sudden sound of shuffling feet and rustling leaves alerts Kate to Luis' mad dash. She turns quickly as he dives for her. She instinctively delivers a smashing blow to Luis's nose, shattering it. Had she struck him with the palm of her hand in an upward outstretched motion, she could have driven cartilage and bone into his brain, potentially killing him. Instead, because he dove at her, she hit him across the nose in a downward motion, breaking it, and causing blood to squirt everywhere. The blow hurts like hell. Luis' brave resolve is broken as quickly as his nose. Kate is irritated.

Minutes later Jon arrives and begins searching for Kate and the guard. Their intercom communication has locked up. Kate whistles once. Jon looks but does not see her until she steps out of the woods and into view. He hurries to her, and finds Luis sitting on the ground holding his head in his hands. No one speaks. Jon shines his red lens flashlight on

Luis. Even in the dark, Luis' swollen face is a mess. There is dried blood on his bare chest. Luis doesn't look at him.

Jon motions to Kate with a head nod, and they step a half dozen paces away. "Did he run into a building?"

"In a manner of speaking." She holds up her hand. "This building."

"Well, what should we do with the little guy?"

"What would Wells say?"

"Kill him."

"You can't be serious!" she says passionately.

"Half serious. Remember what I told you about Wells. Sometimes there are not a lot of easy choices. Sometimes if you work for the devil you become the devil."

"What does that mean?"

"It means take no prisoners."

"Maybe you should ask Wells," she suggests.

"I don't need to ask Wells," he says defensively. "I'll handle it. Let's not get into a moral debate."

"You'll handle it? Or I'll handle it for you?" She feels her temper rising.

"Take it easy," he says calmly. "I am not dismissing your concerns. I'm just saying we need to stay focused."

"Sorry. I'm a bit on edge - and furious. The little bastard deceived me, and pissed me off."

"Ballsy of him. Remind me not to do the same." He smiles at her, and decides to leave it at that. He doesn't know if she sees him smile. "Here is what I would appreciate your doing."

~ ~ ~ ~

Kate approaches Luis, shinning the red beam from Jon's flashlight on his face. He looks up, squinting into the subdued light. The blood has dried, but the swelling is bloating his face around his broken nose, under his eyes, and around his cheek bones.

"Stand up," she commands. As he does so, Jon walks behind him. Luis can see the outline of a pistol in his hand. Her voice is deliberately threatening. "You're a problem. He's going to kill you."

Luis opens his mouth, but only air comes out. He struggles to breath, unable to speak.

"I could stop him," she says in a matter of fact tone, "but you attacked me. I really don't give a mierda about you."

Finding his voice, he whimpers, "I'm sorry. Really, really, sorry."

"Why should I care?"

"My family…my wife and children, my mother…they need me!"

Kate is silent, as if re-considering his plea. "I am a Catholic. I will have to live with this sin. Unless…"

"I am Catholic, too!" he says hopefully, he voice suddenly stronger. "Unless what?"

"Unless you do exactly what I tell you," she says in a controlled monotone.

"Any…any…anything," Luis stammers, fear gripping him.

"Give me your wallet." She holds out her left hand.

Luis keeps his wallet in the side pocket of his pants, and retrieves it quickly. It is a cheap and thin wallet, with only a few small bills and three plastic cards: a national identity card, a driver's license, and an employee card. She removes the driver's license and puts it in her pocket. "I'll keep your driver's license. If you do exactly as I tell you, we may spare your life. If you do not, we will know it. And I promise we will come back here, hunt you down like the dog you are, and kill your family. Every one of them. Do you understand me?"

"Yes, I will do what you say. God bless you, senorita." He falls to his knees and makes the sign of the cross.

"I will always know where to find you. You understand?"

"Si, claro, senorita."

"Say it."

"You will know where to find me."

"Sit down," Kate says gruffly as Jon steps next to her, facing Luis.

"Any minute now, the building you work in will explode. Everything in it will be destroyed in a giant fire. You will hear it. You will see it. When it is no more, you will go back – before anyone arrives – and wander around the flaming ruins in a daze. Your survival will be called a miracle. People will say you did not die because Saint Barbara protected you. And she asked God to spare your life. You will become famous. Newspapers and television will want to know your story. Unfortunately, you will not know what happened. You will have no memory. One moment you were going about your duties, and the next moment, you found yourself outside the building, your shirt and gun belt torn from your body, your face bleeding. And missing a shoe. You don't know what happened. Can you do that?"

At 2:53 a.m. the sleeping campus is shaken awake by a huge explosion. Flames leap four stories into the air, and an angry black cloud climbs hundreds of feet into the night sky. Pieces of cement, building materials, classroom and lab equipment, rocks and dirt fall from the air, landing within a hundred feet of the former building. Three hundred yards distant, Kate shoves Luis off toward the brightly burning building. "Remember what I told you, Luis."

"God as my witness, I will. Thank you Senorita." He limps into the night with one shoe on and one shoe off.

Jon is confident Wells has a video ringside seat of the strike. Probably a lot better than he and Kate's. Nevertheless, he keys the upper button on his watch. "H-bird. Firefly. Over."

"This is H-bird. Go."

"H-bird and Navigator. Ground level BDA is a perfect 10. Over."

"Firefly. Navigator. H-bird BDA confirms your observation. Time to get moving."

"No rest for the weary, Navigator. Out."

Berrien and her drone co-pilot sneak a look at each other and smile. Newton and Gilmer head for an in-flight refueling.

~ ~ ~ ~

The night air cools as they hurry along the jungle river path in the darkness. The river is a major tributary of the San Juan River. The San Juan is several miles north of their position, and flows west to east. The river is the focal point of a long standing border dispute between Costa Rica and Nicaragua. Jon is wearing the NVG and leading the way. Still, their progress is slower than walking speed. For the following person a quarter moon doesn't help much, and every few minutes low clouds block the light entirely. It's like a blind person following a sighted one. The night gets darker, it begins to drizzle, and the night vision goggles blur. Finally, they reach the intersection of the tributary and the San Juan. They turn to the right.

"Firefly, H-bird. You're on track."

"How far?" Jon asks.

"About two mile, Firefly."

"Roger." Jon doesn't think the male voice sounds as comforting as the woman's voice.

He hears a crashing sound behind him and turns ready to engage. It's Kate. She has stumbled in the darkness, but jumps up. "I've fine," she says. He stops and drops to his knees. "Let's dump the non-essentials." He removes the water from his rucksack and tosses them to Kate. "Drink up. Dump the rest." Kate drops the water to the ground, and slips out of her rucksack. She unzips pockets of her first-aid kit looking for noncritical items: iodine wipes, burn cream, safety pins, eye pads, tongue depressors, hand sanitizer, and eye wash solution. She stuffs these for disposal in her rucksack. Jon tosses her the remaining MREs from his rucksack, then puts the medical supplies and extra ammo clips in his rucksack. He rechecks to make sure his MP7 has hollow points loaded, and puts the armor piercing in the rucksack. The knife is in his calf pocket. He smashes the robobees with the butt of his MP7. Should have done this before now, he thinks. He gets to his feet, picks up Kate's now disposable rucksack, with throw-a-ways, and slips and slides his way through the wet and muddy underbrush to the river bank. In short order he finds enough loose sand and river rocks to fill the pack. With a mighty heave he throws the rucksack and his jungle knife into the fast moving river. The knife sinks instantly, but the rucksack doesn't sink completely before attracting the attention of large river caiman, the South American crocodile.

"Your turn to take the lead," Jon says, climbing up the bank and handing her the NVG. Back on the path, relieved of one pack, and lightening the remaining one, Jon feels refreshed. He shifts his thinking to tactical matters. Kate picks up the pace. Jon is calculating the time to overtake their prey, and then the best way to engage them. His thighs are beginning to burn. He ignores whether it's cramps or fatigue. Kate doesn't complain. He wonders if she is experiencing any problems but doesn't want to ask her. Being the follower is harder than being in the lead. He refocuses. He hopes to kill everyone in the group ahead as quickly as possible. By then Wells will have instructions about what to do with the deadly cargo.

Kate is also planning ahead. She wonders about the containers. Are they bullet proof? If the vials are punctured, will the steady wind from the river carry the spores down river? How far? Dr. Screven said anthrax – carried on the wind - could kill for more than a mile. Maybe further. He also said some lethal gases spread by the wind could kill up to forty-five miles away.

"Firefly, H-Bird."

"Go ahead H-bird."

"Targets gone, Firefly. Over."

Kate stops and turns, pulling her NVG off. Three steps later Jon is next to her. He holds his wrist up so both can view the dim light of the mini screen. In R2 and the Conference Room, Wells, Soperton and others are also looking at the screen.

"How is this possible?" ask Jon. "Navigator?"

"Navigator here. We're checking for a malfunction. Standby." Berrien turns around in her pilot seat and looks at Wells. He turns around to look at anyone that might have a notion of what has happened. Berrien says, "We have no indication of a malfunction, sir."

"You're absolutely sure?" Wells asks.

"All the equipment is working fine…we just don't have a thermal image anymore."

Wells says to everyone in the room, "What would explain that?"

"They are being shielded by something would be my guess," answers Berrien.

Everyone in R2, plus all the resources of those in the Conference Room, swings into action in search of an answer. General Burke orders controllers in R1 to feed the satellite images on Screen 7 (Nicaragua, Costa Rica and Panama) into the Conference Room.

"Firefly, Navigator."

"This is Firefly. Over."

"Firefly, we are working on it. Take a break and we'll get back to you in a minute or two," says Wells. "Over."

"Firefly standing by."

Kate and Jon sit down in the middle of the path to wait. "Any ideas?" asks Kate.

"Not really."

"Something is blocking the camera. Unless it's a malfunction."

Minutes pass in silence.

Jon says, "I didn't know you were Catholic."

"I'm not. Do you have any of those energy bars left?"

He reaches into his parka jacket for the last one, and hands it to her. "What was that about a Saint Barbara? Did you make that up?"

"Of course not." She unwraps the bar, and slips the wrapper into her pocket.

"How did you come up with that bit of trivia?"

"Well, my mother was a Catholic before becoming a Methodist. Not a lot of Catholics in Kansas when I was growing up. Anyway, she read me stories about all the saints. Not all the saints, but a kid's book about saints."

"So there really is a saint named Barbara?" Jon says.

"There are thousands of saints. I just happen to remember Barbara because she is one of the "Fourteen Holy Helpers", and my uncle was a fireman in Kansas."

"Holy Helpers, saints and fireman. I don't get the connection."

"Saint Barbara is the patron saint of fireman. And against explosions, fire from above, and patron to a handful of other occupations."

"Firemen have a Patron saint?"

"You betcha."

"Is there a Patron saint for our kind?"

"I don't know. What's "our kind"? There's a Patron saint of miners. I remember that. And for protection from lightening. And against sudden death." Kate gets up on one knee. "Wish we had kept some water."

"Firefly, Navigator. Over."

"About time," Jon says to Kate. "Go ahead, Navigator."

"We think we have the answer," Wells begins. "Here's the short of it. We think those in front of you have dropped into a river cave. Over."

"Can you give me something more specific, Navigator?"

"Be advised there are a number of river caves from your position to the ocean. We think they are holed up in one. This is why we can't get an image. Why and for how long is anyone's guess. Over."

"Okay. We'll think about it and get back to you. Out."

~ ~ ~ ~

The Conference Room players are milling around, watching the H-bird live feed, listening to the exchanges with the team and Wells, discussing the operation, and drinking more coffee. Wells and Soperton are quietly talking in a corner. "This is beginning to have more drama than I expected - or need," says Soperton, glancing around the room. "Are you worried?"

"This new development has me concerned," he admits. "Why are the bad guys holed up in a cave? Are they waiting for daylight? Are the bioweapons being stashed in the cave? How are Jon and Kate going to destroy the bad stuff without confronting the bad guys? Yea, I'm worried."

"Know what worries me most?" Soperton asks.

"What?"

"Getting them out of there."

As Wells and Soperton turn to refill their coffee cups, General Burke enters the room in the company of another Army four-star. Before anyone can call the room to attention, Burke says in a voice louder than normal, "As you were, gentlemen. May I suggest we return to our seats for urgent news?"

When everyone is settled, Burke –still standing – says, "Some of you may know General Henry Hart commands N.S.A. General Hart and I are old friends," Burke says gently. There are tired smiles of tension around the table.

Soperton and Wells have had their professional ups and downs with N.S.A. Covertly, with C.I.A. assistance, N.S.A. made "electronic modification" to cell phones sold by ICE (Corporativo del Instituto Costanicense de Electricidad), the telephone company, in Costa Rica, and NICACEL (Telefonia Celular de Nicaragua). The modified circuitry (extra circuits) in the phones allows N.S.A. to monitor calls into and out of Costa Rica and Nicaragua to its two million square foot installation at Ft. Meade. The calls are digitally recorded and passed to NTOC – N.S.A.'s Operations Center. Intelligence officers listen to suspect communications in real time, 24/7, and report the information to the Center within 10 minutes. The accuracy of the data is confirmed within 20 minutes.

Hart stands. He has intense eyes hidden behind wire frame glasses, and thin lips. For a man in his mid-fifties, he is extremely fit. His appearance projects self-discipline. "We've been following this – that is to say – N.S.A. and the Agency have been working together on this operation. I have new information."

Wells and Soperton are anxious.

"About 15 minutes ago," Hart says, clearing his throat, "we intercepted, translated and transcribed cell phone traffic between the group in Nicaragua, and the one in Costa Rica."

Oh shit! thinks Wells.

~ ~ ~ ~

Beside the swift river, and beneath the rain forest floor, are many undiscovered limestone caves. Scientists believe the caves were created millions of years ago when volcanic action fractured the terrain and moved rivers, creating underground rivers. Some of the caves are so cavernous that large buildings would easily fit inside them. Many run for miles and miles. The entrances to the caves are hidden by thick vegetation that grows in the jungle. Because of the remoteness of northern Costa Rica, few people have ever been in one of the caves.

The plan is for H-bird to tell Jon when they are several hundred yards from where the bad guys disappeared. At that point Jon and Kate will get off the path and work their way toward the cave. Moving through the dense jungle will be painfully slow, but safer than taking the path. Jon believes the most direct way is often the most deadly one. He learned that lesson from an uncle who was a dog handler (Labrador Retriever) in Viet Nam. Shortly past 5 a.m. H-bird makes contact and reports one thermal image about 200 meters ahead. Slightly to the right side of the path. Jon and Kate hunker down in the dense overgrowth to talk.

"They have a watchout," Jon suggests. "We need to take him out. I'll take the NVG and make the approach to the target. You stay here."

"I could go with you a little further," she whispers. The night is lighter than a few hours ago, but still definitely dark.

"One person is quieter than two." Pause. "Why do they have a guard out? What don't we know?" He eases the rucksack to the ground, removes his holster and puts the pistol in his waistband. He hands Kate the flashlight, confirms he has his knife and picks up the MP7.

"What do you want me to do?"

"One thing at a time. If this doesn't go well, remember the emergency exit plan. Retrace your steps to the campus, and make your way to Point A. One way or another, Wells will come for you."

"Sure you don't want me to come along?"

"This could take a while. When I want you to join me, H-bird will make a low pass over this position. Then come up the path until we meet."

Jon stands up, adjusts the NVG, and slips into the night. He hopes the NVG batteries hold up. To conserve power he has been careful to turn the NVG off when not in use. Kate watches him quickly disappear. She doesn't like waiting any more than most military personnel. Or Type A personalities. She ponders standing or sitting. Which provides more protection from would-be predators – like big snakes? Being in the jungle in the daytime is one thing. But being alone in the eerie jungle at night is something very different. Nighttime hunters wait silently. She plants a "protector" next to her. A large insect bounces off her shoulder, and joins other insects fluttering in the damp foliage. It gives her the willies. Finding a wide spot in the path, she rechecks the suppressor on the MP7 and clicks the safety off. Soon Jon will be too far away to hear if she fires her weapon. She knows talking softly registers about 50 decibels (dB). Hand clapping registers about 65 dB, and firing a standard rifle about 165 dB. In a closed room, firing a suppressor equipped MP7 would sound loud. But outside a person with good hearing would not hear it from 50 feet away.

~ ~ ~ ~

"The Nicaragua controllers are in contact with the group in Costa Rica," continues General Hart. He pauses with his encrypted cell phone to his ear. "Apparently they are planning to rendezvous today at 1200 hours."

Wells impatiently jumps in. "Excuse me, General. Are you sure that is our group?"

"We believe so," Hart replies. "As you and Mr. Soperton know, we have intercepted their cell phones, and been listening for a considerable time."

Soperton speaks up. "I don't suppose you know where the rendezvous is to take place."

"They have been careful to disguise locations. Learning a rendezvous time has been a breakthrough. I wish I could tell you more." Hart sits down, but General Burke remains standing in place.

"We don't have a lot of time," Burke says. "I suspect we need to discuss alternative courses of action – maybe involving special ops – now that the situation has changed."

"With respect, general," says Soperton, "this may not be an option."

Wells scribbles a note to Soperton while he is talking and slides it in front of him: The hell you say! I'm not hanging my people out to dry!!!

"Let me continue," says Soperton. "Clearly our joint effort relies on close cooperation with the military. But the intent has always been to get support from the military, not direct, ground level, boots-on-the-ground action. I'll have to talk with Washington." Soperton writes on Wells note and returns it: we need to think this through.

~ ~ ~ ~

"H-bird, Firefly. Over."

"Go Firefly. Over."

"H-bird, how far am I from the target. Over?"

There is a short pause. "Firefly, H-bird. Five hundred meters. Over."

"Roger, H-bird. I will not acknowledge any further transmissions until the target is eliminated. But I have my ears on. Keep me advised. Over."

"Copy, Firefly. Target is stationary and solitary."

Jon does not respond. Instead he studies the image on his wrist screen. Five hundred yards is a long way when moving quietly. He would prefer to use the MP7 when closer. That would be an easy kill. But he doesn't know how far the man is from the entrance to the cave. Would the shot be heard? What if the man is wearing a Kevlar vest? Would he have to get a head shot? Would the target have time to alert the others? The better solution is to use the knife. Jon decides to out flank the target by moving inland, through the dense jungle, at a faster pace. His plan is to make a move before first light, when the target should be less alert. Being physically fit may give Jon an edge. Surprise is the biggest advantage. Jon's superior upper body strength should tip the scales in his favor. At least he hopes so.

Back in the SOUTHCOM Conference Room, the discussion of an alternative plan is proceeding. At the same time, nearly everyone keeps watch on the screen. It is a drama about to unfold, although there is nothing much to see. Marine general Clay McIntosh muses, "It's kind of like watching one of those California highway patrol chases on the television. It's boring as hell, but hard to not watch."

Several of the brass look at McIntosh, but no one comments. Others nod agreement. The focus is on the next step. Special Operations Admiral Lamar is speaking softly. "I can get a SEAL team in there, but I understand Mr. Soperton doesn't think we can get approval. Correct Mr. Soperton?"

"We have two challenges, Admiral. At least two." Soperton holds up his index finger. "First, how do we carry out this operation and not invade the sovereign territory of Costa Rica?" He adds his middle finger to his index finger, forming the V sign: "Second, who can do what, and by when?"

Wells speaks up. "May I suggest challenges three and four? What do we do with the recovered bioweapons? And how do we safely extract our people?"

~ ~ ~ ~

"Firefly, H-bird. Target is still stationary. Looks like you are 25 meters out."

Jon stops. He considers whether it is better to creep up on the target from a standing position or low crawl until he can pounce. The thought of low crawling where Anaconda and Bushmasters may be low crawling is not appealing. The boa thing runs through his mind. On the other hand, he leaned long ago that when he is not afraid he is less effective. Fear is a motivator. He pauses to form a mental image of the target, to visualize the attack. Then he moves ahead at a dead-slow pace. He looks at the video feed. Only he and the target show any thermal image. Unfortunately, Anacondas are cold blooded.

"Firefly. You are 10 meters from target. Target is stationary."

Jon takes a half step and stops. He covers the video feed watch with its Velcro strap. The NVG provide vision excellent. He studies the target. The man is standing and unmoving, his right arm hanging loosely at his side. In his hand is an AK-47. Creeping slowly closer, the answer becomes clear. The man is leaning against a tree. Whether or not he is asleep, Jon can't tell. Six quick steps and he could be on him. Haste is not a good idea.

In SOUTHCOM, all eyes are watching Jon approach his prey. Marine general Clay is glued to the screen. He fidgets. "The guy is a hell of a stalker," he says. He feels an adrenal rush just watching the video feed.

Jon would prefer attacking the man from behind. That's not possible. Objective one: prevent any outcry or alarm that could alert others. In all likelihood he is not more than 25 yards from the cave. Any outcry would bring quick trouble. That leads to the second objective: kill quickly. Stabbing the man in the heart, through clothing and whatever else he may be wearing, is out. Eliminating any sound means slitting the man's throat, quickly and deeply. Jon looks in all directions in case someone else is approaching. He listens for any sound. If the man is disturbed or hears anything, he is most likely to look around at chest-high level. Jon decides to go in low. The devil may be in the details, but so is success. Quietly he eases the MP7 to the ground, and adjusts his NVG. He thumbs open the knife and silently slumps to the ground. He low crawls a few inches and stops. All is quiet. He is not "skull-dragging", as the Army might say, but he is low. He crawls another few inches. He can see the man's legs and feet, and the tip of the AK-47. The jungle provides good cover. He creeps silently forward another few inches. The man coughs once, but doesn't move his feet. Jon stops. Waits. A bead of sweat drops into his left eye. He ignores it.

Now!

With the speed of a Cobra strike, Jon springs upward on the man, pinning him to the tree, hand clapped over his mouth. The man opens his eyes widely in shock and terror. He raises his right arm - finger on the trigger guard of the AK-47 but not on the trigger – to strike Jon. Jon blocks it with his left forearm. The panicked man attempts to claw Jon with his left arm but, like a boxer, Jon blocks his efforts with his right forearm and uses the razor sharp knife. The man is quickly overcome and powerless. Jon draws the blade quickly across his neck, severing the carotid arteries and silencing the vocal cords. He holds the man tightly against the tree until the body goes limp. The AK-47 drops to the wet jungle floor silently, at the foot of the tree. Jon eases the limp and lifeless body to the ground.

In SOUTHCOM the silence in the room is broken when Army general Randolph exclaims, "Jesus! That guy must be a Ranger!"

"Air Force ROTC," says Wells quietly.

"And The Farm," whispers Soperton to Wells, who turns to him and adds, "just trying to teach a little humility."

~ ~ ~ ~

In the predawn light, H-bird swoops down over Kate's position like a giant bird. She gives a sigh of relief, and moves as fast as she can on the path. Meanwhile, beside the body, Jon wishes he were closer to the river to wash the blood from his arms and chest. On second thought that would probably make him a target for hungry predators. The jungle ground is saturated with moisture. An early morning dew clings to the plants and vegetation. He scoops up a handful of damp soil and rubs it on his chest and sleeves. Pulling several large leaves from surrounding bushes, he washes his hands. Halfway satisfied, he retrieves his NVG and searches the body for anything useful. Nothing. No cell phone or pistol. The AK-47 is loaded. The man carried one extra clip. That's it. Jon retrieves his NP7, and stealthfully retraces his steps in search of the path to wait for Kate. He removes the Velcro strip from the video monitor.

"H-bird, Firefly. I'm back up."

"Roger Firefly. Two is on the move. Two hundred meters from you and closing. Should be visible on your screen anytime now."

Jon waits. He is anxious the dead man's relief will arrive before she does, or the morning sun will expose them. He'd rather not take on the remaining five guys without her. Minutes pass. He keeps a close watch on the video feed. When she is nearly on him, he whistles softly to her.

"You okay?" she asks, hurrying to him as best she can in the dark, and looking him over. She sees spots on the front of his parka, but it is too difficult to tell if it is dirt, mud, or something else.

"One down. Five to go," he says.

Kate transfers the rucksack to Jon. He puts it on the ground, and motions for her to huddle near it.

She asks, "Any idea where the entrance to the cave is?"

"Not yet," he answers. "But we must be close. I'd like to find it before sun up."

"Firefly, H-bird. Company approaching from the river. Two targets. Do you see them?"

Jon holds his wrist up. Kate moves shoulder to shoulder to look. The greenish image shows two figures to their right, maybe thirty meters distant. They are in single file, and clearly visible.

"We're in luck," Jon says quietly. "Game on." He feels his pulse kick up a beat. "H-bird, can you mark the spot they came from?"

"Firefly. Pretty close. Over."

"H-bird, keep it handy," He leans into Kate's ear. "Make sure your suppressor is good to go. Let's move apart. I'll go right. You stay here. You get the second target. I'll get the first. You know what these things sound like, so don't fire until I fire. Got it?"

Kate moves the MP7 selector switch to semiautomatic. "Got it."

~ ~ ~ ~

In SOUTHCOM conversations suddenly cease. All eyes are glued to the images on the screen. There is no sound, and no one is sipping coffee. They watch intently as the two figures seem to converse and then separate, one moving to the right of the other and slightly ahead, but not in front.

"Hate to see them separate like that," someone says.

"Probably a good idea at this point," ventures Marine Major General McIntosh.

The two intended targets plod along in single file, unaware of their perilous situation. The early morning is approaching, and a light sky is minutes away. The light is behind Jon and Kate and into the eyes of the

262

targets, if they happened to look to their left. They appear, however, to be focused on the jungle floor in front of them.

Jon selects full-automatic and grips the MP7 firmly. Nothing fancy. He intends to fire a short burst across the target's chest from a standing position. He expects the target to be lightly clothed, as was the first target. It's too hot and humid for body armor. Plus the weight. Kate has lost sight of Jon but, for safety reasons, will fire directly in front of her position, and to the left of center. She re-checks the suppressor. She sees movement through the bushes, and hears the targets approach before seeing them.

The instant Kate hears the soft and rapid puff-puff-puff-puff-puff of Jon's weapon she see her target, closer than she thought he might be. She immediately opens fire, squeezing repeatedly and thinking, too late, she should have selected full-automatic. Her target fires wildly in her direction, perhaps because he had his finger on the trigger, or maybe it was a death grip. She watches him, as if in slow motion, fall backward firing most rounds into the air. Unexpectedly, she feels a painful burning sensation in her leg and falls to the jungle floor as if someone has kicked her leg out from under her.

Jon rushes to his target to confirm he is dead, or to finish the job if he is not. He feels sure he has three hits in the man's chest. He knows where Kate's target went down and he rushes to confirm the kill or finish that job. He is mildly surprised he reached the target before her. The target is obviously finished, but he observes Kate's pattern was not as tight as his. He looks for her.

"Where are you, Kate," he says in a voice louder than a whisper.

"Over here," comes the response. "I'm hit." The voice is calm but urgent.

Jon is at her side quickly. She is bleeding heavily from her upper thigh. "H-bird, one down. Keep an eye on our back." He knows the others in the cave must have heard the AK-47 firing.

"H-bird. Copy."

"Damn!" says Wells, in the SOUTHCOM Conference room. Several of the brass pick up their drop phones and make calls. Aides come to their sides for instructions.

Jon kneels next to Kate. The sun is not fully up, so in the dim light he takes out his red lens flashlight. He shines it on her leg. She is bleeding, but blood is not spurting. So an artery hasn't been hit. He doesn't think it hit a bone because the main bone should be more central in her leg, but he could be wrong. Still, he needs to move quickly. A high percentage of combat deaths are attributable to "bleeding out". He elevates her leg by putting the heel of her boot in his crotch. He considers using her belt as a tourniquet. Balancing the flashlight on a small nearby stick he opens the rucksack next to her, he finds the medical kit and empties it on the ground. Lots of supplies: forceps, shears, tweezers, topical antibiotic and antiseptic wipes, camouflage combat bandages, and sterile gloves. Because they combined their first aid kits, there are also two morphine kits, two UVL pens, two foil pouches, and two white packages, and other items of potential use. He picks up the scissors and cuts off Kate's right pant leg above the wound. It is impossible to wipe enough blood away to see what he is doing. And the red lens makes matters look worse. He remembers their first aid lecture at Hilton Head. ABCs of first aid. She's talking, so A is fine. She's breathing and has a strong pulse. Check off B. Bleeding is the problem. He reaches around to the back of her leg. Her fatigues are soaked. She flinches. With his other hand he sorts through the supplies. The damn bleeding!

"How's it look?" she asks, unable to sit up.

"Like a mess. Do you hurt?"

"Take a wild guess."

"Don't be a smart ass." He opens a white package of CELOX and pours half the granules directly into the wound. He turns her leg and pours the other half on the exit wound. Close to the Celox package is a green foil pouch, with the label written in Korean: STOP BLEED COMBAT GAUZE. He shines his light on the label's smaller letters. Celox is a hemostatic agent, it reads, for traumatic bleeding. Something about the gauze being impregnated with Chitosan. Beneath that, in even smaller letters, he reads it is recommended by COTCCC (Committee on Tactical Combat Casualty Care). Give me a break, he thinks, an ad for a Committee? Eight inches from green pouch is a small box labeled Morphine Tarirate Syrettes – ½ gr. He opens the kit. It contains four sterile syrettes. Each one of the tubes has a hypodermic needle with a single dose of morphine. He removes the cap and pushes the needle half its length into her thigh, then squeezes the tube. Kate doesn't react. He puts the used needle in her parka collar, then secures the gauze bandage around her leg with combat adhesive tape, and applies pressure. He uses both hands. Five minutes. Hold pressure for five minutes was emphasized in the lecture. In his hurry to help Kate, he totally forgets to use the Latex gloves.

"It really stings," Kate says, trying to push herself up on her elbows and look at the leg. "AK-47?"

"Sounded like it." He looks more closely at the entrance wound. It is a small hole. He can't see the back clearly, but it's an exit wound. It is slightly lower and further to the right of her thigh. The bullet must have tumbled, and done a lot of damage before exiting. "Just lean back and relax." He can give her another shot of morphine in two hours. Two hours. That's a long way in the future.

"Is there an exit wound?"

"Yeah. I don't think it hit anything important."

"It hit my leg!" She rolls her eyes and puts her head back. "That's important! Hurts like being passed over for promotion," she says, trying to make light of the situation.

Jon is impressed with her sense of humor, but worried about the wound.

"Did you use the Morphine?"

"May I be the medic?" he scolds her.

"I'll let you know," she says, feeling herself slipping into darkness. "Hope it kicks in soon."

"Any time now," he encourages her. "It's going to be alright." With his free hand he holds and reads the instructions on the container. It says the morphine will take effect in 20 to 30 minutes. The instructions also caution motor control may be impaired with the morphine. He translates that to mean she won't be walking soon. Not good.

~ ~ ~ ~

Meanwhile, in the SOUTHCOM conference room, the calm is more reflective of professional military training than lack of concern. N.S.A.'s General Hart is the first to speak. His remarks are intended for everyone, but he addresses them to General Burke. "We've intercepted another cell phone conversation."

Hushed conversations with aides and each other stop, and calls on drop lines and secure PDAs cease.

"The people in the Costa Rican believe they are being pursued by a rival gang intent on stealing drugs. They think three have been killed. The people in Nicaragua are telling them to hold on. When they arrive they will hunt the druggies down and kill them."

General Burke addresses his comments broadly, but looks at Soperton and Wells while he speaks. "We need a good plan, and pretty damn fast. Let's do it!"

Wells stands in place and says, "May I suggest we first get our people out. Let's see what each service can bring to the table on that. Secondly, we'll need to deal with the bad guys. Lastly, we'll need to decide what to do to remove or neutralize the bioweapons. Unless someone has a better idea, may I suggest the Navy and Marines meet in that corner"–he points to his left–"the Army next to General Burke and the Air Force in the middle with General Whitfield. The rest of us with Admiral Lamar and Admiral Haralson next to me. Let's regroup in 15."

~ ~ ~ ~

Jon is sure the people in the cave heard the AK-47. The last thing he wants is to be in a position unable to fend them off. "Kate," he says, lips next to her ear, "everything is going to be okay. Just lie still and let me make sure we're safe. Then we'll get out of here."

"Don't be gone long," she mumbles, slurring her words.

"Ten minutes. Tops." He thinks she is concealed in the underbrush. And she will be behind him, so he moves in the direction of the cave entrance. He puts her out of his mind to focus. Dawn is minutes away. "H-bird, anything?"

"Firefly, you're close. Entrance seems to be on the river side. Down from your position. Over."

"H-bird. Hard to tell. I may see what an entrance could be." Studying the vegetation, it appears ground cover and bushes have been disturbed. There isn't a path, but someone has carelessly brushed aside and broken small limbs and stepped on large ferns. Jon drops to the jungle floor, intending to creep forward. Unexpectedly, he is startled to hear a loud roar like a waterfall, except it is growing louder. He can't identify the direction or the source of the sound. The dawn light darkens as thousands of bats pour out of the sky, seemingly from all directions, wings flapping loudly, returning to their cave dwelling.

Jon stands up in a crouched position and hurries back in the direction of Kate. "Navigator, Firefly. You on the channel?"

"Navigator here," Wells answers. "We're working on the problem," he says, "and we want you to get on the other side of the river. Over."

"What?! You know what's in the river?"

"Roger. It's still the best option. Over."

"Roger," he responds, wondering what other options could have been considered. Moments later he is at Kate's side. She hasn't moved. She opens her eyes when he takes her hand and says, "How you doing?" Her response is incoherent, like someone who has had too much to drink. He puts her hand down and checks her leg. It doesn't seem any different. The blood has caked beneath the bandage. He doesn't feel any leaks.

"H-bird, Firefly. You in on this plan? Over."

"That's a rog. I have a good place for you to cross. It's about a mile from your position. Get back on the river path. Head east. To the right. I'll tell you when you arrive. Over."

"Thanks, I know east from west. Out."

Jon puts on the rucksack, then rolls Kate to her stomach, lifts her to chest and quickly ducks under her, draping her over his shoulders in the fireman's carry. Her left leg and left arm join together at his chest, and he secures her with his left arm and hand. Her injured right leg hangs down. He slings her MP7 upside down on his left shoulder, and carries his MP7 in his right hand.

~ ~ ~ ~

At SOUTHCOM a plan is coming together. Admiral Jake Lamar says, "I think we have a workable plan. General McIntosh has Phase One.

Marine General McIntosh leans back in his chair. In a clear, confident voice he says, "The Pentagon and the Joint Chiefs are communicating with their counterparts in Costa Rica, requesting permission for one helicopter, one time, to conduct a navigation exercise - mostly over the Western Caribbean, but touching a small part of Northeast Costa Rica. It will be an unarmed helicopter conducting a navigational training exercise. While we wait for permission, I am having a team put together in Panama to execute the recovery, if that's what we decide."

"Thank you," says Soperton.

Admiral Lamar speaks again. "Woody and I agree we will need some help from the Navy and Marines. And the Army."

Vice Admiral Woody Haralson decides to participate in the planning. He slowly gets to his feet, looking grim. "We have a covert platform in the general area." He stops.

Silence.

Wells waits, then says, "Can you give us a little more detail, Admiral?"

Haralson looks to Jake Lamar, who gives a slight nod.

"The platform is highly classified," he begins. Only politeness keeps everyone from calling bullshit. Everyone in the room has, at least, a Top Secret clearance. Haralson clears his throat. "It's a few hours away, but has orders to proceed at best speed to a position closer to our people. There is a team on board, and we believe we can effect whatever action may be required."

"Thank you, Admirals Lamar and Haralson," says Soperton, "and General Burke. May I assume our task now is to refine our plans, and establish timelines as quickly as possible? "

"Correct. Let's do our best, gentlemen," echoes General Burke.

As everyone returns to service-specific tasks, Soperton and Wells take Lamar aside. "Admiral Haralson was sort of cryptic, Jake," Soperton says. "Do we have an Ace in the hole or not?"

"Woody's an outstanding officer. I'm sure you appreciate, by virtue of his responsibilities, how sensitive he is about covert ops."

Wells says, "We do appreciate that," rather than "Give me a break," which is what he is thinking.

"Our 'Ace in the hole', as you put it, is under the operational control of the Naval Forces Southern Command – 4th Fleet. That's Woody's command. A few years ago, the Navy developed a Carbon fiber boat called Stiletto. It's small, only 88 feet in length, and fast."

"Fast is classified, I suppose," ventures Wells.

"Yes, but you and Adrian have clearances. Fast means speeds exceeding 55 knots – say, 65 mph."

"Impressive," says Soperton.

"We've been testing its "M-Hull" design in open water conditions in the Caribbean.

It can launch a 7-man RHIB in shallow water."

"RHIB?" questions Soperton.

"I'm sorry. I sometimes assume everybody knows naval vocabulary. RHIB means Rigid Hull Inflatable Boat. "

"SEALS?" asks Wells.

"Maybe, but not necessarily. Could be Rangers. Special Ops people. It's a joint Army-Navy craft. In recognition of the Army's role, the ship is named Bayonet. The Army mariners are from the 10th Mountain Division, 7th Sustainment Brigade."

"And Bayonet is headed to assist in exiting this operation."

"That," says Lamar, "would be my recommendation."

"How long, Jake?" Soperton says.

"I'll check."

Wells looks at both men. "Time is short. I think we need a backup."

"Let me talk with McIntosh again. He has some assets in the area," says Lamar. While Lamar goes to find McIntosh, Wells and Soperton return to R2 . They stand together behind H-bird pilot Major Berrien rather than sit. "You understand, Bob," whispers Soperton, "why we have to get London and Breeden on the other side of the river, don't you?"

"I understand what you told me," he says, his brusqueness coming out.

"With respect, Bob, don't get testy. We're on the same side. Washington must be able to assure the Government of Costa Rica that we did not engage in any military operations in their country."

"And what would you call what we just did at the Institute?"

"That was not a military operation, per se. We did not send in the Army or Marines."

"We sent the Air Force in," says Wells, sarcastically. He is more than a little annoyed over splitting hairs.

"You know what I mean. That action was a humanitarian intervention! The President will, if need be, and when appropriate in his judgment, discuss it with the President of Costa Rica. We acted in the best interest of many nations, not just the U.S."

Conversation stops as they both look at the screen with images of London carrying Breeden through the brush on his shoulders. "Time is growing short for getting Breeden out. I'm still unsure of the best course of action," says Soperton. He sounds tired.

"I'm worried. The rubber boat thing may take too long to execute. I do not want to lose either of our people. How are we going to get Breeden out?"

Major Julie Berrien has followed most developments as pilot of the Hummingbird. She overhears Wells say, "…how are we going to get Breeden out?"

"Excuse me, sir," Berrien says, looking back over her left shoulder, "Maybe I can be helpful."

Wells exchanges glances with Soperton. "We'd like to hear what you have to say."

Berrien turns to her co-pilot and says, "Tony, you got it." Then she pivots her seat 90 degrees to the left. Wells and Soperton step to her side when she gets up. "Well, sir, I think I can get her out."

Wells frowns. "How could you do that?" He can't imagine what she means. Soperton is equally perplexed.

"It's really a question of weight, sir. Maybe length."

"Weight? Length? Can you be more specific?" asks Soperton.

"How tall is she, and how much does she weigh?"

"I don't recall height. But weight is one hundred and eighteen pounds, maybe a little less. I fail to see what you're driving at," says Wells.

Berrien licks her lips. "Well, sir, Hummingbird carries a .50 caliber in its nose and belly. The weapon weights about a hundred pounds. Ammunition and a drum to receive spent shells another thirty pounds. I'm guessing. Maybe we could drop the weapon and pick her up." The IF doesn't provide precise height images.

"Is that possible?"

"It's never been done, but I think so, sir."

"But how could you do that? I mean, where could you land? Could you land?" asks Soperton, clearly intrigued by the idea.

"I think I saw a possible place on the other side of the river. Maybe another mile from the crossing place, on the Nicaragua side. And I think I know of a drop off location."

"You think you pull this off?" says Wells, his voice sounding guardedly optimistic.

"Pretty sure. We'd need to get some technical assistance to see if it's feasible."

"Where do we get the TA? Who do we ask?"

~ ~ ~ ~

Wells and Soperton return to the conference room for a group-think, and discussion of an alternative course of action. Everyone from the rank of Colonel down is present, talking and snacking on finger sandwiches, chips, and drinking cokes or coffee. Admiral Jake Lamar is still there, talking with Marine Major General McIntosh, Army Major General Randolph, and Admiral Bibb. The rest of the brass is taking a brief break nearby. Wells and Soperton's entrance goes unnoticed except by the aides. Wells speaks in a normal tone of voice to General Burke's aide, who leaves immediately. He then says in a voice only slightly louder, "Gentlemen, I have asked Generals Burke, Hart and Whitfield, and Admirals Haralson and Wilcox to join us for an update. They should be here shortly. If you haven't had enough coffee and sandwiches already, this might be a good time. You know where the head is." He and Soperton go to their seats to talk quietly and wait. It is not a long wait.

As the conference room door opens, people start to get up only to hear General Burke say, "As you were. It's been a long day." Everyone is in a seat except General Hart, who didn't arrive with everyone else.

"With your permission, General," opens Wells, looking at Burke, "we have a few ideas we've discussed with General McIntosh, General Randolph, and Admiral Lamar, and wanted to get your suggestions. We think we need an alternative course of action, and we need to executive it immediately." Burke nods. Some around the table move closer, others push back. Vice Admiral Haralson takes his glasses off and sets them down. He rubs his eyes.

"What did you come up with Bob?" ask Burke.

"Okay."

CHAPTER 23

If his mother would have allowed it, he would have dropped out. George Upson never much liked high school, mostly because he was bored with English and Sociology and History classes. Shop mechanics was the thing that really interested him. Maybe that was because he was good with his hands. His father died when George was two. That's what his mother said. She never remarried. Anyway, he came of age in the late 1980s, and got his high school diploma in 1991- finishing dead middle in his class. The next day he enlisted in the Air Force.

The Air Force was a life saver. It parented him into adulthood. It gave purpose to his life. George and his wife live in a four bedroom house on base, and have a close group of military friends. His wife plays cards on Thursday evening with other wives. Fifteen hundred servicemen live on base, and 5,000 live off base. Since joining up George has watched the military change a lot. NCO and Officers Clubs are a thing of the past. Base hospitals and base high schools have given way to community involvement and cost cutting. Rent-a-cops man the gates rather than military police. Political correctness impacts traditional military culture. In some cases, whether its weight control or difficult duty – airmen are allowed to "opt-out." That's the PC term for drop-out. Officers seemingly spend more time addressing the marital and family issues of enlisted men – and unhappy ex-wives - than military duties. All the services have on base drug and alcohol counseling. Still, in spite of all the changes, the Air Force has been good to him. His children were delivered by Air Force doctors and nurses, and his family receives good health care. Dentists scare him to death, but his experience with Air Force dentists has been outstanding. Air Force lawyers helped him handle everything from his Will to selling an old car. He banks with USAA and is more than satisfied. And the weather in Arizona is outstanding.

Career wise, the Air Force taught George everything about aircraft. He can disassemble and repair jet and propeller engines with the best, civilian or military. He can repair, service and maintain hydraulic and electrical systems, and he is an expert on aircraft weapons systems, especially those used in UAVs. George was promoted to Senior Master

Sergeant (E-8) after 19 years of outstanding service. Now 38 years old, he is near the top of his game. He expects to make E-9, and complete 25 years. After that he can be a civilian contractor with the Air Force, or hook up with a major defense contractor. Because of his knowledge, technical skills, hard work and leadership abilities, he supervises and manages all drone systems at Davis-Monthan Air Force Base.

His call is through the Chain of Command, beginning with Lieutenant General Lucas Whitfield, and flowing rapidly down through channels to him.

CHAPTER 24

In 1979 the President of the United States – with approval from the Congress – relinquished control of the Panama Canal Zone. In 2000 the Republic of Panama took full control of the canal and the Zone. A year earlier, in 1999, all U.S. military bases in Panama were closed. Subsequently, two Panamanian bases were leased to the U.S. Navy. One base is located 217 miles west of Panama City at Punta Coca. The other base is 280 miles east of the capitol at Bahia Pina, in the Gulf of Panama. Bahia Pina is famous for Black Marlin fishing. The U.S. Embassy is located in Panama City.

Shortly after his morning swim in the embassy compound, Defense Attaché, Army Brigadier General Robert Meriwether, is putting his shoes on in the men's locker room. Major Thomas Appling, the ranking officer among the Marines detailed to the Marine Security Guard stationed at the embassy, rushes in. "Excuse me, General, but there is an urgent conference call scheduled in the Ambassador's conference room in fifteen minutes." The Major waits for a reaction.

"What's up, Tom?"

"I don't know, General. It's a VIP conference call for you and Ambassador Dooly."

"Thank you," he says knotting his spit-shined leather shoes. Old habits die hard, and Meriwether doesn't wear patent-leather girlie shoes. "Lead the way."

The Ambassador's conference room is located on the top floor of the embassy, next to the Ambassador's safe room. At approximately 6:45 a.m. the conference call begins. Ambassador Susan Dooly arrives just as the roll call of participants begins. She looks sleepy. The call last fifteen minutes, and is more aptly characterized as "give" then "take". Major Appling is waiting as Meriwether comes out of the conference room. He follows the general to the Defense Attaché's Office (DAO) on the second floor. "Hold my calls, please," Meriwether says to his executive assistant, an Army captain, as he and Major Appling go into his office and close the door.

"Here's the drill, Tom." He then proceeds to share the essence of the conference call. "The Ambassador has released the Marine's Pave Hawk to us. When is it due here?"

"May I assume you are talking from Coca, sir?"

Meriwether says, "You may."

"1000 hours, sir. For the Ambassador."

Meriwether looks at this watch. "Good. Change of mission. The Ambassador will not be needing it today. Instead, I want you to lead a Medevac mission."

"Yes, sir," he says as calmly as if he does this every day.

"It's a rescue mission. As soon as the chopper arrives, brief the crew. Located the embassy doctor and take him with you. Tell him to bring along any medical supplies he may need to assist a wounded person."

"Yes, sir."

"Select the best mechanic on your duty roster and have him aboard. Pull any armament. Might want to take along a couple of men to assist in case there is any heavy lifting, if there's room."

"Sir."

"You know a Gunnery Sergeant Victoria Coweta?"

"Yes sir. That is to say I am aware she arrived here a couple of days ago – TDY for a classified assignment. She wasn't gone long. I think she is due to leave today or tomorrow."

"Find the Sergeant and take her with you. She's the only person who can identify the person we want."

"Yes sir."

"I'll call the CO at Coca and follow up on other details. The chopper will need in-flight refueling."

"General, if I may, the Navy prefers the term 'helo' instead of 'chopper'," he says in a good natured way.

"I'm in the Army, remember?" The general forms a pistol with his hand and shoots at the major. "In about an hour we'll have exact coordinates. You'll brief the crew."

"I'm on it, General."

~ ~ ~ ~

Back in SOUTHCOM's conference room, General Burke and Admiral Lamar discuss the plan of action. There are more details to work out.

~ ~ ~ ~

It is more difficult than expected, and it is taking longer than he hoped. Jon stops several times to readjust Kate across his shoulders, and to give her and him a break. She complains, somewhat incoherently, about wanting water. He promises water soon. The monkeys scream loudly at them, jump from limb to limb and violently shaking tree branches. Had the damn primates evolved further, Jon thinks, they would have picked up rocks and stoned them. In several places the narrow path simply ends. He can't think of any rhyme or reason for it. The path just stops. Discarding the jungle knife was a mistake, he acknowledges to himself, and the price is detouring time and again.

It is approaching 7:45 a.m. when Jon and Kate reach the designated spot for crossing the river. Time is rapidly slipping away. He is beginning to feel fatigued. The terrain is different. They are at the edge of the jungle, and a swarm of insects are hovering nearby. Low grass and a white sandy shore meet at the river's edge. The sandy shoreline is 20 feet wide, with jungle trees extending 10 or 15 feet over the water's edge. A few large trees have branches overhanging the river by 25 feet.

Jon eases Kate from his shoulders onto the sand and props her head up on his rucksack. She appears dazed, weakened, and dehydrated, but not in any pain or distress. The bandage looks okay. Maybe a little bleeding. The back wound seems to be leaking blood or something else. There is more swelling. He doesn't want to dwell on it, but he is deeply concerned. He will check her leg and re-bandage it on the other side. She is quiet. He will find water after they cross the river. If they get across. He looks at the muddy-colored river. The moderate current is strong enough to carry a raft or canoe downstream, but too strong to swim against upstream. From where he is standing, it looks moderately shallow, and about 50 yards wide. Only 50 short yards of opaque water. Impossible to tell what dangers lurk beneath the surface. Half way across the river is a small sandbar. Then another, narrower, sandy bank on the other side. Unfortunately, there is a "sand trap". He is mildly amused with the unintended pun. The "sand trap" is the sandbar and the half dozen crocodiles sleepily sunning themselves, looking docile, and awaiting their next meal. He looks closer at the bank where he stands, watching for ripples on the surface that might indicate any hidden or immediate danger. At first he thinks he sees something, but then blames his imagination. His eye catches a large crocodile on the sandbar slipping quietly into the water without making a splash. Its a few minutes after eight-o'clock. Time to get off the dime.

"H-bird, Firefly."

"H-bird, Go." Everyone in R2 and the SOUTHCOM conference room stops to look at the screen.

"Okay, H-bird. We're at the place. Lots of company in the water. Can you see them?"

"Firefly, Navigator," interrupts Wells. "We see the company. Maybe if you just take it real slow and easy. Over."

"Navigator. Do you believe that?" he says, but thinking, I sure as hell don't. "Over."

"What's your plan?"

"I'm hoping you have a plan."

"We are checking data bases and sources," Wells says automatically.

"Great. Firefly out."

Every source available to those in the conference room is interrogated. Question: How dangerous are crocodiles in Central America? Within five minutes Wells calls Jon. "Firefly, Navigator."

No answer.

"Firefly, Navigator," says Wells, a bit more urgently.

"Go ahead Navigator."

"We've been assessing the situation. Over."

"Me, too, Navigator. Over."

"Okay, Firefly, good news. The consensus is only a handful of crocodiles in the world are really dangerous." Pregnant pause. "And they are Nile or salt water crocodiles. Over."

"So I shouldn't be worried about these giant, pre-historic, cold-blooded bad boys? Over."

"Technically, they are caiman not crocodiles. But all wild animals are dangerous. Over." As soon as he says this, he regrets it.

"Navigator, whatever you call these things, they are humongous food chain champs! Over."

"Roger that, Firefly. What's your plan?"

"I'm working on it," Jon replies, sounding clearly irritated. "Firefly out."

Jon watches the crocodiles. They are huge. Two of the biggest ones probably weight half a ton. He doesn't think they have moved an inch. From all appearances they could be stuffed animals in a museum exhibit. Growing up in south Florida he knows something about alligators. Just because they are often somnolent, doesn't mean they don't wake up in a hurry when they hear the dinner bell. He knows crocodiles and caiman are worse…ambush hunters, just waiting for food to get close enough to strike. To have any chance, he will have to feed or kill the monsters. Or they will kill and feed on him! He is glad Kate is essentially unconscious. Time for him to cut bait and go fishing. He returns to the corner of the jungle, watching the angry, jumping and screaming monkeys protesting his presence. There are plenty of them in the trees, almost daring him to invade their space. He switches the MP7 selector to full automatic. This isn't target practice; he needs to have success rapidly. He fires a short burst at a group of monkeys on low lying branches. As the weapon fires, the monkeys scream and scatter in all directions. All but one. It comes crashing through the limbs to the ground. Jon works his way to the animal, nudges it with the barrel of the MP7 to make sure it's dead, then grabs the tail and drags it to the bank. When he is 10 feet from Kate, he is alarmed to see an Anaconda slithering out of the water toward her. He drops the monkey and tattoos the giant snake from head to mid-body with 20 rounds. It recoils and does a half roll. Jon's heart is beating noticeable faster. The creature must be fully 20 feet long, as big around as his neck, and is still half in the water! He shutters to think what might have been in another five minutes. He approaches the snake with caution, and fires another round into its oversized head just to be sure. With considerable effort he pushes it into the water. The big crocodiles don't yawn or open an eye. But under a low lying branch near the river's edge, a smaller croc quickly snaps it up. Two threats gone.

~ ~ ~ ~

The Navy Special Ops version of the UH-60 is a four-blade, twin turboshaft engine, modified for diplomatic use, meaning it is classified as a utility variant for VIPs. The UH-60 type was used in Grenada and Panama, and is currently used in the Middle East, including Afghanistan. It was the helicopter of choice in the bin Laden operation. It has a cruise speed of 173 mph, and a maximum speed of 182 mph. Major Appling has the coordinates for the mission, and an in-flight refueling.

The 10 a.m. planned departure is delayed because the embassy doctor is attending to one of the embassy staff in a local hospital. He arrives at 10:25 a.m. and is confused why he has to go with the helicopter. He reminds the ambassador how important it is for him to remain at the embassy in case of emergencies. The ambassador suggests he go. End of discussion.

Inside the cockpit the pilot – Marine Captain Jim Dawson - runs a gloved hand over instruments in front of him and over his head. Like a large gray spider, his left hand lightly glides over various nobs and switches on the center console, and moves on. He turns one nob as if adjusting volume on a radio. Satisfied, he twists the throttle on the collective stick to the left. Then he turns it back to the right. Then back left again. With his right hand he rotates the cyclic stick in a circle the size of a dinner plate. He appears patient and unhurried. Moments pass until he starts the engines and increases the RPMs. The blades whirl and whine, and the cockpit vibrates. Dawson gently pulls the collective up, changing the angle of pitch, and lifting the UH-60 off the helipad. Meriwether and the ambassador watch from the window as the helicopter lifts up, dips its nose, picks up speed and altitude, and turns to the right toward the Western Caribbean. A light drizzle begins to fall. "Looks like rain clouds," says Meriwether, looking at the Ambassador. She nods. If all goes well, the chopper should be on location in two plus hours.

~ ~ ~ ~

Jon doesn't have time to dwell on the snake, and hurries back to the same spot at the jungle's edge to bag a second monkey. He returns to Kate as quickly as he left her, dropping the monkey next to the first one. Kate seems to be stirring slightly. He ejects the clip of hollow points from his MP7, and replaces it with a clip of armor-piercing rounds from the rucksack. He hopes shooting crocodiles with armor-piercing rounds is better than hollow points, but is unsure. And he is not going to call Wells and ask for any more advice. He puts another clip in his parka jacket. Then he pauses. Experience tells him to take a second to think. He takes two seconds, ejects the clip from Kate's weapon, puts it in his calf pocket, and throws the MP7 in the river. He takes a knee beside Kate, and takes her right hand in his. He says, "Squeeze my hand, Kate. Hard!"

Kate responds to his demand, but her squeeze is weak. He repeats the test with her left hand. "Squeeze my hand like you're mad at me!" he says. Her response is weaker than with her right hand. He retrieves the rucksack and confirms it contains the extra clips of ammunition, UVL pens, and the combined medical supplies. There is one high energy bar, a pair of socks and a small container of foot powder, overlooked until now, and two protectors. The rucksack is light and relatively flat. He removes the laces from Kate's boots and loosely but firmly ties her wrists together. Her boots are not going to fall off because she's not walking. He lifts her head enough to remove her boonie. He flings it into the brush. Next he takes the first bait monkey and heaves it as far as he can in the direction of the sandbar. It lands with a sizable splash, 40 feet in front of the sandbar, but not as far as he hoped. The current moves the carcass 30 feet further before four of the five crocodiles hoist themselves up on short primeval legs and dash into the water, quickly closing on the meal as it drifts down river. The largest crocodile – granddaddy croc - doesn't show any interesting in competing for the snack.

Time to move. "Kate," he says, leaning close to her ear.

"Yes," she answers, obviously in an altered state.

"I'm going to have you hold on to me. Can you do that?"

Pause. "Can I do what?" she slurs.

"Let's get in the water," he explains, almost parentally, "and you hold onto me. Can you do that?"

"Yes."

Jon turns her on her stomach, picks her up under her arms, and drags her to the water. He stretches to get the second monkey next to his MP7. He slides Kate into the water, turns around and ducks under her arms. Then he takes the monkey and MP7 from the bank. The entry to the river is gradual at first. Knee-deep. Quickly he is waist deep in the current, and leaning into it. The next step he sinks to chest level. He half turns to make sure Kate's head is above water. "You okay, Kate?" he calls.

There is an incoherent grunt. He is eager to get rid of the monkey before the crocodiles detect it, and to get his balance in the river. The current is manageable. Kate is fine. It's easier to move with her than he expected. She is almost floating behind him. He assumes water will not affect the weapon. A little late to worry about that now. The crocodiles are on his right - downstream - fighting over "parts" in a feeding frenzy as he slowly moves toward granddaddy croc. It gives no indication of interest or concern in him. Maybe it's ill? Dead? Old? Full? Whatever.

Jon wants to reach the sandbar as quickly as he can without the crocodiles on it. When he is 15 feet from the big creature he lamely launches the second monkey. It's a fair throw, landing 40 feet in front of the monster. It still does not move, but the splash draws the attention of smaller crocodiles on the far bank. They swiftly head for the monkey.

Jon's options are down to one. He considers for a nanosecond where to shoot the crocodile. Granddaddy crocodile is still unmoving. Its eyes are unmoving. Jon can't aim very well from a head high position in the water, but fires two long burst at the beast. Probably 20 rounds. Most rounds hit the crocodile, but a few rounds kick up sand near its belly – clear misses. The big crocodile absorbs the other shots, much like a heavyweight fighter taking body blows. It flinches, swings its mighty tail, and then paddles rapidly with its short legs into the water, where it does a roll and dives like a submarine. Other crocodiles rush to the opportune feast, and the water boils with primal blood lust. Jon doesn't have time to watch, and scrambles onto the sandbar, stumbling with Kate, but recovering his balance. He immediately plunges into the river again, heading to the far bank. His feet don't touch the bottom, but he swims as quickly and strongly as possible with Kate around his neck, splashing wildly, with the big crocodile no longer a threat. Two stokes from exiting the river his sixth sense kicks in. He feels he is being hotly pursued. He reaches the sand on the bank, falls to his knees and spins with his finger on the trigger. A smaller crocodile – maybe six feet in length – is within two feet and closing. Jon empties the remainder of the clip into the reptile, then double times through the low grass for ten yards before dropping to his knees again. Kate is hanging limply around his neck. He ducks under her rather than lifting her off.

"Have we been swimming?" Kate murmurs. "I'm thirsty." Morphine has a strange effect on her. It's not something she is consciously aware of. She seems in a dream state, disconnected from reality. But she doesn't appear anxious or in pain. She's relaxed, but unable to connect the dots, and apparently unconcerned about it.

"Gonna get water in just a minute, Kate," he says, breathing heavily. "Can you hold on for a minute?"

"I like swimming with you," she answers.

Jon gets to one knee and stops, looking around and catching his breath. He inserts a fresh clip into the MP7.

"Well done, Firefly," says H-bird.

"H-bird, take five and then point me in the right direction." His watch reads 9:30 a.m.

~ ~ ~ ~

"Hot damn," exclaims Marine General McIntosh, slapping his hand forcefully on the conference room table. Admiral Wilcox jumps at the loud and unexpected noise, almost like it was a gun shot. "That's my kind of guy," he says.

Admiral Lamar quietly adds, "3B-SEAL."

Soperton leans his head closer to Wells for an explanation. "Brains and Brass Balls SEAL," he says.

~ ~ ~ ~

Ten minutes later: "H-bird, Firefly."

"Go Firefly."

"Where is the promised land?"

"Half a klick north. Can you get through the bush?"

"Gonna try, H-bird. Any suggestions gladly accepted. Over." Jon is feeling more comfortable on dry land, away from the river, and closer to his immediate objective.

"Straight line. Over."

"Roger," he responds. He checks Kate's leg. When they arrive at their destination he will change the bandages. The rucksack's waterproof capability seems to work. Turning Kate face down again, he picks her up to his chest, ducks under her, and lifts her to his shoulders. He stands for a moment to get her weight evenly distributed across his shoulders, and then bends to grabs the MP7. It's back into the jungle, zizzing and zagging, and twisting and turning to avoid branches and bushes that might hit Kate in the face. In the process he picks up painful lacerations and cuts on his hands from sharp fibers on palm fronds. Within minutes, his hands bleed and look infected.

Finally, long minutes later, he steps out of the jungle into an open space. He eases Kate off his shoulders and leans her against a tree stump. He checks to make sure there are no ants around. Kate's face has several small bleeding cuts from their passage. He removes the rucksack from his back, leans his MP7 against it, and stretches. Then he frees Kate's hands from the boot laces. She barely opens her eyes, and doesn't speak. It's after 9, and the morning rain has come and gone. The plot of open land has been clear-cut, probably by loggers. Or maybe locals for pasture or crops, and then later abandoned. There are hundreds of large tree stumps. He takes Kate's parka off, walks a few paces, and spreads it over a stump in hope of drying it. In the stump is an indentation filled with water from the morning rain. He returns to Kate and removes both boots, then goes back to the stump. He scoops up water with one boot, and pours it into the other. It's probably a cup full. He returns to Kate and his rucksack and removes the UVL pen. Its battery operated and takes only a minute to purity water. He takes the cap off, turns the power on, and dips it into the boot. He'll give it 90 seconds. "Kate," he says, removing the pen and putting the boot to her lips, "drink some water." She opens her eyes as he pours water into her mouth, spilling at least half. He repeats the process. She closes her eyes again.

Unexpectedly, she says "My leg hurts."

Jon repositions her onto her left side, and pulls the rucksack next to him. He carefully removes the bloody bandages from her leg. He has zero knowledge of wounds other than the "sucking chest wounds" drilled into him when he was in the service, but it looks ugly. He gets up and goes to another tree stump for more water. Once back at her side he uses the UVL pen again, waits 90 seconds and pours half the water on the front of her leg, and the other half on the back. Her leg looks even uglier when dried blood is washed off. The entrance wound is a clearly defined circle. That doesn't look too bad, except her thigh is swollen, red and irritated. He assumes infection has set in. The exit wound at the back of her leg looks larger, less circular and more damaging. It's leaking. He reaches into the first aid kit and takes out the Neosporin, morphine, Celox, gauze, and tape. He empties the Celox directly into her wounds, front and back, and wraps gauze around her leg several times. Using the adhesive tape he tightly binds the new dressing. Kate grimaces, but doesn't complain. He gives her another shot of morphine, and sticks the needle in her fatigue collar. Making a mental note to take the first needle out of her parka collar and re-stick it in her fatigues collar. He gets more water and attends to her facial wounds, then applies the Neosporin, and rubs some on his scratched hands.

High in the sky Hummingbird hears the call: "H-bird, Firefly. Over."

"Firefly, this is H-bird. What's your status? Over."

"H-bird, does Navigator have a plan? Over"

"Firefly, this is Navigator. We have a plan. H-bird has stage one. Go ahead, H-bird."

"H-bird, roger. Firefly, do you see an old road or level area about a hundred meters north of your position?"

"Negative. The ground is level. Hard to see over the grass and scrub."

"Roger. Go due north for a short distance and try to locate it. Over"

"Roger. Give me a few minutes."

"H-bird standing by."

Jon has no intension of letting Kate out of his sight again, so he repeats the process of getting his gear and her before striking out in a northern direction. Minutes pass until he finds what was once a road. He eases Kate to the ground. No visible ants or spiders around. The morphine has taken hold of her.

The road is a single lane size piece of red clay, sand and dirt. Years earlier it had been a logging road. It started in the west, and stopped where the jungle began in the east. In the ensuing years, the beginning end of the road filled in and grew over, but with relatively low ground cover. From a distance it looks mostly level, but on closer inspection it is irregular at best.

"H-bird, Firefly at the place. Over."

"Outstanding, Firefly. How does it look?"

"How does it look for what?"

"To land."

Holly shit, thinks Jon. I never even consider that! "H-bird, you can land, but I don't know about getting airborne. It will be rough. Over"

"No problem. Do you see any obstructions? Over."

"Stand-by." Jon jogs a short distance in both directions without losing sight of Kate. First he goes north, kicking a few softball-size rocks to the side. Then he turns around, passes Kate, and does the same thing in the opposite direction. The ground is higher or lower by three or four inches in several places, but no drastic deviation. Lots of weeds and low grass, but no obvious obstructions.

"H-bird, Firefly."

"Go ahead, Firefly."

"H-bird, I'd estimate length at hundred to a hundred and fifty yards - straight line. Maybe a little more. Over."

"Firefly, it might be a little tight, but I think it's possible. Navigator, what do you think? Over."

"Stand-by H-bird and Firefly," says Wells.

~ ~ ~ ~

Back in SOUTHCOM, Wells and Soperton confer a few minutes longer with Hummingbird drone pilot Berrien, and then return to the Conference Room. Nearly everyone has been there all night, although a few of the highest ranking took catnaps while aides stood in for them. The room is full. Hot coffee is in abundance.

In Room 1, Screen 7 (Nicaragua, Costa Rica, and Panama) is focused on the river separating Costa Rica/Nicaragua, watching for river traffic moving upstream or downstream toward Jon's position. While other screens are being carefully monitored, headset traffic in the room means everyone is aware of the drama unfolding on Screen 7. Meanwhile, the Conference Room's primarily monitor displays Hummingbird's live feed.

Admiral Lamar has assumed the operational command for the military, subject to agreement with Soperton, his CIA counterpart. "We have a workable plan, but we are not completely confident in timing. I'm going to ask Mr. Soperton and Mr. Wells to explain." He turns to Soperton, who defers to Wells.

"Good morning, General Burke and Gentlemen. I trust everyone had a good night's sleep," Wells says. His comment is greeted with a few false smiles - and fewer chuckles. "Thanks to a lot of people, but especially General Whitfield, the primary objective has been achieved. We've have had a few unexpected glitches, as you are aware. But all in all, it has worked out. What we did not know, and did not anticipate, was the movement of some very dangerous bioweapons."

The room is quiet.

"Consequently, the original exit strategy has changed." Wells pauses to allow for any comments. There are none. "We have two remaining objectives. First, extract our people. Second, destroy or recover the biologicals." He pauses again. Soperton raises an index finger. Wells recognizes him with a nod.

"As simple as these two tasks seem, I would simply remind everyone of two complicating factors. One: Washington's sensitivity to the political ramifications of military action in Costa Rica. And two, timing."

"Thank you, Adrian," Wells says. "Soon we will attempt extracting our wounded team member. The next step is tricky at best. In fact, it has never been attempted before. But we have a cautious level of confidence. General x and Admiral have an excellent plan, developed with Admiral Lamar, to successfully accomplish our objectives. Questions?"

Admiral x says, "Mr. Soperton mentioned timing. What's the status of that?"

"The status is uncertain," Wells answers. "We are trying to get assets positioned, but to a large extend there are several variables, including Mother Nature. The next several hours will tell the tale."

"How things go," adds Soperton, pointing to the screen, "we will see momentarily."

~ ~ ~ ~

"Firefly, H-bird."

"Go ahead, H-bird."

"Firefly, do you have a visual?"

"Negative, H-bird."

"We'll be making our approach east to west. When we come to a full stop, it would help if you could turn us around for an East to West departure. Copy?"

"Copy that. Still negative visual. Over."

"Standby, Firefly."

It often time takes a trained eye to spot an airplane, even when it is heard. ATC people have an edge because they know where to look, and at what altitude to look. And they have the added advantage of radar. Hummingbird is a small object, and painted to make it difficult to see from the ground, even though it is designed to fly unseen at high altitude, and at night. Jon continues to scan the sky, looking at an altitude he estimates to be between 1,000 and 3,000 feet. Looking into a sunny eastern sky doesn't help. Minutes pass.

"Firefly, I'm on final."

Jon strains to see the drone. He thinks he sees something – really low. Maybe 500 feet. It's the drone. Three hundred feet and descending. It seems to flutter, then float, and then softly drop over the trees onto the road. He runs to the far end of the field as Hummingbird throttles back. As he runs he keys the transmit button on his wrist. "Nicely done, H-bird," he complements.

"All in a day's work," deadpans the pilot.

Jon is surprised at the size of the drone. He has never seen a drone before, but had an image of them as large radio controlled model airplanes. Wrong. The slender 43-foot wing span seemed huge up close. He gentle pushes on a section of the rear fuselage to turn it around. The crew had no visual of Jon because of his position. "Okay, H-bird, ready to go."

"Roger," the pilot says, and nudges the throttle to get the craft rolling. Jon jogs behind it. The crew has forward vision, but limited up-close vision around the drone. As close to the end of the road as possible, the drone stops. Jon repeats turning it around for takeoff.

"H-bird, you are good to go," he says.

"Thanks. We're going to shut down and patch you into control. Over."

"Roger that. Standing by."

~ ~ ~ ~

While Jon is being patched to Davis-Monthan AFB in Arizona, Berrien, Soperton and Wells huddle in R2. Wells asks, "How long will it take en route to the landing point?"

Berrien answers, "Probably 20 minutes." She looks to her co-pilot for confirmation. He nods in the affirmative.

"Then you double back and give Firefly and the Navy support."

"Yes sir," she says.

Soperton says, "Thank you. You're doing a good job." He and Wells head to the Conference Room.

~ ~ ~ ~

Firefly control is passed to Davis-Monthan and Senior Master Sergeant George Upson. "Firefly, this is Control. How do you read? Over."

"Loud and clear, Control. Over."

"Roger. We're going to be working together for a while. Just call me George. Over,"

"Roger, George."

"Can you get under the craft?"

"Affirmative." The drone sits shoulder-high above the ground on its landing gear.

"Outstanding," says Upson, who is standing under a sister drone in a hanger with several airmen, and several officers standing nearby. "The fuselage has three sections," he explains. "The first section is immediately behind the engine. The second is in the middle, and the third runs toward the tail. See that?"

"Affirmative."

"Section 1 is six feet and contains the weapon. Section 2 is the power section. Its eight feet long. Section 3 is the electronic suite and is four feet long. We are concerned only with Section 1. Copy? Over."

The Conference Room has no visual, yet everyone is listening intently and watching the image from Screen 7 in R1. It has zoomed in on the vacant field and clearly shows the drone. Near it is a prone body.

"So far, so good, George," Jon says, eyeballing the underside of the drone.

"Okay, Firefly. Section 1 is held in place by 12 fasteners – screws. Do you see 'em?"

"Yeah. Four on each side, and two on each end."

"Right. You've got to remove this panel by taking out the screws. Can you do that?"

"I can try. Let me get back to you."

"Standing by." Upton turns to the audience of on-lookers and says, matter-of-factly, "this could take some time so you might want to have a seat." Several airmen hurry away to find some folding chairs for the officers.

Jon is not at all confident about removing the panel. His only tool is the knife. And it isn't one of those Swiss knives with blades for seemingly every task. His hands are beaten up and he wishes he had gloves. Starting at the far end, the end toward the tail section, he inserts the knife and starts to turn it when it slips out. He tries again, pushing strongly upward. It slips out again. He tries the screw next to it. The knife slips but stays in place. It has some traction. He feels the screw loosen, and then turn slightly. He turns it several more times. He'll be able to get that fastener out. Then he starts down the far side of the panel. The first screw turns, the second one doesn't. He continues down the panel. Fifteen minutes pass.

"Firefly, this is George. How's it coming?"

"Slowly." Jon is glad to drop his arms and get his blood flowing again. "Some fasteners are more difficult than others. But I'm making progress. Over."

"Great. Let me know when you get the panel off."

"Roger." Jon ducks out from under the fuselage to check on Kate. He puts his boonie hat on her, and takes her hand. "How you doing, Kate?"

She sleepily opens her eyes. "Fine," she answers weakly and shuts her eyes. Jon runs his hand over her leg, front and back. It seems dry. He returns to the drone. Two fasteners later he pops the tip off his knife blade and cuts his finger. It is a blessing in disguise. With the blunted blade, he removes all but the first, incredibly stubborn, fastener in 15 minutes. That fastener come out about an inch, but refuses to come any further. Shit. He tries bending the panel down to put pressure on the lone screw. He puts as much of his weight on the panel as possible, but the screw still won't budge. He'd like to shoot it off.

~ ~ ~ ~

Thirty five miles southwest of San Juan del Norte is a hamlet locally known as El Sauce. At the river's edge five armed men pile into a motorized fishing boat and head upriver. "The Nicaragua Gang is on the move," reports General Hart, head of N.S.A. "Running on Latino Time: late as usual."

Wells says, "That's a break."

"Still," responds Hart, "they expect to arrive by noon – roughly two hours. And they are intent on tracking down our people."

"When can we can get our people out?" asks Burke.

No one answers. Burke nods.

Conversation stops as Screen 7 zooms in on a small boat moving upriver. Intelligence and analytics report the boat is an aluminum sport fishing boat, 19 feet in length. They zoom closer. Two outboard motors are clearly visible. On the side of the larger outboard is YAMAHA. On the back, in smaller white lettering, are the numbers 115. Beneath that Four-Stroke. The second motor, much smaller, has no visible brand. Screen 7 zooms out. The boat has a plastic canopy with plastic windows. Because of the canopy no one is visible, other than one person on the bow of the boat.

"That's our target," says Hart.

~ ~ ~ ~

Shoot it off? Why not? Jon leans on the thin plastic and carbon fiber panel to see how much room he will have to fire his weapon. He releases the panel, and returns to pick up the MP7. Back at the drone, he bends the panel down and puts the muzzle as close as he can – but not directly on - the fastener. Maybe a 4.6 x 30mm, high velocity round will do the job. He switches the safety to the off position and holds the weapon in a pistol grip. From two inches away he fires. Even with the suppressor in place, the noise seems very loud. The fastener is literally blown away. The panel and Jon drop a foot to the ground, nicking a plastic line. A dark liquid like oil spurts out. Still on his knees, Jon jumps up, throwing the MP7 down, and races to the medical kit. It snatches up the combat adhesive tape and races back to the drone. Quickly he wraps the line until all the tape is gone. It's oil, without question. He watches the patch job and then keys his transmitter. "George, Firefly. Got the son-of-a-bitch off! But I nicked a line. Over."

"What kind of line? How bad a nick?"

"It looks like an oil line. But I taped it up. It's not leaking now. Over."

"How much oil leaked?" asks George.

"Ahhh, eight ounces – maybe a little more. Over."

"It will have to do."

It has taken more than 30 minutes. Jon wipes his face. He is covered in perspiration.

"Okay, Firefly, let's off load the .50 caliber, feed mechanism and casing drum." Everyone in the hanger walks behind Upson to look into the drone's belly.

Following George's instruction, Jon removes the 20 pound carousel-shaped cartridge receiver. Then the cylinder-shaped ammunition feed mechanism, and finally the 115 pound .50 caliber machine gun. Each is secured to Teflon-coated racks with high tech thumb screws, and side locks, for easy and rapid removal. Removing the actual racks requires specialized tools. The question is whether or not he can safely secure Kate in the available space. Returning to her side he gathers up her boot laces, again, and removes her belt. Kneeling next to the rucksack he cuts off the straps. He returns to the drone with the MP7. He fires four rounds into the left side of the craft, and another four rounds in the other side, as nearly parallel to each other as he can. He takes the Walther and hammers the exit hole of each round to blunt any sharp edges. Next he takes the shoulder straps from the rucksack and fires a hole in the end of both. He picks up his handiwork and Kate's parka and returns to the drone. He places the parka inside the drone when he plans to put Kate's head. There is enough room for her head and neck, but nothing below her neck. He goes back to Kate and checks her leg again. No change. He looks at his watch. Almost noon. He removes the GPS watch from her wrist and puts it on his right wrist. Then he gives her another morphine shot – the third in six hours – and sticks the needle in her collar. He changes his mind and removes it, and the other needle. He intends to use her parka as a cushion. "George, Firefly."

"This is George."

"George, I have given three – say again – three shots of morphine. Make sure that is passed on, please. Acknowledge."

"Roger. Three injections."

"Okay, George. I'm going to install the package. Standby."

"Standing by."

Kate is semi-conscious as he moves her as gently as he can underneath the drone. "Kate, can you hear me?"

"Ummm," she moans. She doesn't open her eyes.

"Kate, we're going for a ride. You hear?"

"Majorca."

"I'm going to put you in the plane. You have to be very still until we land. Okay?"

"Majorca," she repeats, obviously hallucinating.

"Yes," he answers. "Majorca."

Lifting an unconscious 115 pound person is more difficult than lifting 115 pound dumbbell. A person is more awkward to pick up, balance, move, and control. Jon's considerable upper body strength is a plus. Kate's parka fits nicely in the forward compartment, making a pillow for her head. He secures her to the drone butt down. The improvised shoulder strap and boot laces secure her chest, arms and biceps, the belt from her fatigues secures her midbody. The second improvised shoulder strap and boot lace Jon uses around her upper thigh, above her knees. Lastly, he uses the rucksack waist strap to hold her ankles securely. "Stay real still until we get there. Okay?"

"Okay," she answers softly.

Jon backs from under the drone. There is a lot of clearance between the ground and Kate. She will create drag for the drone, of course, but that is the least of his concerns. Hopefully she will be okay for a short distance. Providing, Jon reminds himself, she doesn't do a lot of moving or struggling against the restraints. "George, Firefly."

"Go ahead, Firefly."

"Okay, thanks for your help. Let's keep our fingers crossed this will work. Out."

"Good luck. Out."

"H-bird, Navigator, Firefly. Over."

"This is H-bird."

"Have you and Navigator been plugged in the whole time?"

"Roger."

"I'm counting on you, H-bird. Package is as secure as I can make it. Over."

"Firefly, Navigator. When H-bird departs you will lose voice communication. But we are watching from the satellite. We plan to reestablish communication soon. We'd like you to do something else. Over."

"Am I going to like this, Navigator?"

"Probably not."

"Go ahead."

"The bad people are in route to your previous location. We expect them within the hour. They will be searching for you. We want you to backtrack and sabotage their boat."

"Is this a good time to re-negotiate our agreement?"

Wells is pleased Jon still has a sense of humor. "It's a white aluminum fishing boat, about 20 feet long, with a white top and Yamaha outboard engine. It should be on the Costa Rica side of the river. Near the cave. Over."

"And something else. I keep remembering your success record with paratroops."

"No paratroopers. In the next couple of hours we'll get you out."

"So I'm on my own?"

"For now," Wells says evenly. For some obscure reason he remembers a poster in the international terminal at the Atlanta Airport. The headline on the poster reads: 'Just Passing Through?' Beneath these words: 'Aren't We All?' In small print at the base of the poster are directions to the airport chapel. He hopes it isn't an omen. "Good luck, Firefly. Navigator Out."

"Firefly, H-bird."

"Go ahead H-bird."

"On your command we are ready for restart."

"Fire it up," Jon says, staying well clear of the craft.

The engine catches on the first try. It sounds smooth. There is a slight breeze in the air. The drone's wings seem to sense it, and flutter slightly. The pilot keeps the breaks locked until the engine is at full power, and then hits the "B" key to releases them. Slow for the first 20 yards, the drone bounces down the old road until after 80 yards it hops effortlessly into the air. Kate doesn't fall out. Very, very gently the drone makes a wide turn to the left. It does not appear to be gaining altitude.

"Firefly, H-bird. We'll be careful. Not to worry. Good luck. Out."

Jon watching the drone until it is no longer visible. There is no sound in his ear bud. He removes it and returns to his rucksack and sits down. For the first time he is aware of himself, the minor but irritating scratches on his hands, and damp feet. The Panama boots are water resistant, but not water proof. He takes boots and socks off. In spite of being totally emersed in water, the boots seem only marginally wet. But the socks are definitely damp. He takes them off and inspects his feet. He throws the socks to the side, and pours most of the foot powder into his boots. He digs out the Neosporin and squeezes some on the back of his hands. Airing his feet out, he eats the last energy bar and takes stock of his situation. Plan A worked fine. Plan B never occurred. Plan C was unforeseen. Plan D was not anticipated. Plan E was another improvise. Plan F is to disable the boat. Plan G is to get ahead of whomever is after him, and Plan H is yet to be developed. He puts on the remaining pair of socks. At least Kate will be okay. Majorca? What was that about?

Morphine dream? Probably. A rumble from the sky and dark clouds signal a coming storm – not just rain. Time to get his feet on.

~ ~ ~ ~

"The Bayonet isn't going to work out," announces Admiral Haralson, looking directly in turn at Burke, Clay, Wells, Soperton, and Special Operations Admiral Jake Lamar. He continues, "But our luck is holding."

"What happened?" asks Burke.

"It's a combination of factors, General. Some technical. Some just bad plain bad luck."

"This is a hell of a time for things to go south, Admiral," echoes Wells.

The Admiral is annoyed by Wells' comment. He doesn't appreciate civilian types who think they know anything about the military, and his face shows it. "True, sir," he responds respectfully, in spite of his personal views, "but we couldn't have asked for better luck."

"Has that, Woody?" asks Lamar.

"As you know, Jake, we have a new class of littoral combat ships."

Wells is growing increasing impatient and struggles to conceal it. "And what is lucky about that, Admiral?"

"The lucky part is the newest ship in the Navy - a LCS – is available."

"Woody," says Lamar, "that is good news. Tell everyone why."

"This ship is perfect for this operation, and it is in the Caribbean in route to the Panama Canal."

Although highly unusual, the Navy Chain of Command can be leap-frogged with the approval of the Chief of Naval Operations. An encrypted communication with the ship from Admiral Jake Lamar is made.

~ ~ ~ ~

Supplies: night vision goggles, binoculars, two UVL pens, ammunition clips, medical supplies, some foot powder, Walther, knife, and MP7. The transceiver pack is in the rucksack. The ear bud and wrist video will be useless for an hour or so. When he gets to his target he'll use the ear bud again. He moves his watch closer to his hand, replacing the wrist video. Kate's GPS is on his right wrist. That's it. Binoculars and NVG he puts in the rucksack. Ammunition clips are stuffed into his parka jacket and fatigue pockets. Walther is in its holster, and he slings the MP7. The UVL pens he sticks in his left calf pocket. Knife in right calf pocket. He will carry the rucksack by its top handle until he can dispose of it in the river. He checks the area for the last time. There are spent cartridge casings, pieces of the drone, and his socks. He has no intention of policing the area. Those after him will have an easy enough time following: there were casings at the cave site, a bloody piece of pants leg, and enough clear signs of broken or crushed jungle for a blind man to follow. There were plentiful more signs where they crossed the river: dried blood on the river bank, a boonie hat nearby, drag marks in the sand, more foot prints on the sand bar, and on the other bank.

It is 11:40 a.m. when Jon strikes out. The thunderstorm is approaching. An hour later Jon hears the sound of the river and turns westward – upstream. The jungle is less thick on the Nicaragua side but there is no path along the riverbank. Instead, every 20 or 30 yards, there is a small path leading from the jungle to the river. The clearings are probably used by local peoples and fishermen. Or worse.

Although he has been expecting the storm, the sky suddenly bursts open and a heavy downpour begins. The rain drums the trees and low vegetation with large punishing drops. Jon turns his parka collar up and continues working his way upstream, pausing at every path in search of the white fishing boat. It is almost 12:30 p.m. when he sees it. Unknown to him, the boat arrived about a half hour before, and a tracking party is on his trail. He ducks into the jungle and continues parallel to the river for another 200 yards, then muscles his way through heavy underbrush to the riverbank. He has passed the boat by at least 50 yards. The rain is still on the Nicaragua side but slowly advancing toward Costa Rica. It forms a curtain of water at the river's edge. Jon lies down in the underbrush; he puts in the ear bud and adjusts his boonie hat to shield his eyes. He focuses the binoculars on the boat. Two armed men are visible on the forward deck. One is standing and the other is sitting, with his legs hanging over the side. Both are looking at the sheet of rain as it starts across the river. The boat is painted white with a narrow red stripe at the water line. It has a removable white plastic top with windows. He's seen a hundred like it in the Florida Keys. Yamaha is clearly visible on the outboard engine. He stares at the standing man. It's hard to tell how tall he is, but three of him could lay head-to-toe horizontally on the decking of the boat. That means the boat is at least 18 feet long, maybe 20 feet. Close enough to the description. The rain suddenly moves rapidly and the two men leave the boat for shelter elsewhere. Probably in the river cave.

The MP7 is a personal defense weapon, not a rifle. Certainly not a sniper rifle. A 50 to 75 yard shot will not be easy because he hasn't "zeroed in" the weapon. The bullet will drop slightly over the distance it travels. How little or how much, he has not way of knowing. Jon's prone position is good. His elbows are dug in securely. He aims dead center at the "m" in Yamaha - establishes his sight picture, takes a breath, holds it, and slowly squeezes the trigger. It's a mild surprise when the weapon fires. He sets the MP7 aside and picks up the binoculars. There is a small black dot below and left of the "m" in Yamaha. Had the men on the boat still been there, they would not have heard the weapon fire. Or, if they had been there, not have seen any muzzle flash because of the suppressor. He puts the binoculars down and picks up the MP7. This time he jerks the trigger. He knows without looking it's a poor shot. The third shot he aims at the top of the motor, and an inch to the right. He fires, and then looks. The black dot is slightly above the "m". He fires four more rounds, varying his aim slightly each time. After inspection through the glasses, he is confident the motor is ruined and he has done what Wells asked him to do. There is no indication of any awareness by anyone near the boat, so he fires a few more rounds at the waterline. Small splashes indicate misses, but five other shots strike the boat. The result may be more irritating then destructive. Soon enough the bad guys will know what happened, and from where it happened. They will find his position, so there is no need for him to pick up the spent cartridges. He just needs to get moving.

~ ~ ~ ~

Hummingbird is making a shallow left turn when a red warning light on the instrument panel blinks once. Both Berrien and the co-pilot see it. They scan the instruments for any obvious problems and wait. There are no more blinks. "What do you make of it?" Berrien says to Captain Wilcox, the co-pilot/systems engineer.

"Maybe an instrument malfunction?" he answers, but suspects it is not.

Berrien gently rolls out of the turn to straight and level flight. Minutes later Hummingbird rolls left again. No signs of trouble. Berrien decides to continue flying low, 500 feet above the rainforest canopy, because she believes the less movement the better for the passenger. Observation of the drone by someone on the ground seems remote. Anyway, anyone seeing the drone probably couldn't care less.

Twenty-two minutes later, Hummingbird nears the landing site. The red light on the panel blinks three more times in rapid succession. Berrien and Wilcox see it.

"Come on, sweetheart," urges Berrien, "you can make it."

They also see an obstruction on the road they selected as a substitute runway. Thirty minutes earlier a used pick-up truck parked on it, illegally dumping trash. The occupants, an old man and young boy, are watching a helicopter in the distance. The old man is sure it belongs to the Guardia Civil of Costa Rica. The boy is spellbound. What a sight!

"Hummingbird, this is Marine 23. Over."

"This is Hummingbird. Go Marine 23."

Captain Wilcox turns to Berrien. "Oil pressure," he says, in an unexcited flat voice. "Clipped oil line."

"Hummingbird, there is a vehicle on the landing site. What's your position? Over."

Berrien continues to look straight ahead but says to Captain Wilcox, "Is it going to hold?"

"Don't know," he answers.

"Talk to Marine 23," she says.

"Marine 23, Hummingbird is on a long final. Over."

"Hummingbird, extend as long as you can. We'll clear the landing area. Over."

"Sooner rather than later, Marine 23. We've got a problem. Over."

"Roger Hummingbird. Will do."

Berrien puts her finger on the keyboard as she speaks to Captain Wilcox. "Let's go in as slow as we can, but no stall landing. Nice and easy. Just need to keep things together." She is talking as much to herself as she is to Wilcox.

Marine helo pilot Jim Dawson keys his mike. "Sir," he says to the officer behind him, "got a truck on the road. Can you clear it?"

Major Appling looks out the side door as the helo turns its side to the road. He motions for Gunny Coweta to lean in and shouts in her ear. "Can you get that truck out of there?"

She looks out the window and shouts back, "Can do, sir!"

Appling says to the pilot, "Can you make a dramatic landing close to the truck?"

"Are you shitting me, Major?" says Dawson, and initiates a power on, side-slipping, stomach-turning, semi-autorotation to the ground. Thirty five feet from the truck.

Gunny Coweta jumps solidly from the helicopter, and runs to the passenger side of the truck. The whop, whop, whop of the blades and powerful rotor-wash get the occupant's full attention. Had Coweta been from Mars she could not have startled the young boy and old man more. She shouts through the open passenger side window, in Spanish, "You are in a restricted area!"

"We did not know," apologizes the shaken old man, when he finds his voice, looking across the lap of the wide-eyed boy.

Coweta says, "We are having Civil Guard exercises. It is not permitted for you to be here!"

"Si, Si," he says, nodding wildly with his head. "We understand. We are going now," he says as he shifts the truck into low. "We are sorry."

She barks. "Don't come back for 24 hours."

"Twenty-four hours. We understand."

Gunny steps back as the truck leaves as fast as it can. Coweta returns to the helicopter and jumps in. It lifts off, backs up, and sets down again, rotors idling. "Hummingbird, Marine 23. Road cleared. Over."

"Roger, Marine 23. We are two minutes out." Hummingbird is making a long, slow approach to the black asphalt road. Berrien trims the drone to descend at 200 feet per minute. She sees Marine 23 to her right, rotors turning slowly. There are no blinking lights on the instrument panel. She smoothly flares the drone and waits. It floats for a short distance before kissing down on the road. Even she is surprised at how gently she put it on the ground. The reception committee is standing outside the helo door when Hummingbird rolls to a stop, and rushes to it as Berrien kills the engine.

It is 20 minutes past 12 when Major Berrien keys the mike button on the joy stick again: "Marine 23, Hummingbird. We've got an oil leak. Can you help? Over."

~ ~ ~ ~

The SOUTHCOM conference room has been running on coffee and adrenalin for what is beginning to feel like forever. But there are no complaints. There have been a few relatively short breaks for admirals and generals, but little rest for the aides. Soperton and Wells have been bouncing back and forth between the conference room and R2. General Hart, who has been quietly talking alternately with his aides and his headquarters, puts his secured cell phone down. "Gentlemen," he says, and the room is instantly quiet. "We've intercepted another cell phone call. The bad guys on the Costa Rica side have discovered the motor on their boat has been put out of operation."

There are collective smiles around the room until Hart adds, "That's not all. The bad guys on the Nicaragua side have decided to give up the chase for our man. Instead, they want the boat loaded and brought to them."

"This thing," whispers Wells to Soperton "is going to be tighter than a mouse's ear."

Marine 23 lifts off smoothly at 12:40 p.m. Several miles away the old man and young lad in the black truck watch it head out over the blue-green waters of the Caribbean. Then it disappears, turning south on its flight to the naval base at Punta Coca. The boy smiles broadly at his grandfather. Inside the helicopter, Kate lies motionless. She is covered from chest to hips in dark oil. The Embassy doctor checks her vitals, and un-bandages her leg to evaluate the wound. Watching closely is Gunny Coweta. She grimaces when she sees the back of Kate's leg. The doctor palpates the wound area, sprinkles something on it, gives an injection, re-bandages the leg, and starts an IV. Coweta figures the bullet must have tumbled through her leg, causing a lot of tissue damage or maybe worse. When the doctor finishes, he shouts into the ear of the Major Appling. Coweta can't hear what he says, but the Major says something into his mike. The pilot turns to look at him as he listens. Turning back, it seems the noise and vibration of the helicopter increases like it's speeding up.

It is the co-pilot's turn for take-off. When the rotors reached a pre-determined number of RPMs, he lifted off. The weather en route and at destination looks good. He tapes the fuel gage, a nervous habit. Marine 23 has a re-fueling probe, and will need to take on fuel in the next 20 minutes. Captain Dawson scans a VFR chart for Costa Rica and Panama. With technology being what it is become, he wonders when aeronautical charts will go the way of navigators and flight engineers on fixed wing aircraft. He looks briefly at his co-pilot, who is looking out his window. It' a nice day for scenery.

Costa Rican territorial waters extend 12 miles from the land into the seas. However, the country exercises jurisdiction over waters adjacent to it for 200 nautical miles. This makes perfect sense on the Pacific side, perhaps less sense on the Caribbean side. Nevertheless, Marine 23 intends to fly 50 miles east, re-fuel, and turn south for another 100 – 150 miles. Dawson plans to make landfall at Chinguinola, Panama, before traveling another 100 miles across land to the Navy installation at Punta Coca.

The Embassy doctor has sedated Kate for the duration of the flight.

Not far behind Marine 23, Hummingbird is struggling to gain altitude. Pilot Berrien and co-pilot/system engineer Wilcox are fixated on the drone's instrument panel as its heads over the Caribbean Sea. The oil pressure indicator light is blinking rapidly. "We're not going to make it back to Firefly. Or anyplace else."

"It's going to blow," observes Wilcox, dryly. It is 12:45 p.m.

"That's a bitch. Only so much duct tape can do," says Berrien. "Better notify the brass we're on borrowed time."

CHAPTER 25

The night is moonless when the USS Coronado passes quietly through the Yucatan Channel between Cuba and the Yucatan Peninsula. Hours later its position is 162.846 nautical miles east of the San Juan River, and 133.127 nautical miles north of the Panama Canal. The trimaran combat ship is en route to San Diego, its soon-to-be home port. It is running fast.

The USS Coronado represents a triumph of technology and politics. The corporate world of mergers and acquisitions - and the military/political world of joint defense contractors - makes it difficult to quickly know who owns what. General Dynamics-Bath Iron Works is a case in point. Bath Iron Works (BIW), of Bath, Maine, is a historic company that builds ships. Mostly combat ships for the U.S. Navy. Several years ago the company won a contract to build Littoral Combat Ships (LCS). However, because of revamped military priorities, tighter budgets, and Congressional/White House politics, the Navy's five-year plan projected $35 billion of cuts. It came as no great surprise that the final number of ships ordered was drastically reduced. It was a surprise when only one LCS order survived. The keel of that ship, and its subsequent construction, took place at the Austal Company shipyard in Mobile, Alabama. Austal is an Australian ship company that partnered with General Dynamics. It took three years and $220 million, excluding cost overruns, to launch. A special mission package for the ship was extra. The Coronado has an unusual shape for a combat ship. Viewed from overhead, and then turned on its side, it resembles a wine bottle with a narrow neck. Perhaps that's because it was originally designed to be a fast cruise ship.

The Navy likes to say a ship comes to life at its commissioning. The ceremonies on that day in Mobile were joyous. The following day, however, the 419 foot USS Coronado began 11 months of less than joyous sea trials in the Gulf of Mexico. Crew training, electronic and combat computer systems checks, propulsion system checks, weapons systems checks, helicopter flight operations, UAV launch and recovery operations, high speed runs, endurance runs, emergency stops and starts, evasive maneuver drills, battle station drills, man overboard drills, fire control drills, and many other operational drills were carried out 24/7. The ship is in and out of port countless times, correcting and testing. Civilian technical representatives lived aboard to train, fine tune, test, correct, change, and calibrate. Again, again, and again. The captain expected – required - a maximum effort by all hands at all times. Faithfully carrying out the Captain's wishes is how the Executive Officer earned the nickname "Maximum Matt".

"Maximum Matt" is really Lieutenant Commander Mathew Irwin, USNR. As Executive Officer of the littoral combat ship, he is responsible for just about everything. Most especially he is responsible for anticipating the captain's wishes, and carrying out his orders. There is no rest for Executive Officers. Irwin loves the Navy and his job, but he is ready to get home.

Home is Coronado Island, California. Famously driven and determined since Naval Academy days, Irwin is Coronado Island's native son, and third generation Navy. His grandfather, retired Navy Captain Thomas Mathew Irwin, graduated from the U.S. Naval Academy in 1941. The year was an exciting one for a young naval officer. More times than not youth is the most exciting time in anyone's life because no challenge is too big, or risk too great. Cagey admirals recognize this. When they must fly in marginal weather, they prefer a pilot that is married rather than single.

Grandfather Irwin settled down when he met the future grandmother Irwin at a Navy officers' dance in the elegant Palace Hotel in romantic San Francisco. In those long ago times parties were lavish and glamorous because of the war. San Francisco was every sailor's favorite port. He fell instantly in love with her, but she wanted to wait. Too many young friends had married only to become young widows. She delayed the wedding until 1945. Four years later Grandfather Irwin received orders to report to the naval base on Coronado Island. Grandmother Irwin was six months pregnant, and clearly of the mind that southern California suited her better then northern Michigan. She decided they would buy a home on the island for the time when he completed his Navy career. They didn't have a lot of money, so it helped greatly that she had income from a small inheritance. They scraped together money enough to buy a charming two bedroom, two baths, home on 3rd Street for $7,495. Originally built in 1924, the 1,480 square feet cottage was adequate for their needs. Over the years its value increased to more than $700,000.

Matt's father, John Thomas Irwin, was born to the house on 3rd street that year - 1949. He followed in his father's footsteps and graduated from the Naval Academy in 1972. Rear Admiral John Thomas Irwin – J.T. - was a phenomenal bridge player, a skill not usually associated with the profession of arms, but a sincere tribute to his patient wife, Laura Irwin, a Life Master. Pursuing his military career, particularly during extended periods at sea, was difficult on the family. But Coronado was family to the Navy. Laura stayed busy being a supportive wife and mother, working at the Episcopal Church, playing bridge, and being a leader among Navy wives. The house brought her deep comfort, and a sense of belonging. When the Admiral worked until one or two a.m. on a Friday or Saturday, they would meet at the nearby Night and Day Café for a burger.

Matt is the third generation of Irwin's to live in the house on 3rd street. Born in 1973, and an only child, he moved with his parents from station to station as his father's career progressed. The house was always rented to Navy personnel in their absence. In 1987, Matt's father received orders to report to the Naval Air Station North Island (NASNI). That's when they decided to settle down for the long haul on Coronado Island. So they moved back into the house on 3rd street, and Matt enrolled at Coronado High School.

Some high school students are superior athletics. Others are superior students. Rarely are students truly superior at both. Matt was the exception. He had a friendly but serious demeanor, and hard science courses came easy to him. So did athletics. In his sophomore year he was first string wide receiver and took every AP course offered. He finished at the top of his class three years straight. When he had spare time, which wasn't very often, he went fishing in the bay near Ferry Landing.

Executive Officer Irwin is lingering in the small Ward Room after lunch reviewing operational data on his laptop. There are a lot of data points to review. The USS Coronado is a modern, complex, and efficient combat ship. It has berthing for 40 crew members, 16 SEALS, pilots and crew for one MH-60S helo and three MQ-8 VTUAVs in the special mission package. And there are other on-board techs and specialists. Captain Schley runs the proverbial tight ship, and he is a stickler for detail. When he wants answers to his questions, he means now. Irwin will have those answers at his fingertips.

"Excuse me, sir," says an Ensign, entering the Ward Room near the Habitability Area and interrupting Irwin. "The Captain requests the pleasure of your company on the bridge." He pauses. "Immediately, sir." He emphasizes the word immediate. Irwin looks up, puzzled. He had lunch with the Captain less than 10 minutes earlier. He can't image what Captain Schley has in mind. Still, like every career naval officer, he has learned to expect the unexpected. It goes with an implacable desire for command.

"Thank you, Tom." He closes the Excel spread sheet and heads to the bridge. When he arrives the captain is standing behind the Captain's chair, looking a bit haggard. Irwin is aware the ship has changed course from a southern heading to a western heading. Something big is brewing.

It is 12:50 p.m. when the USS Coronado successfully launches a MQ-8B Fire Scout VTUAV - Vertical Take Off and Landing Unmanned Aerial Vehicle - with Infrared capability from the stern of the ship. Fire Scout is a fully autonomous, four-bladed helicopter, with six hour endurance and a speed of 145 mph. Its L-3 communications tactical datalink is designed to support littoral operations, and streams video back to the ship for relay to the SOUTHCOM conference room. Fire Scout – call sign Scout One - is flown from the ships' Integrated Command and Control area. It provides surveillance, target acquisition, and overall situational awareness. It also provides real time command and control for the mission, and will locate and reestablish contact with Jon. The launch goes off without a hitch.

More daunting, because of time considerations, is the next task. Captain Schley describes his orders from Admiral Lamar, and the subsequent launch of the ship's VTUAV, to a small group called to the Ward Room. Hanging on every word is the Helo crew, and the officers of the elite SEAL Team 4, Platoon 2. After answering questions, the Captain delegates execution of the mission to his XO, Matt Irwin.

SEAL Team 4 is aboard the Coronado for training en route to the Naval Special Warfare Unit in Panama. Its home base is on the East Coast, but its operational areas are Central and South America. It is the only SEAL team completely language capable – each member of the team has fluency in the Spanish language. Platoon 2 has 16 commandos, led by one OIC (Officer-in- charge), one Assistant OIC, a Platoon Chief, and a Leading Petty Officer. Each of the two squads of eight men, Alpha Squad and Bravo Squad, are composed of one officer and seven enlisted. However, because of helicopter limitations, only five SEALS will be on board for the mission.

The Coronado's MH-60S helicopter – call sign Aztec One – is a multi-purpose, medium lift, helo. The normal crew complement is a pilot, a co-pilot, a tactical sensor operator (TSO), and an ASO (acoustic sensor operator). It can accommodate three others bodies, but the decision is made to leave the TSO and ASO on the ship in favor of adding two more SEALS for a total of five.

Navy Lieutenant Charlie Crisp is the helo pilot. Like most helo pilots, he knows movie-goers think fighter jocks are cool. After all, Top Gun wasn't about helo pilots. Crisp also knows low-level flying is the most difficult flight regime there is. And Helos are an easier target than something flying at mach speeds 50,000 feet above the ground. He jokes that helo pilots are like the guy on the street corner in New Orleans, a harmonica to his lips, a drum on his belly, cymbals attached to his knees, strumming a banjo, and singing between breaths. All at the same time. That's a helo pilot.

Marine Captain Richard Jackson, OIC of the SEALS, and his Assistant OIC, who grew up in Puerto Rico, brief Bravo team on the tactical plan. Bravo team won the coin toss for the mission. Prior to going to the helo, Irwin takes Crisp aside: "Red line it, Charlie. Good luck!"

As the rotors start whirling, Irwin enters the ship's Integrated Command and Control area. He knows the "dash" speed of the MH-60S is 164 mph – but the real maximum speed is closer to 180 mph. With the current headwinds, however, Crisp will be lucky to get 145 mph. But winds change. Out of habit he glances at his watch: 1:05 p.m.

~ ~ ~ ~

Jon retreats from the wet underbrush onto the interior jungle path. He moves as rapidly as he can in a westward direction, frequently consulting his wrist GPS. He stops and takes a knee and listens. Except for an occasional call from a macaw or another type of parrot, it seems quiet. He stands motionless next to the limb of a small tree and notices a small green tree boa. It's probably 18 inches long. Non-aggressive and not verminous, it still has a nasty bite if provoked. It is 12:50 p.m. He thought he might hear something from Hummingbird, some kind of sign off or, at least, letting him know Kate was successfully delivered. The transmission range is limited, but still. Maybe his transceiver is on the fritz. Checking it quickly, it seems in order. It's impossible to know if the ear bud is operational or not. He is more concerned to know about Kate's situation than himself, anyway. The plan now is to find a safe crossing place, hopefully near a waterfall and fast moving water. That would be perfect. Crocodiles prefer calm and dark waters, not clear and more turbulent water near a waterfall. After crossing the river into Costa Rica he plans to double back in the direction of the institute, and follow the original exit strategy. Wells will figure it out, and get him out. No sweat.

~ ~ ~ ~

As the helo is rolled out of Coronado's Mission Bay Lift onto the 3,600 square foot flight deck, Captain Jackson speaks to his team through his headset, "Remember: Three is one, Two is two, Four is three, and One is four. He repeats it again, this time as thirty-one, twenty-two, forty-three, fourteen." He resists adding 'hike.' "Only fire above deck. We want to retrieve two white metal containers. Don't fire on them. Walker and Barrow are swimmers. Questions?"

There are none. Headsets are operational. Most of the SEALS wear elbow and knee pads, and ¾ finger, rapid rappel gloves. Washington and Barrow have a three-point sling for their weapons.

"Let's do it!"

One after the other they climb aboard the helicopter. The rotors are idling in the breeze. As they lift off, the noise level inside the MH-60S increases. What little communication occurs will be minimal. Besides, members of the SEAL Team 4 know what is expected of them. They go about every mission in a professional, practiced, and orderly way. On a mission they tend to keep to themselves, with their own private thoughts, or busy themselves rechecking their weapons and equipment. One member of Bravo Squad likes to doze. Sometimes his mates teasingly call him "Sleepy"; once they put a poster of Sleeping Beauty and The Seven Dwarfs on his locker door. He pretended to be amused.

Bravo Squad is led by Captain Jackson because he decided he would lead the mission. He is armed with a MK23 Mod 0.45 Heckler & Koch pistol, with laser aiming. Many special ops types consider the German made H&K an offensive weapon, as opposed to a personal sidearm. Not an easy weapon to fire accurately beyond 30 feet, Jackson practiced with it until he achieved expert status. Soft spoken and never boastful, Jackson learned most achievements in his life came from personal desire, focused ambition and hard work. Growing up on the outskirts of a small community – Charleston, Mississippi – he was aware of poverty and racial inequality from an early age, but never let it sour his outlook on life. His hero was his optimistic mother, who worked in the Tallahatchie County Court House. She told him repeatedly: "If you can imagine it, you can achieve it." He didn't think that was original with her, but he understood the message.

Jackson was offered a football scholarship to Delta State University, in Cleveland, Mississippi. The DSU "Statesmen" won the 2000 NCAA Division II National Football Championship his freshman year. The following year he was the starting quarterback. Life is sometimes a matter of inches. Had he been six feet tall or taller, rather than five feet ten, he might have been recruited for a Division I school, like Ole Miss. Maybe not everything he could imagine could be achieved. But Jackson was a successful player and won more games than he lost. He graduated in five years with a degree in accounting. Ready to more on after college, he applied for Marine Officer Candidate School (OCS) at Brown Field, Quantico, and was accepted. He imagined being a Marine - the best Marine in the whole world. And he fully intended to make that happen. He set his sights on becoming a SEAL. The training was anything but easy, but there was never, never, any doubt he would be successful. In addition to the physical attributes, Jackson had the mental toughness required to be a SEAL. In addition to the .45, Jackson carries a Colt M4a1 with a 30 round magazine. It fires a 5.56 NATO round. He's an expert with that weapon, too.

Team member Number 1 is Don Walker, from Wrightsville Beach, North Carolina. Raised on the Atlantic Ocean, Walker is the team's most powerful swimmer – by far. He is also a crack shot with the Colt M4a1, a weapon with the ACOG 4x telescopic sight and rangefinder attached. The rifle is fully automatic, weighs 6.6 pounds, and has a maximum effective range of 300 yards. Walker has instructions to wait until the targets are within 50 yards. He is responsible for any targets in the water. Number 1 is 4.

Number 2 is Tim Barrow, from Arizona. Barrow attended Arizona State University on an athletic scholarship. At the end of his sophomore year his girlfriend dumped him, and his grades went south. He wasn't all that happy with his wrestling anyway. Iowa, Iowa State, and Michigan wrestlers gave him all he wanted in the 165 pound weight class. Anyway, as he tells it, one beautiful, humidity-free Tuesday he goes by the Registrar's Office. He tells them he is withdrawing from school. With an enrollment of 72,000 students at ASU, it is immediately obvious one student less isn't exactly significant to them. Frankly, as he tells pals, they didn't give a shit. Leaving campus he knew his life was adrift. His saving grace was the United States Navy.

Barrow carries the new and classified XM25 rifle. It's a smart weapon with smart ammunition. Currently it is being used on a test basis in Afghanistan. The rifle weighs 13 pounds and fires a 25mm round. What makes the rifle smart is that the shooter doesn't have to aim directly at the target, only close to the target. The rifle has an attached laser rangefinder. When the range is known, the shooter presses a button near the trigger to transmit the distance to a small computer in the rifle. The rifle transmits the range to a very small computer in the bullet. When that distance is travelled – measured by the number of rotations the bullet makes – it explodes, throwing lethal shrapnel in a five foot radius. Number 2 will be the second SEAL to fire his weapon. Number 2 is 2.

Nearest the helicopter door is Fredrick Washington, Number 3, and the team sniper. "Ready Freddy", as his teammates jokingly refer to him, has a sniper's temperament. He is calm, unhurried and unflappable. That may have something to do with growing up in Wyoming, the least populated state in the U.S. Staying alive in a combat situation requires snipers to be flawlessly camouflaged and endlessly patient. Survival also depends on the distance a sniper puts between him and the target: the further the better. Mental toughness and perfect body control is essential. Washington has perfected slowing his breathing and heart rate as he gets "in the zone." He can withstand hours – days if need be – lying absolutely still, in all weather conditions, in the perfect firing position, waiting for one shot. Washington is armed with the 31 pound "Light Fifty". The .50 caliber rifle, designated by the Marines as the M82A3, has a mounted scope and a 10-round box magazine. It is a beast of a weapon, with a recoil that can bruise a shoulder if held incorrectly. Some snipers use a padded butt plate for that reason. The .50 caliber round is so powerful it can blow a person's arm off. Usually used against heavy targets such as trucks, the M82A3 penetrates personal body armor and shatters bullet proof glass easily. Washington plans to use just one 10-round magazine. Sometimes, because of its size, the weapon is carried in a soft carry-on bag. He prefers to simply fold the handle and bipod, and lug it with him. He will fire his weapon first. Number 3 is 1.

Sitting across from Washington is his best friend in the unit, Brad Houston, Number 4. Houston is from Montana and shares Washington's love of the outdoors, hunting and fishing, and guns. Not firearms – guns. He carries the Team's M240B - a light weight (27 pounds) machine gun. It fires a 7.62 round at a rate of 1,000 rounds per minute. Usually fired in two to three second burst (200 rounds), the barrel burns out fast…two minutes with sustained fire. Then the barrel has to be changed. And that barrel is hotter than hell, too. Houston doesn't have a second barrel with him. Nanoseconds after Washington and Barrow fire, he will fire clean-up. Flying always makes him sleepy, and he is in a light doze. Number 4 is 3.

~ ~ ~ ~

The white fishing boat, with its undersized outboard motor, sputters down the river at an angle. Luckily, it is going downstream. Upstream would have presented a major challenge. There are four bodies on board when they pick up the other four men shortly after 2 p.m. Five men are too many to have below in the cramped cabin with the containers. Besides, no one wants to be below. They flip the side panels of the canopy over the roof to make room for five in the cockpit well. Two others go far forward, and the remaining one stays on deck nearer the cockpit. The sun is out, and the rains are over for the day. It's a great day for fishing. The little motor is more helpful in directional control than propulsion. The river current is providing sufficient power. They expect to reach their destination by 4 p.m. They will have money in their pockets by evening.

~ ~ ~ ~

The warning light on Hummingbird's panel glows a steady red. The drone is at 6,000 feet over the Caribbean. Those in SOUTHCOM's conference room are aware of the situation via the split screen monitor. The decision of what to do is never in doubt. The question is at what altitude to do it. R1 scans the immediate area to determine if any ships are in the area and, if so, how far away. The distance is important to avoid witnesses to the event, or create any unwanted videos, or encourage any attempts to recover wreckage. The final decision is made in minutes and communicated to the pilots in R2.

"Okay," says co-pilot Wilcox. "Powering down." Gently he moves the joy stick forward.

"Expensive adventure," comments Berrien. She doesn't say what she really thinks. Machines sometimes take on a human persona, particularly when they perform well. Pilots and car drivers frequently talk to their machines to encourage them or damn them. Sometimes it's a person's car. Other times it's as common an object as a lawn mower, computer, or sewing machine. It's not unnatural that Berrien developed a certain fondness for the Hummingbird drone. But she not about to admit it. "When we're at 600 feet, if we get that far, I'll let her go."

"If it holds together that long," replies Wilcox, noting they are descending at a rate of 500 feet per minute.

Eight minutes later, passing through 1,000 feet, Berrien lifts the protective plastic cover over the Esc key on the computer key board, finger poised. At 600 feet she presses it three times. The screen goes blank. The time is 1:05 p.m.

~ ~ ~ ~

Back in the SOUTHCOM conference room, Wells looks at the Admiral. "When is the earliest we can establish contact, and get on the river?"

"Any time now."

Anytime turns out to be 2:15 p.m. Coronado's VTUAV - Scout - arrives on station looking for the target first and, depending on time, the operative – Jon London - second. In the SOUTHCOM conference room everyone is watching the feed from Screen 7 in R1, and the feed from the VTUAV. They followed the saga of Hummingbird and its destruction over the Caribbean. Its drone crews in R2 stood down about an hour earlier.

Minutes later. "Aztec One, this is Scout One. Over."

"This is Aztec One. Go Scout One."

"Scout One is on site. Target is moving. Over."

"Roger. Understand target is moving. We are close. Out."

The visual from R1 is amazing. Zooming tightly the white fishing boat is seen in detail. Because the larger of the two outboard motors is inoperable there is minimal wake as the boat moves downstream. Clearly visible are two men at the front of the craft, AK-47s hanging loosely over their shoulders.

The boat can't move fast enough for Wells. He is anxious for the intercept to occur, the containers to be recovered, and the search and contact with London to commence. He sits and watches as calmly as he can. Soperton sits quietly beside him. Marine General McIntosh watches the monitor with the intensity of a football fan who's favorite team is about to score the go ahead touchdown. He is clicking his ballpoint pen at an increasing rate. Air Force General Whitfield sits quietly, hands folded in front of him. His face is angelic calm, as if he is recalling some agreeable event. Admiral Jake Lamar is leaning forward on both elbows, clearly projecting himself into the mission as much as if he were there.

At 2:22 p.m. Aztec One arrives on location, minutes downstream from the boat. As planned, the helo flies first to the Costa Rica side of the river. Because of overhanging trees it hovers 40 feet above the ground. Without hesitation, Washington and Barrow rappel down the rope as effortlessly as trapeze artists, their hands protected by gloves. Their weapons and equipment are on their backs. The helo turns left, swooping away from the approaching boat, and flying to the Nicaragua side of the river. It hovers about three feet above the ground as Jackson, Walker and Houston jump out. Then Aztec One turns steeply to the right, flies 13 miles out to sea, and waits.

Washington takes a position upstream and a few yards left of Barrow. He scratches out a small spot in the undergrowth for the weapon's bipod. Prone and concealed, he consults his handheld ballistic computer. Four times larger than a smart phone, the computer provides a firing solution by doing the math for range, elevation, temperature, humidity, and windage. Confident he is ready, he settles into a comfortable prone position, takes the safety off, and begins his ritual to "zone-in". Within a minute he reports: "Number 3 in position." He slows his breathing and heart rate. Mentally, he blocks out peripheral vision. His mind is focused through the scope.

"Number 2 in position," reports Barrow, seconds later. He stretches his neck, pulls his gloves tight, and pops his knuckles. He's ready.

On the opposite side of the San Juan River, Jackson, Houston and Walker are making sure their field of fire will not endanger Washington and Barrow. Houston is to the right of, and upstream from, Jackson and Walker. He is well downstream from Washington and Barrow. Walker is the last man downstream and left of Jackson. Through his telescopic sight he locates Washington and Barrow across the river and makes note of his line of fire. "Number 1 in position," he says.

"Number 4 ready," follows Houston.

"Okay, mates," says Jackson. "Just like the script."

~ ~ ~ ~

The in-flight refueling of Marine 23 is flawless, welcomed by none more than the Embassy doctor. He doesn't like flying. And he really doesn't like flying in military helicopters. It's a control issue for him as much as anything else. He monitors Kate's vitals frequently and checks to make sure the IV is working properly. She is not in mortal danger, but the leg wound is infected and the tissue damage is considerable. There is possible nerve damage, but without further evaluation it is hard to tell how extensive it might be. He suspects the Navy will send her to the states for more specialized treatment. She's quiet and not in distress. That's a good thing. He needs to get back to the Embassy.

Mother Nature decides to reward the helo for a good in-flight refueling performance; the winds shift, and the ground speed increases substantially. As Marine 23 makes a turn over land, Gunny Coweta marvels at the natural beauty of the land. She is glad Mrs. Echols is going to be okay, but wonders what kind of mission she was on, and for which agency. Probably something to do with drugs, she reasons, perhaps the D.E.A. or Homeland Security. The guy – Mr. Echols, that is – is probably D.E.A., too, but had military in his background. He must be okay. Coweta's biggest concern is whether or not she can get back to the states from this Coca base.

For the next hour Marine 23 flies over seemingly unpopulated terrain. No one speaks. The pilots communicate with controllers and, perhaps, each other. The air is calm and the ride is smooth. Soon they begin a descent toward a marked helipad. They land with a gentle bump. As the rotors wind down a Navy M-ATV tactical ambulance pulls up. That's a bit of a surprise to Gunny Coweta because the vast numbers of M-All-Terrain Vehicle ambulances are sent to Afghanistan, and rightly so. A Navy doctor and two corpsmen exit the rear of the ambulance to take the Embassy doctor and Mrs. Echols to a nearby Navy ship. Everyone else wanders into Flight Ops. It is 2:50 on a glorious afternoon in Panama.

CHAPTER 26

The fishing boat moves slowly in the current, closer to the Nicaragua side of the San Juan River, a few miles west of the Caribbean Sea.

SEAL Team 4 is waiting. Everyone in SOUTHCOM's conference room is quietly waiting, too. On the fishing boat there is no quiet. The men are laughing and arguing loudly about the upcoming FIFA World Cup. Their voices are heard well before the boat comes into view.

"El Pescadito!!" shouts a loud voice, bouncing off the water.

"Who's that?" questions one of the SEALS over his headset.

"Ruiz," someone answers. "Guatemala's all-time scorer."

"How do you know that?" says another voice.

"Knock it off, you guys!" says Jackson.

Washington checks his ballistic computer and makes a minor adjustment to the M82A3. He repositions himself again and gets his breathing under control. As the boat comes into view, he doesn't like his line of fire. He waits patiently. A full minute passes. The boat is 10 degrees left of his position. He focuses on the driver and squeezes off a round. "3," he says as soon as he pulls the trigger. Then he rapidly shifts his aim to the man standing in front of the cockpit and fires a second .50 caliber round.

Two things happen between Washington's first and second shot. The first thing is Barrow fires as soon as he hears "3" in his ears. He aims his smart bullet for the man at the far left back of the boat. The second thing is Washington doesn't have time to see the result of his first shot. Not that he had any doubt about it. Barrow's smart bullet sprays shrapnel 360 degrees, killing three men outright. A fourth man is knocked overboard, serious wounded but still alive. "Two," he says instantly, and decides against firing a second time.

Washington would like to fire again – at the small motor – but neither he nor Barrow do. The boat is turning toward the far side, moving further downriver, and neither wants to take any chances of a "friendly fire" incident. On the far bank, Houston lets loose a short burst from his M240B at the men on the front of the boat. Both go down, one on the deck and the other over the side.

"One," he reports.

Walker watches the water. Through his telescopic scope, the red laser dot is on a man's head in the water to his right. So are the eyes of several crocodiles swimming toward him. Walker considers for a nanosecond whether to shoot the man or let the crocs finish him. He decides to let nature take its course, and shifts his attention to where the other man went into the water. He's not visible, but the feeding frenzy at his last location is. The water boils red with blood. Machaca are Costa Rica's piranhas. They make short work of human flesh. Walker doesn't discharge his weapon, but says, "Four."

The cockpit of the white fishing boat is white no longer. As it passes Jackson's position, the little motor still running, Jackson says to Walker, "take out the motor."

Walker says, "Sir," and holes it perfectly with one 5.56X mm full metal jacket NATO round. All is quiet.

"Aztec One," calls Jackson, "standing by. Over."

"Roger that," comes the crisp response.

~ ~ ~ ~

The SOUTHCOM conference room is quiet. There is no bravo, no hurrahs, no congratulations, no nothing. They watched the monitor with morbid fascination and professional interest. The special ops was perfect; but there is no pleasure in witnessing a man's head being blown off, as Washington's shot did, or seeing men eaten by wild animals. All men of arms know how fragile and momentary life is. Their innermost thoughts are about those they send in harm's way – in Afghanistan, or Iraqi or on an unknown river in Central America.

~ ~ ~ ~

Aztec One recovers Team 4 in reverse order: Jackson, Houston and Walker first, and then Washington and Barrow. The fishing boat is adrift in the current, sometimes bumping into the bank on the Nicaragua side and then bouncing back toward mid-river.

The helo hovers over the boat. Jackson and Walker rappel down the swinging rope to the cockpit. Houston stands in the open door of the helo to provide cover.

"Jesus," says Walker, landing on the deck and slipping on things he'd rather not think about. He is momentarily transfixed by the scene.

"Give me a hand here, Walker," says Jackson, bringing Walker out of a trance. He is pushing the first of two containers through the shrapnel scared cabin door.

"I'm going to throw up," Walker says.

"No you're not!" commands Jackson. "Just hook the damn box up, and get it out of here!" He hopes shouting at Walker works. The bottom of the boat and the shattered bodies look like the floor of a slaughter house. Jackson feels none too well himself.

Walker does as ordered, all the while breathing through his nose. Jackson slides the second container through the door. Walker hooks it up. Then he gets the dry heaves. That almost makes Jackson blow chunks. "Get out of here," he tells Walker and sends him up in the harness. The sight in the cockpit of the boat is gruesome and disquieting. Jackson blocks it out, and is hoisted to the helo. Inside the door he turns to Houston and says, "Empty your clip into the boat." Turning to Washington, who is standing on the far side of the helo, he shouts, "Throw me a couple of 'therms'!" Therms are thermite grenades, also known as incendiary grenades. They burn at 3,992 degrees Fahrenheit, even under water. Because they are not intended to be thrown, and don't explode in the traditional sense, they have a delay fuse of 2 seconds.

After Houston's weapon clicks empty, he steps back to make room for Jackson, who pulls the pins on both and drops them into the boat. The molten metal will quickly burn through the bottom of the boat. "Let's get outta here," he says to Lieutenant Crisp, the pilot.

Aztec One touches down on the USS Coronado at 4:30 p.m.

Scout One returns to the ship almost an hour later, on fumes, having been unsuccessful in locating Jon London.

CHAPTER 27

About an hour after Hummingbird destructs, Jon's jungle path swings back along the river. The ground is softer on the path after the heavy rain, but narrower and high above the murky river. Moving fast, Jon hopes to out distance any followers. Or at least discouraged them. Perhaps they will give up and turn back. He is beginning to feel his chances of getting out in one piece have improved. He is unaware the "bad guys" have been picked up, loaded the containers on the boat, and are no longer in pursuit. If all went well with Kate, he believes this adventure will end happily. He is mildly surprised he hasn't heard from Hummingbird. Thinking about Kate and getting out gives him an energy boost. Maybe Kate is his destiny. Time will tell.

Minutes later Jon encounters a dark cloud of swarming insects. His briefing led him to believe insects stayed away from the swift river in favor of the interior. So much for that. He swats them away with the MP7. The insects are too small to be mosquitoes, so he quickly eliminates them as a real threat. More like blind sand fleas. As a precaution, however, he pauses momentarily to pull down the netting in his boonie hat. That's when he feels a sharp bee sting on his neck. Because he hadn't seen any bees he dismisses the bite – if that is what it is - as an irritant and moves on. Probably a Central American cousin of the bee, he concludes. A few steps later he stops a second time, feeling slightly disoriented and unbalanced. He is short of breath, sluggish, suddenly fatigued. He staggers a few steps further and falls forward at the extreme edge of the riverbank. His boonie hat topples off in front of him. Reaching for the hat he loses his balance and tumbles off the bank.

It's like a dream in freeze frame, not slow motion. Frame 1: falling in space, loose rocks and earth falling with him. Frame 2: right hand open to grab something not visible. Frame 3: left hand reaching for the floating rucksack. Frame 4: a small boy walking along an empty beach, followed closely by a Fox Terrier. Time is suspended. Jon realizes he is about to die. Perhaps, he wonders, time has stopped so he may know how his life ends. He is mildly surprised, but not frightened. He never thought he would die in this place. It seems so pointless, so inexplicable, to die now!

Real time returns when he violently hits the water. The impact knocks the breath and consciousness out of him. At that moment he ceases to wonder, or question, or understand - or exist. For short seconds he floats on the surface of the river, drifting in a forever current. Darkness envelopes him. His luck has runs out.

Destiny trumps luck.

CHAPTER 28

With the bioweapons secured and en route to the U.S. Coronado, a sigh of relief seems appropriate. But it's not that simple. The unspoken concerns of everyone in the conference room are multiple. A deadly attack against the United States has probably been prevented. Are there others they don't know about? Where? When? How? By whom? It might even be argued they are lucky this time. Sober thoughts. Soperton feels a great responsibility on his shoulders. He knows he shares the burden with many others, in and out of uniform, but that is no comfort. Adrian Soperton is a well-educated and extremely well read individual. He and Wells are both Harvard products – he the law school and Wells the Kennedy School – but more than a few years apart. Both were more the intellectual than cloak-and-dagger types. But Wells can be tougher than Soperton on people who didn't live up to his standard.

"Thank you, Gentlemen," says Adrian Soperton, breaking the silence. "Our country owes a great debt of thanks to you and all of those under your command. It will be my pleasure to inform the President of your success." While he says one thing, he is thinking another. He harbors an inner conflict about what the nation should do to address evil in the world, if anything. The world is unlikely to ever be a democratic one. Yet, someone has to step up and do the right thing. Moral courage is important to Soperton. But the price is high.

He looks to Bob Wells.

"Well," says Wells thoughtfully, tugging at his ear lobe, "this success is due to the team effort made possible through those you lead. I am hopeful, General Burke, Admiral Lamar, Admiral Bibb, we can finish the operation by locating and recovering our remaining operative. It would be good if we could keep satellite surveillance on the immediate area until we can get some kind of closure."

"We'll do everything we can, Bob. You know that," says General Burke, answering for Admiral Lamar who sits quietly next to Admiral Bibb, head of the Special Operations Command, and across from Air Force Lieutenant General Whitfield.

"Thank you, gentlemen, I'd appreciate that," Wells concludes.

"What's the next step? After we recover your man, that is," asks Major General Randolph, sitting next to Vice Admiral Haralson.

Soperton looks to Wells and nods for him to answer the question. "First, general, we need to air evac our person. Second, we'll want to off-load the containers as soon as they arrive in Panama, and fly them immediately to Fort Detrick for biological and forensic analysis. After that it's up to the President, Secretary of State, Secretary of Defense, Joint Chiefs, and others as he decides, to determine the next step."

CHAPTER 29

All naval vessels have medical facilities, but larger ships have more space than smaller ones for expanded medical services. However, the most extensive medical services afloat are found on the USNS Comfort – a non-commissioned hospital ship crewed by civilians. Originally an oil tanker launched from San Diego in 1976, the ship was later given to the U. S. Navy. Whether by sheer luck or a welcomed twist of fate, the USNS Comfort is on another humanitarian cruise to provide medical services to those in need. This time to the Caribbean and Central America. The USNS Comfort has 1,000 beds, 12 operating rooms, intensive care units, and everything else found at the typical hospital. On board are doctors, dentists, nurses, techs and many specialties, from orthopedics to plastic surgery. After departing Naval Station Punta Coca, it will sail to Colombia before – ironically – turning north to make port in Nicaragua.

Kate is conscious when she is carried aboard the USNS Comfort. She is taken immediately to the intermediate care unit for evaluation. The medical team has been awaiting her arrival. The care she receives is outstanding, and she is expected to make a speedy and full recovery. After the doctors approved her for travel, the Navy will immediately fly her to the States, probably to San Diego. It is the largest Navy base on the West Coast, and the location of the highly regarded Navy Medical Center (NMCSD). It's closer than Norfolk. Wells expects to be there when she arrives.

The generals and admirals return to their usual bases and commands. The last few days have seemed more like a few weeks. Their only reward for a job well done is personal satisfaction. To most professionals in government that's good enough.

Wells and Soperton stay at SOUTHCOM with General Burke. The hours drag on as they watch the satellite search for London. It's a mystery.

"What do you make of it?" asks Burke.

"I don't know," answers Wells. "We know he headed upriver after sabotaging the boat. We saw the IR boonie hat, obviously dropped. Then he disappeared. Vanished."

Soperton says, "You know him better than anyone. What was he thinking?"

"He probably thought we'd communicate again. He had no way of knowing what happened to Hummingbird. When we didn't make contact, I think he reverted to the original exit plan."

"Going back into Costa Rica, you mean?" says Soperton.

"Right. I think he crossed back into Costa Rica and made his way to that institute. And from there…I don't know," he sighs.

"But we looked for him – for anyone, really – on the CR side," reminds Burke. "And we never saw just one person…by themselves."

"Do you think he was or is hiding out in a river cave?" ask Soperton.

"Doesn't make sense for him to do that. I mean, he knows we can't spot him if he is in a cave. And he knows I would never leave him. I'm at a loss."

"Our guys will mobilize in country. We'll find him," consoles Soperton.

"Right," adds Burke. "We'll lay on a joint military training exercise and find him."

"I want to be positive," Wells says. "Maybe he'll show up in a day or two. If not, I want to go down there and find him. I owe him that."

"And the Agency does, too, Bob."

"Let's meet Breeden and make sure everything is being done for her. Then let's go get London."

CHAPTER 30

Since the Panama-California Expedition in 1921 San Diego has been a Navy town. The city has a long history of being supportive of active duty military, their families and veterans. Off and on since World War I, the city has provided civilian facilities in beautiful Balboa Park to the Navy. During the Viet Nam era, Balboa Park and the surrounding area constituted the largest military hospital in the world.

After consultation with a team of military and civilian doctors, it is decided Kate will begin rehabilitation at the Navy Medical Center San Diego (NMCSD) in the park. Many veterans are treated at this hospital, some for wounds that are difficult to heal. Kate's excellent physical condition, youth, positive attitude, and desire to heal, speed her healing. The sunshine, low humidity and beautiful surrounding help. When Soperton and Wells arrive for a visit, they find her outside the facility under a cloudless sky and bright sun. Her spirits appear high. The doctors report she is walking with a cane while tissue and muscle regenerate. They expect her to throw the cane at them in another week or ten days. She has clearly charmed doctors and nurses alike with her high energy and can-do spirit.

Kate spots Wells coming with another man, but doesn't know who the civilian with him is. She stands as they near. As soon as Wells sees her stand, he waves for her to sit down. Fifty feet later they stand in front of her.

"Good to see you, Kate," Wells says in as up-beat a tone as he can muster.

"And good to see you, sir," she answers, extending her hand. Wells takes it.

"This is Adrian Soperton, Kate. We work together."

Soperton steps forward and shakes her hand. "He was my boss when the earth was forming," Soperton says. "Any bad habits I have, I learned from him." He has a great smile, warm and sincere.

"You look great, Kate," Wells says. He wants to ease into the real reasons he's visiting. Kate knows that. And he knows she knows. That doesn't make it easier.

"I've had excellent care, sir. The Navy knows how to look after their people." She, too, has a warm smile and inviting face. The chit-chat continues for another ten minutes, praising what a great town San Diego is, with all the things to do and places to see. That topic exhausted, it is time to talk of the past, present and future.

"Kate, I'd like to talk about a few things, if you feel up to it."

"Certainly, sir," she says. She blots Soperton out of her mind.

"First, thank you for all you did. The operation was a success, and we were able to recover the containers."

"That's good to hear, sir. I was sort of out of it at the last."

"But you were very much in it when it mattered. Jon couldn't..." He hesitates in mid- sentence, regretting mentioning Jon's name so quickly. "Ah...couldn't have done it without you. You know that."

"He's a very capable man," Kate says. Her gaze is steady, eyes unblinking. Her face does not reveal what she is thinking.

Wells wonders what she is thinking. "Yes indeed. Very capable."

"What's his status, sir?"

Wells clears his throat and looks at Soperton. Kate looks at both of them, intuiting something is amiss but hiding her feelings.

"There's a problem, Kate." Wells looks hesitant.

In a strong voice she says, "With all due respect, sir, please cut to the chase."

Wells sighs. "We don't know where in the hell he is!"

"Sir?" Kate says her eyes widening in amazement. "I don't understand."

"Excuse me," interrupts Soperton, "we don't either."

Quickly, Wells jumps in to explain. "After you were evacuated, Jon carried out another assignment – sabotaging the boat with the containers. We concentrated our assets on stopping the boat and capturing the containers. When that was successful, we went back to locate Jon and get him out – only we couldn't find him."

The silence is loud. Wells thinks Kate inhales more deeply than usual. Soperton checks the knot in his silk tie. Finally, Kate says, in a non-emotional and controlled voice, "This doesn't make sense."

"Did you two discuss the alternative exit strategy in case things went…went differently than we planned?"

"There was never a doubt in either of our minds that might be necessary."

Wells says, "Jon is a resourceful man, and a survivor. I'm sure you know that. We're going to North Island from here. Then I'm going to Costa Rica to find him."

"I'm still on annual leave, sir. I can go with you."

"That's not necessary, Kate. Finish rehab. Then we'll talk. I'll find him and bring him back – and I'll keep you informed."

"I'd appreciate that, sir. I would really appreciate that."

As Wells and Soperton leave, talking quietly as they walk away, Kate suspects they have not shared all they know. Still, if Jon were dead they would have told her. The loss of a colleague is difficult. But this is different. Her mind is telling her one thing. Her heart is telling her something else. "Steel yourself to shield yourself," the Academy chaplain advised the cadets when she was a student. "Protect your heart." Deep down she knows Jon's death would be heartbreaking.

Soperton and Wells walk silently for a considerable distance before pausing outside a museum. "What do you think the chances are we will find London?" asks Soperton.

Wells looks at the immaculate landscaping surrounding them as if he doesn't hear Soperton. After a few moments he says, "Not good. Sometimes things don't end well."

"So you think he's lost?" Soperton asks.

"I think he is resourceful and mentally tough. We'll just have to see."

"However it turns out," Soperton says softly, "we did the right thing."

"That's what you're going to be judged on, Adrian. Bioweapons are more subtle than a nuclear attack. And I think more likely."

They resume walking to the car.

"Glad you aren't cursing anymore," observes Soperton.

"Un-huh. My tkumah," he says in Hebrew, meaning "rebirth."

"Right."

CHAPTER 31

Ten days later, the Vice President of Development quietly knocks on the open office door. Looking up from his desk, the Chief Executive Officer of the Association of Graduates (AOG) at the United State Air Force Academy waves a hand and says, "Come on it."

An attractive middle-aged woman approaches his desk and says, "Thought you'd be interested in this." She places a standard sized envelope on the edge of the desk.

Looking over his rimless bifocals, he picks it up and asks, "What is it?"

"It's unusual. That's what it is." She stands quietly waiting for a response.

The envelope was opened minutes earlier with a sharp knife. There is no return address on the envelope. He removes a single sheet of cream-colored stationary. As he is unfolding the letter a check falls out. He picks it up and stares at it. It's a Cashier's Check in the amount of $250,000. "Wow!" he exclaims. Placing the check to one side, he again picks up the stationary. There is no letterhead and no watermark, but the paper is of high quality. Typed on it is a short message: "In honor of Lieutenant Colonel Katherine Breeden. Restricted to U.S. Air Force Academy Mock Trial Team."

Puzzled, he asks, "Do we know Breeden?"

"Class of 94. Last I was able to find out she was assigned to the Pentagon."

"I think we need to find her." He returns the letter and the check.

~ ~ ~ ~

The President of the University of Sint Maarten receives an anonymous letter three days later. It reads: "In memory of Dr. Kim Lake. Restricted to academic scholarships for 'B' students." Attached is a Cashier's Check for $250,000. She puts the check on her desk and pats it like her Labrador Retriever puppy. She is happy to receive the generous gift, but reflective and saddened remembering Kim. She was a wonderfully positive influence on students, and a first rate intellect. The president wonders what became of Dr. Jon London. He and Kim made a great couple. That calls to mind the tragic loss of Dr. Douglas Clayton in a terrible storm in Bermuda. It's a sad day all around.

She picks up the phone on her desk and pushes a three digit extension. "Kaatje, I'd like for you to make a deposit at the bank today."

ACKNOWLEDGEMENT

Special thanks to my editor, Dr. Clifford Bee, professor emeritus at San Diego State University. Cliff is an outstanding Rotarian, a friend of the Library, a friend of the Navy, a friend of the Federal Bureau of Investigation, and a friend of San Diego State athletics, especially basketball. As a Peacock Bass master, fish from Alaska to Michigan, from Mexico to Panama, and from Panama to the lakes and rivers in the interior of Brazil fear him.

In addition to Dr. Bee's many awards for distinguished service and professional achievements, he is the recipient of the prestigious Monty Award. He is an Ambassador Extraordinary and Plenipotentiary of San Diego, and my longtime friend.

I also want to thank several people who have contributed to this story without knowing it. I am grateful for the memories, encouragement and suggestions of Katherine Alsop, Jennifer Bartlett, Athena Braio, Ray Burgos, Brian Clarkin, Robert Comer, Victor Corrigan, Bob Dawson, Harlan Davis, Joe and JoAnne DeSantis, Justin Dobson, Stuart Fleming, James Hill, Camaron Isbell, George and Alice Kalafut, Steven Macheers, Maureen McGrath, Thomas Pettit, Dees Reesman, Bob Rowland, Bob Shaw, Linda Smyth, Victoria Turney, Art Warman, and Herb Zoehrer.

Special recognition is due the Kalafuts. They provided me with valuable feedback about the characters and the book's story line. And they always bought me coffee.

-JAF

Georgia, 2023